Will put down the mug and half rose from his seat. "Where? When did you see her? You must tell me . . . !"

"Sit easy, Sky rider." The eldest of the trio made calming motions with his hands. "We didn't actually see her ourselves. But we met and talked with others, human and saurian, who in the course of conversation mentioned encountering a strange human female traveling alone in a little-visited part of the canyon."

"I'm not sure I follow you," Will confessed.

"We'll give you all the details," the olive-skinned Ollyanto assured him, "but first you have to do something for us."

"Don't bargain with me in this." Will spoke sharply. "A woman's life may be at stake."

The world of Dinotopia is revealed in these epic adventures:

# DINOTOPIA LOST
by Alan Dean Foster

# DINOTOPIA: A LAND APART FROM TIME
written and illustrated by James Gurney

# DINOTOPIA: THE WORLD BENEATH
written and illustrated by James Gurney

# THE HAND OF DINOTOPIA

*by*
*Alan Dean Foster*

*Illustrations by*
*James Gurney*

**Foundations for the
Future Charter Academy**

**AVON BOOKS**
*An Imprint of HarperCollinsPublishers*

*For Mike Triebold—*
*With thanks for the*
*Rex biscuit. . . .*

Dinotopia® is a registered trademark of James Gurney.
www.dinotopia.com

The Hand of Dinotopia
Copyright © 1999 by James Gurney

Library of Congress Cataloging-in-Publication Data
Foster, Alan Dean, 1946–
    The Hand of Dinotopia / by Alan Dean Foster ; illustrations by James Gurney.
        p.        cm.
    "Based on the Dinotopia books by James Gurney."
    Summary: Will and Sylvia search for the mysterious Hand of Dinotopia, which will supposedly lead to a safe sea route to and from the hidden island where people and dinosaurs live together peacefully.
    ISBN 0-06-028005-0 — 0-06-051851-0 (pbk.)
    [1. Dinosaurs—Fiction.   2. Islands—Fiction.   3. Adventure and adventurers—Fiction.   4. Fantasy.]   I. Gurney, James, 1958–      ill.   II. Title.
PZ7.F795Han   1999                                                                          98-27814
[Fic]—dc21                                                                                          CIP
                                                                                                        AC

Typography by Matt Adamec
❖
First Avon edition, 2003
AVON TRADEMARK REG. U.S. PAT. OFF. AND IN OTHER COUNTRIES, MARCA
REGISTRADA, HECHO EN U.S.A.

Visit us on the World Wide Web!
www.harperchildrens.com

*Advancing slowly and with great dignity
toward the two astonished travelers was a most
extraordinary procession.*

GURNEY

ylvia's missing."

The words echoed in Will Denison's head as he repeated them to himself, over and over. No matter how many times he spun them through his mind, they still made no sense. The force of repetition could not hammer them into anything that *made* sense.

The utterly unexpected and irrational revelation had hit him hard, all the more so because everything had been going so well: not only between them, but in his new life in general. As if that were not enough, it was an exceptionally beautiful day.

Now, the assertion on the tiny message scroll that had been delivered to him had shattered the feeling of peace and contentment that had been luxuriating within.

The other passengers on the ferry ignored the silent, brooding skybax rider. A few took notice of his distraught expression and were sympathetic, but no one approached him. It would have been impolite to interrupt his contemplation. Not knowing the cause of his distress, it would have been presumptuous of any of them to offer any kind of solace or condolences. Privacy was a valued commodity in Dinotopia, one no one could put a price on.

The ferry was embarked on its regular morning run between Belluna, the principal town on Grand Isle, and Sauropolis, the capital of Dinotopia. The large, square canvas sail of the modified Roman galley billowed in the steady breeze that blew down the Polongo River as her oars rose and dipped in time to the beat bleated out by the energetic young *Parasauralophus* in the hold. The customary winsome drone was clearly audible up on deck.

As the ferry cruised close to the north shore, humans and dinosaurs could be observed working side by side to gather the bounty of the great river. Using their flat bills, hadrosaurs, edmontosaurs, krittosaurs, trachodonts and others slogged their way through the reed-choked shallows, probing the sand and mud in tandem with swimming humans.

Upon locating a cluster of oysters, clams, or crabs, the duckbills would proceed to root them out. Those shellfish not gathered gently in long, flat bills would be netted or pulled from hiding places by the human divers. Heavy canvas sacks strapped to the backs of the big duckbills bulged with the river's abundance. Young men and women armed with flat-tipped knives were busy prying the more recalcitrant shellfish from their underwater perches.

Farther inland, where the shore became even more marshy and the footing difficult, humans riding camarasaurs and apatosaurs filled sacks suspended from massive flanks with hand-gathered wild rice. While the great sauropods were not averse to devouring the harvest right out of the marsh, like their human companions they much preferred the final, threshed product.

As they grazed, men and women riding on swings suspended just above the waterline used delicate primate fingers to pluck the rice. When gathering baskets were full, they were hauled up onto the lumbering, slowly rolling broad saurian backs by other humans waiting there, and the accumulated rice dumped into larger sacks secured to small storage buildings. In this fashion a single sauropod and its attendant human crew could harvest an area that would take dozens of humans working from many boats an entire day to process.

The shellfish gatherers and rice harvesters looked up frequently from their work to wave to the passengers on passing boats, including those aboard the ferry. Children and parents watching from the railings waved back, but Will did not join them. His thoughts had been turned to unpleasant possibilities.

The message had arrived, literally, like a bolt from the blue. Well, like a sheaf of paper from the blue, anyway, he corrected himself. The ferry had hardly left Belluna when Will, soaking up the morning sun on deck, had heard the little girl standing just forward of him cry out, "Look, mother—there's a skybax without a rider!"

While it was not unusual to see the great skybaxes at play or simply out exercising their vast wings, this was not a common sight in the immediate vicinity of Sauropolis. The skies above the capital were usually filled with resolute riders either departing for or returning from the distant corners of Dinotopia. Lifting an idle glance skyward, Will was shocked to see that the circling, soaring *Quetzalcoatlus* was none other than his very own skybax, the noble great-winged Cirrus.

While visiting friends in Belluna, he had left Cirrus behind at the main Sauropolis skybax rookery. What had prompted his membranous partner and companion to come looking for its rider on his own?

Utilizing the whistling calls he had learned from Oolu, the master skybax instructor, Will had finally managed to gain Cirrus's attention. To the delight of the human and saurian youngsters on board the ferry, the skybax had responded with a direct dive at the boat, folding its wings and dropping steeply, only to open them again at the last moment to sail majestically past the bow. The plunge was designed to do more than spawn squeals of delight from the assembled children on board, however.

The tightly bound scroll that Cirrus dropped on deck was caught by a fast-moving crewman, who was quickly joined by Will. Sure enough, it was intended for him. Expecting to find himself reading some sort of official communiqué, he was stunned to discover that the enclosure was a personal message directed to him. He read it twice to make certain he had not misunderstood.

Now the import of it churned his thoughts as he stood at the railing, watching the teams of humans and dinosaurs harvesting the bounty of the riverbank, seeing but not hearing the men and saurians handling the smaller river craft like dhows and paddleboats that hugged the shore. One small fishing boat pulled alongside the ferry while several handsome jawless fishes were passed to eager customers on board. Will paid no more attention to the brisk commerce than he had to a passing, frolicking school of ichthyosaurs.

Sylvia was missing.

According to the report, which was already days old, she had taken a leave of absence from her career as skybax rider to engage in some private research in the vicinity of distant Canyon City. That much he already knew, because she had told him all about it before leaving. Teasingly, she had refused to give him any details, promising him a full report on her return. But according to the scroll, she had failed to report back on schedule to the relevant authorities in that distant community.

Now she was more than a week overdue, and preliminary inquiries were being made. While it was not the intent of local officials to induce any panic, it was standard procedure to notify family at this point. As her fiancé, that included Will.

As he and his father had discovered on more than one occasion since their arrival in Dinotopia, just because a place was civilized did not mean it was devoid of danger. From the primitive carnivores of the Rainy Basin to the precipitous Forbidden Mountains and sometimes raging rivers, the wondrous forgotten land of enlightened humans and cultured dinosaurs still contained perils enough to snare the unwary. Had his beloved Sylvia, in the course of pursuing her hobby, encountered one? And if so, what?

One thing he knew for certain: he was not about to wait on slow-moving authorities to find out.

The ferry had been designed and built for stability and carrying power, not speed. Right then, the need for speed was paramount in Will's mind. If the boat would not go any faster, he would have to secure other means of transportation. Fortunately, there was one at hand. Clutching the scroll tightly, he turned away from the railing and went in search of the ferry's captain.

He found him on the raised rear deck, conversing amiably with his helmsman. A somewhat portly individual of Sinhalese descent, he eyed his plainly agitated passenger uncertainly.

"Well, well, young man, what brings you away from the delights of the deck and carries you into my company? Is everything all right?"

"No, sir, everything is not all right." Seeing the concerned look that came over the kindly gentleman's face, Will hastened to explain. "It has nothing to do with you or your boat, I assure you."

The captain was clearly relieved. "Gracious me, I am glad to hear that, certainly! What is your problem then?"

"It's nothing that concerns you. But I unexpectedly find myself in great hurry. I have to get to Sauropolis at once!"

The captain exchanged a glance with his oriental helmsman, who shrugged helplessly. "We are traveling as fast as the current and wind allow. I cannot raise the beat below except for an on-board emergency." He eyed Will steadfastly.

"There's an emergency, all right, but I'm not asking you to stress the rowers on my behalf. I just need your permission to carry out a pickup. A skybax pickup."

The captain's forehead crinkled. "A skybax pickup?" He gestured forward. "But there is not enough room on my deck for a skybax's wings to clear."

Will's expression was determined. "I know. I wasn't thinking of trying it on deck." Turning, he pointed. Upward, toward the small lookout bucket that was poised at the top of the high mast.

The captain tracked the gesture. "Shiva knows I am no skybax rider, but isn't what you are proposing rather dangerous? If you miss, it is a long way down to the deck, and the planks are not as yielding as the water."

Will met the older man's gaze evenly. "I'll be the one taking the risk. I absolve you of any responsibility, or consequences." He glanced at the helmsman. "This I do in the presence of witnesses." He started to plead. "Please, sir, I have to go now. But this is your boat, and I need your permission as captain to make the attempt."

"You must be greatly troubled to consider so risky a maneuver."

Will's gaze fell. "The woman I love may be in grave danger."

The captain considered this briefly, then nodded. "Go and try, then. You have my permission. But let me clear the deck in that area." He inhaled deeply, chest and belly swelling. "It would reflect badly on me if you were to fall on another of my passengers."

Will barely lingered long enough to nod and mumble his thanks before whirling and racing toward the mast. High overhead, Cirrus circled on thirty-eight foot wings, his cries falling urgently on the slow-moving ferry.

Heedless of the unyielding deck receding beneath him, Will went up the rigging as fast as he could, the scroll now tucked safely away in his shoulder pouch. As he neared the vacant lookout basket, the wind began to pick up. Here in the shallows, the ferry was steady as a rock, but the pickup was still going to be tricky. Perfect timing between human and pterosaur would be required.

Reaching the basket, he paused for a moment before

climbing even higher, scrambling up the remaining section of mast. Moments later he was teetering precariously on its very apex, his feet balancing on spikes that extended out sideways two feet below the top, his thighs clutching the smooth hardwood. Spreading his arms wide for balance, he tilted back his head and looked up until he located the circling skybax. Then he whistled the command for pickup. Without a clean landing site in view, would Cirrus correctly interpret his partner's intent? Will knew there was no way he could make a leap for the saddle. The mast and rigging would foul the skybax's wing. This, he knew, was the only way.

Had Cirrus heard? Pursing his lips, Will whistled sharply a second time, nearly losing his balance in the process. Enthralled by the little drama centered on the top of the mast, attentive passengers on the deck below sucked in their collective breath.

Doing his best to stand upright while maintaining his precarious perch, Will saw that Cirrus had begun to circle lower. The skybax had commenced a long, swooping descent that would bring him in low over the stern of the ferry. Will struggled to stand as straight and tall as he could. He knew there was no margin for error either on his part or that of the skybax. River-whipped wind eddied around the top of the mast, threatening to topple him from his tenuous roost. Supported on rising currents of air, the vast membranous wings came toward him. Closer, closer—until the great shadow was almost upon him.

*Now!*

Forsaking any further attempt to hold his balance and casting cautions as well as his body to the winds, he lunged upward with both hands. The left one missed, desperate fingers just scraping the cord. But his right hand hooked cleanly over the braided rope that hung beneath the sky-bax's bony keel. Part of the sky saddle tack, it always hung a little bit loose in flight. His fingers clutched convulsively and he felt himself forcibly yanked from his perch. Instantly, he reached with his free hand and felt his fingers coil around the now taut cord.

Beneath and behind him, he heard first a concerted gasp from the watching ferry passengers and then their applause. Dangling fifteen meters above the water and rising as Cirrus strained to gain altitude, he thought the cheers premature.

He could kick, but only a little lest he throw Cirrus off line. Using only his hands, arms, and shoulders, he slowly worked his way up the tack until he made his way around to the front of the great wing. Without putting any pressure on the thin, delicate membrane, he dragged himself up onto the *Quetzalcoatlus*'s back and into the lightweight saddle anchored there. Stretching himself out in the prone flying position to minimize air resistance, he patted the great pterosaur affectionately on its neck.

"That's the way to give wing, Cirrus! That's the way Oolu trained us!"

The pterosaur spoke only its own language of croaks and chirps and squawks, but it readily recognized the tone of its rider's voice. Responding with a sequence of ascending vocalizations, the skybax continued its slow but steady climb as they soared eastward, leaving the ferry, a cluster of awed passengers, and one very relieved captain behind.

By skybax, the distance to Sauropolis was comparatively short, and Cirrus stayed low. There were no mountains to cross here, no hills to dodge. The lush fields and villages of the Polongo inlet spread out beneath him. Human and saurian workers alike paused occasionally to wave at the passing skybax.

Someone had sent out the unmanned Cirrus with the message instead of another skybax and rider, knowing that a rider's mount would be the more likely to find and recognize his partner quickly. Will was grateful for the forethought. He tried not to imagine Sylvia's situation as they neared the outskirts of the capital.

Then they were crossing the harbor, with its sturdy artificial breakwaters and finger-like boat slips. Beyond, imposing structures whose origins lay in Hindu-Greek-Arabic architecture gleamed prominently in the rising sun, their pillars and cornices white with finely chiseled marble and granite. Saurian shapes large and small filled the busy streets. Elegant sauropods and ceratopsians bedecked in colorful embroidery filed by in one long noisy cortege, the music from the procession audible even at the skybax's current altitude.

The kaleidoscopic cavalcade of dinosaurs and humans was heading for the parade grounds, Will decided, or perhaps the grand amphitheater. A circus, by the looks of it, and he felt a twinge of regret that he would not be able to attend. A Dinotopian circus, with its acrobatic humans, ornamented ceratopsians, musical hadrosaurs and strength-displaying sauropods, was always a special treat. But there was no way he could relax and enjoy himself knowing that Sylvia was in difficulty and possibly even in real danger.

He did not have to direct Cirrus to the skybax rookery. Without guidance from his rider, the *Quetzalcoatlus* headed there automatically, descending on a rising wind toward the high wood and masonry structure. Other skybaxes roosted there, with quarters for their human riders nearby. As this was the primary rookery for the capital, it was the biggest on Dinotopia, with room for many skybaxes. Cirrus had no trouble finding an open platform on which to land.

As soon as Cirrus touched down with his hind feet, Will leaped clear to remove his weight from his friend's narrow back. Freed of his human burden, Cirrus folded his immense wings and came to rest not only on his feet but on the hollow-boned fingers of his wing-supporting arms.

"Sorry, my friend, but I've no time to waste. The attendants will see to you." Concluding his hasty parting with a reassuring hoot, Will turned to go. Disdaining the sauropod-powered lift, he rushed down the nearest spiral stairway, heading for street-level ten stories below. Behind him, Cirrus cocked a great, querulous eye at his rider's retreating back and wondered at the emergency that could spark such anxiety in his usually easy-going human.

*Something in that message I delivered*, the skybax thought. Whatever it was, it should not provoke such unseemly haste. He had felt the tension in his rider's body ever since they had accomplished the tricky snatch from the top of the ferry boat. All that hurly-burly, and not even time for a rub-down after landing. Ah so, the skybax cawed throatily to no one in particular. It knew well from experience that humans, while fun to have around and work with, were all too often driven by impulse. Pivoting carefully on feet and knuckles, Cirrus turned to confabulate with his fellow mounts. As usual, riders and their oft-incomprehensible human concerns were quickly forgotten as the conversation turned, inevitably, to the weather and the week's flying conditions.

Breathing hard, Will stumbled out of the base of the rookery tower and nearly ran into a lumbering ankylosaur loaded down with produce from a suburban dairy. Bottles of thick milk rattled and jangled from sideways-protruding spikes. By the time they reached the intended delivery point, they would be well on their way to becoming butter.

The ankylosaur turned its armored head and barked at him, but Will had no time to respond to the well-deserved chiding. Pushing past, he found himself running down Pterosaur Way in the direction of Centrosaurus Central.

Not for the first time, he realized that streets designed to accommodate the stride of sauropodian titans like *Brachiosaurus* made for protracted going by humans. This wouldn't do, he decided as he halted, bending over as he tried to catch his breath. Most of the national bureaus, including communications, were located in the great administration complex on the northwest side of the capital. The skybax rookery was situated on a hill off to the east. He still had nearly the entire city to cross.

In mid-wheeze he spotted just what was needed— a raptor rickshaw. The two velociraptors were chattering softly, waiting for a customer. Leaping into the seat, he barked out his destination as best he could in their rasping tongue. He was hardly fluent in raptor, but all the principal streets and structures in Sauropolis had names that both saurians and humans could recognize.

Chittering back at him, they settled themselves into their harnesses and took off, their powerful hind legs and agile bodies allowing them to weave in and out of the bustling traffic at high speed. When he urged them on to even greater efforts, they took it as a challenge, negotiating the crowded avenues with such speed and skill that it was all he could do to hang onto the rickshaw and not fall out. Once, he was even forced to duck. Disdaining a detour, the raptors roared right under the road-blocking bulk of a sluggish *Tenontosaurus*. Will felt his hair brush the drooping belly of the big plant-eater, but other than a couple of startled expressions and accompanying exclamations on the part of both human rider and sauropod, no harm was done.

As for the raptors, they chattered away nonstop, submerging themselves in the excitement of the challenge. Too many of their regular passengers wanted to travel in leisurely style. Now this anxious human had given them freedom to run! And run they did, the wheels of the rickshaw banging and bouncing off the pavement. On more than one occasion Will actually became momentarily airborne without the aid of his skybax.

Breathing hard, their small but powerful saurian hearts pounding, and thoroughly exhilarated, the raptors finally pulled up outside the requested offices, nearly rolling the rickshaw in the process. Will had to do a highside left to keep the spindly vehicle from turning over. He had no one to blame but himself for the wild ride. He should have known better than to ask a couple of raptors to put on all possible speed.

Climbing shakily out of the wickerwork contraption, he thanked both of them profusely as soon as he could catch his own breath. Then he turned and headed up the wide stone stairway and into the huge, colonnaded structure.

Within, dinosaurs and humans moved to and fro on floors of polished, inlaid marble and granite, intent on the business of administration. Benign Dinotopia's might be, but there was still plenty of administrative work to be done. It took him several stops and multiple queries before he was directed to what he hoped would be the proper office in the depths of the Bureau of Communications.

Despite the size of the building, the room itself was light and airy, a small triumph of Dinotopian architectural design. The back looked out on a small garden, while the opposing walls were lined with scrolls to twice the height of a man. A large portal near the garden led to unseen chambers.

The slim, elderly man who rose from a desk piled high with scrolls appeared preoccupied. Given his position, the attitude was understandable, but at the moment Will was decidedly short on patience. Removing the scroll from his shoulder pouch and slapping it down on the wooden counter, he addressed the clerk in clipped tones.

"Is this the latest? I need to know!"

"Know? Dear me." The clerk adjusted his rectangular, half-size spectacles as he picked up the scroll and spread it out before him with careful deliberation. "Everyone needs to know, young man. That is why they come to the Bureau of Communications. We are in the business of helping people to know." Arranging the scroll on the countertop, he perused the contents.

When he had finished, he let the scroll roll back up as he glanced over the top of his spectacles at his edgy visitor. "You should learn to relax more, young man, or you will not live to the ripe old age to which you are entitled."

Will gestured at the scroll. "You read that? Then you know why I can't relax. Is there any more recent information?"

"Just a moment, just a moment." Appearing slightly flustered by Will's insistence, the clerk turned and emitted a sound between a grunt and a low, musical hoot.

A reply, deeper and richer, came from beyond the portal. Moments later a massive shape ambled in on all fours. The *Iguanodon* wore the identifying tassels of a senior clerk. Perched on her snout was a pair of large spectacles little different from those worn by her human colleague. Will found himself staring. It was unusual, though not unprecedented, to see a dinosaur wearing corrective lenses.

Filling most of the room, the saurian clerk peered over the shoulder of the old man and studied the scroll he unrolled before her. The slightly incongruous spectacles only enhanced her natural resemblance to an enormous olive-green basset hound. Almost immediately, she looked up at Will and nodded.

Standing back on her hind legs so that she rose to her full fifteen-foot height, she began searching the upper shelves on the left side of the room, using the thumb-spike on her left foreleg like a page-turner to shift scrolls aside rapidly and efficiently. After several minutes spent scouring two bins of recent communications, she dropped back down to all fours and eyed Will regretfully. Though she and he could not communicate verbally, her expression was eloquent. For emphasis, she let out a short series of mournfully modulated honks. Then she turned, all thirty feet of her, and tiptoed lightly back through the rear portal, returning to her own office.

Her human associate set a sorrowful gaze on Will. "That's it. You heard Ereweth. I'm afraid there isn't anything new. If anything had come in subsequent to this"—he tapped the scroll that lay half open on the counter—"she would know about it."

Will's frustration was bounded only by the physical limits of Dinotopia. "But this is impossible!" It was his turn to tap on the maddeningly uninformative scroll. "People don't just vanish in Dinotopia. They have accidents and get hurt, or even die, but they don't just go missing!"

Unperturbed, the elderly clerk pursed his lips as he regarded his agitated visitor solemnly. "Apparently that is just what the lady in question has gone and done." He did his best to sound reassuring. "I can see by your attitude and hear by your tone that you are a worrier. Recently arrived in Dinotopia?"

Will could barely contain his impatience. "My father and I were shipwrecked on the northwest shore only a few years ago, near Romano's hatchery."

The clerk's expression brightened. "Ah, you are one of the redoubtable Denisons! Your father has gained quite a reputation since his arrival here."

Always my father, Will thought crossly. What about *my* reputation? He forced that line of thinking out of his mind. This was not why he had come here.

"There has to be more recent news. An official update on the search."

"Search?" The clerk indicated the scroll. "I read nothing in here about a search. It is merely individual notification of an awkward circumstance that has not yet progressed to the point where others are required to take action. The authorities wished you to be aware of the situation. Evidently they are not yet concerned enough to progress to the next step."

"Well, I am!" Picking up the scroll, Will turned to leave.

"A moment of your time, young man."

Will paused restlessly. "What is it?"

The clerk was at once concerned and philosophical. "I do not know how much of Dinotopia you have seen since your arrival here, Will Denison, but while this land is long settled and much civilized, there remain many places that have never been visited or explored. And I am referring to regions besides the Rainy Basin, where the wise man or dinosaur does not set foot alone."

"What's your point?" Will gazed longingly in the direction of the beckoning doorway.

The clerk nodded at the scroll Will clutched tightly in his right hand. "Mark well where your lady friend was last seen. Canyon City is the gateway to the vast gorge of the Amu River. The great canyon has hundreds, perhaps thousands of offshoot branches and side fissures. Most are too steep for even the smallest of our saurian brothers and sisters to negotiate. They have many skills, but rock climbing is not one of them. That requires the flexible hands and feet of a primate. A human.

"If there is any area on Dinotopia that remains unknown to our prehistoric friends, it is the great canyon and the lands that surround it." He smiled. "Perhaps that is why your friend went there. What was she seeking in so dangerous and empty a place?"

"I don't know." Frustration was making Will irritable. "She wouldn't tell me."

"Ah! Then perhaps she wished her intentions to remain a secret. She may not want anyone, even one motivated by the best of intentions, to seek her out."

Will waved the scroll. "Even if that were the case, she was still supposed to report regularly to the local authorities. That's a minimal necessary precaution."

"Just so, young man, just so. But in the distress of your admittedly laudable concern, you assume that she has encountered some exigency. I think you may have overlooked the other possibility."

Will blinked. "Other possibility? What other possibility?"

For a second time, the clerk peered sagely over his glasses at his apprehensive young visitor. "That she may have found something."

# -II-

he clerk's words clung to Will's worry, festering and refusing to let go as he exited the office. What if the old man was correct and he was panicking needlessly? If Sylvia was all right and nothing was wrong, descending on her in the middle of the wilderness with a team of rescuers might be the last thing she'd want. Her reaction to such a maladroit intrusion might be less than appreciative.

But she ought to have reported in as scheduled, he insisted to himself. Sylvia was not the flighty type, and she would know that others would be worried about her. He renewed his resolve to find out exactly what was going on, even if it meant incurring her displeasure. Let her yell at him and shake her finger in his face if he was proven wrong. At least he would know that she was all right.

But where to go to carry the matter further? Around him, humans and dinosaurs strode through the hallways and cupolas, beneath ceilings high and wide enough to accommodate even the largest sauropods. Like expectations, building in Dinotopia had from the first been on a grand scale.

Blocking the path of a trotting *Struthiomimus* on courier duty, he made inquiries by referring to specific lines on the scroll. Chirping encouragingly at him, the courier turned to indicate the way with lean, strong fingers any pianist would have been proud to call their own. Familiar with several words of struthie from earlier experiences, Will was able to thank the courier in her own language.

Hurrying through the administrative complex soon brought him to a high archway inlaid with fine mosaic that identified the offices beyond as belonging to the Bureau of Public Assistance. Pausing only briefly to make certain he was in the right place, he hurried onward and began searching for an uncrowded office or an official who did not look unduly occupied.

He found several in a large, spacious room where hundreds of small scrolls consisting largely of work orders were being filed or distributed. Fast-moving coelophyses would grab messages from human or saurian staff to disburse throughout the administrative complex, while a steady stream of dispatchers kept coming and going with backpacks and side pouches full of communiqués that needed to be filed in waiting niches in the walls

Among this organized hubbub and grand confusion Will singled out a pair of twins of Javanese descent who were working in conjunction with a medium-sized *Centrosaurus*. Possessed of multiple horns on his face and a row of sharp spikes lining his neck frill, the centrosaur could carry enough paper to keep any bureaucrat content. In addition to his pair of side-mounted files, numerous loose bits of paper and message were stuck down on his horns and spikes, turning the hefty herbivore into a virtual walking filing cabinet.

The two demure, petite young women looked up as Will approached. "You require assistance?" the nearest member of the duo addressed him in wee, bell-like tones. While her figure might be fragile, there was nothing but steel in her voice. Compassionate steel, he hoped.

"See this?" He unrolled the scroll before them. "The Bureau of Communications insists there's nothing here to worry about yet. I know this lady, and I have to disagree."

The two women paused in their filing to study the scroll. The horned head of the curious centrosaur pushed between them to peruse the writing.

"Communications is probably right," declared the second twin. "What do you want of this department?"

"Why, to mount an expedition to find her, of course!"

The two women and the single ceratopsian exchanged glances. "Expeditions are expensive affairs, Mr. . . ."

"Denison. Will Denison."

"To look for a single missing person in the canyon of the Amu would require a great deal of preparation and many searchers." The woman indicated the scroll. "This report has the flavor of a courtesy, not an emergency. Could it be that you are overreacting?"

Of course it could, Will knew, but he was not about to confess to that.

"She's overdue to check back in. The report says so. It's time to go and find her."

As the other twin spoke up, the *Centrosaurus* turned away with an unmistakable sigh. There was important work to be done.

"Not if it requires the utilization of excessive resources that can't be justified."

"Then you won't help me?"

The women looked at one another, as if deciding who was going to reply. "Help is given where help is needed, Will Denison. The information contained in that scroll does not state that this is so. The Bureau must allocate its resources according to a sliding scale of needs. Yours would, I regret to have to say, appear to lie near the bottom of that scale." She smiled encouragingly. "Of course, the relevant circumstances could change rapidly."

"Don't patronize me." He rolled the scroll tightly. "If Public Assistance won't help me, I'll try one of the other Bureaus. And another, and another, until I find one that'll take me seriously."

A blast of warm, mildly fetid air mussed his hair. Whirling, he found himself staring into the face of an irritated *Pssiticasaurus*. The disapproving saurian stared hard at him for a long moment before shuffling off to continue with its deliveries. Will hesitated. It had been a while since he had been on the receiving end of the dinosaurian equivalent of a dressing-down. He realized that from the moment he had entered the room his attitude had been less than courteous.

"Listen," he murmured, turning back to the twins, "I'm sorry if I've been impolite, but this is my betrothed we're talking about. I can't help it if maybe I seem a little insistent. I'm worried about her."

"Of course you are," replied one of the young women. "You have every right to be. But your concern doesn't give you the right to make unreasonable demands on your fellow citizens, be they human or saurian."

"You can try the other administrative offices," her

bright-eyed double acknowledged, "but as soon as you show them that scroll, the tenor of its contents will produce the same results. Without a declaration of realized emergency, they will all advise you to wait for further news, or at least until more time has passed. This may not prove a satisfying response, but it is the most likely one."

"He's in love," her sister murmured. "You can't expect him to act rationally."

Will had the grace to blush. "I hear what you're saying, but now that I've read this message"—and he gestured anew with the rolled-up scroll—"I can't just let it lie, can't just wait around for the next official follow-up." He made no effort to conceal or disguise the tension in his voice. "I have to do *something*."

The twins deliberated. Achieving consensus, they sought out their lumbering ceratopsian co-worker. After much grumbling and snorting and exchange of Dinotopian script, they returned to confront Will.

"We put the question of your dilemma to Jesmacha." Behind them, a paper-laden centrosaurian head turned to look in Will's direction. The eyes were kind, belying the unavoidable brusqueness of the *Centrosaurus*'s heavily glottal commentary.

"If you are irremediably set in your intentions," the other twin continued, "Jesmacha suggests that you request a formal leave of absence from your assignment as skybax rider so that you can pursue this matter on your own."

Will hesitated. "I could do that. I have some accumulated leave time due me. But then how would I get to Canyon City? How would I organize a search party?"

The clerk shrugged. "How do any of us do anything in

this world? By doing, while those who do not get anything done do nothing but talk. Good luck to you, citizen." She turned away.

Aware that he had already taken up more of their time than he was entitled to, Will left the office. In his mind, if not his heart, he knew that the twins were right. Until the appropriate office got around to issuing a formal proclamation of personal emergency in Sylvia's case, he was not going to be able to obtain any official help in ascertaining the true nature of her present situation. That meant everything was up to him.

To reach distant Canyon City from Sauropolis would take many days—except by skybax. But if he took a leave of absence from his duties, then he could not expect to be able to make use of Cirrus's services to cross half of Dinotopia.

Unless—unless there was a routine delivery scheduled for that city some time in the near future.

His return rickshaw trip to the rookery was more sedate and less harrowing than had been his rocketing ride earlier. Just as well, because it gave him time to think. As soon as he was dropped off at the base of the rookery tower, he went straight to the skybax service offices located in a separate building nearby.

Several dromaeosaurs were working at scroll readers, powering the well-greased treadmills at a steady pace. The wall file for incoming packets and messages was off to the left, those intended for outgoing on his right. Since he was still wearing his skybax rider uniform, no one questioned his presence in the distribution center.

Sure enough, there were a couple of small, neatly wrapped

packets and a number of scrolls in the Outgoing box marked Canyon City. Leaving the distribution center, he strode purposefully into the base of the rookery tower. The strong smell of skybax permeated the sturdy structure from top to bottom.

Half a dozen skybax riders had congregated in the ready room. In smaller cities and towns there might only be one or two at a time, but as the main skybax distribution center for the capital, this rookery was always busy.

Acknowledging the waves and hellos of the other riders, some of whom he knew personally, others who were strangers to him except by profession, he went straight to the assignments board. The smooth, erasable slate showed the assignments for the rest of the day. Tomorrow morning it would be wiped clean and rescribed.

Gentoo Paik, two p.m., to El Qubbanukka, Khasra, and several rural drop points in between. Flight terminating this evening in Canyon City. That was the man he needed to talk to. He recognized the name, but did not know the individual. When he put his inquiry to a married pair of riders, they quickly pointed out a neatly dressed rider seating at a table by himself. The man was in the process of making short work of a large lunch.

Paik was small and slim, that being a general requirement for at least two Dinotopian professions: that of jockey, and of skybax rider. He smiled as his fellow rider sat down opposite him. Both wore the embroidered patch of full-fledged riders.

Will extended a hand, palm upward, and Paik met it with the one not holding a pair of chopsticks. "Breathe deep, seek peace."

"You also, Rider." Paik's voice was kindly, almost deferential. Pinioned between the bone chopsticks, exotic vegetables found their way to his mouth. "What news?"

"Clear conditions across the Polongo," Will responded conversationally. "That's all I've seen for this morning. Speaking of good flying weather, I have a favor to ask."

The older man gestured with his paired utensils. "Consider it fulfilled, if it is within my means."

Will nodded in the direction of the assignments board. "I see that you are scheduled to make a run this afternoon to Canyon City."

Paik delicately slurped vegetables and nodded. "A long, hard flight, and a tricky one. The winds off the eastern slopes of the Forbidden Mountains are always calmer than those to the west, but they can be tricky if not as strong. And you must know what it's like at the canyon."

Will smiled. "Landings there are always touch and go." He leaned forward. "I have reasons of my own for wanting to get to Canyon City as quickly as possible. It would be a great help to me if I could take your assignment."

An uncertain frown shadowed Paik's face. "For this afternoon's flight? That's very short notice."

"I apologize for that, but the news that takes me to Canyon City reached me by my own skybax only a little while ago. It's kind of a personal matter in which the officials at Administration see no reason for urgency."

"But you do, eh?" Paik smiled understandingly. "Well, never let it be said that a skybax rider refused to help a colleague in need."

Will struggled to control his excitement. "Then you'll trade with me?"

"Not so fast, not so fast, my young friend!" Paik's grin widened. "What's *your* assignment?"

Will blinked. "You know, I've been so wound up in this personal matter that I haven't even bothered to check. It's not on the board."

"Come." Paik carefully wiped his engraved chopsticks on a cleaning cloth as he rose from his seat. "We'll find out together."

"But you haven't finished your lunch," Will protested.

The other man shrugged. "I was getting full anyway. Don't worry, it won't be wasted. There's a sauropod Commonality a few blocks away that takes all the table scraps from the rookery." He stepped back from the table.

Will's next flight assignment, as forwarded to him by a duty officer in the tower, called for him to fly several packets of fruit tree seedlings from the Sauropolisian developmental farms to several Rainy Basin plantations at Carnassus, with the usual mail stop at Waterfall City.

"A standard run up the Polongo." Paik put a comradely hand on Will's shoulder. "Nice views, plenty of places along the way to stop for refreshment, and easy air. It's shorter, too. I'd be a fool not to swap with you. Consider yourself put on the afternoon run to Canyon City, friend Will."

"Thanks!" Will's expression of gratitude was heartfelt. He was on his way, and without having to break custom.

"I am curious, though." Paik held his hands behind his back as they headed off toward the ready room. "What motivates you to trade an easy flight for a much more difficult one?"

"It concerns a friend of mine," Will explained. "She may be in trouble."

"Oh-ho! As always, the operative word is explanation enough."

Will eyed him uncertainly. "Operative word? Oh, you mean 'trouble'?"

Paik grinned through teeth that were half gold. "No. I mean 'she'."

The dispatch clerk's brows narrowed when Paik explained that they were swapping flight plans, but as neither of them was an apprentice she saw no reason to present any kind of formal objection. The messages and packets for Canyon City, El Qubbanukka, and Khasra were stowed in separate delivery pouches while mail for rural drop points was consigned to sturdy plunge containers. Will bent slightly under the resultant load as a cheerful Paik bid him farewell and good flying.

Cirrus had been groomed and fed well in his absence, and had enjoyed a good rest while Will had been visiting friends in Belluna. The short flight out to meet the ferry with the message about Sylvia would not have taxed the great *Quetzalcoatlus*. Will spoke softly to his mount as he carefully secured the delivery pouches to the saddle with buckles and straps.

"It's Canyon City this time, Cirrus. A long flight, and we'll be lucky if we get there before dark." They would have to, Will knew, because attempting a landing at Canyon City at night was a task for a master skybax rider, and he was far from achieving that status. They would have to fly fast, and make no mistakes during intervening drop-offs.

Rookery staff attended to last-minute checks of Cirrus's tack. One youngster chatted while concluding some last minute grooming of the skybax's long, narrow chest.

"In a hurry, Rider?"

"Very much so. Got a sack of urgent messages."

The attendant nodded knowingly. "I've put in for apprentice myself. Maybe some day. . . ."

Will smiled at him as they walked Cirrus to one of the four landing-and-takeoff platforms that jutted out into open air from the top floor of the tower. "Study hard, practice well, and remember: you are dependent always on your skybax—your skybax is not dependent on you." By way of illustration he stroked Cirrus's neck, and was rewarded with a shrill burble of approval and affection.

Around them the rookery rang to the conversational cries of other skybaxes, the babble of busy human attendants, and the occasional sharp, parrot-like *chirr-rup* of an arriving or departing message-carrying *Rhamphorynchus*. As they approached the edge of the platform, the attendant stepped back.

"Smooth air, Rider!"

"Thanks." As Cirrus leaned forward slightly, Will mounted by placing his left foot in the appropriate stirrup and swinging his body over onto the skybax's back. Finding the other stirrup with his right foot, he stretched out flat on his stomach between the saddle's side braces. They had been contoured to fit his body and he squirmed slightly to slip down snugly between them. His hands slid through the arm stirrups, securing his upper body to the saddle.

Following a last-minute check of the pouches, secured to either side of the side braces, he whistled at his mount, concluding with a comforting stroke and pat of the long neck. Cirrus answered with a piercing cry and waddled awkwardly to the edge of the platform. Ten stories above the

29

hard pavement, the skybax spread gigantic wings—and stepped off.

Instantly they plunged groundward, but Will did not even swallow hard. At the level of Floor Seven they stopped falling and began to level off. At level five a powerful downward wing thrust straightened them out. At level three they began to climb as Cirrus instinctively sought the nearest column of rising warm air.

Moments later they commenced a long, slow curve, angling northward and continuing to climb as the skybax, under Will's knowledgeable direction, eventually adopted an easterly heading toward the farming community of Jupe and the southern terminus of the Forbidden Mountains.

As the neat plaid of extensive agriculture unfolded beneath them, it struck Will that except for his fellow skybax rider Gentoo Paik, and the flight director at Sauropolis rookery, no one knew where he was or where he was going, much less his intentions. His father would have to be notified, and friends at home in Waterfall City, but nothing could be done until he reached his first touchdown at El Qubbanukka. There he could consign a message to a skybax traveling back to Sauropolis, from where the missive could be forwarded on to Waterfall City.

That would take two days at least, he decided. Enough time so that his father would not feel overlooked, long enough so that neither he or anyone else would have time or opportunity to talk Will out of his plans. He smiled to himself as Cirrus's path was crossed by a formation of raucous ravens. The big black birds were energetic and agile, but none came close to approaching the majesty of a full-grown *Quetzalcoatlus* in flight. Will found himself wondering if, despite his father's experiments with heavier-than-air powered flight, anything ever would.

Below him he could clearly make out sauropods and hadrosaurs, ceratopsians and ankylosaurs and others, busily at work in fields and orchards. With more difficulty, he could distinguish their human companions, tiny dots when set alongside their immense saurian compatriots. Together they perpetuated the fertility and fruitfulness of Dinotopia. Everyone had enough to eat, plenty to do, outlets for individual creativity and personal satisfaction. It was truly a wondrous place, he reflected, even if all the resident humans and their ancestors had arrived as castaways and not passengers on some grand transpacific clipper.

But civilized as it was, the land and countryside was not always safe, and once more his thoughts turned to Sylvia.

The southern edge of the Forbidden Mountains soon came into view. Keeping the main east-west road between Sauropolis and Chandara beneath him at all times allowed him to relax. Like any well-trained skybax, Cirrus would automatically follow the most obvious path between delivery points without requiring constant guidance from his rider. Only occasionally did Will vary the route, saving time where the road bent or twisted. Unlike a road, a skybax rider did not need to follow the contours of the land.

He executed a hasty drop-off at El Qubbanukka, shouting apologies for the speed of his departure. After barely allowing enough time for both Cirrus and himself to slake their thirst, they launched from the rookery and turned north in the direction of Khasra. With an eye on the sinking sun, he barely left himself enough time for drop-off and pickup before starting on the final, long, desolate leg northward to Canyon City.

Here too they followed the trade route. Not because it was the most direct, but because it was the safest. As impatient as Will was, he knew that if they had trouble and were forced to land, they could expect assistance only along the north-south road. A direct flight path would have taken them over the Ancient Gorge, the major tributary of the Amu and the great Canyon. No one lived there and in the event of an emergency touchdown no help could be expected. It would do Sylvia no good if they ended up lost and helpless themselves.

So while he chafed at the lost time, he forced himself to exercise the minimum of caution, at least in his choice of routes. Along the way they made several drops to isolated trading outposts where humans and dinosaurs maintained the road or provided services to the infrequent traveler. This involved diving low over fine mesh nets suspended at a forty-five degree angle from poles fixed securely in the ground. At the last safe instant, Cirrus would pull up sharply while Will tossed out the mail container. He prided himself on hitting not just the catching net, but its exact center. In the annual competition among skybax riders from all over Dinotopia, he and Cirrus had finished eleventh in overall drop accuracy. No winning ribbons for them, but many compliments, and much praise for the future for such a young team.

Contrary to Gentoo Paik's admonition, the winds off the steep eastern face of the mountains were cooperative, almost gentle. For this, Will was as grateful as Cirrus.

Even though it was too late for them, second thoughts

kept picking at his mind. What if the *Centrosaurus* Jesmacha and the twins at the Bureau of Public Assistance turned out to be right? What if Sylvia was fine, secure in her chosen isolation, and angry at being interrupted? He would come off looking foolish not only in front of her, but in front of the entire skybax guild. Not to mention his father. He could see old Nallab the librarian's face now, chuckling softly at Will's youthful recklessness while chiding him for charging off without thinking things through.

Too late for recriminations now, he told himself. Wind streaming past his face, he looked to his left. Too late for many things, it seemed. For despite Cirrus's best efforts, the sun was beginning to set behind the Forbidden Mountains. They were not going to make Canyon City before nightfall.

Not if they hewed to this route, anyway. They were still a good distance from the Trilobite Towers. Off to his right and below, the first branches of the Ancient Gorge probed the foothills of the mountains like stealthy brown fingers. Surely if he and Cirrus followed the Gorge as it grew steadily wider and deeper they would soon strike the main portion of the canyon.

In chirps and hoots he queried his mount as to his condition. Cirrus responded with a vibrant, drawn-out honk and by climbing higher. That was enough for Will. Better to risk a sudden, unlikely collapse or failure of strength than to have to chance a landing at Canyon City in the dark. Tapping the great *Quetzalcoatlus* on the right side of its neck, Will guided his mount until they were gliding north-northeast. Below them, the Gorge began to widen. As Will peered over the side of the saddle, the deeply shadowed depths of the canyon began to take on more and more the appearance of a gaping mouth.

Finding the view (not to mention the metaphor) unpleasant, he lifted his head and stared straight ahead, past Cirrus's rudderlike red crest. Somewhere ahead in the vast maze of great fissures and chasms that splintered the Earth lay the safe haven of Canyon City. They would find it before dark.

They had to.

# -III-

The setting sun attacked the fortresslike formations of the canyon with fading light, throwing fantastic shadows on butte and pillar, crevice and cleft. The great canyon of the Amu was a fracture on the shoulder of Dinotopia, at once a geologist's paradise and a traveler's nightmare. Flushed by storm-swollen rapids and waterfalls, the Amu itself was barely navigable for only short stretches at a time. Eventually it was swallowed whole by the underground maw in the middle of the Great Desert known simply as The Portal.

It was no place to have to land and spend the night, Will knew. He could feel the trembling in Cirrus's wings. Even his seemingly tireless mount had limits, and the skybax was rapidly approaching his. Dark as it was becoming, Will realized, they might have no choice but to set down to give the straining *Quetzalcoatlus* a few precious minutes rest. Despite the well-known dangers landing late at Canyon City entailed, it would certainly be better to arrive after dark than not to arrive at all.

Beneath him, he felt Cirrus falter slightly. The next brace of wing strokes were hesitant and brief. For some time now, the skybax had been relying on his gliding ability. He would not demand to rest, but would wait instead for his rider to make the decision.

Scanning the horizon immediately in front of them, Will thought he saw a possible landing site still illuminated by the fading light. It was no skillfully woven rookery platform, with its soft carpeting of easily grasped heavy-weave matting, but at this point they could not be choosy. Leaning forward, he whistled to his mount and tapped him in the appropriate place. Cirrus hooted a soft response and slowly, gratefully, began to descend.

As they dropped lower, both saw that not only was the site Will had selected adequate, it was also already occupied. But not by another skybax.

The camping party consisted of three humans and one family each of dryosaurs and hypsoliphodons. The human sized dryosaurs and their slightly smaller cousins glanced up in astonishment as the winged shape of the skybax glided toward them. The younger hypsoliphodons in particular were jumping up and down excitedly, clicking their horny beaks and urging their larger dryosaur friends to join them as they raced to the edge of a precipitous drop-off. Stubby, clawed hands waved in greeting, and decorative tassels and streamers fluttered from the neatly braided collars favored by both species.

Meanwhile the adults, human and saurian alike, continued to work on the campfire they were assembling. Will heard one dryosaur adult wail warningly at the youngsters to keep back from the edge of the cliff.

Behind them, Will could now see the faint outline of a walking trail, like a lighter thread absently dropped on a mass of darker fabric. Clearly, the three families had walked here, but for what reason? If they had been in the area for any length of time, they might know something of Sylvia's whereabouts. Any individual traveling alone in the vicinity of the Amu was sure to spark comment among those she encountered.

A great rusty-red sandstone arch, one of the thousands of spectacular natural formations that made the great canyon a geological wonderland, loomed before them. Rapid calculations raced through Will's mind. As tired as Cirrus was, asking him to rise and circle was all but out of the question. Choosing to say nothing, but instead to let the experienced skybax choose his own course, he clenched his fingers tightly around the saddle grips and kept his head down.

Warm wind whistling past his streamlined body, Cirrus sped beneath the arch, his wingtips clearing the rock by only a meter or so on either side. Then it was clear gliding all the way to the flat-topped promontory Will had espied from the air.

As soon as the skybax touched down, Will slipped his feet clear of the stirrups and swung himself to the ground. Relieved of the weight of his rider, Cirrus folded his wings and relaxed, breathing hard, his narrow chest pulsing in and out as he sucked air.

Almost immediately they were surrounded by half a dozen young dryosaurs and hypsoliphodons, the latter nearly as tall as Will, their smaller cousins barely coming up to his waist. Their macaw-like beaks clacked and rattled rapidly as they assaulted the unexpected visitor with a flood of questions he could not answer.

Slower runners than their saurian playmates, the three human children in the party were late arrivals to the greeting. Everyone pushed and shoved for the best view of the skybax rider and his mount. Among the saurian squeals, Will could now make out queries he could understand, but he pushed through the cluster of excited youngsters without answering as he headed for their camp.

The adult members of the party awaited his arrival. By now they had the fire going, a tiny point of warmth and light in the gathering darkness. Several of them were setting up a pair of large tents; one for humans and the other for the saurian members of the group.

An energetic young man not much older than Will walked over to confront him. "What brings you here, Rider?" He chuckled softly. "I know there is such a thing as special skybax mail delivery, but this is a bit much." Turning, he shouted back at his busy companions. "Anyone expecting a birthday scroll?"

Good-natured laughter greeted this query. Despite his impatience, Will mustered a smile. "We haven't stopped here on official business." He gestured behind him. "My skybax had to have a rest. We're on our way to Canyon City on a matter of some urgency."

His host's expression grew solemn. "I see. It must be urgent, to bring you here this late." Looking past his visitor, he studied the evening sky, now as full of golds and reds and pinks as the surrounding rocks. "No matter how long you rest with us, you won't have much light left for making a landing in the city."

"I know, but we had no choice."

"Well, we'll do what we can for you. Would you like some dinner?"

The man's words reminded Will that he'd had nothing to eat but some lutefisk since leaving Sauropolis. "If it's ready, I'd appreciate it more than I can say. As for Cirrus, I think he'd like something to drink more than anything else. It's not good for a skybax to fly tired on a full stomach."

"Done," declared his host. "Come with me."

While Will gobbled down a hasty snack of dried fruits and nuts, the youngsters in the party took turns carefully pouring water from gourd canteens into Cirrus's pelican-like mouth. The skybax drank with steady gulping motions, his head back, the long bill pointed skyward.

"We can't thank you enough for your hospitality." Will addressed his hosts as they rested, human and saurian side by side, around the crackling campfire. "What are you doing away out here, anyway?"

"Just as you see," replied an older man from the other side of the fire. He was leaning back against the flank of a dryosaur. One of the dinosaurs short, thick arms lay draped lazily over the human's shoulder. "We all work together in the city. Garment cleaning and mending, mostly."

Will knew that the fingers of human hands would do the majority of the fine work while their saurian colleagues would handle the heavier aspects of the occupation, including the delivery of finished product.

"What do you mean, 'just as you see'?"

"We're on a camping trip," explained the woman seated next to the speaker. "It's for the children, mostly, but we all enjoy getting away from the city for a little while." She lifted her gaze skyward. "It's so peaceful out here. Quiet and calm. All you can hear at night is the river, far below. It's very good for the youngsters." She murmured something to the dryosaur lying on its belly next to her and it chortled a musical reply. Neither actually understood the other's language, of course, but it was always possible to exchange obvious sentiments.

The light was nearly gone when Will finally rose. Once the fire had been conjured to life it had been possible for the campers to grill some of the delicious river fish they had brought with them. His stomach full and his spirits refreshed, Will knew it was time to take his leave if he ever expected to reach the city tonight.

"Thank you again," he told the campers. "Your help means a lot to us."

The senior human among the group waved diffidently. "We would have done the same for any wayfarer. As would you, Rider, had our positions been reversed. I hope you succeed in your mission."

"Be careful, cloud shaper," a girl of about twelve warned him. "Between here and Canyon City there are many arches and rock spires."

"Yes," added the ten-year old boy seated cross-legged on the ground next to her. "My dad says that the Earth here has many fingers."

"We'll do our best to avoid them." Will turned and strode purposefully toward Cirrus. The rejuvenated skybax was waiting for him, having already turned to face the sandstone abyss at the edge of the promontory. He too was anxious to conclude the final portion of their long journey.

As Will stepped up into the saddle, saurian and human children crowded close, remarking on everything from the detail of the finely-worked saddle to the sweat stains on Will's previously immaculate skybax rider attire. Then Cirrus unfolded his immense wings and they politely retreated.

Unprompted, the *Quetzalcoatlus* took a couple of awkward strides to the edge of the precipice, stepped off, and plunged down into darkness.

Landing in the canyon was not the problem that had faced Will and Cirrus in searching for a place to set down. Choosing a location that would give a skybax enough room to drop, spread its great wings, and gain air and altitude before smashing into a pinnacle or wall greatly reduced the number of possible landing sites. The campers' promontory was narrow and protruded conveniently into a spacious section of unobstructed canyon.

Still, it was touch and go as Cirrus was forced to circle below the canyon's rim until he had gained enough altitude to turn once again toward Canyon City. Once, his left wingtip actually scraped the rock of the unforgiving sandstone escarpment. But he banked sharply, regained his equilibrium, and continued his steady climb.

Their other concern involved the onset of night. As the sun dropped, so did the ambient temperature. The cooler the air became, the more difficult for Cirrus to gain altitude. That was one of the problems that would face them when they prepared to land in the city. During the heat of the day, a missed approach could be dismissed and another easily attempted. Hot air rising from the canyon depths would immediately lift an errant skybax cloudward for another try.

Without rising air currents to fall back on, they would almost certainly have to succeed on their first attempt.

Unable to gain lift, Cirrus would have to set down wherever he could and await either the arrival of morning or an actual rescue. That would be unbearably embarrassing for them both, Will knew. He was determined to avoid it. Had he not learned his trade from the master Oolu himself? Had not he and Cirrus practiced night landings dozens of times before?

Of course, that was practice. They had yet to actually perform one. It was an oversight, Will ruminated, shortly to be rectified.

It was not long before lights came into view. From the air, they presented a wondrous aspect. The spires and formations of the canyon seemed to be alive with jewels, sparkling and twinkling in the depths of the multi-hued sandstone itself. They were the candles and lanterns and fireplaces of Canyon City, a fantastic community whose homes and businesses had been hewn, down through the millennia, out of the solid rock itself.

The tall towers below had not been raised by human or saurian hands, but by the natural action of wind-blown particles and cutting water. Within these eroded stone monuments humans and dinosaurs had worked together to excavate bedrooms and porches, stairways and parapets, nurseries and storerooms. In many instances, the settlers had found naturally-occurring caves and tunnels that had only to be enlarged and modified. Sturdy, swaying rope bridges linked apartments and workplaces of carved sandstone together in a single, thriving community. Soil laboriously carted in down through the centuries from the foothills of the Forbidden Mountains had been neatly packed in everything from cliff-face gardens to flower boxes. In

Canyon City, it was said throughout the length and breadth of Dinotopia, even the rocks bloomed.

No sauropods or camarasaurs lived here. No great-horned ceratopsians tip-toed along the rope bridges, no hadrosaurs carefully picked their way along the paths that lined the cliffsides. Canyon City was for the slight of body as well as the nimble of foot. Here only the smaller dinosaurs could exist comfortably side-by-side with their agile primate cousins.

It would have been much easier and more comfortable for Cirrus had they continued on to the skybax rookery at Pteros. Will felt a pang wondering if his instructor, master Oolu, was there, teaching another class of young would-be skybax riders. But the matter that had brought them all the way from Sauropolis, now far to the south, lay here in the city, and not still farther to the northeast. Once he had assured himself that Sylvia was all right, even if he did not actually have the opportunity to see or talk to her, he would be able to relax. Only then could he and Cirrus contemplate paying their respects to the school where both had learned their trade.

The mix of blossoming artificial and fading natural light was confusing. His eyes burned from long hours in the saddle. If they had not encountered the campers and taken advantage of their generous largess, he knew, both he and his mount would be in a bad way by now. As it was, they were simply exhausted.

"There!" he shouted, even though he knew Cirrus could not understand the word. But the skybax knew the tone, and shared the excitement in its rider's voice.

Ahead and slightly to their right, the Canyon City skybax

rookery rose in imposing isolation. Taller than its equally impressive neighboring spires, it boasted several natural protruding ledges that took the place of the thick artificial platforms that were required elsewhere. The smooth stone footing was not as secure as an intricate, heavy fiber weave, but what the landing site lacked in comfort it more than made up for in spaciousness.

Provided, of course, one could see it clearly. With its hollow bones, even the strongest skybax could not risk a crash landing.

In the near darkness Will could barely make out the outlines of tiny figures running around on the landing platform. Do they see us, he wondered? And if so, are they preparing for an emergency? Teeth clenched, he urged his mount onward and down. From here on until touchdown there was nothing more he could do. His life lay in the long, thin hands of his mount. All he could do was hang on and rely on millions of years of pterosaur instinct to bring them down in two pieces.

All at once, light appeared ahead of them. Multiple lights, small but oh so brilliant against the night. It was the rookery attendants setting out firebaskets! They had been seen, Will realized. Recognizing the peril inherent in their night-shrouded approach, appropriate measures had been taken to help the nocturnal arrivals. He exhaled sharply.

With blazing firebaskets delineating both sides of the landing platform, Cirrus made a perfect approach, touching down gently equidistant between the two flickering lines. Will half jumped, half fell to the ground. It had been an epic flight, and one he had no desire to ever repeat.

But they had made it, they were here in Canyon City.

Now he could inquire personally after Sylvia's whereabouts, now he could put the question to authorities who should be in a position to know. No more bureaucratic obfuscation, no more shunting him off to still another department, another official. He would find what he came for, and find it now. He would . . .

"Hello, Will Denison. I always thought you intelligent, and courageous. But I never thought you a fool."

Looking around, Will found himself gazing back at a rugged, no-nonsense face framed by a truly daunting set of blonde but graying muttonchop whiskers.

"Greetings, Master Oolu. The air—the air was good to us."

And with that he collapsed, completely drained, into the strong, supportive arms of his old instructor.

He awoke to the sound of a cloud singing. It was not the cloud outside his window that was producing the jaunty tune, however, but rather an apprentice seated cross-legged outside the door to his room, tootling on a flute carved in the shape of a skybax's long, narrow head.

Sitting up in the bed, Will stretched exquisitely. Before he could venture so much as a "good morning," the apprentice had seen that he was awake and had ceased his playing to dash off somewhere out of view.

Rising from the intricately carved bed, Will walked to the window. Outside, Canyon City defined both sides of the gorge. Trails and bridges were alive with people and small dinosaurs intent on the day's business. The sun was warm, flowers limned the rock ledges with bursts of color, and beneath his window was a sheer five-hundred meter drop. He was in Canyon City, all right.

He was only half dressed when the imposing figure of Oolu appeared in the doorway, pushing through the beaded curtain.

"Master, I only just awakened and . . ." Trying to put on his pants, Will fell backwards onto the bed.

"Rest easy, Rider." Oolu entered the room and courteously stood staring out the window while Will hastily finished dressing. "That was quite an arrival you contrived last night. The rookery attendants and the riders currently in-house are still talking about it. Your manifest shows that you left Sauropolis late, yet you completed the entire journey in one day." He turned from the window. Morning light showed gold on the curly blonde hair that coated his muscular, exposed forearms.

"What engenders such haste, Will Denison? What message was critical enough to drive you and your skybax to near collapse? Nothing so urgent was found in your saddle pouches."

"It's no message, Master Oolu." Usually confident to the point of brashness, in the presence of his old instructor Will found himself clumsy and tongue-tied. "It's a—personal matter."

Eyebrows like gold wool rose questioningly. "A personal matter? You used your position to facilitate a personal matter?"

"Oh no, Master!" Will protested. "I would never do that. If you've seen the saddle pouches then you know that I was bringing the regular mail from Sauropolis." His tone grew more subdued. "It was just a fortunate coincidence that I was given this assignment, because there is indeed something personal here that I need to follow up on."

Oolu was rubbing his chin and staring penetratingly at his former student. "'Coincidence,' is it? I wonder. . . ." Then his stern visage cracked and a smile as broad as the Blackwood Flats spread across his rugged, wind-scoured face. "You always were a clever one, Will Denison."

A sudden remembrance prompted Will to interrupt. "Cirrus . . . !"

Oolu made placating gestures to calm his former student. "Your skybax is fine and resting comfortably in the rookery. No thanks to the way you pushed him."

Oolu or not, Will was moved to protest. "Cirrus could have refused my direction at any time. You know that, Master. The feelings and opinion of a skybax always take precedence over those of their rider."

"True enough. But I've yet to encounter the skybax whose greatest desire was not to please their partner and companion." Having said this, the older man seemed to put the whole matter out of his mind. Will knew from experience that Oolu's moods could change as abruptly as the wind.

"Come then; out with it. What is this 'personal business' that brings you to Canyon City in such a rush?" Waiting expectantly, he sat down in the single wooden chair close by the window that had been cut from the solid rock, and crossed one leg over the other. The chair was carved in the shape of a skybax; its head back, its outspread wings forming the arms.

"My fiancée. She was working in this area, and according to the authorities here she hasn't checked back in the way she was supposed to. Since no one else seems to think it's worth investigating, I decided to do so myself." Self-consciously, he straightened his belt. "If you saw the other messages in the pouches, you should have found that one as well."

"There were several secured with privacy ribbons," Oolu responded. "Naturally no one opened them."

Of course they wouldn't, Will thought. He was still too tired to think clearly.

Oolu rose from the chair. "Are you rested enough to come with me?"

Will blinked. "For what, Master?"

The instructor's irresistible grin returned. "For a skybax rider's breakfast, of course. Come—the other riders are anxious to hear of your epic little flight. Epic with a small 'e', it is true, but epic nonetheless. And that landing! What would you have done if you had not been seen on approach and the firebaskets had not been set out to guide you in?"

As they started for the entrance Will felt a powerful, comforting arm come to rest across his shoulders. It was the kind of gesture one would expect from a colleague, not a teacher. He straightened a little, pride beginning to replace uncertainty.

"It *was* quite a landing, wasn't it?"

Oolu continued to smile, but his tone turned cool. "Indeed it was. Now, don't let it make you cocky. The skybax rider whose head is always in the clouds is the one who flies head-first into the low-hanging branch." With his free hand he brushed aside the beaded curtain that hung in the doorway.

Will discovered that he was ravenous, devouring everything the kitchen assistants placed on the table before him. Oolu ate more moderately, watching his former student with amusement.

When he was convinced that his guest had eaten his fill

(or at least was starting to slow down) he led him into reminiscences of their days as student and teacher. Will held his own in the conversation, but much preferred to listen to the Master. Oolu was full of the most marvelous stories about skybaxing around Dinotopia.

After bringing his old teacher up to date on all that had been happening in his life, Will eventually came around to the reason for his frantic flight from Sauropolis. Oolu listened intently until his visitor was finished.

"No, I don't know the lady. Haven't seen her around the city myself, though that doesn't mean anything. Recently I've been spending most of my time up at Pteros."

"I'll start with city administration," Will informed him. "If they won't help me . . ."

"They won't," Oolu interrupted him. "If the authorities in Sauropolis didn't feel there was an emergency, neither will the administrators here."

Looking down at his plate, Will wiped up the last vestiges of nutritious brown yeast extract with the remaining half of his sourdough quinoa roll. "I was afraid you'd say that. But I don't know what else to do."

"Try the taverns and the visitor's hostels," Oolu suggested. "See if you can find out where she ate while she was here, and where she stayed. It's likely that someone remembers her, and despite what you say is her penchant for privacy, she may very well have told someone where she was heading. Oftentimes travelers who wish to keep their intended destinations or purposes private will tell a concierge what they'd never tell an official."

"That's right." Will perked up. "Sylvia loves to talk. Yes, I can see her not filing an official plan of travel but mentioning her intentions to a total stranger seated next to her at dinner." Pushing back his chair, he rose from the table. "I'll start immediately."

"Good luck to you, Rider." Oolu stood also. "I'm sure you'll find her well. Myself, duty calls me back to Pteros." Coming around the table, he put both hands on the shorter, younger man's shoulders. "Take care in your searching. Canyon City is a bad place in which to miss a step."

A couple of friendly taps on the back, and Oolu let his former student go. With a sigh Will resumed his seat. There was still time for another cup of Bent Root tea before he had to depart.

Though it was the largest community in the eastern half of Dinotopia, between Chandara to the south and Proserpine to the north, Canyon City still retained the feel of a frontier community. Hewn out of the solid sandstone, it relied on trade, crafts, small-scale mining, and specialty farming to survive. There were none of the extensive farms and fields that surrounded either of the great coastal cities. As a result, Canyon City suffered somewhat from its isolation from the mainstream of Dinotopian cultural and economic life—but its citizens reveled in it as well. It was unique, a place like no other in Dinotopia.

Where else could one dine overlooking a thousand-meter sheer drop broken only by hanging gardens of flowers embedded in the rock, or cross a bridge in the company of busy, scurrying coelophyses while pterosaurs of all shapes and sizes flew past in formation *beneath* one's feet? Where else could one shower under a spring-fed waterfall twenty meters high but only a few centimeters wide, the wash water sprinting away through a narrow cleft in the base of the stall to feed ornamental bouquets on the outside of the hostel in which you were staying?

It reminded Will of Treetown, only here a misstep would prove even more serious than in one of that Arcadian hamlet's inhabited redwoods. And here there were no massive sauropods or ceratopsians to break one's fall. There was only the ancient course of the Amu, winding its way along the canyon floor far below.

Unlike some visitors to Canyon City, traversing the narrow rope bridges and natural stone arches that connected various parts of the community did not trouble him. He was used to more extreme altitudes—though there were moments when he missed the warm, comforting length of Cirrus beneath him.

He tried the hostels first, but no one could recall a traveler of Sylvia's description. Canyon City was a busy place, the proprietors invariably avowed, and many humans and dinosaurs passed through on their way to somewhere else.

"She might have stayed with friends," he was told following more than one inquiry, "or camped out on her own."

He had forgotten from his studies how large the stone warren known as Canyon City actually was. Furthermore, unlike Sauropolis or even Waterfall City and because of the heights involved, to get around required more climbing and descending than in any other large community in Dinotopia. Discouraged but refusing to give up, he moved on to the taverns. Weariness and hunger combined to make him pause in one long enough to order some lunch. The young woman who brought him his food wondered at the melancholy of the handsome young rider seated in her establishment. In response to his question, she had no more information as to his fiancée's whereabouts than had anyone else he had talked with.

But others were listening.

As he was finishing the last of his meal, two men and one woman sat down across from him. All three were more or less his age. He looked up hesitantly.

"I don't know you, do I?"

"No. And we don't know you," responded one of the young men instantly, "but we know why you're here." He nodded in the direction of the now absent waitress. "We were at the table behind yours and we overheard your question."

Polite but preoccupied, Will sipped from the now nearly empty ceramic mug that had been brought with his food. "I don't suppose you have any information, either."

"But we do." The young woman indicated the youth seated next to her. "Ollyanto and I think we've heard about the woman you were asking for, and not so very long ago at that."

Will put down the mug and half rose from his seat. "Where? When did you see her? You must tell me . . . !"

"Sit easy, Sky rider." The eldest of the trio made calming motions with his hands. "We didn't actually see her ourselves. But we met and talked with others, human and saurian, who in the course of conversation mentioned encountering a strange human female traveling alone in a little-visited part of the canyon."

The woman nodded energetically. "That's right. They came into my parents' store to get certain supplies they can't grow or make for themselves." She made a face. "I think they're kind of funny, both the humans and the dinosaurs, but lots of people have funny ways about them. They're accepted here, of course."

"I'm not sure I follow you," Will confessed.

"We'll give you all the details," the olive-skinned Ollyanto assured him, "but first you have to do something for us."

"Don't bargain with me in this." Will spoke sharply. "A woman's life may be at stake."

"According to the ones we talked to who had seen her, she was in excellent condition. Certainly nothing was said about her life being at stake, or even of her being in any danger." Maddeningly, the senior member of the group smiled at Will.

There was nothing he could do. Without an affidavit of emergency from a recognized authority he could hardly claim that Sylvia's life was in danger. He forced himself to relax in the chair, though he couldn't quite bring himself to smile back.

"All right, what is it you want me to do?"

The two men hesitated, leaving it to their attractive female companion to speak first. "It's nothing time-consuming or difficult." She smiled encouragingly at him. "We just want you to win a little race."

# -IV-

ill's brow furrowed. "'Win a race'? I'm pretty good at the short distances, but nothing to beat a sprained *Gallimimus*. As for distance, I'm afraid I never did have much wind."

"The distances involved are short," Ollyanto assured him, "and while speed is required, balance and good judgment are far more important."

Will eyed the attentive trio cautiously. "'Balance and good judgment'? What kind of 'good judgment'?"

"You'll see." Rising from her seat, the young woman took his hand and led him toward the door.

As they made their way along the breathtakingly narrow trails cut into the sides of the cliffs, and crossed gently swaying rope bridges that connected one inhabited pinnacle to another, Will learned that his three new acquaintances had lived all their lives in Canyon City. Feeling better about his companions the more they told him about themselves, he returned the courtesy by regaling them with stories of Waterfall City, of Sauropolis, of his adventures in the Rainy

Basin, and of his perilous encounter with the castaway crew of the pirate Brognar Blackstrap. They listened raptly, occasionally chiming in with questions or anecdotes of their own. The young woman in particular held tight to his hand, giving it an occasional squeeze that carried with it a hint of more than mere guidance.

At last they reached the destination they had in mind for him as well as for themselves. It was a tiny hanging valley set into the west side of the canyon wall. Composed of particularly soft stratified sandstone, it had been eroded into a fantastic assortment of spires and rocky blades. All exhibited wide bands of color ranging from cream-white to deep ochre or rich mauve, showing where different types of sediments had been laid down eons ago.

A number of other youths had assembled on the ledge nearest this geological pincushion. Several had removed all their clothing save for briefs and running sandals. A few glanced up as the newcomers approached.

"Well," declared one aloud, "who's going to run for your habitat this time?" The speaker eyed first Will's female companion, then the youth next to her. "Going to give it a try this time, Terena? Or will it be you, Ollyanto?"

"Neither," replied the trio's senior speaker. He gestured jauntily at their guest. "This is Will Denison. He'll be competing for Sharsteep habitat."

"Will will?" The inquirer chuckled easily and turned away, shaking his head slowly.

"Just a minute, wait a minute." Will vainly tried to keep his newfound friends (or were they his friends, he found himself beginning to wonder?) from picking at his clothes. "What are you doing?"

"You certainly can't wear all this," Terena informed him in clipped, no-nonsense tones. "You'll get too hot."

"While I'm doing what?" Outnumbered as well as confused, Will decided not to resist as they removed his outer attire.

"Racing to pick up the totem," Ollaynto informed him perfunctorily.

"What 'totem'? Where?"

"Over there, of course." Lifting a hand, he pointed across the pillar-filled valley.

While efficiently helping Will off with his light but tough long-legged skybax rider's pants, Terena explained. "Look across the tops of the spires. About two-thirds of the way to the canyon wall. See it?"

Blessed with excellent eyesight, Will had to confess that he still saw nothing out of the ordinary. Terena fought to constrain her impatience. "A little more to your right. On top of that mostly all-white pillar."

Will squinted harder, trying to focus on the indicated spot. Yes, an irregular shape seemed to rest atop the smooth rock. "You mean that piece of wood?"

"That 'piece of wood' is what we compete for. It's a branch that was found lying on a bridge." She gestured upward. "It must have fallen from above. To us it represents the big trees we can never have here in Canyon City as well as the endless branchings of the Amu and its canyon. Groups of us compete every two-week for the right to call it our own."

"You said something about a 'race'." Standing naked before them except for his briefs, Will experienced only a tingle of discomfort stemming from his early, non-Dinotopian

56

childhood. Air rising from the depths of the canyon warmed his exposed skin.

"That's right." The eldest youth was studying the heavily eroded little valley. "Each habitat picks someone to run for them. Whoever reaches the branch first gains possession of it for their friends for a two-week."

"I told you," Will protested, "I'm not that fast."

"And we told you," Ollyanto reminded him, "that balance and good judgment are just as important as speed, if not more so." Approaching their newly designated, reluctant champion, he stretched out his left arm to point while putting his other around Will's bare shoulders. "Look at the race arena. The competition is not to the swiftest so much as it is to the smartest and the most daring. Because the distances between pinnacles varies, there is no straight-line route to the totem." Stepping back, he smiled at the skybax rider. "To reach the branch first demands someone who is good not only in the sprints but at chess."

"I see." Will found himself becoming interested in the contest. "So the runner has to choose whether to take the shortest route—or the safest. Or the best combination of the two."

"Now you understand." Smiling, Terena stepped back. "The runners have to make decisions quickly. Not only about which way to go, but how far they can jump."

Glancing down, Will noted that in places the gaps between the eroded pinnacles plunged the height of a full-grown *Brachiosaurus* and more to the ground. A runner missing a jump could easily fall far enough to break a leg. Or his neck.

Across the small flat-topped butte, the other runners

were grinning at him. Will straightened. He might be an outsider, and a stranger to this peculiar canyon competition, but he had never been one to back down from a challenge. And if he didn't run, they wouldn't tell him what they had found out about Sylvia. Assuming it was Sylvia they had information about, he reminded himself.

Might as well give it a try, he decided. It was not as if he had a dozen leads to pursue.

"When do we start?" he asked.

His newfound friends looked delighted. "Nestor, over there, will blow a lambeosaur trumpet. You can begin from anywhere on the edge of the butte." Ollyanto gestured. "I would recommend starting over there, where Pollux and Hiroshii are waiting. It's an easy beginning, with short jumps, and you can . . ."

Will was already assessing possible routes to the totem. "I'll start right here, if you don't mind." He walked forward, the sun-warmed rock smooth beneath the soles of his featherlight skybax boots.

Terena eyed the initial gap doubtfully. "If you miss this jump, the race will be over for you before it's barely started."

He locked eyes with her. "Who's running—you or me?"

She looked a little startled, then backed off and offered no further suggestions.

He waited tensely for the horn to blow. He'd run many races, both with and against dinosaurs and other humans, and had done well, if not spectacularly. But this was something he might excel at, a venue where his agility and indifference to heights would stand him in good stead.

The young man raised his trumpet, cast in the shape of

an adult male *Lambeosaurus*'s colorful crest, and blew a single long, bleating note. Immediately, those who were only spectators raised a cheer and the race was on.

Taking a good running start, Will planted his right foot, pushed off, and leaped, high and long. Behind him, he thought he heard Terena let out a gasp. Her companions cheered.

He cleared the gap easily, landing with half a body length to spare, and immediately sought out his next landing site. His choice of a difficult starting point had placed him in the lead already.

His rarefied status did not last long. Utilizing their knowledge of the canyon, his local competitors were soon vaulting ahead of him, choosing pinnacle tops with care. Soon Will was working hard just to keep from falling farther behind.

Searching for an easier route, he saw that he had no choice but to continue on the path he had already chosen. Three of his competitors were already going that way. According to the rules of the race, no more than two runners could occupy the top of a spire at the same time. Anyone else trying to share the same space would be disqualified. The competition was a unique, and dangerous, combination of long jumping, running, gymnastics, and chess.

An unoccupied pillar lay just off to his left. Reaching it would not only allow him to make up most of the ground he had lost in the past several minutes but might even put him in the lead again. But it was too far away. Glancing down, sweat streaming across his body, he saw that the gap was more than forty feet deep. There were protruding ledges to grab if one missed, but still, it was a potentially dangerous drop. Behind him, the excited onlookers continued to shout encouragement to their favorites. He did not hear his name among them, nor did he expect to.

Steeling himself, he sprinted forward, trying to muster as much speed as possible in the limited space available to him. Fortunately, he'd always been a good starter. The nearer he came to the gap between the pinnacles, the deeper the chasm between them seemed to grow. Trying to remember the instructions of Mankorua, the champion *Struthiomimus* runner he had done some training with at Treetown, he planted his right foot hard and pushed off, felt himself soaring through the air. Behind him, a roar came from the crowd.

There was no Cirrus waiting to dive beneath him now and rescue him from a case of bad judgment. There was only rock, hard and unyielding. He felt himself falling, falling, for what seemed like an eternity. Then he hit, hard, his foot slipping. He scrambled for a handhold and dragged himself over the hot sandstone until he was lying prone on his belly on the top of the pinnacle he had aimed for. He'd made it. From here it was only a short hurdle across two small spires to the pinnacle where the totem waited.

Rolling over, he rose to his feet and prepared to resume his run—only to see one of the other runners standing atop the spire, oh so near, holding the honored branch aloft. Behind the winner, the members of his habitat cheered.

Will could not believe it. He had never seen the other runner approaching. What direction had he come from, what sinuous route had he utilized? It didn't matter. He had lost, and only by seconds.

Crestfallen, he made his way back to the flat staging area

atop the butte, choosing a return route that required little more than a series of safe, short hops. Most of the other youths were crowded around the winner, who was holding the branch over his head and waving it in slow, triumphant circles.

Ollyanto, Terena, and their older companion were waiting for him.

"I'm sorry." With a half-hearted shrug he began to slip his clothes back on. "I did my best, but I'm afraid it wasn't good enough."

"Good enough?" Ollyanto's expression was not that of someone who had lost. "You did great! That last jump of yours had everyone holding their breath."

"You bet it did," agreed his companion. "I didn't think you'd make it. If Severn had been half a step slower, you would have beaten him to the totem. And on your first try!"

"But I didn't beat him," Will murmured. "He beat me." He began to button his skybax rider shirt. "I guess this means you're not going to tell me what you know."

"Don't be silly." Stepping forward, Terena put both hands on his shoulders. Then she leaned forward and, to Will's astonishment, kissed him full on the lips. Nearby, her two companions hooted loudly.

As she stepped back, Will could only stare. "You must love your lady very much to come all this way on your own to try and make sure she is all right. I hope she appreciates how lucky she is. Did you really think we would withhold that kind of information from you just because you didn't win?" She smiled. "You ran a great race, Will Denison. One that I, certainly, will never forget. You brought honor to Sharsteep habitat." Turning, she nodded at the eldest among them.

"Kharan, tell them what the shoppers spoke of when they were stocking up on supplies in my father's store."

The older youth nodded and smiled at Will. "They were a funny lot, they were. Humans and oviraptors, children as well as adults. The humans wore very little and the oviraptors sported less in the way of ornamentation than any civilized dinosaurs I've ever seen."

"I was there too," Ollyanto put in, reminiscing. "They went away loaded down, as if they only visited town once in a great while." He glanced at his friends. "But before they left, we had a chance to talk to them for a little while." He eyed Will significantly. "In addition to finding out something about them, we also found out a little about someone else."

Will was fastening his belt as Terena took up the narrative. "I had forgotten all about it, until we overheard you in the tavern asking about a missing woman who might be traveling through the canyon on her own."

"I remember," Will told her. Anticipation overcame his exhaustion.

"One of the adults spoke of a beautiful young woman they encountered who was hiking down the main canyon that parallels their own. Her manner was cheerful and open, she was dressed for walking and rock climbing, and she carried a sizable pack." Terena pointed to a nearby band of red-orange rock. "Her hair was that color."

Tired as he was, a surge of excitement raced through Will. "Sylvia!"

"The shoppers did not give her name."

"It's her. It has to be her." Will smiled knowingly. "I don't know many people besides Sylvia who would strike off on their own down the canyons of the Amu." His forehead wrinkled. "But what can she be looking for?"

Ollyanto shrugged. "Maybe they know, but the shoppers did not say."

"How can I find these people?" Will asked him anxiously.

"It's a bit of a trek, but not a particularly difficult one." The other youth turned and pointed. "You go back to the city portal, turn left and down two walking levels at the east wall reservoir, then down . . ."

A smiling Terena cut him off. "We'll make you a map, Will Denison. To someone unfamiliar with these canyons, one turning looks the same as another. The Amu has thousands and thousands of tributaries."

Will glanced skyward. "I wouldn't have any trouble from the air."

"I see what you're thinking, but that won't work. Not if you want to find these people. My father says that the canyon in which they live is so narrow that in places you can stretch out your arms and touch both sides at the same time."

Will frowned. "Doesn't sound like there's enough room to live in."

"I can't imagine it myself, but clearly they do live there. In any case, it's obviously much too narrow for your sky-bax to enter." She put a hand on his arm. "Come. You must be thirsty after your valiant effort." Her fingers squeezed. "Let's get you something to drink, and while we're toasting the runner-up, we'll make you that map." She indicated the older youth. "Kharan is a fine draftsman."

"Don't worry." The older boy put a comradely arm around Will's shoulders. "We'll see to it that you don't get lost."

Equipped with map, pack, food and water, Will set off the next morning in search of the peculiar family his new friends insisted might be able to help him pinpoint Sylvia's whereabouts. By the time he was out of sight of Canyon City, he was glad of the hand-drawn map they had made for him. Just as Terena had said, each canyon seemed to have half a dozen branchings, and each of those as many more. Without Kharan's deft cartography, he would have been lost within an hour.

The trail he found himself following led downward at a gentle angle, following the curves of the canyon wall. Twice, he crossed bridges fashioned of rope imported from the east coast. They swayed and rocked as he made his way across, small streams tumbling beneath him in their rush to join the stately current of the Amu itself.

Nourished by springs that trickled from the porous sandstone, small oases supported extensive plant and bird life. According to what he remembered from his studies, many of these miniature environments were unique to the canyonlands, their inhabitants endemic to the valley of the Amu. He frequently heard bird songs he did not recognize, more than once encountered a profusion of flowers whose perfumes were as unfamiliar as they were intoxicating.

One critical turnoff nearly escaped him, so constricted was the entrance. He remembered what Terena had said about being able to reach out and touch both sides of the chasm where the family dwelt. As he made his way along the narrow trail that paralleled the anxious creek at the bottom of the slot canyon, he wondered how anyone could live in such an environment. In places there was barely room enough to turn around in, much less find room to sleep. And what would dwellers in such a locale do in the event of a sudden summer storm and consequent flash flood, when the level of the deceptively tranquil creek at his feet might rise a foot a minute?

Answers, he knew, lay at the end of the canyon. High overhead, sunlight crept uncertainly down the upper flanks of the chasm in a futile search for the bottom.

An hour later a sound made him hesitate. It was distinctive and familiar. The narrow canyon magnified the noise. Picking his way carefully, he turned a corner—and found himself staring at a face that combined the most prominent features of raptor and parrot. He let out a startled exclamation.

Equally surprised, the *Oviraptor* made a sound halfway between a hoot and a tweet and took a couple of startled steps backward. Then she relaxed and cocked her head sideways. A few cautiously modulated *wheets* came from her heavily-beaked mouth.

"I'm sorry—I didn't mean to startle you like that." Will smiled reassuringly. "You surprised me too, you know."

Straightening, the svelte dinosaur stood about a head shorter than Will. She chattered querulously at him, perhaps unaware that he could not understand a word she was saying, before turning and beckoning for him to follow. Hefting his pack higher on his shoulders, Will complied.

They did not have far to go. Quite unexpectedly, the canyon opened up onto a sizable circular dead-end, like a sheer-sided bore-hole in the earth. At the far end of the box canyon was the source of the sound he had been hearing for several hours. The crystalline cascade that tumbled over the upper cliff was twice the height of the tallest brachiosaur but no wider than the span of Will's arms. A citizen of Waterfall City would have classed it as a mere trickle, but here in this dry, isolated place it was as conspicuous as any Niagara.

It spilled into a pool the color of Persian turquoise and from there tumbled over a series of exquisite travertine dams where it reformed into a single stream before vanishing down the narrow canyon.

More remarkable than the dazzling little waterfall was the series of rope and bark hammocks that criss-crossed the canyon. At once Will saw how the inhabitants lived; working and eating alongside their miraculous pool and sleeping in the oversized hammocks draped above. In the event of a flood everyone could find safety in a hammock, suspended well above the raging waters below.

There were trees in the dead-end canyon as well; trees he did not recognize. Young children and dinosaurs were gathering nuts from the ground at their bases while older youths worked up in the branches to shake them loose. Bushes clinging to the canyon walls yielded berries and edible flowers.

A man clad in sandals and shorts swiftly greeted the new arrivals, exchanging a couple of crude hoots with the *Oviraptor*. He reminded Will of his own father. Then the greeter extended a hand, palm up and facing Will.

"I'm Peralta." He indicated the *Oviraptor*. "This is Chinpwa. Welcome to the home of the Family Helth."

"Thanks." Unslinging his pack, Will laid it gratefully on

the ground and sat down next to it. At his feet the stream rushed past, full of energy and gurgle. Chinpwa settled down on her haunches alongside them, studying the unexpected visitor with open curiosity.

As they rested, a boy and girl brought them a flat woven basket full of nuts and berries. While a grateful Will sampled the vividly colored berries, Chinpwa helped herself to the nuts, using her heavy jaws and parrot-like beak to crack the tough shells with ease.

"What brings an outlander to our little canyon?" Peralta wanted to know. "We don't get many visitors."

Clearly the three dozen or so humans and dinosaurs within view placed great value on their privacy, or they would not have chosen to live in such an isolated place. "I hope I'm not intruding."

"Not at all," Peralta assured him. Chinpwa added a comforting hoot before she cracked another nut. "The Family Helth isn't antisocial. We simply prefer to live outside the mainstream of Dinotopian life and on, you might say, a sidestream." He indicated the creek at their feet. "We follow a singular philosophy of living that involves much meditation as well as a special diet."

Which you are not above supplementing with occasional visits to the shops of Canyon City, Will mused. Aloud, he said nothing. Many were the ways and philosophies of living, and Dinotopia had room for them all. Even for the willful peculiarities of the self-isolated Family Helth.

"I came in search of someone," he replied.

Peralta chuckled. "There are no strangers here and, as you can see, no place for one to hide."

"Not here," Will explained. "I was told that you might

have encountered her outside your own canyon, between here and Canyon City."

Peralta glanced at Chinpwa and hooted crudely. The *Oviraptor* made him repeat the words (even the most linguistically adept humans being poor approximators of dinosaurian speech) before replying. The man listened, nodded, and turned back to Will.

"We occasionally do encounter travelers headed up or down canyon, though most are making the crossing from Canyon City to the Pteros side on their way to the coast, or back again. Who was it that you have come looking for?"

Will described Sylvia, then had to endure another coarse exchange between human and dinosaur. In response, Chinpwa rose from her haunches and bounded lithely off in the direction of the waterfall. Will could hear her hooting at each of her fellow saurians as she passed.

Peralta tried to be encouraging. "Chinpwa is putting the question to her family and friends. The oviraptors tend to travel outside farther and more frequently than the rest of us. They're always looking for more Yengu trees." He indicated the pile of empty shells where the small dinosaur had been sitting.

"I don't think I could live here." Will made polite conversation as they waited for the *Oviraptor* to finish her rounds.

"It's not for everyone," Peralta agreed, "but there is a peace, a contentment, that often escapes those who live in the cities. And we believe it to be healthier."

"How old is your senior family member?"

The other man grinned. "Ah, you see, that is one of the fallacies of life outside. The notion that a healthy existence is determined by how long one lives. We believe that there are other, more important hallmarks." He rose as Chinpwa rejoined them.

Will listened intently, even though he understood less of what the *Oviraptor* said than did Peralta. As a skybax rider, Will knew a number of useful phrases in several saurian tongues, but that of the oviraptors was alien to him.

Peralta was nodding, which Will chose to interpret as a hopeful sign. Before the conversation concluded they were joined by two more oviraptors, both slightly smaller than Chinpwa.

"This is Jemot, and next to her is her sister Wiwiri," Peralta explained. As their names were mentioned, each of the sisters extended a clawed hand palm upward and touched it to Will's. "They think they saw the lady you seek."

"Where?" Will demanded to know, more sharply than he intended.

Peralta put the question to the saurian siblings, who faced each other and argued briefly. There was much pointed jabbering and gesturing of clawed fingers before they quieted. The nearest, Jemot, put a hand on Will's arm and turned him to face the canyon's distant mouth. As she held him she chattered, and Peralta did his best to translate.

"Jemot says that she and Wiwiri were just returning from a walk of many days down canyon in search of food supplies when they came face to face with a single young human female. The woman talked to them with signs and drawings in the sand, and a few words." Peralta paused. "She had very red hair."

Will nodded excitedly. "That's Sylvia. Tell them to go on."

The oviraptors did so, barely leaving time for Peralta to translate. "They camped with her that night, which gave

69

them a chance to talk. The woman seemed healthy and unharmed."

For the first time in days, Will felt a great uneasiness leave him. "I can't tell you how glad I am to hear that. Where was Sylvia going?"

Again Peralta queried the young oviraptors. When he looked back at Will he wore a strange expression. "It's very odd."

"What is?" Will prompted him.

"I'm pretty sure I am understanding them correctly, but it doesn't make any sense. They say that the woman told them she was making her way to the east. But nothing lies to the east of where they were camped. No towns, no villages, not even other solitary kith like the Family Helth. Beyond a few small, steep side canyons east of that place there is only one thing."

Will frowned. "What one thing?"

If anything, Peralta's kindly expression grew even more mystified. "Why, the Great Desert, of course."

Though he'd never been there, Will knew well the location of the Great Desert. A competent skybax rider had to have an encyclopedic knowledge of Dinotopian geography. Certainly Peralta was right. Saying that the Great Desert lay to the east was the same as saying that there was nothing there.

"I don't understand." He eyed the two saurian sisters, who gazed back at him out of round, slightly bulbous eyes. "That can't be right."

Peralta restated the inquiry, and for a second time the two oviraptors replied identically. Their questioner shrugged. "They insist that is what she intended. The woman drew them a map in the sand."

"But it doesn't make any sense!" Will accepted a swallow of water from a cup held out to him by the thoughtful Chinpwa. "Why would Sylvia—why would anyone want to walk out of the Amu, away from the safety of Canyon City, and into the Great Desert?"

Through drawings and handsigns Jemot made it clear that the woman they had encountered was in search of rare, early fossils, of which Dinotopia had many. Will could not recall hearing of any substantial deposits having been found in the great canyon, but that did not mean they didn't exist. He was a skybax rider, not a paleontologist.

When had Sylvia developed this sudden interest in early fossils? Certainly she'd never spoken to him about it.

Apparently the oviraptors had experienced similar concerns. While Wiwiri kept snapping her powerful beak shut and then gently slapping the sides of her jaws with both hands, Jemot was pointing to the stick figure of a human woman she had drawn in the sand with one long claw.

"Close-mouthed?" Will stared hard at the two saurians. "Guarded?" Peralta tried to help with a few awkward hoots of his own. "That can't be right. Sylvia's one of the most open people I've ever met."

But the sisters clung to their story, insisting that whenever they tried to pin their visitor down to specific locations she might be heading for, they were discouraged. Charmingly, but discouraged nonetheless.

Why would Sylvia deliberately withhold such information? The knowledge contained in the fossil record was valuable to all. Something here made no sense. Several somethings.

He had Peralta query again. This time, Jemot approached Will. With her clawed but careful fingers she pinched up bits of Will's cheeks and gently tugged them in several directions. At this demonstration Wiwiri tootled her laughter, and Peralta had to smile.

Jemot stepped back, nodding and gesturing while Will felt of his face where she had manipulated him. "What was that all about?"

"I think," a grinning Peralta told him, "that she was demonstrating how flexible human faces are. Flexible, and expressive. Jemot is trying to tell you that while they were listening to your lady friend's words and looking at her drawings in the sand, they were also reading her face. Her gestures and sketches said one thing, but her face another." The grin vanished. "They're not saying that your lady was lying to them outright, but they believe that she was definitely concealing something.

"And if it makes you feel any better," he added as he accepted some nutmeat from Wiwiri, "it doesn't make any sense to them, either. Or to me. So we all stand confused together, my young friend."

What was going on here, Will wondered? For a moment he considered the possibility that the oviraptors had encountered someone else on the trail. But the physical description was too close. It had to be Sylvia. It just didn't sound like *his* Sylvia.

She *could* be hunting fossils, but why be cagey about her intended destination? If he were the one traveling alone in this country he would want everyone and anyone to know where he was going. His head was starting to hurt trying to make sense of it all.

"I have to go after her," he informed Peralta. "I think she may be in trouble."

"Well you certainly can't go like that." The older man indicated Will's small daypack. "The canyons are full of springs, but you still need something to carry water in. And your friend was headed east. You'll need food, and some kind of sleeping gear." He spread his hands and smiled apologetically. "We would be glad to help, but as you can see, the lifestyle we have chosen requires very little in the way of physical goods."

Will rose. "That's all right. You've already helped me a great deal. At least now I know where and in what direction to search." He looked back down the slot canyon, back the way he'd come. "I'll have to return to Canyon City and stock up on supplies."

"Why not wait for her?" Peralta urged him. "According to Jemot and Wiwiri she wasn't in any difficulty."

"I can't do that," Will told him. "You're probably right and there's nothing wrong. That's what everybody's been telling me all along. But too many things don't add up. This isn't like her. I have to know what's going on, and see for myself that she's all right."

Peralta nodded gravely. "Then we wish you good luck, and safe walking."

They bade him farewell, Wiwiri presenting him with a bag full of shelled nuts, and a big oviraptor hug. Jemot was more circumspect, pressing palms with the visitor in the accepted manner. Will waved to them as he started back down the slot canyon. The music of the thin, high waterfall and the laughter of human and dinosaur children lingered in his ears long after he had lost sight of the isolated paradise.

He dared not run on the narrow trails, but he lengthened his stride, anxious to return to the city and prepare. Jemot and Wiwiri had made certain he understood how to find the place where they had parted ways with Sylvia. He did not anticipate any trouble finding it. Tracking Sylvia from that point would be more difficult, but he knew he at least had to try.

# -V-

xhausted and wearing a fine coating of trail dust, he reached the outskirts of the city early the following morning. The sympathetic proprietor of the inn where he literally fell in had his clothes washed and cleaned for him while he showered. Much refreshed after a big breakfast, he made inquiries and was directed to a shop three levels up and across one bridge.

Tall and muscular, the outfitter looked more like a blacksmith or wrestler than a shop owner. He wore his jet black hair in a long ponytail behind him. His skin and attire of choice both suggested a south Mediterranean ancestry.

"So you're really determined to go hunting this young lady of yours, then?"

"That's right." Will was trying to decide between two large backpacks fashioned from tough fabric. He had not seen their like before. Some local manufacturer had devised a method of placing metal brads at strategic places to reinforce the seams. He found himself wondering if other handwoven commodities could be similarly strengthened. Pants, for instance. But that would never do, he decided. Who would want to wear pants with metal brads sticking out of them?

Settling on the larger of the two packs, he added a water-bag before moving on to the section of the store that stocked trail foods that had been dried in Canyon City's strong sun. The intrigued proprietor followed, looming over his smaller customer.

"But according to what you tell me," he said pleasantly, "you cannot even be sure that it was your lady these sisters met on the trail."

"Their description was too accurate to be mistaken." Will studied the shelves of dried fish and fruits, the little sacks of dehydrated vegetables. "Besides, it's the only lead I have."

The proprietor scratched at the back of his head. Save for an occasional regular visitor, the shop was empty, and this young skybax rider interested him.

"You're not going to be able to carry sufficient supplies, you know."

Will glanced back at him and smiled. "I don't eat much. I'll manage. Maybe I can convince someone else to travel with me."

"Not where you're going," the shop owner replied feelingly. "Those side canyons can be deep, and narrow. These rocks aren't like those in the Forbidden Mountains. Sandstone is tricky, and tends to crumble under a climber's hands. If she was headed east from the point where those oviraptors last saw her"—the aquiline profile nodded in the appropriate direction—"she'll run out of trail quickly. So will you. How then do you propose to track her?"

As Will considered his reply, the proprietor leaned over and whispered something to the woman perusing dried flowers at the middle counter. She glanced briefly at Will, then turned and exited the shop. Since she hadn't spoken to him, he thought nothing of it and continued with his shopping.

"I've had some training," he informed the proprietor. "I'll look for marks. Footprints, scratches on the rock walls, stones that have been disturbed. If she continued on up the side canyon where the two sisters encountered her, she should be easy to follow."

The owner nodded gravely. "It's not an easy thing you are proposing to do, my young friend." He stepped forward. "Here. This fish will last longer than the species you are handling."

"But this one tastes better," Will countered.

They discussed his purchases for what seemed to Will like a very long time, but he knew that the owner was only trying to helpful. His concern for Will's welfare was obvious, and Will appreciated it. He was not sure, however, that he appreciated what followed.

He was settling the bill with what remained of his barter credits when a tall, lean man accompanied by a *Hypsoliphodont* entered the shop. Both were clad in bright gold and blue. Will at once recognized the unmistakable emblems of municipal office.

The gaudy *Hypsoliphodont* stared unblinkingly at Will while her human associate glanced from the skybax rider to the proprietor. "Is this the youth, Talifrez?"

The shop owner nodded. "This is him, Borla."

Will didn't know what to say. "What's going on?" He

eyed the proprietor accusingly. "I thought you wanted to help me."

"I do, young rider. That's why I saw to it that the authorities were notified. What you are proposing to do is foolish and dangerous. While it is not for me to pass judgment, that is a responsibility that does fall to others. I'm sorry if you feel betrayed. Believe me, I have only your best interests at heart."

"But Sylvia's already out there," Will protested.

"Myself, I would not send a fool to rescue a fool." The big man turned away. "But as I said, this is not for me to decide."

The *Hypsoliphodont* stepped forward. Putting a clawed hand on Will's arm, she tugged gently.

"You are to come with us," her human companion informed him.

"Come with you?" Will gathered up his purchases, struggling to keep small packets from spilling onto the floor. "Come with you where? I'm a free citizen. Am I under arrest?"

The tall man looked shocked. "Certainly not! We are to take you before the Canyon City Director of Public Safety. Having heard of your case, she has taken a personal interest in it. Believe me, everyone has only your welfare in mind."

"That's fine," he countered, "but what about Sylvia's welfare?" Again the gentle but firm saurian tug on his arm.

"I do not know the lady in question. We were told only to bring you."

Seeing that he was not going to be able to argue his way out of it, Will allowed himself to be escorted from the shop.

A few curious inhabitants of the city watched as he was led away. Behind him, the shopkeeper stood in the entrance way and followed the retiring back of his young customer with concerned dark eyes.

There being a decided paucity of flat, open space in Canyon City, its municipal offices occupied a series of vertical habitats fashioned from the eastern cliff face. Far smaller than comparable offices in Waterfall City or Sauropolis, they were nonetheless fully occupied and busy.

Will was led to a sizable chamber in the middle level. As he waited to be admitted to the inner sanctum, he contemplated the scene outside the hand-hewn window. One thing about living and working in Canyon City, he reflected: unlike in other communities, here it was impossible to find a dwelling *without* a view.

After what seemed like an eternity but was in fact only the usual bureaucratic delay, the receptionist directed him to enter. Inside he found himself staring across a desk fashioned from finely worked flagstone and slate that had been decorated with stonework inlays. An elderly woman sat behind while off to her left a *Dromaeosaurus* stood ready to take notes on a scroll-writer.

"Come in, young man." The woman's voice was a surprise, cool and youthful. A singer's voice, Will decided as he complied.

"Look, I don't want to cause trouble and I don't want to involve anyone else." He took a seat in the single empty chair. Off to one side, the scroll-writer whirred as the *Dromaeosaurus* got to work. "I just want to make sure that my fiancée is all right."

"Yes, that's what I was told," the official replied briskly.

"According to my report, she was heading east, out of the canyon and toward the Great Desert. I would imagine she will turn back before that point is reached."

"You don't know Sylvia," Will told her. "If she thinks she's onto something interesting, she'll forget everything else—including where she happens to be at the time."

"I see." The official folded her hands on the stone desk. "You must realize that as the Director of Public Safety the health and well-being of everyone in Canyon City is to a greater or lesser degree ultimately my responsibility. That responsibility extends to travelers passing through." Her expression hardened slightly.

"What you intend is very dangerous."

Irritated, Will replied with a distinct lack of diplomacy. "I wasn't aware that subjecting oneself to danger was a punishable offense in Canyon City."

"It's not," she replied instantly. "Neither, for that matter, is youthful foolishness."

"Are you going to forbid me to go?"

Sitting back in her chair, the official sighed deeply. "That is thinking from the outside world. In Dinotopia we do not forbid. We can only suggest."

Will was immediately abashed. "Sorry. It's just that I'm so worried about her, and anxious to be on my way."

"Yes, I can see that." She stared out the window, at the panorama of homes and shops, bridges and walkways that decorated the canyon walls. "Personally, I think your little one-man expedition a waste of time. But it isn't my place to rule on that. Your safety, however, is another matter. I cannot let you go alone." These last words were uttered with a force and finality that belied the official's age and slight stature.

Will shrugged. "It'd be great to have company, but no one will go with me." As if to make up for his earlier discourtesy, he offered a lopsided grin. "Strangely, they all seem to think my going after Sylvia is a waste of time."

It brought a hint of a smile to the Director's deeply lined face. "That should tell you something, young man, but I can see from your expression that it's not going to change anything. Very well then. Since you are determined to do this, and since no one will volunteer to go with you, a suitable companion will be appointed. At city expense."

"I'm grateful," Will replied frankly.

"You will need a translator and packer. One with experience and some knowledge of canyon tracking, small enough to follow you into the narrow places. I have taken the liberty of choosing one from the available staff." She looked past him, to the *Dromaeosaurus*, and whistled something in the high-pitched tongue of that species. Will admired her facility with the language even though he knew that, like most humans, she doubtless commanded only a very few words and phrases that would be comprehensible to the dinosaur.

Nodding and replying with a much sharper whistle than any human could manage, the dromaeosaur stepped down from the scroll-writer and loped out through the doorway.

"I cannot stop you from making a fool of yourself," the woman was telling Will, "but with luck I can prevent you from killing yourself."

"Then we both want the same thing." He smiled again.

"It will be very important that you. . ." She broke off and rose from her seat. "Your companion is here."

Will quickly rose from his own chair, anxious to greet

whomever the city had assigned to assist him in his hunt for Sylvia and to reassure them that he knew what he was doing and was not simply some addlepated youngster utterly ignorant of the potential difficulties involved. A smallish, hog-sized dinosaur was waddling through the doorway.

He was not surprised to see that it was a *Protoceratops*. The official had told him he would need a translator, and that meant the only one of the ceratopsian species that could switch easily between the human lingua franca of Dinotopia and its multitude of dinosaurian tongues. The sturdy four-legged *Protoceratops* could also carry plenty of supplies not only for itself but for another.

He was surprised, however, to find that he recognized this particular representative of that estimable species. Recognized him instantly, in fact. At the same time, the arriving dinosaur caught sight of the young skybax rider. His reaction was probably not what the Director of Public Safety had anticipated.

"You!" he blurted, almost forgetting to translate.

Will was too astonished to smile. "Hello, Chaz," he replied simply.

The intrigued director looked from saurian to sapiens. "You two know each other?"

"Know each other?" The ornately ornamented *Protoceratops* stomped into the room, making as much noise on the stone floor with its stubby feet as it could. It was a ceratopsian way of adding emphasis to its words. "This—this reckless young human was all but the end of me a dozen times over this past year. Did word of the intrusion by antisocial humans on the north coast not reach here?"

The Director looked thoughtful. "It seems to me I may

have heard something of the incident. You were both involved?"

"*He* was involved." Raising one foot, Chaz indicated the amused skybax rider. "*I* was dragged along, very much against my better judgment. A judgment, I may say, that was more than vindicated by subsequent events.

"And now you wish me to accompany him? I don't want anything to do with him, Madame Director. I don't want to walk with him, I don't want to talk with him, I don't want to eat with him and I don't want to sleep with him!"

"Nice to see you, too, Chaz," Will murmured.

"But it is the judgment of the city council and the recommendation of this department that you do so." The Director eyed the petulant translator sternly.

Approaching the desk, the *Protoceratops* raised up on its hind legs and laid both stubby feet on the edge of the finely worked stone. "On being informed of the nature of the journey I thought it a waste of time, and dangerous to boot." Chaz looked toward Will and nodded. "And now that I see who is involved, that feeling is reinforced tenfold."

"Don't get so overwrought," Will advised him. "We're just going for a little walk."

"'A little walk,' he calls it." The translator lowered his front feet to the floor. "Up unvisited side canyons to the edge of the Great Desert." He glanced back at the Director. "I am telling you, Madame, that unpleasant things have a tendency to occur in this young man's vicinity, and I want no part of it. Send someone else."

"There is no one else," the Director replied quietly. "Not with your qualifications."

"Send Esmac. She can pack four times what I can."

"That's because Esmac is a *Centrosaurus* and she is four times bigger than you. Not only do her translation skills not approach yours," the Director admonished the reluctant *Protoceratops*, "but she is too large to negotiate the more narrow trails and bridges. This assignment has been given to you, Chaz. Do you refuse it?"

The translator's head dipped slightly. "No. No, of course not. You know I cannot do that." One round eye swiveled to regard Will. "I am telling you in advance, Will Denison, that this time I will not be drawn into any of your wild shenanigans or youthful tomfoolery. We will go and have a quick look for this Sylvia female of yours and then we will return straightaway to Canyon City."

Will made a show of considering the *Protoceratops*'s terms before nodding slowly. "Sounds fair to me."

Still unsatisfied, Chaz turned to face the youth. "No mad adventuring this time?"

"Absolutely not. We're just going to have a look for Sylvia to make sure she's all right."

"According to what I just heard from the receptionist in the outer office, the authorities already think she's all right."

Will smiled engagingly. "Then in that case, there's nothing to worry about, is there?"

Chaz snorted, producing a sound like a miniature buffalo. "Very well then. I will see to the necessary supplies, though I still think this is a jeopardous waste of time."

"Everyone else seems to agree with you." Walking over to the muttering *Protoceratops*, Will put a friendly hand on the top of his frill. "You have the weight of opinion behind you."

"Yes," Chaz retorted mulishly, "but unfortunately, it looks like I am going to have you in front of me."

# -VI-

"heer up," Will told his grumbling four-footed companion as they left the soaring stone arches and graceful gardens of Canyon City behind. "It's a beautiful morning, and I'm sure we'll find Sylvia's camp within a few days."

Trailing behind, the *Protoceratops* glanced owlishly up at the ebullient biped striding along confidently in front of him. "I seem to recall you being 'sure' about a great many things in the course of our experiences last year, only to find yourself captured by uncivilized humans and indebted to outraged tyrannosaurs. Among other trivialities. With me hauled along in the bargain."

Will looked back over his shoulder. Though as concerned as ever about Sylvia, he was in high good spirits this morning. He refused to accede to Chaz's pessimism.

"Don't be such a grumble-beak! Everything turned out all right, didn't it?"

"Thanks be to a kind Fate," the *Protoceratops* groused. Willful ceratopsian eyes considered the vast chasm of

the Amu. Far below the trail, the great river roared and growled against ancient rock. According to his companion, soon they would be turning off up a tributary, and then making their way into a smaller canyon still. There they would be truly alone, and on their own. Already Chaz missed the conviviality of the sleeping barn and the always interesting multilingual conversation of mature humans and dinosaurs.

Instead of being there, here he was yet again, stuck with nursemaiding the entirely too impetuous Will Denison. His left hind foot slipped on the gravely sandstone and he staggered under his load. Irritated beyond measure, he snapped reflexively at it with his beak.

"No telling how far we'll have to walk," he muttered.

This time there was a twinkle in Will's eye as he looked back. "Would you rather fly?"

With their less flexible faces, dinosaurs were not capable of a full range of facial expressions, but Chaz's reaction was articulate enough.

"Very droll, Will. As you perfectly well know, my one previous airborne experience in your company was sufficient to last a lifetime, thank you." The translator emphasized his response with several extra-heavy foot stomps. "All ceratopsians are built low to the ground for a reason, and my kind are built lower than most. If it is all the same to you, I will keep my feet where they belong and leave the flying to hollow-boned pterosaurs and hollow-headed skybax riders."

Chaz's response caused Will to think of Cirrus. In his absence, the great *Quetzalcoatlus* would be well looked after in the rookery at Pteros, and would enjoy the company of his own kind. But the special bond that existed between Rider and Flyer was strong, and Will knew that the skybax would long for its human as much as the human pined for his mount.

No more of such thoughts, he ordered himself firmly. From this point on he should be thinking of Sylvia and what he would say when he saw her again. Especially, he told himself grimly, if she was not in any trouble.

As much to distract his mind from melancholy as to break the lengthening silence, he asked Chaz to bring him up to date on the *Protoceratops*'s doings since last they'd met. That request, at least, was one that his reluctant four-legged companion was predisposed to fulfill.

"After recovering from our 'little adventure,' as you call it," the *Protoceratops* informed him dryly, "I returned to my work and to my studies. I am now a full-fledged translator." Dinosaurs were not particularly prideful, but Chaz could not keep a hint of it from creeping into his voice as he made the pronouncement.

"Like Bix." Will scrambled over a cluster of rocks that had collapsed onto the rapidly narrowing trail.

"Yes, like Bix, only without her experience." Chaz carefully picked his away around the fresh scree.

"So that means you're now qualified to talk nonsense in twenty tongues?" Will teased playfully.

The *Protoceratops* glanced up. "Dinosaurs do not talk nonsense. We leave that to humans." Warily, he peered over the edge of the steep drop. The trail ahead was withering rapidly to an occasional ledge underfoot. "As a diplomated translator, I have better things to do than waste my time on wild gallimimus chases into the wilderness."

"Why not reserve judgment until we've found Sylvia?" Will had to turn sideways to navigate a narrow shelf. Exhibiting better balance, the four-legged Chaz suffered no such hesitation.

"Why? I am certain she is well. No one, human or dinosaur, would head off alone into country like this without being properly prepared. Is she an idiot?"

Will looked back sharply, but his companion was not being accusatory. "Of course not. Sylvia's one of the most intelligent women I've ever met."

"Then why not credit her with some of that intelligence and assume that she is all right?"

They continued to argue as they made their way deeper and deeper into the contracting maze of canyons. If nothing else, the interminable, unresolvable debate helped to pass the time. The ledge along which the vanishing trail ran grew progressively narrower and steeper, the dangerous drop-off more and more shallow, until the stream that was responsible for it trickled along less than a few body-lengths below them. Overhead, the sun was a distant memory, having long since set behind the narrowing canyon walls.

"How can you even be sure this is the right chasm?" Chaz was arguing.

Will examined their surroundings carefully. "It's the right canyon," he replied unequivocally. "All the signs are here."

"What signs?" Chaz looked from left to right. "These fissures all look alike to me."

Will peered back over his shoulder. "That's why you're a translator and I'm a skybax rider." Scrambling up a steep slope, he turned to give his companion a hand, reaching down to grab the *Protoceratops*'s harness and yank hard.

Grunting and puffing with the effort, Chaz surmounted the incline and they continued on.

"If we could move a little faster," Will commented, "we'd be done with this sooner, and could return to Canyon City."

"I am doing the best I can," the quadruped snapped. "Am I a skinny monkey like you? I think not." He indicated the twin supply packs strapped to his back. "It would be interesting to see how agile you would be with this load resting on your shoulders."

Will was at once contrite. "I'm sorry, Chaz. I don't mean to criticize." He gazed anxiously toward the head of the canyon, whose walls were beginning to peter out on both sides. "I'm so worried about Sylvia that sometimes I forget what I'm saying."

"Hmph. Well then, I forgive you. After all, it is well known that infatuated humans lose one percent of their intelligence quotient for every week they are in love." Less brusquely he added, "I truly hope that we will find your lady healthy and in good circumstances."

"Thanks," Will told him warmly.

"But that does not mean I still do not believe this to be anything other than a brachiosaurian-sized waste of time," the *Protoceratops* added quickly.

Will's grin widened slightly. "As always, your opinion is duly noted."

At the top of the canyon they paused to take stock of their surroundings. The stream they had been following emerged from a cleft in the rocks and both human and dinosaur used the opportunity to drink their fill and replenish the waterbags Chaz carried. Ahead lay low ridges of crumbling, broken sandstone and beyond, the Great Desert.

And still no sign of Sylvia.

Maybe Chaz was right after all, a tired Will thought. Perhaps they should simply make their way back to Canyon City and wait for the proper authorities to decide when it was time to take action. But having come this far, he was loath to return without obtaining at least some indication that Sylvia had passed through this canyon. So far they had only the hermit family's word for it that she had even come this way.

Climbing past the spring, he continued eastward, choosing the simplest path more for Chaz's benefit than for his own. Once they surmounted an unavoidable slope that loomed just ahead, the hiking appeared to become easier. Chaz would needed help getting up the modest wall, he knew. Preparing himself mentally for the effort of hauling the chunky *Protoceratops* up over the top, he put his right foot on a thin ledge, boosted himself up, and grabbed an outcropping with his left hand. A quick kick upwards, a strong pull, and he was up and over the top.

To find himself staring directly into a pair of eyes that were purely reptilian and utterly devoid of saurian intelligence.

In response to his sudden appearance, the eyes drew back sharply and a loud buzzing filled the air. It was instantly joined by at least a dozen similar rattlings. The diamondback Will had surprised was a good twenty feet long, with a body as thick around as his own, and it was by no means the largest of the snakes that had chosen to make the wide ledge their present home.

Will remained frozen on the edge, his legs still dangling

down. He could let go and drop, he knew, risking a potentially ankle-shattering fall. Even that was no guarantee of beating the huge snake's strike. Unable to move forward, uncertain whether to risk falling backward, and hardly daring to breathe, he remained frozen on the edge of the slope.

Below, an unwitting Chaz shouted up at him. "What are you waiting for? Climb the rest of the way up! And what's that noise—another spring?"

Will dared not reply. Even the slight movement of his lips, much less the sound of his voice, might be enough to alarm the snake he had surprised. Behind it, its equally imposing companions were beginning to settle down, the animated warning sounds generated by their vibrating tails to hush. But the snake nearest the stunned climber continued to watch him intently.

If it began to coil, Will knew, he would have no choice but to let go and risk the drop. A snake that size packed enough venom to kill half a dozen men or a fair-sized dinosaur. If he was bitten, there was nothing Chaz would be able to do for him. Or anyone else, for that matter.

Beneath him, the *Protoceratops*'s impatience was growing. "Are you going to hang there all day like a ripening banana, or are you going on up? Why don't you answer me?"

Slowly, ever so slowly, the great snake relaxed. Its tail ceased quivering and the rattles grew still. Silently, emotionlessly, it lowered its head to the warm rock and slithered off to join the rest of its sun-worshipping clan. Like so many intricately patterned, scaly cables, they lay close to and on top of one another as they soaked in the heat of the afternoon.

With infinite patience, Will let himself down, feeling for the little ledge with his right foot and never taking his eyes off the coiled mass of weighty reptilian bodies.

"What was that all about?" Chaz demanded to know as his lanky companion rejoined him. "Is the way ahead too difficult?" Ceratopsian eyes evaluated the slope. "With a little help I am sure I can make it to the top."

Will looked down at him. "I'm sure you can, but you don't want to."

"Why not? Isn't this the way?" The *Protoceratops* paused suddenly. "Why, you're trembling."

Glancing down at himself, Will noted that this was indeed the case. Angry, he forced himself to relax. There was no danger now. Rendered torpid by the temperature, the nest of serpents had shown no inclination to pursue the intruder who had inadvertently disturbed their afternoon nap.

"There are snakes up there," he finally explained. "Poisonous snakes."

"Oh," whispered Chaz.

"Large poisonous snakes. Extremely large poisonous snakes." Looking to his left, he nodded. "I think we can get around them if we go that way, but we still need to be careful. There may be more."

Chaz nodded somberly and turned. "I do not like snakes. Especially extremely large poisonous ones." He tilted his head back. "Are you sure you are all right, Will? You can ride for a while if you like."

"No. No, it's okay, Chaz. Thanks anyway." As they crossed the headwaters of the canyon-cutting stream, he squinted upward. The ledge above remained deserted. "I was just surprised, that's all. In country like this one should expect to encounter snakes. I just didn't think they'd be quite so big."

"Any size is too big for me," Chaz insisted, decrying the living representatives of his own ancestry. More gently he added, "I am sorry that I snapped at you, but I had no idea what was happening."

"I know." As they started up the alternate path, Will kept a wary eye on the high ledge that was now behind them and to their left. "I appreciate your concern."

"I am not insensitive." The *Protoceratops* struggled up the slope. "Only practical."

"We'll need plenty of that before we get out of here." Grabbing a double fistful of the little ceratopsian's harness, Will tugged hard, helping his companion up the incline.

"You mean if we get out of here," Chaz muttered as he fought to surmount the difficult grade.

By the time they had made it up the last of the most difficult slopes the sun was threatening to set for the night on the far side of the great canyon complex. They did not find another spring, but their waterbags were full and Will chose a spot where eddying rainwater had bored a series of perfectly round pits in the smooth rock. All were filled nearly to the brim with recent rain.

Instead of drinking, he promptly divested himself of his clothes. After helping Chaz out of his harness and pack, each of them chose a suitable hole and settled down for a long, invigorating fresh-water bath. After the long climb up out of the canyon, Will found the rain-filled potholes as relaxing as the finest public bathhouse in Sauropolis.

Leaning back against the smooth stone, he spread his arms out onto rock on both sides to keep himself above water, his lower body floating motionless in the sun-warmed natural pool.

"See, Chaz? This isn't so bad."

The *Protoceratops* looked up from the shallower, wider natural basin in which he reposed. "Compared to what? Though I must admit," he added grudgingly, "that this is a truly beautiful spot. Perhaps we should give thanks to the snakes that sent us in this direction."

"You thank them. One confrontation was enough for me." Will closed his eyes, allowing the water to support his tired body, letting its warmth penetrate sore muscles. After a while he let out a long, contented sigh. Using his arms, he boosted himself up and back and sat with only his lower legs dangling in the clear pool, letting the setting sun dry him.

"All we have to do is take our time," he assured his companion, "and everything will be fine." Whereupon he promptly leaped into the air and began flailing frantically at his rear end.

Unlike the rattlers, the scorpion that had stung him was of ordinary arachnid proportions. None of which did anything to mitigate the searing pain in his backside. For his part, Chaz enjoyed the impromptu dance hugely, chuckling uncontrollably as his human companion danced frantically across the rocks. Eventually, surfeited with hilarity, he finally lumbered out of his own bath—only to step on the surly scorpion's nearest next of kin.

Hopping madly on three feet, the *Protoceratops* joined his friend in a futile attempt to shake off the pain. Hastily they reassembled Chaz's harness and loaded their supplies once more onto the *Protoceratops*'s back. They quickly discovered that the pool-pocked sandstone mesa was a favorite haunt of the nasty little stingers and with the coming of night, they were now starting to emerge from their well-camouflaged lairs. It took some careful tip-toeing and a few anxious moments before the vulnerable intruders were able to leave the beautiful but arachnid-infested site behind.

As they made camp in the shelter of a less attractive but considerably safer rock overhang, human and dinosaur ruefully compared injuries.

"How's your foot?" Will methodically stoked the small fire they had built.

By way of reply, the *Protoceratops* lifted the outraged member off the ground and flashed it at his friend. The redness and swelling were clearly visible in the light from the fire.

"It feels like I stepped on one of those glowing embers," Chaz told him. "Fortunately, it stung me on top of my foot, so I can still walk. But it burns most unpleasantly." The stout ceratopsian nodded meaningfully at Will. "And along the same lines, how is your butt?"

His human companion grimaced. "Why do you think I'm squatting here like this instead of sitting?" He poked at the cheery blaze with a long stick.

"I think I would rather have trouble walking," Chaz replied thoughtfully. Remarking the seriousness with which this observation was pronounced, Will couldn't help but break out laughing.

When all was quiet once again, he allowed his companion to inspect the wound he himself could not see, and to treat it with a small bottle of salve. After Will unscrewed the cap, the *Protoceratops* manipulated the container efficiently with his beak. Then it was Will's turn to return the favor, ministering to Chaz's swollen foot.

The stings proved not only educational but bonding, mutual suffering creating common ground between them. From then on, Chaz's bickering (though never dying out completely) was less vitriolic, while Will in turn teased his four-footed companion more gently.

None of which did anything to improve their prospects of finding the missing Sylvia.

It wasn't long before they lost even the pretense of a trail. The slopes that barred their way eastward continued to flatten out and become more gentle, until they found themselves walking down a dry arroyo little different from the dozens of similar washes that flanked it. His original determination sapped by exhaustion and the steadily increasing heat, Will reluctantly found himself inclining more and more to officialdom's line of thinking. There was no question that to properly search the surrounding hills and gullies demanded the services of a real expedition.

Chaz was something of an expert at reading human expressions (it was, after all, part of his job) and he could see the resignation developing in his friend's face. His tone became gentle instead of admonishing.

"Are you ready to say 'enough,' Will Denison? If we press on like this there's a good chance that an expedition will have to be sent out to rescue *us*. Skybax rider you may be, but on the ground you can get just as lost as anyone else." The diminutive *Protoceratops* glanced back the way they had come. "Best we turn back now, while we still have some steps to retrace."

Will halted. Dust settled around his feet. The surrounding layered, multihued sandstone offered him neither surcease nor clue. The air was still, devoid of comforting human chatter and familiar saurian hoots and bellows. Somewhere a bird cried out, isolated and forlorn.

A glimmer of red caught his eye. Peeping out from a crack in the rocks off to his left, it suggested the presence of some unknown desert flower. Behind him, Chaz shifted impatiently from one foot to the other.

"Come on then, make up your mind. Do we turn back now or not?"

"Just a minute, Chaz." Excitement rising within him, Will moved forward. As he neared the crack, the bright red gleam was joined by one of deep blue. It would be an unusual flower indeed that boasted two such contrasting colors within the same blossom.

The scarf was grimy and wrinkled, but its origin was unmistakable. As he held it up to the light, Chaz ambled over to join him.

"*Now* what have you found?"

Will turned and let the fine silk, with its embroidered scenes of Dinotopian life, flutter in the slight breeze. "It's Sylvia's! So she *did* come this way." Fully alert once again, he scanned the distant horizon with anxious eyes. "She wouldn't have thrown this away, Chaz. It was a favorite of hers."

"That does not mean she is in any particular difficulty," the *Protoceratops* reproached him. "Probably it blew off her neck, or she simply dropped it, and did not notice that it was missing." So saying, he proceeded to inspect the hard ground in the immediate vicinity of the crack where the scarf had lodged.

"There is no sign of a struggle here, no indication that

anything untoward took place on this spot."

"That's a relief, anyway." Cramming the scarf into a pocket, Will started forward. "Come on, Chaz. She might be sheltering just up ahead, waiting for help."

"Or she might not." Grumbling, the *Protoceratops* struggled to keep pace with his long-legged friend. "What makes you think she continued on in this direction? We are at the very edge of the Great Desert. No one in their right mind willingly enters that country. It is the worst place in all of Dinotopia, emptier even than the Forbidden Mountains. Why would anyone, especially someone traveling alone, want to go there?" Gesturing with his beak, he indicated the surrounding maze of gullies and fissures millions of years of runoff had cut in the rock.

"More likely that she is wandering about right here. We should search these dry hills first. It may even be that she has started back to Canyon City."

"Not if she came up that side canyon." Will was adamant. "I know her. She'd head home by the same route. She couldn't have passed us."

"As usual, your misplaced confidence does not comfort me. Will, this is crazy. We should return to Canyon City and inform the authorities of what we have learned." He indicated the scarf that trailed from his companion's pocket. "Now that we have proof she came this far, they will surely mount a proper expedition to search for her."

Will spoke without looking at his friend, his eyes searching the hills ahead. "Sylvia may not have the luxury of that much time, Chaz. I have to find out. I need to know."

"You are a stubborn, *pachy*-headed primate, Will Denison!"

Will halted. "If you want to go back, Chaz, I'll understand. But I have to go on."

The *Protoceratops* squinted up at him. "Fine chance you'd have traipsing around out here all by yourself! Besides, you know that I was assigned to you." He let out a resigned snort. "Very well. I will accompany you to the edge of the Great Desert, but no further. My mandate from Public Assistance ends there. I absolutely, positively, will go no farther! It is far too dangerous, much too risky, certainly too reckless." His voice rose sharply. "Do you hear me, Will Denison? *Are you listening to me?*"

The outskirts of the desert were given more to rock and gravel than sand. Tough, scrawny plants eked out a circumscribed existence in hollows and the shelter of dry hillocks—wherever there was shade or a promise of dampness. Overhead, slow-moving clouds flecked a cerulean sky. In its austere, bleak fashion it was a beautiful place, Will thought. Chaz's comments on their surroundings, of which the *Protoceratops* kept up a steady flow, were other than charitable, his observations less than laudatory.

"Nobody comes here," he muttered darkly under his breath. "Nobody! And with good reason. There is nothing here to see, or to do, or to inspire." His feet shuffled mechanically across the hard-baked surface.

"Do you realize, Will, that nothing of civilization lies between us and the coast trade route? Nothing at all? Even along the coast it is scattered and small. There are only the tiny supply stops of Neoknossos, Meeramu, and Hardshell. Beyond them is the ocean.

"Far to the north of here there is a road from Pteros to Kuskonak on the coast. South of that there is no road, no trail, not even a recognized track. Nothing until one reaches Chandara, a place where the desert is no more. There are reasons for this, Will."

"We still have food, and plenty of water." Will's gaze continued to sweep the horizon in all directions, searching for a suggestion of color, a hint of movement.

"For now. That too, will change."

"I'm not a fool, Chaz. When we've drawn our waterbags down halfway, we'll turn back. No matter what kind of situation Sylvia's gotten herself into, it won't do her any good for us to die of thirst out here looking for her."

"Well! Brace me on both sides and use me for a couch! A sensible statement at last. Very well, then. I will monitor the water level in the bags closely, and hold you to your affiance."

*We'd better find her before then,* Will told himself, knowing that he had made the promise only out of a need to mollify his critical companion for the time being.

As they moved out into the Great Desert the signs were anything but encouraging. In fact, Will would have welcomed signs of any kind. They searched in vain for tracks, boot marks, scraps of clothing, spoor, broken branches and disturbed gravel. Nothing they saw or encountered suggested that Sylvia, or for that matter any other human, had recently passed this way.

Any hints of her passage might well have been erased by the wind, Will reflected. The wind that was even now beginning to rise, tickling their faces with tiny particles of sand. Looking longingly back over his shoulder, he resolved to keep searching. Having come so far, he felt he had no other choice. Chaz would have instantly disagreed with such an assessment, of course. Humans were notoriously headstrong beings.

Having only half promised to turn back when the water-bags were half empty, he now found himself reluctantly coming to terms with his own casual evasion. If they had not found Sylvia by the time specified, they would truly have no choice but to return to Canyon City and seek the help of the authorities.

The wind continued to rise, picking up larger bits of sand and hurling them forcefully in the direction of the distant Amu. Reaching into a pocket, he withdrew Sylvia's scarf and wrapped it carefully around his face to shield his mouth and nostrils. Since he had her scarf, what would she be using to ward off the wind-blown grit? He forced himself not to imagine her stumbling aimlessly through the desert, her smooth pale skin burnt brown, her eyes red and watery, her lungs filled with choking dust.

He felt a tapping at his leg. "If you don't mind . . . ?" Chaz requested dryly.

"Oh, sorry." Digging through one pack, he found an unadorned, heavier length of fabric and carefully fastened it over the *Protoceratops*'s face to shield him from the effects of the driving sand. "I was thinking of what Sylvia must be going through right now."

"Better to think of what you and I are going through," Chaz admonished him. "I warn you, I won't stand for much more of this."

"I know."

His four-footed companion blinked in surprise as they trotted on. "You mean you agree with me?"

"Yes. There's only so much we can do. If we haven't

found her by tomorrow morning we'll start back." Raising his left arm to shield his face, he squinted beneath its protection. "If this gets much worse we could pass within a few yards of her without seeing anything. I told you that I wasn't a fool."

"Praise be." The *Protoceratops* cast a thankful glance skyward.

Will's prediction proved more accurate than he could have anticipated. Within the hour the wind had intensified to the point where they were unable to see more than a short distance ahead. Taking shelter behind a low, weed-covered hummock, they huddled together to ride out the storm.

"I'm sorry I got you into this, Chaz." Arms wrapped around his folded legs, Will tugged the scarf a little higher over his face.

"So am I," the translator replied without hesitation. Laying his head in Will's lap, he used the human's folded legs for extra protection from the driving sand.

Bundled together as best they could manage, they surprised themselves by falling into a deep, wind-massaged sleep.

Will awoke to a stillness the likes of which he had only experienced in the World Beneath. The sun was not merely out, it was positively holding court in the morning sky. All suggestions of cloud had been banished and the sky was a pure, intense blue from horizon to horizon.

"Chaz. Chaz, wake up!" Will nudged the leathery, heavy skull lying motionless in his lap.

"*Snaf*, what . . . ?" Bestirring himself, the *Protoceratops* wakened from his unexpected nap. His rear legs lay buried in wind-driven sand.

Shaking off as much of the accumulated dust and grit as they could, they proceeded to take stock of their surroundings. Around them, the air was silent and utterly still.

Then a soft, guttural cry drew their attention to the sky.

The *Argentavis* was beginning to circle. It was soon joined by a second, and then a third, the twenty-foot wingspans of the great vultures forming black spirals in the sky. Will watched them uneasily. Equipped with beaks that could shear through dinosaur bone, they would make short work of a much smaller human corpus.

But *Argentavis* was strictly a scavenger: opportunist, not predator. If there was one thing a skybax rider knew well, it was the habits of those who shared the sky with him. He and Chaz would not be bothered until it was clear to the morbid circlers that human and dinosaur could no longer offer any resistance.

He put a little extra spring into his step as he started forward. "Let's get moving." He jabbed a finger skyward. "We don't want to give our airborne audience any wrong ideas."

"Indeed," Chaz agreed as he shuffled off a bit too hastily in Will's wake.

The three argentaves followed, wheeling silently overhead as they patiently kept track of the two travelers. The great scavengers were in no hurry. They knew they had plenty of time. There was no need for them to mount an attack on their chosen quarry. Sooner or later the Great Desert took all creatures down.

"How's our water?" Will had stopped to brush dust and grime from his face. Though late afternoon was shading into early evening, the heat was still oppressive. Memories of Canyon City and its cool underground chambers and gurgling cliff-face springs assailed him mercilessly. He was just about ready to admit defeat and start back.

Shaking himself to sample the reduced weight on his back, Chaz made an estimation of their supplies. "Half left. Look for yourself, Will." He gave another calculating shake. "Perhaps even slightly less than half. If we do not start back immediately, we may not get there. If we were to encounter another of those disorienting sandstorms now, it could prove fatal. I beg of you—let us turn back."

Will wiped sweat from his forehead. His clothes were sodden with perspiration and the heat threatened to cloud his thoughts as well. Chaz was right, he knew. As weary and worn out as they were, they had better start for Canyon City right now, before their judgment became impaired.

"All right, I give up. Let's go."

"That's more like it. I assure you, Will, I will be right there by your side to help you plead your case for a full-scale search and rescue expedition."

"I know you will. But just to make sure we don't get lost, let's ask these people for directions."

The *Protoceratops* gaped at him. Had the insidious sun finally begun to affect his companion's state of mind? After all, a human had no blood-filled frill to help him shed excess heat. "I beg your pardon? To just whom are you referring?"

"Why, to them, of course," Will replied, and he pointed.

Shuffling forward a couple of steps, the translator now saw the inspiration for his friend's comment. The nearer they came, the less certain the *Protoceratops* was that he and his friend should have any contact with them.

"Are you so sure, then," he whispered in the still, dry, sand-blasted air, "that they are *people*?"

# -VII-

dvancing slowly and with great dignity toward the two astonished travelers was a most extraordinary procession. The *Stegosaurus* in the lead was followed by several kentrosaurs, a *Tuojiangosaurus*, and then two more stegosaurs. That in itself was remarkable enough, but what made the parade far more extraordinary was the fact that humans were not only living with the armored saurians, but on them.

Slim poles had been securely fastened to the dinosaurs' upstanding back plates, rising vertically and protruding horizontally. Tough cords held the poles together, with lightweight cloth stretched between them to form walls and ceilings. Woven fiber floors provided places to sit within. The colorful, outrageous structures resembled the howdahs the young Will had seen in pictures of Indian elephants, or the tents that the Bedouin of Arabia mounted on the backs of their camels.

Only, these elegant edifices were much larger and more elaborate. It would have taken more than a dozen camels to provide as much back space as a single mature *Stegosaurus*—and camels did not come equipped with built-in room foundations in the form of horny triangular back plates.

Each fabrication was richly embroidered with vividly colored thread. Streamers and pennants flew from the tops of tents while stegosaur tail spikes were capped with gold. Located just above the front legs of each saurian was a much smaller tent where a single rider could travel in comfort. The great stegosaurs in particular had been turned into veritable walking apartment houses. It all looked quite grand and comfortable, if one did not mind the slight but steady rocking motion that underlay this matchless mode of travel.

Huge waterbags hung down from the largest back plates, slapping against the sides of the dinosaurs as they walked and not incidentally helping to keep them cool. Catching sight of the two solitary hikers, the lead *Stegosaurus* bleated a halt. Instantly, the bearded man riding in the small tent above the armored dinosaur's shoulders dismounted and beckoned for them to approach.

"What do you make of this?" Will asked his companion.

The *Protoceratops* ruminated. "Desert nomads. There are stories about them. It is said that they choose to live apart from the rest of Dinotopian society, sharing the fraternity of their own spirit. Not many dinosaurs are inclined to lead such an isolated life." The translator nodded in the direction of the now halted procession. "It seems that the stegosaurs are among those who are."

Again the lead rider gestured at them. Behind him Will could see others, including women and children, peering out from the openings of high-riding tents. Wondering, no doubt, what a single young human and *Protoceratops* were doing wandering alone in their country. Lately, he had been given to wondering that himself.

"We might as well find out what they want." Chaz started forward.

"Maybe they have news of Sylvia." Will followed close behind his friend, acceding to protocol by allowing the translator to take the lead. Despite their outré appearance and eccentric choice of living arrangements he never hesitated. The notion that these remote desert dwellers might be hostile never entered his mind. Among all known dinosaurs only the primitive carnivores of the Rainy Basin represented any real threat. Easy-going, plant-loving stegosaurs should welcome them.

His assessment proved not entirely accurate. While never less than cordial and polite, the perambulating dinosaurs and humans were correctly formal. The kind of uninhibited greeting a stranger would receive in Treetown or Chandara was absent.

Edgy under the penetrating gaze of the human who had dismounted, Will waited while Chaz conversed with the lead *Stegosaurus*. After several minutes spent exchanging muted bleats and honks, his companion turned back to him.

"They do not quite know what to make of us, I think."

"The feeling's mutual," Will replied readily.

"They wonder what we are doing out here, with so few supplies, in country that is so hostile to life."

Nodding, Will found himself searching drawn-back tent flaps for faces half-concealed within. "Well, did you tell them?"

The *Protoceratops* responded with a subtle shake of his head. "As our welcome has been less than effusive, I thought it best to avoid making requests at first greeting. We have been invited to share their camp for the night. It would be impolite of us to refuse."

"Why would we refuse?" Frowning, Will found himself suddenly swaying on his feet. A look of alarm flashed from Chaz's eyes.

"Will, are you all right?"

"I—I'm not sure." He wiped at his forehead and let his hand linger there, feeling the heat. "As a skybax rider I'm used to having a cool breeze blowing in my face most of the time. This hot, motionless air is kind of new to me." He forced himself to stand straight. "I'll be okay."

Still dubious, Chaz resumed his conversation with the *Stegosaurus*. "Ahminwit says you are welcome to join the other humans in riding on his back."

"No thanks. I'll walk. Unless of course," he added quickly, "turning the offer down would brand me as 'impolite'."

"No. The offer was made purely out of courtesy." After a pause he added, "I would ride if I could. But then, I have four legs and am not as likely to fall over with heat prostration."

"Do I look prostrate?" Will challenged him.

Chaz studied his young human companion thoughtfully. "What you look like is someone in need of a serious bath, but I am sure my appearance is no better. Walk, then, if you prefer."

After conveying this information to Ahminwit, the *Protoceratops* moved a couple of paces off to one side. The senior *Stegosaurus* promptly turned her head and bellowed at those waiting patiently behind her. Having settled to their knees to rest and wait, the other members of the caravan now straightened and turned. Dust rose from beneath heavy feet and tents joggled on support poles and projecting horn armor as the line of massive bodies turned south and west. Curious eyes continued to peer at the newcomers from behind the security of woven tent flaps.

Will and Chaz chose to walk just to the left of Ahminwit's head. Her bearded rider leaned out of his compact shelter to peer pointedly at Will.

After some fifteen minutes of this unrelenting scrutiny the skybax rider looked sharply at the older man. "Tell me, sir—is it my face or my attire that so intrigues you?"

"Neither." The stegorider's voice was cracked with age and rusty with accent strange. "I am much more interested in your state of mind. What ever would possess a city dweller like yourself to come walkabouting in the Great Desert with only an inexperienced translator for company?"

Will remembered Chaz's caution. "Time enough later to explain all that, after we've reached your camp. Meanwhile, my friend and I are fascinated by you and your people. Could you tell me something about your—tribe?"

The elderly stegorider inclined his head in a sort of half bow while accompanying it with a strangely sweeping hand gesture Will did not recognize. "We are the Orofani; the Wandering Ones. Descendants of those humans and dinosaurs for whom the cities were too confining, the lowlands too damp, and the seacoast too open. Our ancestors fled an ancient tragedy in the islands of the eastern sea and made the Great Desert their own, free of bureaucracies and civilized constraints. Here," he declared with obvious pride, "we make our own laws and render our own judgments—on food, philosophy, procreation, each other, and life." For the second time, he bowed slightly from the shoulder.

"I am Yannawarru, of the Orofani."

Something in the stegorider's tone called for a response. "I'm Will, Will Denison, and this is my friend Chaz."

"You seek something." It was not a question. "No one comes to this place who is not in search of something, either within themselves or without."

"I said that I'd tell you when we reached your camp." A dry cloth seemed to pass over Will's eyes and for a moment he found he could not see anything. He staggered slightly. Then his vision cleared, and with it came the return of his balance.

"Then tell." Raising an aged, sun-browned arm to point, Yannawarru indicated a low rise composed of compacted and fractured shale just ahead. "Because here is the place where we will make camp for the night." Knowing eyes crinkled at the young human. "And from the looks of you, pilgrim of a modest mien, not a moment too soon."

"Don't be ridiculous!" That was strange, Will found himself thinking. While he hadn't been paying attention, some mischievous sprite had gone and tilted the horizon. "I'm perfectly fi—"

He awoke staring up at a ceiling which, he decided, was both an interesting and unexpected phenomenon to encounter in a desert. It had the sheen of fine yellow silk but with a slightly coarser texture.

Pushing himself up on his elbows, he saw that he was lying in a tent. The ceiling rose to a central peak, cleverly supported by poles that crossed and re-crossed in a fluid pattern. Beneath him was a thick, soft mat of some fibrous brocaded material. His head had been supported by a small, rectangular pillow that was filled with something less forgiving than cotton.

There was no furniture in the tent: only another couple of mats. While far from spacious, it seemed too large to ride on the back of even a very large *Stegosaurus*. The surface beneath him was hard and unyielding, and nothing moved. The implication was that he was lying on the ground and not atop some supportive saurian spine.

He sat up, preparatory to rising, and remembered. Had he passed out, less secure in body than in mind? And where was Chaz? The thirst he had worked so diligently to repress returned with a vengeance, and he found himself licking dry lips. There was no sign of food or water in the room.

The latter appeared moments later in the shape of a ceramic jug borne by an even more pleasing shape. The young woman was clad in a blue gown belted with gold cord. Gold and red tassels hung from the ends of the waist cord and fine filigree trimmed sleeves and cuffs. They swayed as she approached him. A striking red and gold headpiece covered her hair and faded to a dark blue veil of chiffon that mysteried her face. Like the tassels, the veil was a mosaic of small pieces of fabric cut-outs that took the shape of stegosaur or kentrosaur back plates.

Producing a squat, wide-mouthed handleless cup, she filled it to the brim and passed it to him. He drained it gratefully, careful not to spill a single drop, and handed it back with a thankful smile.

"Could I have another one, please? I guess—I guess I was a little thirstier than I thought."

Without a word she refilled the cup and passed it back. This time he drank more slowly, pausing between long swallows, until he had drained the contents. Handing the receptacle back to her, he nodded appreciatively. Her eyes never left him.

"I guess I must have passed out." After the unrelieved starkness of the desert, the embroidered arabesques of his surroundings struck him as unnaturally sumptuous. "Thank you for the water."

Lowering her eyes, she curtsied delicately. He found himself peering past her, toward the entrance. The sounds of busy people and dinosaurs created an unhurried sussuration outside.

"My four-legged friend, is he all right?" In response to his query, she nodded. He prepared himself for an attempt to stand up. "I guess I'd better go and find him and tell him I'm okay. You know, I hope you won't mind my saying this, and I wouldn't normally, but I've just come through some very harsh country that I didn't find especially attractive, and you sure are a charming contrast to it."

She said nothing, but ducked her head slightly. Then she looked back at him and, with consummate grace and ease, dumped the remaining contents of the water jug squarely on top of his head.

Sputtering and spitting and more than a little startled, he scooted back on his hands while gawking up at her. But his initial surprise was nothing compared to his reaction when she pulled the veil aside. His lower jaw dropped.

"Sylvia? *Sylvia!*"

"'Charming contrast,' am I? 'Wouldn't say it normally,' would you?" Putting the jug down, she folded her arms across her chest, causing red and gold tassels to flutter.

He scrambled to his feet, hands at his sides, palms imploring. "Sylvia, I'm sorry. I'm hot, and I'm tired, and I didn't mean anything by . . ." he paused. "What are you laughing at?"

"You, of course. You look like a limp *Mesosaurus* that's just been dragged out of the mud."

He glanced down at his sodden clothing. She had one hand over her mouth, trying to subdue her laughter. With a grin, he shrugged off some of the water and approached.

"Well, you don't. You look wonderful. Sylvia, I can't put into words how worried I was when I found out that you'd disappeared!"

Her laughter faded as her expression turned serious. "And you came all this way to check up on me. Will Denison, when will you learn that I can take care of myself?"

They embraced, and he kissed her tenderly but firmly enough to know that she hadn't dampened his spirits. "Then you haven't been in trouble?" He took a moment to contemplate her exquisite, expressive features, luxuriating in the feel of her once more in his arms.

"I didn't say that. Actually, I got a little carried away with what I was doing and before I knew it, I found that I'd put myself in a difficult position. Fortunately, the Orofani found me, just like they found you and Chaz. I can't tell you how amazed I was to find people actually living full-time in this country."

"Same with Chaz and me." He considered his surroundings more closely. "Where exactly are we? Yannawarru said something about a camp."

"So you've met him. He's a nice old bird, but formal as

a librarian. This is one of their waterholes. They'll stay here for a while before moving on to the next one. The dinosaurs of the Orofani need a lot more water than their accompanying humans. They have to keep migrating between oases or they'll exhaust the water supply at each one. Incidentally, the water here comes from seeps, not springs. It's enough to satisfy their needs, but hardly what we'd call plentiful."

Stepping back, he looked her carefully up and down. "That outfit would sure turn heads in Waterfall City. What happened to your own clothes?"

"Climbing out of the canyon of the Amu wasn't exactly like taking a walk in Hopleg Park. Seeing the state I was in when they found me, the Orofani offered me these." She executed a slow pirouette for him. "They're cooler, and unlike what was left of my hiking clothes, in one piece, so I accepted. They've been very kind to me, only . . ." Her words trailed off.

Will hesitated. "Only what?"

"It's a little hard to explain. Everything's fine, except that they won't let me leave."

Will was aghast. "What do you mean, they won't let you leave? That's—that's un-Dinotopian!"

Putting a finger to her lips to caution him, she glanced quickly in the direction of the entrance. "It's not like I'm a prisoner, Will. They would simply prefer that I didn't leave them. I'm sure if I wanted to just walk out into the desert, no one would try and stop me. But they won't help me, either, and without water and food it would be foolish of me to try. But now that you and Chaz are here, maybe we can contrive something." She eyed him unblinkingly.

"They won't want you two to go, either. They didn't even

want me to come see you, but neither did they try to stop me. That really *would* have been un-Dinotopian. These people are unusual, they're not part of normal Dinotopian society, but they're not barbarians. They just have—different priorities. It's something to do with what made their ancestors come here in the first place, I think." She looked thoughtful. "I've asked Yannawarru and a few of the other tribesfolk about it, but their answers are either evasive or they claim not to know."

Will was not sure he could believe what he was hearing. "It doesn't make any sense. Travel in Dinotopia is open and unrestricted to all. I can't imagine what might have happened in their past to make them this way."

"Neither can I," she replied simply.

His expression hardened. "Why don't they want you to leave?"

Glancing toward the entrance for a second time, she lowered her voice deliberately. "It's because of why I came here, Will. Why I came all this way and put myself in real danger. It's because of what I've found."

He shook his head uncomprehendingly. "Found? You know, that's something I've been wondering about from the start. What you were looking for out here in this empty wasteland."

By way of reply she teased him with her eyes as well as her words. "It's not as empty as you might think."

He remembered the recollections of the canyon-dwelling family Helth. "Strange fossils?"

She laughed delightedly. "No, not fossils. Something else. Something much more wonderful."

There was a shuffling at the entrance and her eyes flicked

quickly in that direction. Her voice dropped even further, to a whisper. "Tell you later." With a nimble kiss and a final lingering smile she turned and was gone.

He took a step in her direction. "Sylvia, wait!" As she passed through the tent flap, a trio of older women entered. They too were clad in embroidered, tasseled clothing. Two of them were large, verging on the imposing, and they carried water jugs, brushes, and bundles of soft fabric that might have been towels.

Concluding an analysis of the inferred presentation, he reached a hypothesis in short order and took a wary step backward. "Ladies? Now just a minute, ladies. I'm not exactly sure of what you have in mind, but . . ."

Later, cleaned and refreshed (if severely over-scrubbed), he emerged from the tent. Spread out before him were the tents of the Orofani, arrayed around a broad, shallow pool of murky water fringed with cycads, palms, cattails, and other water-loving desert plants. Eroding sandstone walls sheltered the oasis on three sides. Children played on the rocks, among the bushes, and chased each other along the edge of the pool. Youthful stegosaurs and other back-plated dinosaurs gamboled with them, not as agile as the young of other dinosaurs but with the energy and enthusiasm common to the children of all species.

Both four-footed and bipedal adults looked on indulgently, engaged in tasks that ranged from repairing tent fabrics to the preparation of stored food for the forthcoming afternoon repast. The latter required only a modest effort, as very little was eaten during the heat of the day. The Orofani took their main meals in the cool of early morning and late evening.

Beyond the oasis, the Great Desert marched off in all

directions. Only a few scrub-splotched hillocks broke the surface of a level plain composed of gravel flats and wind-swirled sand. The panorama brought home forcefully to Will how close he and Chaz had been to making a potentially fatal mistake.

He found the *Protoceratops* squatting in water up to his beak in a shallow arm of the pool, chatting amiably with a young *Kentrosaurus*. The small-headed dinosaur acknowledged Will's arrival with a polite nod, murmured something else to Chaz, and then turned and ambled off.

"Well, you don't look like you're suffering too much," Will told his friend.

"Thanks to the kindness of these outlandish people, no." The *Protoceratops* stirred slightly, small eddies rippling out from his short but stout legs. "You will be interested to know that we no longer have to wander aimlessly in the wilderness. Your lady friend is here."

"I know." Will sat down in the shade of a small cluster of palms and rested his arms on his knees. "She's already explained to me how she came to be here, but not why."

"I barely had any opportunity to talk to her myself. Except," he could not resist adding with evident relish, "to learn that she is fine, that nothing is wrong with her, and that our presence here is entirely superfluous."

Will looked around to make sure no one was listening. "Not necessarily."

The little translator cocked a curious eye up at him. "What have you found out?"

"It's what I haven't found out that has me intrigued, Chaz. And not a little puzzled. Also, things may not be as 'fine' as they seem."

The *Protoceratops* smacked his tongue against his upper palate. "I trust you can elaborate on that eccentric observation in greater detail?"

Will took another look behind him. None of the Orofani, human or dinosaur, were within hearing range. Nevertheless, mindful of Sylvia's counsel, he kept his voice low.

"She says that she's found something."

"Found what, pray tell?" A small fish went lazing past beneath the *Protoceratops*'s beak and he took a casual snap at it.

"That's what's so intriguing. She won't tell me. I also got the distinct impression she didn't want any of the Orofani overhearing us talking about it. Whatever 'it' is."

"Peculiar indeed." Clearly Chaz was as puzzled as his friend. "What did you mean when you said things might not be as good as they appear?"

Will's brows drew together. "That's even more confusing. She said something about the Orofani not wanting her to leave—or letting us leave, either."

Now Chaz was more than simply puzzled. "That's absurd! No Dinotopian would restrain another against their will." Even as he uttered this conviction, the *Protoceratops* found himself glancing surreptitiously at the members of the tribe playing and relaxing around the waterhole.

"That's what I told her. But take a good look around, Chaz. This isn't Sauropolis, and these aren't your usual city or country people. They exist outside the pale of Dinotopian society as we know it. Who knows what they're capable of?"

"Piffle," Chaz growled irritably. "Purebred piffle. They've been nothing but courteous and kind since they first found us wandering in the desert."

"We weren't wandering," Will objected. "We were tracking Sylvia."

"Whatever," the translator barked impatiently. "How to you reconcile this rubbish Sylvia has told you with our kind treatment thus far at the hands of these Orofani?"

"I don't see any contradiction. She told me that they've treated her equally well. They just don't want her to leave."

"That makes no sense, Will Denison."

"I agree." Lifting his gaze, he looked past his bemused companion. "It must have something to do with what she's found, with what she didn't have an opportunity to talk to me about."

"Then you'd best get some answers out of her, Will." The *Protoceratops* settled back down into the tepid water. "Until then I, for one, intend to enjoy our hosts' hospitality." So saying, he lowered his frilled head beneath the surface and commenced to blow a succession of long, loud, exclamatory bubbles.

It was fascinating to watch the Orofani at work when it came time to pack up and move to another waterhole. These periodic changes of campsite kept the water and vegetation at each location healthy by allowing them time to recover from the impact of so many humans and dinosaurs.

Children scurried about as the adults loaded tents and other goods onto the backs of their large, armored saurian companions. A few of the younger stegosaurs, kentrosaurs, and their companions carried miniature packs or tents on their own immature backs in preparation for the day when humans would not only live but ride between their horny dorsal plates.

When all was in readiness the lead *Stegosaurus* let out a

sharp hoot. This was followed by the appropriate equivalent human shout, whereupon the elegant caravan began to move southeast. Tents swayed on massive saurian backs and brightly-hued pennants fluttered gaily in the occasional desert breeze. Several humans tootled on flutes hewn from desert branches while others beat out a modest, unhurried pace on drums slung on either side of an accommodating *Kentrosaurus*'s neck.

Will and Chaz strode alongside the stegosaur on which Sylvia rode, keeping pace with the children of the tribe. Thus separated from her according to tribal custom, they had no chance to converse privately. They could only exchange meaningful glances; his burning with curiosity, hers full of promise.

The brief pause for the light midday meal did not afford them any opportunity for conversation, but when the evening campsite was reached and the Orofani busied themselves building cookfires and unharnessing their saurian companions, the two humans were joined by Chaz in an unobtrusive rendezvous in the shade of several striking pillars of striped sandstone.

"Now then, Sylvia," the *Protoceratops* harrumphed importantly, "what's all this about? Why the mystery?"

Taking one last look around to make sure they were not being overheard, she lowered her voice and leaned forward. Despite his intense curiosity, Will could not keep from thinking how beautiful she was in her exotic Orofani garb.

"It's because of what I found. Not here, but in the great library at Waterfall City." She smiled at the wholly attentive Will. "You know how I like to spend a lot of my free time poking through the old scrolls, trying to make interesting associations?"

He nodded, grinned down at Chaz. "She drives head librarian Enit crazy with some of her requests. I can hear the translations of his whistles now: 'This and that, that and this—what *are* you looking for, young woman?'"

She chuckled softly at the remembrance. "Of course, I don't *know* what I'm looking for. That's where the fun of it is, and that's what drives Enit to frustration. He's so logical. Playing around with random choices and free associations strikes him as a waste of time. Usually, it is."

"But not in this instance," Chaz concluded hesitantly.

"No," she agreed more solemnly, "not this time. Nallab was a great help to me. On a professional level I'm sure he'd agree with Enit, but person to person he was more sympathetic. He understood that what I was doing was more for my own entertainment than for any serious purpose." Her expression tightened. "At least, it was until I started to make some unexpected connections."

Will leaned back against the gritty, sun-warmed surface of the banded rock. "What did you find, Sylvia?"

Her tone grew slightly distant as she reminisced. "There are so many old scrolls—records, histories, narrative poems, tall tales—that nobody bothers to read these days. I found a reference in one that caught my interest, and then a corresponding reference in a completely different place, and after that I just started looking for corresponding mentions. The longer I looked, the more I became convinced I'd stumbled onto something truly important.

"I kept notes as I went, but it was really frustrating to only be able to do research part time. Whenever I'd be able to make time for a visit to the library and I'd ask Nallab for some old scroll that hadn't been touched in decades, he'd just smile tolerantly at me and gently suggest I spend my time reading something more interesting. I'd smile right back and him and then he'd cluck his lips and dig into the stacks to find me the scroll. I was so *sure* that I'd found something, Will. I kept digging, kept researching. I felt certain that all these seemingly unrelated mentions I kept coming across had to be based on something real."

"Mentions of what?" The idling *Protoceratops* made circles in the sand with one front foot.

"I'm getting to that, Chaz." At a gust of wind, she gathered her flowing raiment more closely around her. "When I felt that I'd made a convincing case for my discovery, I took my conclusions to Nallab. He listened and just smiled and told me that it was a nice story, and wouldn't I like to read some of the more exciting chapters of the original version of the Marabayata Sauriensus instead?"

Will adopted a rueful expression. "What did you do then?" He found his attention straying to the nearby mob of humans and dinosaurs. Having established camp, the highly efficient Orofanis were preparing for the evening meal.

"I took my conclusions to people outside the library, but the response I got was the same everywhere. It was a nice story, a pleasant fantasy tale for young humans and dinosaurs, and maybe next I would spend my valuable time on a more practical, worthwhile project." She shook her head disconsolately at the memory of many repeated rejections. Then her tone and expression firmed.

"It was clear to me that the only way I was going to convince anyone that what I had discovered was real was to provide incontrovertible proof. That meant coming up with something more cohesive than inferred connections between scattered references in old scrolls. So I asked to take my accumulated time off, saw to it that Nimbus got a good spot in the rookery at Pteros, and made my way here, following the hints and references I'd put together from my research."

"Senseless folly!" Chaz was unremitting in his condemnation. "To come to the Great Desert by yourself. This is no place even for experienced solitary travelers. What if you had broken a leg, or run out of water?"

She patted the *Protoceratops* on his curving snout, behind and above the nostrils. "Thanks for your concern, Chaz, but as a skybax rider I'm used to working alone. I was careful in my preparations, and as you can see, I'm perfectly all right."

"The good fortune of fools," the *Protoceratops* grumbled, but not very harshly. "What's all this Will tells me about the Orofani not wanting to let you go, or for that matter, not willing to let us leave, either?"

She looked past her two companions, to where busy tribesfolk were setting out feeding baskets of selected grasses, grains, and nuts for the waiting armored dinosaurs to eat.

"Understand, they've been nothing but kind to me. But they know about what I found, and they're not so isolated and ignorant of general Dinotopian society that they don't realize word of it would bring dozens of researchers running out here. They value their isolation and their privacy and they don't want it invaded. I think they're afraid that if their children spend much time around city people that they'll no longer want to live out their lives migrating through the Great Desert, following the ways of their parents."

Will nodded knowingly. "It's hard to keep 'em down on the sand once they've seen Sauropolis."

"Exactly. They're instinctively wary of outside influences. So the longer they can keep me, and you, among them, the longer that isolation will be preserved. I'm sure the ethicists among them are having trouble rationalizing their position."

Will frowned. "Have they used force to prevent you from leaving?"

She shook her head sharply. "I haven't tried to force the issue, yet. I don't want to, if I can help it. I was kind of waiting for the right time to try and make my break. Then you two showed up, complicating matters."

"Terribly sorry if our attempt to rescue you has proven inconvenient," the little translator jibed.

"Oh, stop that, Chaz. You know what I mean." She turned back to Will. "I think we can slip away tonight. We have to try, anyway, because starting tomorrow the tribe will begin moving in the wrong direction, away from what I discovered."

"Yes, this discovery," Chaz demanded to know. "Just exactly what is it that you have found out here?"

This time she did not meet his unbroken gaze. "Well, that's a little hard for me to say, Chaz. You see, I haven't exactly found it yet."

The *Protoceratops* lowered his head, his eyes staring up at her. "You haven't found it yet?"

"No. I was on my way to it when I started having water problems and ran into the Orofani."

"So," the translator concluded, "your 'discovery' is still nothing more than a series of hypothetical conclusions that you have drawn from fumbling through a bunch of old scrolls in the Great Library?"

"I didn't 'fumble,'" she shot back. "I was following a definite trail."

"Oh yes," the *Protoceratops* agreed, "a definite trail that led you here, to the outer reaches of the Great Desert, where to this point you have found nothing at all."

"Take it easy, Chaz," Will reproved his friend.

"Easy indeed! How can I take it 'easy' when we find ourselves at the mercy of a band of antisocial nomads who, I now find out, may or may not strenuously object to our ever leaving their company."

"Yes, think about that a moment, Chaz," Sylvia instructed him. "If there's nothing out here to hide, then why try to keep us from telling others about it?"

"Not being Orofani, I can not answer that." The translator snorted curtly. "If you are correct in your assumptions about them, then they have their reasons. They may simply be reasons different from those you choose to ascribe to them."

She shook her head slowly. "No, Chaz. I'm sure about this. As sure as I've ever been about anything." She leaned her shoulder against the *Protoceratops*'s companion. "As sure as I am about my love for Will."

The trenchant translator started to reply and this time Will rushed to forestall him. "Don't say it, frill-necked brother. Think of it if you must, but don't say it."

Chaz sniffed, but obligingly swallowed his budding retort. "Very well then. Let us assume, for the moment, that these people have something they wish to keep a secret, and that even less likely, it is the same thing you plan to discover. Clearly they have no intention of showing it to you. Therefore if we are to see it and verify your, ahem, discovery, we must find a way to withdraw from the company of our hosts. As you have obviously had time to give the matter some thought, what would you suggest?"

"Tonight," she reminded them. "After a long day's march everyone is tired, and will want to rest."

"That's easy enough, then," Will decided. "We simply wait until everyone is asleep and then slip out of camp. You know what direction to take?"

"Yes," she replied, "but it's not going to be that easy. They always mount lookouts at night."

Chaz's lower jaw dropped. "Just to keep watch on you and ensure you do not slip away?"

"No, silly. To make sure dangerous animals don't slip into the tents."

Will nodded, remembering his encounter with the nest of giant rattlesnakes. Who knew what other dangers a place as mysterious and empty as the Great Desert might hold within its unexplored boundaries?

"We'll have to move very carefully and very quietly," she told them. "Slipping out of camp should be fairly easy. The lookouts' attention is directed away from the tents and out into the desert, not back towards them. But once past their positions we'll have to be careful they don't see or hear us." Stepping away from the smooth rock against which she had been leaning, she pointed eastward.

"That's the way. Once safely out in the rocks we'll be all right. This ground is too hard to leave much of a trail, and the sand blows around late at night and covers everything."

"Surely you don't think they'll follow us?" Will commented.

She chewed reflectively on her lower lip. "I don't think so, Will. That *would* mean holding us against our will. But I'd rather not find out."

Chaz nodded vigorously, his head bobbing up and down. "I am in full agreement with you, Sylvia. Let us do our utmost to leave that particular question unresolved."

"And if they do?" Will could not help but think the situation through to every possible conclusion.

Sylvia's expression was flat. "Then we'll have a most interesting variation of basic Dinotopian law to report to the authorities once we get back to Canyon City."

"If we get back," the always pessimistic *Protoceratops* proclaimed dourly.

# -VIII-

he moon was three-quarters full and one hundred percent helpful when Will and Chaz stole out of their tent and went in search of Sylvia. She was waiting for them at the pre-selected spot: the striking pillars of sandstone they had talked beneath earlier in the day. In addition to casting dramatic highlights on every rock ripple and rill and throwing the stone spires into sharp relief, the moon seemed intent on filling heavily shaded hollows with watchful, disapproving Orofani shapes.

Will found himself glancing sharply at shadows. Footsteps trailed on every sigh of the wind. A nervous Chaz trotted along beside him, the translator's steady breathing sounding far too loud in the still of the night. Surely they would be seen or heard.

But no curious Orofani intercepted them as they made their stealthy way out of camp. Beneath the appointed rocks a sylphlike shade awaited, swathed in moonlight. Behind her legs Will could just make out several woven sacks filled with supplies and a pair of bulging waterbags.

At the sight of Sylvia standing safe, alone, and unchallenged, Will allowed himself to relax. A little.

Wasting no time congratulating them on their arrival, she looked anxiously past them. "It doesn't look like you were followed. I think we're all right, so far."

"'So far.'" Chaz struggled to catch his breath. "That is precisely how I desire to be in relation to these Orofani oddities—so far, as in away." Turning his head, he looked back toward the somnolent camp. As near as they could see, there was no movement save the final flickerings of the cookfires. "I suggest we congratulate ourselves later, when we are sure of our escape." He indicated the jumble of rock that formed the eastern horizon.

"You claim there is something out there, Sylvia. Let us go and find it."

She smiled down at him as she and Will loaded the precious water and supplies onto his broad back and secured them with the makeshift harness straps she had brought.

"What a coincidence, Chaz. That's just what I was going to say."

"Hmph!" Having delivered himself of that particularly succinct comment, the *Protoceratops* started off into the moonlight, only to halt when he realized that he did not have the faintest idea where he was going.

As the glow from the Orofani camp fell behind them, it was gradually replaced by the dimmer, cooler light of the moon and stars. The longer all remained silent and still behind them, the more confident they became in their flight. When an ever pessimistic Chaz questioned the ease of their escape, Sylvia informed him that the Orofani were an especially vocal tribe. Had their absence been noted, she insisted, a voluble hue and cry would surely have been raised by now. Instead, only the querulous creaking of nocturnal insects broke the desert stillness.

By sunrise even the dubious *Protoceratops* was convinced. "Don't get me wrong. I'm pleased at the ease with which we made our departure, but I am also surprised."

"Think about it a moment, Chaz." Striding along with a cool, lumpy waterbag on his back, Will was feeling expansive. "We weren't captives in a historical sense. It wasn't that the Orofani wanted to imprison us: they just didn't want us to leave."

"And now that we've gone," added Sylvia, "it will take them a while to try and decide how to cope with what for them is an unprecedented situation. By the time they come to a decision, we'll be well on our way." She waved at the hilly horizon. "No matter what they decide, it'll be hard for them to follow us out here. And taking the time to chase after us would mean diverging from their traditional migratory route. That should lead to even more arguing among the tribal elders." She looked back the way they had come. "No, I think we've made good our departure."

Reaching down, Will gave the translator a friendly pat on the curved upper rim of his frill. "Listen to Sylvia, Chaz. If she's right and the Orofani don't usually come this way, I don't see them altering their whole lifestyle just to come and look for us."

The translator favored his bipedal human friend with a jaundiced eye. "And why do you suppose that is, Will? Perhaps it is because there is nothing out here."

"Oh, there's something out here, all right." Sylvia adopted the expression favored by Lewis Carroll's notorious cat.

"And we're going to find it." Drawing a large piece of paper from one of the sacks on Chaz's back, she proceeded to unfold it and study the contents intently. Occasionally she looked up to check the dark scribblings against natural landmarks on the horizon.

"What, exactly, are we looking for?" Chaz trudged along steadily, doing his best to stay on the shady side of the two humans.

"It's a secret," Sylvia chided him playfully.

"See here, woman, I've had about enough of these games! Will and I have had a long, difficult journey to find you, and I think we deserve a full explanation, or at least the rationalization, for your so far unjustifiable presence here."

Sylvia laughed softly. "All right, translator. I promise that I'll tell you everything—at supper tonight."

And try as both he and Will might, that was all the additional information they could elicit from their ebullient and elegantly gowned traveling companion.

Bits and pieces of her attire either fell off of their own accord or were removed by Sylvia herself as they advanced deeper into the desert, the costume of a traveling Orofani lady being more suitable for riding in a stegosaurian howdah than for traipsing on foot over gravel and sand. By the time Will spotted the red flash, her free-flowing raiment had been much reduced in volume. This was fortunate, since long skirts and gowns were unsuitable for running.

And if Will was correct in his identification of the flash's origin, there was a good chance they were going to have to run.

"You're sure that is what you saw?" Chaz stood squinting

at the place Will had pointed out. "I don't see anything."

"Neither do I." Sylvia used a hand to shade her eyes from the sun as she studied the horizon.

Their implication was that he had imagined it. But much as he wished he had, he knew he had not. A skybax rider was trained to identify as well as detect.

As he scanned the rocky outcroppings a flicker of bright blue appeared, fanned the air briefly, and then vanished, ducking down behind the jagged boulders. He gestured excitedly in its direction.

"There! There it was again!" Turning, he pondered possible escape routes anxiously. "We have to find a place to hide."

"From what?" The translator remained dubious. "I still haven't seen anything."

"I saw it this time, Chaz. Will's right." Sylvia stood next to him, one hand resting on the *Protoceratops*'s frill.

Moments later several more of the distinctive red and blue shapes appeared. Popping up like flash cards from behind rocks and ridges, they would twitch and wriggle a few times before ducking back down out of sight. Will knew at once what they were, but only from his studies. He had never actually seen the phenomenon in the wild.

The only place one would expect to encounter such a display was the Rainy Basin, and their present surroundings were about as different from those humid, tropical environs as could be imagined. But Dinotopia was full of surprises. Clearly the Great Desert contained its fair share.

As the frequency of the intermittent displays increased, even Chaz was able to pick them out. "I hope that is not what I think it is."

"I'm afraid they are," Will commented grimly. "*Dilophosaurus* snout flourishes. They're signaling to one another. And since there isn't much else out here to palaver about, I imagine they're talking about us."

"I do not like this at all," Chaz muttered nervously. "Dilophosaurs are large, lightly-built carnosaurs. It is thought that they originally lived by scavenging because their jaws are too lightly built to kill anything sizable. But no pacifying parties pass through the Great Desert to tame the ancient instincts of any predators that live here with offerings of fish." He looked on as another pair of the brightly colored double skull frills rose above the rocks to flash hidden meanings in the direction of unseen companions.

"They're not allosaurs, much less T-rexes," Will concurred, "but if they're uncivilized they're still plenty big and strong enough to bring us down." Again he searched the terrain in the opposite direction from the decorative, semaphoring frills. "We don't even know if we can talk to them, and we've little food to spare with which to try and buy safe passage."

"Maybe," Chaz ventured hopefully, "they are just discussing our presence here and intend no harm."

"I'd like to believe that, Chaz, but its been my experience that when you encounter friendly travelers in open country, they usually come right up to you and tender greetings. They don't hide behind rocks and signal each other surreptitiously. We'd better see if we can find a safer place. We're awfully exposed out in the open like this."

They began to move faster, Will and Sylvia breaking into a jog while Chaz trotted alongside. Fortunately the ground was relatively level and the squat *Protoceratops* had no trouble keeping pace with his lankier human companions.

Will glanced back over a shoulder. The snout flourishes were more frequent now. Once, he was sure he saw a lean, toothy skull appear from behind a ridge of red shale. Like miniature sails, the membranous red-and-blue head frills extended from just behind the nostrils at the tip of the snout to the top of the skull. A bright yellow eye blinked, and Will imagined that it was peering in his direction. There was nothing civilized about the *Dilophosaurus*'s attitude. Its posture hinted of controlled power—and hunger.

They were in an area of broken ground surrounded by rocky hillocks, none of which boasted slopes precipitous enough to discourage the relatively agile dilophosaurs. They needed to find something steep to climb, even if he and Sylvia had to pull Chaz up with them by his tail. Such desperate gymnastics might mean abandoning their supplies, but the alternative was much worse. He had not come this far only for the three of them to end up as dinner for a pack of wandering desert carnosaurs.

Realizing that their presence had been discovered, the meat-eaters gave up any pretense of subterfuge. No longer using their colorful frills to silently signal one another, they were calling loudly to maintain contact as they began to pursue. With their long, powerful legs they would soon overtake the fleeing trio, Will knew. It was imperative that he and his companions find someplace to isolate themselves, or preferably to hide.

If they could not climb out of the dilophosaurs' reach, maybe they could find a cave or a cleft in the rocks too narrow for the big carnosaurs to enter. They searched desperately as they ran, but nothing bigger than a rabbit hole presented itself.

"Ahead!" Sylvia shouted.

Will saw what she was pointing at. A narrow canyon wound through the landscape slightly off to their right. It was too wide for a *Dilophosaurus* to jump and the nearer they drew, the more it became apparent that its sides were too steep for the big carnosaurs to climb down. There were plenty of human-sized hand- and footholds that could be used to descend into the gorge—but what about Chaz? As he himself had pointed out on more than one occasion, ceratopsians were not built for climbing.

The same thought occurred to the translator as they neared the opening in the earth. "You two go on and save yourselves! I will distract these barbarians for as long as I am able."

Will looked down at his friend as they raced on, side by side. "Not a chance, Chaz! You're coming with us!"

"But how?" The *Protoceratops* was puffing hard, like a miniature rhino. "There is no way I can negotiate a wall like that. I am not afflicted with your hook-like primate hands."

"We'll think of something," Sylvia told him, "but Will's right: we're not leaving you behind."

Ropes, Will thought frantically. If only they had some ropes they could try lowering the *Protoceratops* to a safe ledge. Then he realized it did not matter. They didn't have the time. The stalking dilophosaurs were closing ground too fast.

They would try *something*, he knew. He just didn't know what.

The canyon was very close now, its promise of salvation from pursuit marred by the seeming impossibility of bringing Chaz with them. They would not abandon the little translator, he vowed, even if it meant making a stand against the dilophosaurs with the precipice at their back. What they could do against a determined band of ravenous carnosaurs he could not imagine. Even accurately thrown rocks would not discourage them for long. They were too big, and too strong.

Then he saw the arches. There were three of them, of varying size, set close to one another where they spanned the canyon. The narrowest of the fragile sandstone traverses was hardly wider than his foot, but the broadest—the broadest was perhaps half a yard across. It might support his weight, and even Chaz's. Whether it would hold a much bigger *Dilophosaurus* was open to question.

It didn't matter. They had no choice, as he quickly pointed out to his companions. Angling to their left, they tried to increase their speed as they made a desperate dash for the arches. Divining their intent, two of the dilophosaurs simultaneously lengthened their stride in an attempt to cut off their intended prey from this possible avenue of retreat.

A couple of stony outcroppings lay in the predators' way. Powerful legs enabled them to clear the first in a single bound, but the second was higher and steeper, forcing them to go around. The brief delay provided just enough time for the retreating humans and their ceratopsian companion to reach the edge of the canyon.

Looking down, Will saw that even he and Sylvia would have had trouble negotiating the vertical wall. The handholds were not as prominent as they had appeared from a distance, and the sandstone would have made for footing that was crumbly and treacherous. Behind them, the pursuing dilophosaurs began to ululate shrilly as they closed on their prey. Along with the primitive, bloodcurdling shrieks that harkened back to earlier eons, dust from their pounding, clawed feet filled the air.

Now he understood why the Orofani had chosen stegosaurs and kentrosaurs and their cousins for traveling companions. In addition to providing broad backs for carrying people and supplies, the armored, spike-tailed dinosaurs could mount a stalwart defense against a pack of dilophosaurs. No such formidable natural weapons protruded from his considerably smaller tail end, and Chaz's beak was too diminutive to do any real damage to a large carnosaur.

But one thing humans were very good at was taking refuge in hard-to-reach places.

"Hurry!" Already Sylvia was halfway across the narrow arch and beckoning to her companions.

Will imagined he could feel the dilophosaurs' hot, fetid breath on his neck, could envision the slim but sharp teeth biting through the flesh of his shoulders and into the bone.

"Come on, Chaz! Move it!" He smacked the *Protoceratops* sharply on his hips.

Taking a tentative step out onto the narrow sandstone bridge, the *Protoceratops* glanced down and let out a moan. "Heights! You know how I hate heights. All my kind do, from the torosaurs right on down to the protoceratopsians."

"Just keep your eyes on Sylvia and the far side of the canyon," Will instructed him. "Don't look down." Trailing his friend, he kept slapping him encouragingly on his broad, leathery behind. "That's it—you're doing great!"

"Ohhhhh." Eyes half closed, the stocky translator advanced by forcing himself to put one foot in front of the other. Pebbles and grit slid away beneath his stumpy feet to vanish into the depths below. The largest of the three arches was barely wide enough for him, and the load of supplies shifting on his back did nothing to improve his equilibrium.

But as he so often complained, he was built low to the ground, and it was almost impossible for him to lose his balance. Vertigo was something else again, but with Will nagging him from behind and Sylvia beckoning from the safety of the far side of the canyon, he kept moving.

The precarious traverse would have given most humans pause, but as skybax riders, neither Will nor Sylvia had any fear of heights.

After what seemed like an age but had really been only a few moments, *Protoceratops* and primate reached the other side. While Chaz collapsed onto his belly from relief and nervous exhaustion, Will embraced Sylvia.

"When you two have finished your greeting ritual," the translator wheezed, "I would greatly appreciate something to drink."

Smiling, Will slipped the waterbag he had been hauling off his back and presented it, drinking spout unfastened, to his four-legged friend. Head tilted back, Chaz drank gratefully. But not too much. As Sylvia hastened to point out, they were entering unknown territory well off the usual Orofani migration routes, and there was no telling when they might find water again.

On the far side of the canyon, the assembled dilophosaurs

were bellowing their frustration. They paced back and forth along the edge of the drop-off, pawed at the unsympathetic ground, and snapped at the swirling dust with powerful jaws. A single leap would have brought them within biting distance of their prey. Fortunately, it was a single leap just slightly beyond the range of the strongest jumper among them.

Driven beyond reason by rage and hunger, one of the smaller members of the pack started across the sandstone arch Will and Chaz had just traversed.

"Watch out!" Sylvia shouted, "it's trying to cross!"

Hurriedly Chaz scrambled to his feet and they resumed their flight. It was too much to hope that there might be another canyon spanned by arches anywhere ahead, but the character of the landscape had now changed from gravel and sandy plain dotted with low hillocks to higher, rockier ledges and gullies. They might yet find a place to climb to safety, or a narrow cleft to hide in.

Neither proved necessary. From behind them came the sound of crumbling rock, accompanied by a strident squeal. Halting, they turned in time to see the frantic *Dilophosaurus* disappear into the depths of the canyon, accompanied by the crumbled remains of the stone bridge that had in the end proven too slender to accommodate the sinewy carnosaur's weight.

They stood there, motionless and silent. Seconds later, the distant echo of broken rock smashing into unyielding granite rose from the bottom of the ravine. Then all was stillness, ascending dust, and the intimation of death.

On the far side of the gorge several of the dilophosaurs walked cautiously to the edge and peered down. Then they threw back their heads and began to howl. Will was reminded of the dog packs that had haunted the streets of his boyhood home town back in New England. Only this sound was deeper, sharper, and far more poignant. The dilophosaurs, after all, were intelligent. Primitive and outside the mainstream of Dinotopian society, but still intelligent. The death of one of their own affected them profoundly.

With a few final, murderous stares in the direction of their now unreachable prey, they turned away from the chasm and, one by one, strode off back the way they had come.

"Back in Sauropolis they'll want to know all about this encounter," Sylvia declared. "It's generally believed that all the uncivilized carnosaurs live in the Rainy Basin. Finding a pack of them here, in the Great Desert, is a sociological discovery of some importance."

"Pardon me if my interests at the moment are less than scientific." Taking deep breaths, Chaz plodded along between them. "We were fortunate to escape with our lives."

"Well, you can relax now." Will patted his friend fondly on the flank. "The canyon we just crossed seems to run for quite a ways off to north and south, and I didn't see any other way of getting across."

"That is true enough," the *Protoceratops* agreed. "Of course you realize that means there is also no way of our getting back."

"Um, that's right," Will had to admit. "I hadn't thought of that. Didn't have the time."

"It doesn't matter." Sylvia's confidence was unshaken, and Will found himself wondering if anything ever bothered her. She was by far the most confident woman he had ever known. It was the first thing that had attracted him to her. Well, one of the first things, he corrected himself.

"And at the risk of sounding obtuse," Chaz inquired dryly, "might I ask why it doesn't matter?"

"Because we'll find another way out, even if we have to cross all the way to the ocean."

"Of course," Chaz muttered darkly. "Why didn't I think of that? A simple traverse on foot of the whole breadth of the Great Desert, with no road or trail to guide us, and then we'll be at the sea. Nothing to it. How daft of me to overlook the obvious."

"Now Chaz, don't worry." Smiling encouragingly, she put her arms around his frilled neck and gave him a hug. He struggled to pull away—but not too strenuously, Will noted. "Didn't we save you from the dilophosaurs?"

"Geology saved us from the frilled meat-eaters. Geology and luck." He studied the increasingly steep and rocky terrain ahead. "I hope both are still with us when our water begins to run low."

"It'll be all right, Chaz," she promised him. "You'll see. There'll be plenty of water where we're going."

"Will there indeed?" Turning his head to one side, the *Protoceratops* peered up at her. "And just how can you be so sure of that?"

She strode along confidently beside him, swinging her arms and enjoying the solid ground beneath their feet. "Because the old records say there is."

He continued to eye her steadily. "We are speaking of the same old records that have led you to this barren place?" When she nodded he added, "Then there can be no reason to doubt our eventual success. Our survival is assured."

Will made a face. "You know, Chaz, you might find it a nice change to be a little positive for once."

"Of course. I don't know what I was thinking," the *Protoceratops* responded. "Alone in the Great Desert, with only the food and water we carry on our backs, pursued by aboriginal carnivores, our whereabouts unknown to the rest of civilization, I should naturally saunter along buoyantly. How else could I think, with such a fine prospect before us?" He snorted.

"I am here, aren't I? Hauling food and water for you? That should be enough for you. I should not be required to be 'positive' as well. Be content that you can only understand your own language, because I can be sarcastic in nearly thirty distinct tongues and dialects, and right now I feel like making use of them all!"

# -IX-

rue to the translator's concerns they did not find water, but in many other respects the site they settled on for the evening's camp was more than suitable. Situated part way up the easily negotiated left side of a broad gully, the cleft they had found was high, narrow, and deep, affording protection from the elements as well as possible marauding predators. While they unpacked their supplies and built a fire near the entrance, overlooking the dark winding swath of the ravine below, it was a great comfort to know that in the event of a visit by unfriendly nocturnal predators they could retreat further back into the rock to places where nothing larger than a *Protoceratops* could reach.

Feeling comparatively safe and secure for the moment did not make Chaz forget his concerns. Taking an occasional mouthful from the basket of dried mixed fodder Will had set out beneath his beak, the translator waited until his human companions were well along with their own evening meal before speaking.

"You knew this place was here too, I suppose," he teased Sylvia.

She shook her head, looking past him to the dark, deserted wash. "Not at all. I do know that this is the right way to go, but stumbling across this campsite for tonight was just a fortunate coincidence." She dug into her own food.

"It seems to me that we have been depending entirely too much on fortunate coincidences." Chewing methodically, he continued to stare at the young woman. "I wonder if you really do know where you are going, or where you are, or if this little excursion of yours is based more on hope than knowledge."

"Chaz!" Will responded sharply. "How can you say that? Do you really think Sylvia would come all this way and expose herself to these kinds of risks without being absolutely sure of herself?" He looked to his left. "You wouldn't, would you?"

She laughed softly. "If the philosophers are right, no one can be absolutely sure of anything. But I didn't make up the information I found in the old records, and the ancient scrolls aren't fakes." Setting her supper aside, she put her hands on her knees and leaned forward slightly.

"I promised I would tell you where we're going and what we're looking for at tonight's meal, and so I shall." She looked meaningfully from attentive fiancé to curious ceratopsian, letting the silence linger until both of them had begun to fidget.

"Have either of you heard of the tomb of Mujo Doon?"

Will and Chaz exchanged a glance. It was the translator who replied.

"I think I once read something about it, in a general

history of this part of Dinotopia. The site is located some-where in the coastal mountains, not terribly far from the sea. Some preliminary excavations have been carried out there, but the location is too remote and difficult to justify full-scale archeological work when so many more easily accessed and promising sites are still to be developed."

Will chipped in. "I've heard of the place, too. Isn't it sup-posed to house the remains of some early ruler of that part of Dinotopia? One of the ancient civilizations that preceded the present form of universal government, like Poseidos or First Chandara?"

Sylvia nodded. "That's right. Nobody's entirely sure, because as Chaz pointed out, only preliminary excavations have been carried out at the site. There's no disagreement about the location, however. It's shown on most maps of Dinotopia." She leaned back against supporting stone and regarded her expectant companions.

"There are other archeological sites of importance in the Great Desert that have only been casually noted, and which have never been studied."

"So that's what this is all about." Chaz sniffed. "A simple scientific expedition to study ancient civilizations. There is only one problem with that, young lady." He eyed her evenly. "To the best of my knowledge, none of those sites is located in this part of the Great Desert. Like Mujo Doon itself, they are all in the south, while you are leading us decidedly eastward."

She pursed her lips as she considered how best to reply. "The operative part of that observation, Chaz, is 'to the best of your knowledge.'" That's what I've been saying all along. There is more knowledge in the ancient scrolls than has ever been studied. What I did was to pull together seemingly unrelated references from different sources."

"And these sources identified what?" The *Protoceratops* remained skeptical. "The tomb of another unknown ruler? Some overlooked vestiges of coastal Neoknossosian civilization? The site of early Poseidosian inland trading routes?"

"No," she replied quietly. "They hint at the location of a successful sea route away from Dinotopia itself. One that would let capable sailors leave and return in relative safety."

Will gaped at her. "That's crazy, Sylvia! Everybody knows that the currents around Dinotopia prevent any vessel from leaving its immediate oceanic vicinity. Even the new steam-powered craft that were starting to be built when my father and I were shipwrecked here couldn't do it. And any ship that tries to land ends up wrecked on the reefs. You can't make a safe landfall on Dinotopia, and you certainly can't sail away from it."

"What I found in the old scrolls and tablets suggests otherwise," she countered simply.

"Pardon me for stating the obvious," Chaz interrupted, "but if it is an impossible sea route you seek, what are we doing in the middle of the Great Desert?" With a raised forefoot he gestured at the moonlit gully below them. "This seems to me the wrong place to be debating the abilities of ships and sailors."

"It doesn't matter," Will stated flatly. "There is no such route. There can't be."

"Why not?" Aware of the radical nature of her conclusions, Sylvia was patient with her companions.

"Because if it existed, it would be known," he replied

with confidence. "Think what it would mean to Dinotopia! Ships from other countries might not be aware of such a route, but there are boats in Sauropolis and Chandara that are capable of making an open ocean journey. If the ancestors of today's Dinotopian sailors ever made such a voyage, why did it not lead to regular trade with India, say, or the Spice Islands?"

She tilted her head back to gaze up at the stars. "That's one of the questions I'd very much like to have an answer to, Will. If it can be done, why isn't anyone doing it? It seems strange indeed that people would make such an incredible discovery and then just forget about it. Perhaps they wanted to keep the knowledge secret so that only they would benefit, and before they could, something happened to them."

"That's a very un-Dinotopian supposition," he pointed out.

"It certainly is," Chaz agreed, "but it took time for today's society to develop. In ancient days old habits of self-ishness lingered among some humans. We dinosaurs had to tutor you in the ways of sharing and seeking peace." Though he remained no less suspicious of her claims, he looked upon Sylvia with new respect.

"It is a plausible bit of psychological theory, but mean-ingless if this mysterious ocean path does not in fact exist."

"I agree, Chaz, but I'm convinced that it does, and that we can rediscover it."

He chuckled softly, his beak clacking as light from the fire danced in his eyes. "Well then, I suppose we should start gathering wood to make a boat."

"Yeah," Will put in. "How do you find a safe path over

the sea anyway? It's not like looking for a trail among the rocks."

"I know this looks silly," she told them. "Searching in the middle of a desert for a way across the ocean. But I'm only following the clues that were in the scrolls." She waved at the rocky terrain surrounding them, her arm encompassing the ravine and the hills beyond.

"We're looking for an actual physical indicator. A great monument that was raised by the ancient and now forgotten Dinotopian civilization that discovered the water route. According to the old records, it points the way over the sea, and in unmistakable fashion."

"And what is this mysterious monument called?" Chaz wanted to know.

"The Hand of Dinotopia."

It was Will's turn to chuckle. "That seems straightforward enough. We just keep walking toward the sea until we stumble over a giant hand." He grinned at Chaz.

Sylvia's patience with her sardonic companions was beginning to wane. "I don't know that the monument takes the form of a giant hand. It might be something else entirely. The description might be allegorical. It might be a spit of land, or a cluster of ancient trees."

"If it is trees, they may long since have fallen down," Chaz pointed out. "Which would explain why no one else has stumbled across the discovery. Assuming it actually exists, of course," he hastened to add.

"I know that," she admitted. "But I felt that it was potentially such an important finding I couldn't just forget about it. That's what the historians and archeologists I consulted about it told me to do." Her voice fell. "They were no more encouraging than you two are."

His smile slipping in the face of her dejection, Will moved close to put his arm around her. She didn't look up at him. "I'm sorry, Sylvia. We didn't mean to make fun of you."

She looked up at him. "Yes you did."

He did his best to make light of it. "Well, okay, we did. But no harm was meant." He gave her shoulder an affectionate squeeze. "You have to admit, it's a pretty extreme concept to ask someone to swallow."

"Yes." Chaz ambled over to place his head gently in Sylvia's lap. "Did you really expect us to be more encouraging than the experts who told you to put the idea aside?"

"I suppose—I don't know," she murmured finally. "I guess I hoped that when I told you, you might at least show some enthusiasm."

The *Protoceratops* removed his head from her lap. "Right now I am enthusiastic about a warm bed of clean straw and a basket of fresh fruit, but considering the present situation, that is something of a waste of time. In lieu of that, I suppose I might as well be enthusiastic about your quest. At least until it has been conclusively disproven."

Her lips twisted slightly and she regarded the little ceratopsian with affection. "Not exactly a ringing endorsement of my research, but right now I'll take what I can get." She turned her attention to her fiancé. "Will? What about you?"

He sighed resignedly. "At this point we might as well go on as go back. Especially with those angry dilophosaurs behind us. Besides, I admit I'm curious to see if this monument of yours exists. Never mind the impossible sea route. But you still haven't explained what we're doing looking for clues to an ocean route in the middle of the desert."

"According to the old records," she explained, "the civilization that discovered it was devastated in the same great earthquake that caused Poseidos to sink beneath the sea in what is now Sapphire Bay. Only their most distant outposts survived, and these were too scattered and weak to sustain the original culture. Over time, the survivors merged with other Dinotopian societies, and much of the original knowledge of their parent civilization was lost."

"Including this hypothetical safe sea route," Chaz commented.

"Yes." Once more she gestured at their silent surroundings. "That's what we're doing out here, in the middle of the Great Desert. In the ancient scrolls I think I found the location of one of their last outposts."

"And you hope it will hold clues to the location of this enigmatic Hand of Dinotopia," Chaz finished for her. "Well, if nothing else, young lady, it is quite a story." Ceratopsian eyes considered the moonlit ravine, a river of shadow spread out beneath their feet. "The question is, is it only that? Nothing more than a story?"

"That's what we're going to find out in the next few days." Will settled himself against Sylvia, and she did not push him away. "It'll have to be in the next few days, because we don't have supplies enough to go wandering around in the Great Desert for weeks. We're only three people; not an expedition."

Smiling fondly down at him, she began to toy with his hair. "Speak for yourself, Will Denison. Right from the start, I've always thought of myself as an expedition."

"If that is the case," commented Chaz as he paced in

tight circles and tried to find a soft rock on which to spend the night, "then I am afraid your relief column is sadly lacking in the material necessary for extended archeological exhumation."

"That may be so," she replied, "but in its place I have your always bright and cheerful personality to sustain me."

Chaz responded with an articulate snort. Finding a smooth section of sandstone, he flopped onto his belly with a soft, heavy thump, closed his eyes, and did his best to abet the onset of sleep. On the other side of the fire, Will and Sylvia snuggled a little closer together, and not just because the night was turning cold. It was simply time, they decided by means of unvoiced agreement, to deal with matters other than ancient lost monuments and the caprice of unknown seas.

The followng morning, the difficulties of simply walking through the rocky hills, much less finding anything, were compounded by the comparative sameness of their surroundings. To Will and Chaz one stone outcropping looked no different from the next. When they queried Sylvia about their concerns she would reply that her notes were copious, her research extensive, and that they should trust her lead because she knew where they were going. This they did, not because they were convinced of her findings, but because they had no other choice.

Still, Will reflected as they made their way along what seemed like the tenth (or maybe it was the twentieth) rock-lined ravine, it would have been greatly encouraging to him and his ceratopsian friend if they had found so much as a shovel point or a broken piece of pottery. But in two days of continuous hiking and searching there had been only rocks, and scrub, and a plethora of desert insects not all of whose intentions had proven benign.

Stumbling along behind Chaz and his fiancée, he reached down to scratch at the bites that had raised itching welts on the backs of both legs. The perpetrators of these irritations to his person remained at large and incognito, having initially disguised themselves as harmless, colorful beetles. He had ignored them, a decision that in retrospect seemed naive. Very little life survived in harsh climes that did not bite. It was a lesson he ought to have heeded.

Chaz's thick skin protected him from all but the most voracious arthropods, and Sylvia seemed not to have been affected. Why should they trouble her, he thought sardonically, when they had already feasted on him? More to the point, his traveling shorts had provided easier access to flesh and blood than had her trimmed-down but still extensive Orofani garb.

Grousing over his misfortune, he caught up to her, and she slowed to walk alongside instead of in front of him. The look on his face alarmed her.

"You don't look like you're feeling very well, Will."

"Oh, I'm okay. It's just that these blasted bug bites are driving me crazy."

She peered into his eyes. "I know you better than that, Will Denison. What's wrong? Tell me."

He hesitated, turning away from her and making himself study the rim of the ravine they were currently traversing. "Sylvia, we've been wandering around in these dry hills for days now without finding anything. Not a potsherd, not a hieroglyph, not so much as a bone bead, much less some grand exalted illustrious Hand of Dinotopia." He gestured ahead, at the packs secured to the back of the lumbering *Protoceratops*. "Our supplies are starting to run low." Turning back to face her, he gazed earnestly into her eyes.

"Maybe—maybe it's time we started looking for a way out of here, Sylvia, instead of for some ancient mythical cenotaph that may or may not exist."

She made no attempt to conceal her surprise and disappointment. "Will! And I thought you believed in me."

"I do, Sylvia, I do. Honest. But believing and finding are two different things. We don't have the resources to go scrambling all over the Great Desert in search of an artifact that may or may not be where you think it is—or even exist. I came all this way, against everyone's advice, to make sure that you were all right. Not to head off on some dangerous, extended archeological search. If—if we die out here, your research will hardly be vindicated."

"We're not going to die," she insisted primly. "I know where I'm going." She indicated the increasingly narrow, high-sided ravine in front of them. "We'll find water up ahead, you'll see."

"But what if we don't?" He pleaded his case as gently as he could. "Sylvia, if there are ruins out here, think how much easier it would be for a fully-equipped expedition from Chandara to find them. They could avoid the Amu entirely and come up the coast road from Chandara, then strike inland."

She shook her head angrily. "The scrolls were emphatic about one thing. All the hints and the clues lead inland eastward from the canyon, not westward from the coast. That's why I came the way I did. An expedition coming up from Chandara would never be able to find the place."

"What if they were accompanied by skybax riders? Say, you and I on Cirrus and Nimbus. We could overfly the whole area and scout on ahead. Wouldn't that be more efficient?"

It made her hesitate, but only for a moment. "We don't have an expedition at our disposal, Will, and we're not likely to ever have one. I tried that route, remember? So did you."

"Then maybe we should try again." The insect bites, the heat, the throbbing in his legs from endless hiking up and down hills and along gravel-laden gullies, all had combined to sap his strength as well as his patience.

Hearing it in his voice as well as seeing it in his face, she was moved to reluctant compromise. "All right, Will. As important as this is to me, I don't want us to fight over it. It's not as important as you and I." She took a deep breath. "If we don't find water by tomorrow morning, we'll either turn back or strike straight for the coast."

He swallowed, thirsty but unwilling to take a drink out of turn from their shrinking supplies. "You mean that?"

She nodded tersely. "Perhaps you and Chaz are right. Maybe I read too much into the old scrolls. Maybe I wanted something like the Hand of Dinotopia to exist, and so I saw hints where none existed, invented connections impossible to justify." She straightened slightly. "You're both right about one thing: we can't keep searching in ever-widening circles and spirals without replenishing our water supply."

"That's fair enough." Satisfied with her decision, he said no more about it. "I'd sure like to find even a muddy water-hole, but I'm afraid we're going to have to make what we have left last all the way to the coast. If we were walking on sand I'd say our chances were better, but the likelihood of finding water in rocky ravines like this one are pretty close to ze—"

He was interrupted by a loud yelp of surprise from the trail-breaking Chaz, followed immediately by the translator's complete disappearance from view. The yelp was followed by another noise, sharp and distinctive. Both Will and Sylvia knew instantly what it was. They simply did not believe it.

Their disbelief was dispelled moments later as they rushed to the edge of the unexpected drop-off. Below, the *Protoceratops* was paddling furiously to get back to the place where he had fallen in.

"Hang on!" Fully clothed, Will leaped in to help his friend. Like all ceratopsians, Chaz was a fair swimmer, but the load of supplies on his back was weighing him down. Will pulled and tugged furiously at the ropes until the burden was released. A grateful Chaz immediately bobbed higher in the water.

As the relieved translator paddled back to the trail head, Will was treated to the highly incongruous sight of their precious half-full waterbags bobbing up and down in a clear, deep pool. Treading water while hanging onto the sack that contained most of their food, he turned—and nearly swallowed an unintended mouthful.

The sight that greeted his startled eyes was as spectacular as it was unanticipated—and it was not even the legendary Hand of Dinotopia.

Chaz had fallen not into a pool but an enormous cistern, for it was immediately apparent even to Will's untrained eye that the water catchment was artificial in origin. Each about the size of a human head, intricately carved stone blocks lined the sides of the rectangular repository. Above these the ravine walls were chiseled with deep bas-reliefs showing humans, dinosaurs, and mythological half-breeds engaged in all manner of water-related activities, from fishing to sailing to simply enjoying the sea. The sea, which was far from the place where he and these artistic representations of a vanished age now cavorted.

Looking down between his feet through the crystal-clear water, he saw that the commodious basin was lined with dark blue tiles. The style and glaze was unfamiliar to him, as were the abstract yellow and gray patterns that had been baked into the glistening finish. Tile would hold water better than stone, he knew. Whoever had fashioned this remarkable catchment had been masters of their craft.

"Will!" It was Sylvia, yelling at him. "Are you okay?"

"Yes."

Next to her Chaz shook himself dry, the motion not unlike that of dogs Will had known as a child. Standing at the place where he had tumbled in, the *Protoceratops* turned to eye the pool and its single occupant. "Well, are you going to stay in there all day? Come out, and let us see what we have found."

"What you've found, you mean." With easy strokes Will made his way back to the end of the trail. Pulling himself up out of the water, he sat down next to Chaz and considered the prospect before them.

"I told you we'd find water." Sylvia could not resist celebrating her vindication.

"You might have warned a person." Grumbling, Chaz

shook himself again, inadvertently watering Sylvia and re-soaking Will.

Brushing droplets from her face and arms, she studied the tile-lined catchment. "The old records said there would be water here. They just neglected to say how much."

"I only wanted to be able to drink my fill," the *Proto-ceratops* observed. "Going for a swim was the farthest thing from my mind." He looked up at her. "What is this place?"

"An entrance—I hope." Scanning the far side of the basin, she suddenly knelt and pointed. "There! All the way on the opposite side, off to the left."

"What?" Will stared at the place where she was pointing. Then he saw it—or thought he did. "That dark area?"

"Yes. It's just as it's described in the records. A conduit. It should lead us the rest of the way."

"The rest of the way where?" Chaz tilted back his head to examine their surroundings. The basin was completely enclosed on all sides by sheer, unclimbable rock walls. The only way in or out was via the trail they had stumbled down.

"Let's not waste any time!" So saying, the excited Sylvia promptly jumped into the catchment, sending water flying.

A startled Will tried to shield his face. "Hey! You didn't answer Chaz's question."

But she had already taken the waterbags in tow and was kicking toward the far end of the basin. "Come on! We're almost there."

"Almost *where*?" Chaz barked loudly, but she did not reply. He turned to Will, who could only shrug helplessly.

"Almost to someplace, I guess." Whereupon he followed

his fiancée's lead by jumping into the water, pushing the buoyant sack of food and the rest of their meager supplies ahead of him.

"Now wait a minute!" the translator began. He halted when he saw that neither of the young humans was paying any attention to him. "Oh, bother!" he muttered. Unable to hold his nose, he kept his snout as high as he could as he leaped back into the pool, raising a splash that was bigger than Sylvia's and Will's combined.

The dark shadow Sylvia had spotted from the trail head turned out to be a tile-lined tube or pipe with a low ceiling. A very low ceiling, Will decided uneasily as he approached it. As a skybax rider, he preferred wide, open spaces to tight, enclosed ones. Paddling close behind him, Chaz was of like mind, but the enthusiastic Sylvia seemed untroubled by their claustrophobic surroundings.

The light faded fast as they swam inside and the entrance to the conduit slipped farther and farther behind them, a fact that Chaz was not hesitant to point out.

"Am I a struthie that I can see in the dark?" he complained. Though he spoke softly, his voice echoed loudly off the enclosing tiled walls.

"Just a little farther," Sylvia called back to him from up ahead.

"A little farther to what?" Chaz kicked on, wishing he could feel the bottom of the conduit with his footpads. Darkness, damp and cold, closed in around him.

Then a shout from in front of him. "Light! I can see light ahead of us. We're coming out."

Will listened intently for the sound of falling water, but that was one threat they did not have to worry about. No waterfall or dangerous rapids awaited them at the end of the conduit. What did await them was marvelous in the extreme.

Illumination returned and his eyes struggled to readjust to the bright light. As his vision cleared he found himself gazing in amazement at the incredible surroundings. Off to his left, Sylvia had emerged from the water and stood standing on a stone walkway inlaid with tiles fashioned from jade and agate and lapis-lazuli. The dust of ages covered the tiles and in places piles of wind-blown sand had accumulated, but they could not dim the beauty and the glory of what those who were no more had left behind.

She was grinning triumphantly at him as he pulled their food supplies out of the water and turned to help Chaz.

"Welcome to Ahmet-Padon," she proclaimed gleefully.

**-X-**

ven Chaz was awed by the sights that surrounded them. "You told us you had found evidence for some kind of lost artifact or monument, Sylvia, but never even in my most concessionary moments did I expect anything like this." Overwhelmed by their new surroundings, the *Protoceratops* turned a slow circle, and in so doing nearly fell into the water for a second time.

"It's magnificent." Will's voice was hushed, as was only appropriate in the presence of something truly remarkable.

"To tell you the truth," Sylvia confessed as they started into the lost city, "I'm kind of thunderstruck myself. The old records hinted that this was someplace special, but they weren't very descriptive. They just said there would be water, and places to rest."

"Places to rest, indeed!" Chaz murmured. "Palaces would be more like it."

Soaring sandstone cliffs rose on all sides of them, forming a multitude of narrow canyons and clefts. Apartments, temples, granaries, workshops, stables, schools, offices and baths, passageways and water conduits; all had been hewn out of the solid rock. It reminded Will of Canyon City. The difference was that Ahmet-Padon had been built to a more elaborate scale. Far more elaborate.

Though they supported nothing but the canyonsides of which they were a part, pillars and arches had been cut from the solid rock to supply decorative architectural detail. Facing cliffs had been deeply incised so that their surfaces would resemble individual building stones even though no mortar had been utilized and the "stones" were part of the same solid cliff-face. Hinges of faded brass and copper still supported heavy, weathered wooden doors. Unbroken windows contained numerous inserts of cut quartz, prisms that would carry sunlight from the narrow chasms deep into cavernous living quarters.

Several avenues paved with neatly cut stone showed signs of having been widened to accommodate the larger dinosaurs. Ahmet-Padon had been a true Dinotopian civilization, home to a full range of saurians as well as their consorting humans. Steps and staircases wide and strong enough to serve broad, flat feet were further proof of the city's cosmopolitan past.

Several of the stables were expansive enough to have housed the largest sauropods in comfort. Their entrances were marvels of the stonemason's art, filled from ground to crown with intricate bas-reliefs depicting daily life in ancient Ahmet-Padon. Will and Chaz found themselves wondering how humans and dinosaurs could have found room to share some of the narrower streets, until Sylvia pointed out the catwalks cut from the solid rock high above their heads. Humans could stride along on these elevated paths in comfort while leaving the lower concourses to their more cumbersome fellow citizens.

Apartments varied in size from cozy cubbyholes excavated from the rock to spacious venues large enough to accommodate smaller saurians as well as humans. There was crumbling furniture and fine metalwork, all of it covered with dust or sand and showing the ravages of time. Despite this, the dry desert air had preserved much of the city's wood- and metalwork. Anything organic, such as leather or cotton clothing, had long since bowed to the attentions of efficient desert scavengers, from insects to small rodents.

The stonework, from the bas-reliefs to the incredibly detailed false temple faces, was remarkable. But it was not the exceptional quality of the carvings that overwhelmed the three visitors so much as it was the quantity. No stone was unetched, no cliff-face undecorated. Every square foot of sandstone to a height at least halfway up each cliff was covered with carvings and reliefs.

Every aspect of life in the ancient city was wonderfully depicted, from processionals and sporting events to religious ceremonies and nuptials. Even the smoothly paved stone streets boasted detailed carvings, though down through the centuries many of these had been worn smooth by the tramp of heavy dinosaurian feet. Each street was slightly V-shaped, with the center of each reserved for a covered drainage ditch.

Water was piped to the inhabitants by means of stone flumes that linked an elaborate and ingenious system of storage cisterns. Some, like the one Chaz had stumbled into, were located at or near street level, but most had been hewn from rock higher up, enabling the pipes that joined them to supply the habitations below by means of simple gravity feed.

Strolling along one magnificently decorated sandstone corridor, Will tilted his head back until his neck complained and pointed toward the rim of the nearest cliff, high above.

"I'll bet the tops of these bluffs are pockmarked with a whole network of storage cisterns designed to collect and store runoff."

"It must have been interesting here during a storm." Chaz shuffled along between his two human companions, lost like them in wonder at the beauty of the lost city. "Flash flooding would fill some of the narrower streets quickly."

"Their drainage system must have been a marvel of ancient engineering." Sylvia paused to finger a bas-relief that showed ankylosaurs and humans working side by side to cut a storeroom from solid rock. Some of the finer details had been lost to wind erosion, but it was still possible to follow the sequence of events as they had been laid down hundreds of years ago.

"There are doubtless storage cisterns for runoff also located beneath the streets," Chaz pointed out. "Whole subterranean lakes, perhaps." The sudden thought made him tread a little more lightly on the seemingly solid pavement underfoot.

"Theirs was an industrious and talented culture," Sylvia remarked. "I wonder what happened to them?"

Chaz gave a ceratopsian shrug, his frill twisting slightly with the gesture. "Many ancient Dinotopian societies rose and fell, until the finest accomplishments of all gave rise to the community of humans and dinosaurs we know today. Some of the ancient cultures left extensive histories behind. Others, like this one, simply vanished or faded away. It may be that we will never know what happened to the inhabitants of this city."

One possible explanation took the form of an elaborate series of decorations that Sylvia spotted inside an ancient granary. The engravings covered one entire wall from floor to ceiling.

They had taken shelter there for the night, and from an uncharacteristically cold rising wind, when she noticed that the reliefs appeared to form a single continuous, unbroken progression.

"See," she told her companions in the fading light as they studied the wall, "it starts at the bottom, here, with a burst of light and an explosion of life."

Chaz nodded sagely. "The beginnings look like your standard creation myth." Leaning back, he was able to balance on his tail and rest his forefeet against the wall, allowing himself to see the higher reliefs. "It does indeed appear to illustrate the history of Ahmet-Padon from the very beginning to a definite end."

"Look here." Will was bending over to indicate a section of wall further toward the rear of the chamber. "This part shows the building of the city."

"And this here," Chaz went on, "the aqueducting of water from springs higher up in these hills." Will joined him in examining the fine sculpture that showed clearly how one ancient engineering marvel after another had been accomplished.

After a few moments Will thought to glance over at

Sylvia. She was sunk deep in thought as she studied the carvings on the highest level.

"These carvings down here are fascinating, Sylvia. Don't you want to see?"

"Later." Her tone was subdued and she did not take her eyes from the reliefs. "I think I've found out what happened to all the people."

Will and Chaz immediately joined her in examining the uppermost section of carving-adorned wall. There was no writing to accompany the incisions, but so obvious was the progression that none was needed. The sequence of events was sharp, unmistakable, and easy to follow, even over the course of centuries.

As the bas-reliefs made clear, a sudden change in the climate had struck this part of Dinotopia. When, they could not tell, but the effects had plainly been devastating to the inhabitants of Ahmet-Padon. Reliefs lower down had shown humans and dinosaurs working side by side to plant and harvest fields of grain. Others had depicted such activities as the gathering of nuts and berries and the netting of fish in vast shallow lakes.

Now the high reliefs depicted scenes of disaster and dismay. Trees were shown without leaves, and fruit withered on vines and bushes. One entire string of some unnamed master of the stone carver's art was devoted to sequences of lakes shriveling up and fish and amphibians perishing on drying ground. Others showed humans and dinosaurs drawing the last water from nearly empty cisterns.

The final reliefs, the highest of all, showed people leaving the city behind. There was no mass migration, no long columns of organized flight. Humans and dinosaurs departed in ones and twos, in family groups and small clusters, until only the magnificent structures remained, unpopulated and empty.

It had grown very quiet in the chamber. For a long time no one spoke. They simply gazed at the intricately carved chronicle of a culture and contemplated its end.

"The masons who carved this must have been among the last to leave," Sylvia finally murmured aloud. "They finished the history of their people and then they packed up their tools and left, just like everyone else."

"They did not do this for themselves," Chaz added compassionately. "They did it so those who came after would know what happened here." He turned to look upon the rest of the very empty chamber. "They did it for us."

Outside, a rising night wind moaned. It sounded more than ever like a dirge, an elegy for a vanished people. Only, they hadn't vanished, Will corrected himself firmly. They had scattered, and their progeny were as much a part of contemporary Dinotopia as Sylvia or Chaz's ancestors.

"I don't think I want to sleep here," he declared abruptly.

"They are only carvings," Chaz reminded him. "It is getting dark outside and this chamber is spacious and comfortable. Why look for another place when this one is perfectly adequate?"

"I just don't want to spend the night in here, that's all." Behind him, Will felt he could hear the voices of vanished inhabitants bemoaning the fate that had befallen their glorious city, believed he could feel the pressure on the back of his neck of vacant stone eyes. Though he was guilty of nothing but being alive, he felt that he somehow stood accused.

Hands slipped gently onto his shoulders as Sylvia came to his side. "I understand, Will. I feel the weight of old memories in this place, too."

"Come on." He started for the doorway. Muttering, Chaz fell in behind.

"Humans. Always so sensitive to the non-existent!"

But as they exited the chamber, he found that he could not bring himself to look back, and he was glad of the keratinous frill that prevented him from looking directly over his own shoulder.

They soon found another comparably sand-free room. Its walls were lined with patinaed tiles showing the children of humans and dinosaurs at various kinds of play. A school-room of some kind, Sylvia decided, or a nursery. What little of the dust-covered furniture that remained gave no clue to the room's purpose, but the smaller than usual entrance blocked out most of the wind and the sand it carried, and made for a comfortable shelter.

They settled down for the night next to the rear wall. Though much reduced in flow, an ancient drinking trough still carried a trickle of clear, potable water. After some discussion, an already damaged piece of ancient furniture served as the foundation for a fire. One was needed not so much to ward off the night chill as to keep lingering spirits at bay. While all three of the travelers repeatedly professed their immunity from superstition, none objected to the presence of the fire, and care was taken to keep it crackling until the last of them had fallen asleep.

Nothing disturbed their rest until the sun, already high in the sky, finally succeeded in making its presence known in the depths of the canyons. Yawning, Will rose and strolled over to the doorway. The wind had died away and the street outside was silent. Behind him, his friends were stirring.

"What I would not give for a decent bed of fresh straw, with some aromatic leaves mixed in to delight the senses!" As Chaz stretched, pushing out on his forelegs, his companions could hear his vertebrae crack.

Sylvia winced at the sound. "I wish you wouldn't do that."

Pulling his upper body forward and letting his hind legs stretch, Chaz glanced over at her. "Find me that bed and I won't."

"We could all use a real bed." Silhouetted by the morning sun in the resplendently carved doorway, Will looked back at them. "But that's something I'm afraid we're going to have to do without until we reach the coast."

"I never thought I would be so glad to see the sea." Shuffling over to where they had piled their scanty stock of supplies, Chaz gestured with his beak. "Come and give me your hands with this. Unless you want to carry it yourselves."

Working together, Will and Sylvia repositioned the bulk of their remaining cache on the *Protoceratops*'s willing back. Snacking on handfuls of the roasted bugs embedded in dried fruit that was a specialty of the Orofani, they exited the chamber.

Standing in the street outside, Chaz looked to right, left, and finally up at Sylvia. "Which way?"

She did not consult her notes. For the first time since they had found her at the Orofani camp, she looked uncertain.

"I don't know," she confessed. "The scrolls say that the key to locating the Hand of Dinotopia lies in Ahmet-Padon."

"Very well," the translator replied amiably. "Here is Ahmet-Padon. Where is this key?"

She scanned the street, the bas-reliefs that lined much of the far wall, the dark enigmatic entrances to long abandoned rooms and chambers.

"The scrolls don't say. I suppose we'll just have to keep looking."

"Pardon me?" The *Protoceratops* eyed her archly. "'Keep looking'? Keep looking where?"

She shrugged helplessly. "In other parts of Ahmet-Padon, I guess. The key is here. All we have to do is find it."

"Of course. Why didn't I think of that? A whole city of who knows what size, extending this way and that into a hundred, a thousand fissures in these hills, and all we have to do is search it all. Not to mention the fact that we have no idea what we are looking for!" He snorted derisively.

Will eyed his fiancée expectantly. "Well, Sylvia? Is Chaz right? *Do* we have any idea what we're looking for?"

"No." She tried her best to radiate some confidence. "But I'm sure we'll recognize it when we find it."

The translator rolled his eyes. "Preserve me from the scientific method!"

"We're wasting time." Exuding determination, if not conviction, Will turned to his right and started up the street back the way they had come. "Let's try this direction."

His companions hurried to catch up. Sylvia eyed him uncertainly. "Will, I thought you were as skeptical about this as Chaz?"

"I am," he replied as he strode purposefully along, "but you were right about this place. The scrolls told you there was something here, and darned if they weren't right. So why shouldn't they be right about the key?"

"I'm sure they are," she agreed, "but Chaz is correct: finding this 'key,' whatever it is, won't be easy."

He had to laugh. "In the past couple of weeks I've flown a skybax all the way from Sauropolis to Canyon City, hiked up and down canyon trails known and unknown, dealt with dangerous animals and peculiar Dinotopians, and crossed part of the Great Desert to find both you and a lost city." He continued to chuckle softly. "I'm not about to give up and stagger home empty-handed. Not yet, anyway. If this key exists, we're damn sure going to find it!"

Much to his surprise, she threw both arms around him and kissed him hard on the cheek. The gesture nearly caused both of them to fall.

"That's one reason why I love you, Will Denison. The more difficult things get, the more determined you become."

"Pardon me, but the word you want is 'stubborn,'" Chaz commented—but without much animation.

Will's energy and enthusiasm began to wane as another night passed and the following morning brought no new revelations. They found wonderful things, for the deserted chambers of the abandoned city were replete with marvels and discoveries, any one of which would have sent the trained archeologists of Sauropolis and Waterfall City into paroxysms of delight. But they found no references to the cryptic Hand of Dinotopia, no description of it, and certainly no key to its location.

Tired and hungry, they selected an ancient temple for the site of their afternoon meal. Even in the shade of the towering canyons whose intricately carved and elegantly ornamented walls comprised the city, it was hot at midday. Cisterns and channels of cool water notwithstanding, they were never able to forget for a moment that they were still isolated somewhere in the middle of the Great Desert, and that beyond the protective sandstone ramparts of Ahmet-Padon the unrelenting sun seared plains of hot gravel and shifting sand.

The entrance to the temple was flanked by gilded wats in the southeast Asian style. Fanciful figures of humans and dinosaurs decorated the exterior to a height that would have provided comfortable viewing for a brachiosaur. As they had come to expect, every sculpture and ornamentive architectural detail had been chiseled from the solid rock wall of the canyon.

The spacious, airy interior gave no clue to the chamber's function. Will thought of it as a temple because its external features suggested a place of supplication, though they encountered nothing inside or out to suggest what, if anything, visitors might have worshipped. The ceiling was honeycombed with abstract traceries in the manner of a Moorish palace. Such unexpected and delightful architectural and aesthetic contrasts were a hallmark of Dinotopian culture, with its polyglot contributions from a multitude of human civilizations. The remarkable environs of Ahmet-Padon were no exception. When Sylvia pointed out a line of exquisitely sculpted hadrosaur heads set atop kneeling human bodies in the style of ancient Egypt, all raised above the floor on cylindrical bases of blue-tinted Ming porcelain, neither Will nor Chaz was surprised.

The central portion of the main room, however, presented them with a puzzle. In a succession of gently curving, irregular, shallow concentric steps, the floor sank to a lower level from whose flat bottom rose multiple lumps and cones.

"What do you make of that?" Standing on the entrance level, Will gestured at the central sunken section of floor.

Sylvia was unable to provide enlightenment. "I don't know. The scrolls didn't say anything about it." She scrutinized the graduated depression that occupied most of the room and tried to make sense of its strange stairs and projections. "At the bottom it looks like some kind of maze, but none of the pieces are big enough to hide behind."

"Some kind of circular ceremonial amphitheater, maybe," Will suggested. "But why such small seats? And if they're stair steps and not seats, why so shallow? Even an infant could crawl up them."

"Maybe that's it," she responded. "Maybe this was some kind of educational play area for young humans and dinosaurs."

Tilting back his head, he regarded the intricately carved ceiling with increasing skepticism. "I don't know. Considering the amount and quality of structural decoration here, it strikes me as awfully elaborate for a nursery."

"Well," she argued, "what else could it be?"

While they rested and ate, they debated what use the vanished inhabitants of Ahmet-Padon might have made of the unusual sunken area and the mystifying, seemingly unrelated lumps and projections that rose from its floor. Unable to sit still for very long, Chaz found himself wandering around the room, studying the inscriptions and bas-reliefs that lined every wall in the by now familiar, florid style of the ancient city.

They were finishing up and preparing to leave when the agitated *Protoceratops* called out excitedly.

"Here, over here! Come and look at this!"

His companions rushed to join him near the back of the chamber. With his beak he indicated the wall relief that had been occupying his attention for the past several minutes. Will looked hard at it but was unable to detect anything out of the ordinary.

"I don't get it, Chaz. Why the excitement? It looks just like dozens of other wall reliefs we've seen around the city. What's so special about this one?"

The translator chuckled, a soft huffing sound that rose from the back of his throat. "Forget the reliefs for a moment, Will, and look at the periphery."

Most, if not all of the wall sculptures they had taken the time to study were rimmed with some kind of decorative margin. Sometimes these took the form of repeated flowers, or insects, or fish. Often they were purely abstract. At first glance that appeared to be the case here, but as Will stared he suddenly realized what this particular edging was composed of, and why it had excited Chaz.

"Hands," he murmured. "The fringe is made up of hands."

"That's right," Sylvia whispered. "They're all twisted around one another to create an abstract pattern, but the individual components are definitely hands."

Inspecting the large chamber they found that many, though not all, of the peripheral carvings that framed the numerous bas-reliefs were of a similar design. Even the rim of the sunken floor area that dominated the center of the room was lined with a pattern of interlocked hands.

"It's not conclusive," Will decided finally. "It doesn't say that this place is the Hand of Dinotopia, or even that it has anything to do with it."

"No," Sylvia admitted, "but it's the best clue we've had so far." She stared hard at the walls, ceiling, and floor, trying to decipher the ancient secrets she felt they must surely hold. "Let's keep looking here a while longer. Maybe we'll find something definitive."

The graceful but innocuous scenes of ancient Ahmet-Padonian life that were depicted on the walls did not provide any clues to solving ancient mysteries, nor was Chaz able to disentangle any of the hieroglyphics that accompanied them. After more than an hour of intense study they gathered together near the back of the chamber to concede defeat.

"The hands are just another decorative design," Will determined. "They don't signify anything special." He looked toward the imposing entrance. "We might as well keep searching the city."

"No." Sylvia was adamant. "This is not only the best lead we've found so far, it may be the only one." Her eyes roved the chamber. On the walls, the intricate bas-reliefs and sculptures seemed to be taunting her. "There has to be something more here than pretty pictures. There has to be."

"Sure there does." Tired and frustrated, Will was unable to keep a touch of irony from creeping into his voice. "Just because we want there to be more doesn't mean that's the case." Glancing down at the sculpture of intertwined hands near his feet, he added, "This could be the key, and we wouldn't even know what we were looking at." He kicked at it derisively.

It shifted and began to sink into the floor.

A low rumbling sound, faint and far-off, reverberated through the chamber. Chaz's eyes flicked from one wall to the next. "I am not so sure that was such a good idea, Will."

Sylvia had taken her fiancé's hand and was pulling him in the direction of the entrance as they eyed their surroundings warily. "Maybe we should leave for a while." The rumbling increasing in volume, but not aggressively.

"No, wait a minute." Examining the walls as he tried to pinpoint the source of the sound, Will held back. From behind, Chaz was pushing at him with his curving snout.

"Sylvia is right. We can proceed with our examination from the canyon outside." Suddenly the distant rumbling grew sharply louder.

Still Will was not panicked. The sound was familiar somehow, and not threatening. He was sure he recognized it.

"There!" He pointed abruptly to his right as they were greeted by the source of the rising din.

From the gaping stone mouths of saurian and human sculptures, water from concealed cisterns burst into the chamber. Cascading down the series of shallow sandstone steps, it gushed into the central depression and quickly began to cover the sunken floor. Sylvia and Will held onto one another while Chaz stood his ground on four solid, stocky legs. The steady, turbulent flow never threatened them. While filling the depression, it never swirled more than a hand's breadth high around their feet.

As the sunken area filled, an astonishing phenomenon manifested itself. In the center of the now water-filled depression, several of the lumps and cones they had assumed were attached to the floor had begun to rise. Attached to the floor by hitherto concealed copper chains so that they would not drift away, these individual sculptures rose higher and higher, buoyed upward by the rising waters.

Gradually the robust flow diminished. By the time the last drops dripped from silent stone mouths, the depression was full to the brim. Instead of a wide, irregularly-shaped sunken area in the center of the floor, the travelers now found themselves gazing at a glistening pool in whose center bobbed one large, misshapen mass and several smaller satellite shapes.

"Now what do you make of that?" Will was impressed by the watery consequences of his action, but no less enlightened than he had been when the depression was dry and its floor easily accessible.

Sylvia studied the bobbing, securely moored sculptures. "Will, I haven't a clue. And I wonder what's making those funny shapes stay afloat?"

"Geology," Chaz asserted. At this unlikely explanation they both turned to their translator. He proceeded to elaborate.

"With all the ornate carvings covering the walls, I did not bother to take a close look before this at the sculptures on the floor, but I see now that they are fabricated from volcanic pumice—a stony material that is actually lighter than water. Note how they are fastened to the floor of the pool so they will not drift freely." He gazed intently at the display. "It is clear that whoever built this intended that they should remain in these predetermined positions. That in turn suggests that the constancy of the overall model was considered to be a matter of some importance."

"But what does it mean?" Eyeing the newly filled pool

and its buoyant masses of patterned pumice, Will struggled to understand what he was seeing.

"Look at the middle of the largest mass," Sylvia suggested. "Isn't that a sculpture of a tiny building or something there?"

Will squinted. "Could be. But it still doesn't make any sense."

"Yes!" Chaz squealed sharply. Dipping his head, he began stomping the floor with all four feet, dancing about as if he was frantic to impress a panel of judges at the annual Waterfall City arts competition. Droplets of water flew from beneath his feet. "Yes, yes, yes!"

Unaccustomed to effusive displays of emotion by his ceratopsian friend, a startled Will eyed the prancing *Protoceratops* anxiously.

"Chaz, have you taken leave of your senses?"

"Hardly, my skinny skybax rider. On the contrary, I have just come to them!" Raising a foreleg, he gestured at the pool. "Sylvia was right. There is more here that meets the eye than pretty sculptures and abstract designs. It was right here before us all the time, only we could not see it. Could not make sense of what was right in front of us— until the pool was filled. Even then it took time for what I was seeing with my own eyes to make sense. Oh, it is most extraordinary!"

"*What* is?" an exasperated Will demanded to know.

"Why, this map, of course!" With his fixed jaw line the translator could not smile, but he managed to convey the impression of doing so nonetheless.

# -XI-

**S**ylvia gawked at the pool. "This is a map?"

Charged with excitement, their four-footed companion executed a ceratopsian pirouette. "Indeed it is, my willowy young woman." Halting after a full turn, he gestured once more with a forefoot. "We have eyes, but we were blind. It needed water to make them clear again. Descry the pumice carvings that float in the middle? They are fixed by their individual chains to the floor of the pool because that which they represent are also immovable in water. The shallow steps and stairs and cones that so puzzled us at first are now underwater. As are the sunken hills and plains and seamounts they denote."

"Underwater contour lines!" Will nodded slowly as the full realization of what they were looking at finally sunk in. "Of course! And the pumice sculptures represent islands."

Dipping his head toward his right leg, Chaz responded with a gracious bow. "Congratulations, Will. Now then: next lesson. Think back to your geography studies. The domain of Dinotopia does not include very many islands. Which of those are these?"

Sylvia answered before her fiancé could. "That little one nearest us must be Bima Kyun, and Boda Kyan next to it. So the larger one above them has to be Ko Veng, near the site of Poseidos itself." A broad smile spread across her face. "The largest one can be nothing other than Outer Island."

She was right, of course, Will knew. Except for Dinotopia itself, the eponymously named Outer Island was the largest body of land associated with the human-saurian realm. The formerly sunken portion of the chamber in which they found themselves was nothing less than an elaborate map. All that had been required to make its purpose clear was the addition of water to simulate the ocean.

"See how the modeled structure in the middle of the Outer Island has a border of tiny hands," Sylvia pointed out. "The Hand of Dinotopia. It *has* to be." She turned excitedly to Will. "We have to go there, of course."

Chaz's tone turned flat. "Now wait just a minute, young skybax rider. Consider carefully your words. Easy to talk one minute about exploring the Great Desert and in the next breath speak of tramping through the Outer Island. To actually do so is a different matter entirely."

"Sylvia's right, Chaz." For the moment at least, Will's uncertainty had collapsed in the face of Ahmet-Padon's reality. The discovery of the map had fired the kind of enthusiasm in him that had led him and his father to undertake the extensive sea voyage that had led to their being shipwrecked on Dinotopia in the first place. While he was not one to wander about aimlessly, they now had not only a map, they had a destination.

"Listen to me, both of you." The *Protoceratops* settled himself back on his haunches and tried to explain. Slowly and patiently, as one would to a group of children newly arrived at school. "It is one thing to go to Outer Island; it is quite another to seek something within its depths. Outer Island is *big*. Not nearly as big as Dinotopia, but plenty large enough to get lost in. Why, it's as big as the Great Desert itself."

"Then it should make for a nice change." Will grinned. "No more sandstorms, no more hot gravel under your feet, no more constantly worrying about water. I'd think it would be something you'd be looking forward to, Chaz."

The translator sniffed. "Outer island is 'outer' in more ways than just geographically, Will. Have you ever been there?" He looked past him to Sylvia. "Have you?"

The two humans exchanged a glance, and it was Will who replied. "No. But it's not like it's an unknown place."

"Merely because a place is shown on a map does not mean it is known, my eager friend. The vast mass of the interior of Outer Island is as unexplored as the Great Desert, perhaps even more so. No trading caravans cross its heart, no exploratory tracks follow its valleys. The center of the island is extremely mountainous and unbelievably difficult."

Will was not intimidated. "I've dealt with mountains before. Dad and I have spent time up in the Forbidden Mountains, and as you should well remember, I've been all through the Backbones."

An apprehensive Chaz beseeched his friend. "The mountains of Outer Island are different, Will. Not so high as the Forbiddens, but steeper and more difficult to negotiate.

These are volcanic escarpments that have been eroded by eons of heavy rain to knifelike sharpness. Like the rest of the island's interior they are blanketed in dense rainforest. Impenetrable rainforest, some say."

Kneeling by the side of the pool, Sylvia scooped water with cupped hands and sipped from the revelatory map. "No forest is 'impenetrable,'" she declared firmly.

Had he possessed fingers, Chaz would have shaken one at her. "Haste to rationalize that which one has not seen is not a virtue."

Bending forward, Will put a comradely hand on the *Protoceratops*'s neck, just behind his frill, and squeezed reassuringly. "Come on, Chaz. We can do it. We conquered the Great Desert, didn't we?"

The translator pulled away from his friend's fingers. "We have not 'conquered' anything, Will Denison. In case you haven't noticed, we are still in the middle of nowhere, short on food and with no prospect of being rescued. No matter which way we choose to go, much empty, difficult country lies ahead of us."

Will straightened. "You're right. Which way do you think we should go? I'll leave it up to you." A flustered Sylvia started to protest, but Will forestalled her.

Chaz eyed his tall friend narrowly. "You're very clever, Will. You know that we are now closer to the sea than to the main canyon of the Amu."

"Not only that," Will added for good measure, "if we try to retrace our steps we run the risk of bumping into our good friends the Orofani again, who might take more care this time that we stay with them awhile. A good, long while. Not to mention," he added for good measure, "a certain hungry, migratory pack of uncivilized dilophosaurs."

"So you leave it up to me to render a decision that logic has already made. I am overwhelmed by your beneficence." This time his bow was mock.

"Don't take it like that, Chaz. It's all part of the adventure, that's all." He put his arm around Sylvia and drew her close. "An adventure's better than a rescue."

"Adventures get people killed," the distraught translator muttered. But he realized they had no choice. Even discounting a potential re-encounter with the unpredictable Orofani or the voracious dilophosaurs, their chances were better if they struck for the coast instead of back inland. He groaned resignedly.

"Very well. Before we start out we should drink our fill here and then top off every waterbag."

"Of course," Will concurred cheerfully.

The pessimistic *Protoceratops* was not encouraged. "I hope you are still smiling when we find ourselves lost in these gullies and ravines, low on water and fatigued from lack of food. Remember also that I cannot perspire as you do."

"Don't worry, Chaz. If your tongue starts dragging on the ground I'll carry it for you."

"How droll." Actually, though the translator was loath to admit it, the image his friend had conjured up really was.

"So, which way, then?" Will asked his sour-tempered friend.

"East, of course. Once we intersect the old trade route that runs along the coast, then we will turn north, toward Hardshell." The translator eyed each of them in turn. "I know we are south of there and we must make certain we do not miss it by drifting too far north. Hardshell is not much of a town, but it is the only one between Neoknossos far to the south and Kuskonak to the north. If we miss it. . . ." He let the implication dangle ominously in the air.

Sylvia was nodding understandingly. "No food, no supplies of any kind anywhere else along the way."

"That is correct. If our luck holds and we do not become too disoriented, we should be able to make it. But to strike directly for Kuskonak itself is too dangerous. We have no map and could easily wander about aimlessly until—until it is too late. If we continue to walk due east we know that if nothing else, we will come eventually to the coast road."

"We might meet a trading caravan there," Will pointed out.

"That is possible," Chaz agreed, "but I would not want to bet my life on it. There is always some traffic along the coast between Chandara and Proserpine, but it is not scheduled. We cannot count on finding a comfortable place by the side of the road to rest while waiting for well-equipped travelers to come ambling along to assist us."

Having imbibed her fill, Sylvia splashed cool water on her face. "We'll make it, Chaz. After all, we've made it this far."

"Fortune favors the bold, they say." The *Protoceratops* shrugged. "We have no choice in any event. We cannot stay here. But if we make it to Hardshell, and then to Kuskonak, I may just squat there and wait for the next caravan heading back to Pteros or Canyon City."

"Now, Chaz," Will chided him. "You wouldn't really let me go on to Outer Island without you, would you? Who else would look out for me and scold me when I'm about to do something stupid?"

"Let the Fates and anyone else who might be listening

183

know that I hereby bequeath that task to your intended mate," the acerbic ceratopsian shot back. "Perhaps she will have better luck at it than I."

Sylvia was less flippant and more earnest in her entreating. "We need you, Chaz. What can be so bad? If the mountains in the center of Outer Island were unclimbable, no one could have mastered them, much less built the Hand of Dinotopia there."

"We do not know that there is anything there," he reminded her. With his snout he gestured at the pumice island floating in the center of the map pool. "All we have to guide us is a bit of ancient sculpture. What if it is allegorical instead of representational? What if there is nothing to be found on Outer Island; nothing at all?"

"Then we will have settled the matter once and for all and I can go back to Waterfall City content in mind," she replied. "But until I see for myself, I'll always wonder what might be hiding there. Come on, Chaz. Aren't you the least bit curious to see if this Hand exists, and if there really is a safe sea route away from and back to Dinotopia?"

"I don't know," he mumbled. "I really don't know if I want to know that."

"Well, we do," declared Will, "and we're going to find out. With or without you."

"You are long on courage and determination, Will Denison, "but short on common sense."

He cheerfully agreed. "That's why we need you to come with us, Chaz. You positively ooze common sense."

The frilled, horned head shook sadly from side to side. "What is it with humans, anyway? With this irresistible need to look behind every tree and under every rock?" He sighed a second time. "There is only one road on Outer Island, and not much of a road at that. Because it sees only local traffic, it is poorly maintained, and though it ostensibly runs around the entire island there are many places even along the coast it does not access."

"What about the interior?" Sylvia inquired.

"I already told you: mountainous, wet, and empty. As far as I know not even exploratory trails cross the central cordillera. Once we set off we will not be able to count on any assistance, much less help in an emergency. On the whole island there is only a single town: Culebra. From the pictures I have seen it is wonderfully situated, but we would not be going there for a vacation."

"But we should be able to get supplies there, and maybe some information," Will contended.

The *Protoceratops* nodded reluctantly, his snout bobbing up and down with the motion. "Perhaps so, but first we have to get there, and before that we have to cross the rest of this infernal desert."

Will's confidence was unbounded. "We'll do it. We know which way we're going now, and we don't have to stumble around searching for anything." Turning to his fiancée, he smiled fondly at her. "Sylvia's found what she was looking for in the desert, and I found what I was looking for."

"I am so happy for you both," Chaz commented dryly. "Well, if we are going to do this thing, now is as good a time to start as any. The sun is beginning to set and we would do well to walk as long as we can after dark, when it is cooler." He shuffled to the edge of the pool and settled down on his belly.

"Check each waterbag carefully for leaks after it has

185

been filled. The middle of the Great Desert is no place for recriminations."

"Surely there are other sources of water ahead of us." Will pushed one of the empty bags under the surface of the pool, holding it down and moving it back and forth as water rushed to fill the thirsty container.

"I have no doubt there are," Chaz agreed, "but suspecting that they exist and finding them are two different things. Better that we carry enough water for the rest of the journey with us, so that we are not forced to speculate on the possible dampness of sandy depressions and inhospitable gulches."

Only when the last bag was filled to the brim and bulging did they set off, Will and Sylvia carrying a single heavy bag each, Chaz hauling the rest of the water and their dwindling supply of dried food.

Will expected that they would find things to eat along the way, but his confidence in the bounty of the desert soon began to fade. Once away from the forgotten city and its protective canyons they soon found themselves trudging laboriously across an unpromising sand-and-gravel plain. Only a few scraggly scrubs were hardy enough to eke out an existence on the sun-scoured flats. As for water, the founders of Ahmet-Padon had not chosen the site for their city by chance. Every drop that fell, or trickled, or oozed through this part of the Great Desert seemed to have fetched up back there.

The transparent blue sky offered no impediment to the rays of the sun, and the trekkers were compelled to drink long and often. With each swallow their burden grew lighter, but at the rate they were going through their supplies, Will knew they would soon reach a point where they would have to begin rationing their consumption. Less water intake would mean slower going. As he slogged along beside Sylvia he sometimes cast longing glances skyward. Stretched out in the rider's saddle on Cirrus's strong, narrow back, he could have crossed this part of Dinotopia in wind-cooled comfort.

But Cirrus was the one who was comfortable, nestled down securely among his fellow flyers in the rookery at Pteros. Feeling something hard and unyielding nudge his hip, he glanced down to see Chaz prodding him.

"Don't deliberate so much. Concentrate on the path ahead."

Will protested. "There's no harm in thinking, Chaz."

"You were daydreaming. You need to keep your mind focused on the task at hand. Feet and legs are not the only parts of the body that can fail in this heat."

"Maybe if I had four of each like you it would be easier," he quipped. But as the day wore on, he kept his friend's warning in mind, and did not waste time pondering anymore on what they did not have.

Sylvia uttered nary a word of complaint. He was unreservedly admiring of the way she strode along, head high, the tattered remnants of her Orofani garb swirling freely about her. She drank less than either of her companions, too, and seemed none the worse for the limited intake. But she was not immune to the heat, and after another full day of hiking, the hardships of the journey began to show in her face as well.

He did not put his arm around her, knowing that any contact that increased mutual body temperature would be unwelcome. But he moved close enough to search her face.

"How are you holding up?"

She smiled back at him through lips that were beginning to crack slightly. "I'm okay, Will. I'll be glad when we reach the coast road, though."

He made himself smile reassuringly. "We all will. It'll be nice to sit in a cafe in Hardshell and have something to eat that isn't dried and preserved."

"Fresh fruit," she murmured. "Chilled and dripping. With honey. Something besides water to drink."

He nodded, licking his lips. "Baked goods, fluffy and sweet. Cold milk with chocolate."

Chaz looked up irritably. "Will you two kindly shut up?" He nodded in the direction they were going. "There is no bread in those hills we still have to cross, and certainly no chocolate."

"How much longer do you think, Chaz?" Shading his eyes, Will studied the low line of hills looming before them. If so much as a single tree made its home in that tortuous warren of rock and stone, it was keeping its location a well-guarded secret.

"To the coast road, you mean? I cannot say. Another day, perhaps. Two, or three if we cannot find a direct route through these bluffs." Lifting his snout, he sniffed conspicuously. "No inkling of salt air yet, or of the sea itself. I would like to say that it lies just over that promontory there, but I do not believe that to be the case."

"Then we'll just have to keep on walking." Her expression resolute, Sylvia deliberately lengthened her stride. Will and Chaz strove to keep up.

The terrain grew rougher and slowed them noticeably. Nor did the gradually sloping gradients provide the kind of shade they had so enjoyed in the constricted environs of Ahmet-Padon. They were compelled to do their climbing and scrambling while exposed to the full force of the sun. This proved far more exhausting than had crossing the hostile but level plain behind them.

Surrounded by barren inclines and crumbled precipices, they did their best to make camp for the night in a dry wash. If the winding, sandy ravine had once been witness to the presence of running water, that blessed phenomenon had left no evidence whatsoever of its passage.

Will checked their waterbags. While now far from full, they still had a decent supply, particularly if they were moderate in their intake. But they were almost out of food. Hiking through empty, difficult country demanded energy. They would either have to hit the coast road soon or find something, however unappetizing, to supplement their remaining stores. Examining the blasted landscape in which they found themselves, he thought it distinctly unpromising. Nor were any of them experienced scavengers.

He was hungry enough to eat a root, he decided, except there were no roots to be had. Troubled, he walked away from where Sylvia was unstrapping the last of the packs on Chaz's back, and took a seat on a crooked, dried-out log.

The log promptly arched upward with convulsive force and threw him six feet sideways.

Rolling over twice, he found himself on his back, looking down his torso and past his feet at a pair of vicious, curved, and very large mandibles. The centipede was a true giant, its body as long as Will's and as thick around as his calf. It was not only of sufficient size to be preyed upon by the huge rattlesnakes that he and Chaz had encountered in the canyon of the Amu, it was big enough to hold its own in any battle with them.

Probably it would have remained motionless and unnoticed until nightfall, had Will not sat on it. Now multitudinous legs scrabbled at the ground as it prepared to strike.

A fast-moving, dun-colored shape interposed itself between the prone skybax rider and the poisonous arthropod. Head down, eyes half shut, the *Protoceratops* boldly confronted clashing mandibles and pointed claws.

"Chaz, no!" Scrambling backward on his hands and butt, Will fought to get to his feet. Off to his left he saw Sylvia clutching a couple of fist-sized rocks. But with the stocky *Protoceratops* in the way she couldn't draw a bead on the writhing centipede.

As Will straightened, it struck, the ghastly flattened head flashing forward with lightning speed. Will tried to yell a warning, and Sylvia screamed, but their cries were too late. The scythe-like mandibles struck the little ceratopsian hard, just above both eyes.

And failed to penetrate. The translator's armored frill gave full protection to his skull and neck. The mandibles plunged no more than a fingernail deep into the solid keratin before sliding off. As they did so, Chaz raised his front feet and twisted to one side. Before the arthropod could scramble clear, both feet descended with the full weight of the *Protoceratops* behind them.

There was a thick crackling sound, like someone mulching dried leaves. Glutinous fluids began to seep from the segment of the centipede's back where Chaz had landed. Heavy ceratopsian feet rose and fell repeatedly, until they finally caught the nightmare head beneath them. The *Proto-ceratops* continued to stomp the centipede until its lethal foreparts had been reduced to an ichorous pulp. Only then did he back off; eyes reddened, chest heaving, head still lowered in ancient ceratopsian defensive posture.

Will and Sylvia united around him. Together they watched the huge centipede's death throes. Loath to surrender its life-force, the powerful body continued to writhe and twist for a long time despite the absence of a functioning skull.

"That was really something!" Bending, Will gave the uncomfortable translator an unyielding hug. "I owe you one, Chaz."

"One what? It is not your fault that humans possess no body armor."

Sylvia bestowed an admiring smile on the self-conscious *Protoceratops*. "How could you be sure that its mandibles wouldn't penetrate your frill?"

"I couldn't," Chaz replied flatly. "I took a calculated risk." Leaning slightly to one side, he peered around her, as if reluctant to believe he had done what he had done. "I have never seen a centipede of that size."

"No one's seen a centipede of that size," Will declared fervently. "There's no telling how many unique and un-known creatures make their homes in the Great Desert." Raising his gaze, he looked across the ravine to the dark line of convoluted hills they still had to cross. "I just hope they're not all as unique as giant rattlers and monster centi-pedes."

"Or as aggressive." Eyeing the writhing corpse, Sylvia shuddered. "Dangerous creatures I can deal with, but I don't like creepy ones. *That* is Olympic caliber creepy."

"Well, we're not going to camp here," Will announced decisively. "There might be others around, and I wouldn't like to wake up in the middle of the night with one crawling across me."

Sylvia made a face at him. "Thank you for supplying that image, Will. It's sure to help me fall asleep tonight."

As luck would have it, in hunting for a safer campsite they stumbled into a copse of something not only benign but familiar. It took Chaz only a couple of seconds to recognize the dense growth of bushes that hugged the little seep. Located in a bend in the ravine they were following eastward, the sandy hollow was lined with the sturdy green-brown growths. These particular shrubs thrived in hot weather, but Chaz had not expected to encounter them here. Only the seep, really no more than a damp stain on the sand, allowed them to survive by providing a reliable supply of subterranean moisture.

Breaking into a run, he nearly stumbled several times as he led his companions in a mad dash toward the densely foliated hollow.

"Jova beans!" he shouted as he ran. "A veritable wild orchard, it is!" Skidding to a stop in the sand, he picked out one heavily laden bush and promptly plucked a cluster of ripe beans from a middle branch. As he chewed, he closed his eyes in pleasure.

"Fwish fid," he murmured contentedly.

"I beg your pardon?" Sylvia slowed to a halt alongside him.

The translator swallowed. "I said, fresh food." Without breaking stride he used his beak to snap off another stem heavy with finger-length, beige-hued beans.

Will bent slightly to examine another of the ripe bushes. "There's more than enough here to fill up our food sacks. It won't make for a very varied diet, but these are really nutritious. I've had them before."

"So have I," declared Sylvia, "which is why I'm puzzled. Jova beans are a domesticated species. How did this lot come to be growing out here, in the middle of the desert?"

"Who knows?" Their unexpected discovery found Chaz, a pure herbivore, positively ecstatic. "Perhaps some migrating bird excreted an indigestible seed or two while flying over this spot. If this seep is perennial, many edible growths besides jova beans could survive here."

"Still, it's quite a surprise to see them thriving like this outside a farm." Despite her hunger, Sylvia was suspicious of the unexpected bounty.

Will was too busy picking ripe beans and stuffing them into one of their nearly empty food satchels to worry. "A real nice surprise. Maybe it's Fate trying to compensate us for the centipede. Come on, Sylvia, don't you want to try some?" Peeling one, he shoved it in his mouth and chewed vigorously.

"How is it?" she asked.

"Sweet. Jova beans have an agreeable buttery-nutty flavor, and these are really ripe. They'd taste better in a soup than they do raw, but we need to keep conserving our water."

"I still don't understand why they're doing so well here." Bemused but grateful, she joined her companions in availing herself of the providential food source.

Having their stomachs full for the first time in days allowed them to fall quickly asleep. With her appetite sated,

193

even Sylvia succeeded in putting all thoughts of humongous crawly things out of her mind.

Which made it that much more of a surprise when they were awakened in the middle of the night.

# -XII-

eeling the hand on his shoulder shaking him, Will rolled over and blinked sleepily. "Sylvia? What's the matter—can't sleep?"

"I will sleep much better when all of you are gone." The gravely voice that had responded most definitely did not belong to his fiancée. Nor were the thick, clawed fingers that had roused him from a sound sleep human.

He sat up very fast.

Not yet the threat that it would become by midday, the sun was just peeping over the eastern horizon, lining the barren hilltops with gold. There was a chill in the air, and a welcome if temporary dampness from early dew that would vanish in minutes under the direct influence of the sun. Stiff and awkward with slumber, he struggled to work the kinks out of his muscles. Nearby, Sylvia was starting to wake and a little further off, Chaz kicked jerkily in his sleep.

The intruder bending over him had a triangular saurian face that terminated in a small, beaked mouth. Large, limpid eyes imparted to the visage a winsome, non-threatening expression. The arms were short but gracile, the rear legs sturdy, the tail heavy at the hips but narrowing rapidly at the tip. Bands of white decorated the snout and belly, which was lighter in hue than the rest of the olive-greenish body.

But by far the most outstanding feature of the unexpected early morning visitor was the solid dome of bone that dominated the rounded skull and gave him the appearance of wearing a top-heavy bowler hat. The sides and back of this smooth mass of solid calcareous material was decorated with a bizarre assortment of knobs and spikes. They allowed Will to immediately identify the intruder as a *Prenocephale*; one of several tribes that belonged to the family pachycephalosauridae.

The prenocephalidae were of average size for their kind, and the one staring down at him was no exception. About eight feet from snout to tail, standing erect he was no taller than Will. By now Sylvia was fully awake and staring, and Chaz had begun to show signs of alertness.

With a startled hoot the little *Protoceratops* rolled over onto his feet and stood up. "What's going on? Who is this?"

The *Prenocephale* turned to face the stubby ceratopsian. To Will and Sylvia's surprise, his human speech was almost as fluent as that of the translator, though far more guttural in its pronunciation.

"I am Khorip."

"Well, Khorip," Will began in an attempt to regain the conversational high ground, "what do you mean by startling us out of a sound sleep like that?"

"What do you mean by gorging yourselves on my Jova beans?" the *Prenocephale* shot back.

"*Your* beans?" With studied deliberation, Chaz stared pointedly at the nearest bush. "I do not see the name Khorip planted here, or engraved on any of these plants."

"Do you think Jova beans grow wild here in the middle of the desert, in packed, healthy clusters, without being nurtured? I dig wells and haul water to them, I provide food and fertilizer, I weed and de-pest them almost every day. It's a lot of work. Then you lot come along and help yourselves without so much as a by-your-leave." Interlocking his leathery fingers, the *Prenocephale* waited stiffly for an explanation.

"We're sorry," Sylvia told him before the two males in her company could offer up another confrontational response. "We didn't know we were taking food from somebody's garden. As Chaz said, there were no signs, or fences, or anything to indicate that anyone lived around here. If it will help to compensate for what we've taken, we have a little salt, and sugar, and some other food items of our own that we'd be glad to share with you."

Will looked alarmed. "Sylvia, maybe we'd better talk about this first."

"No," she declared firmly, "it's the proper thing to do. We've taken from this person's garden and it's only fair that we give back, even if it means turning over the last of our supplies."

"Now just a minute." The bipedal bonehead made placating gestures. "I didn't mean for you to impoverish yourselves. More than anything else, I wish you would just leave."

"Well then," Chaz grumbled, "it seems we all want the same thing." He turned to Will. "Load me up and let us get going. This person does not want us here, and personally, I see nothing to be gained by lingering in his company." *Protoceratops* and *Prenocephale* regarded one another sourly.

As they packed to depart, Will could not help but notice the elaborate tattoo that decorated the *Prenocephale*'s remarkable skull. Inlaid with bits of semi-precious stone and etched by a master engraver, the globular mass of bone had been transformed into a living work of art. Because its owner felt no pain when an artist was working on the thick, solid bone, and since all dinosaurs loved personal cosmetics and decoration, every pachycephalosaur Will had ever met had boasted similar elaborate adornment.

As might be expected, Khorip's was distinctive in design and execution. The incised whorls and glittering mosaics embedded in his oversized skull identified him as an iconoclast, an outsider. The overall aesthetic of his personal body ornamentation was very much in keeping with a solitary lifestyle.

As they packed, Will occasionally paused to check the surrounding hills and gullies, but there was no sign of anyone watching. As near as he could tell, Khorip was every bit the loner he appeared to be.

Similar thoughts had occurred to Sylvia. She eyed the *Prenocephale* as she cinched the last of the translator's harness straps. "What brought you out here, to the Great Desert, by yourself?"

"Drove me out here, you mean." The rough-voiced *Prenocephale* lent a helping hand as she worked to steady the load on the *Protoceratops*'s back. Chaz grunted as the weight settled once more against his spine.

"'Drove'?" Will frowned. "That's a pretty strong insinuation, Khorip."

"What drove you out?" the ever-patient Sylvia inquired as she cast Will a reproving look.

"Boredom, mostly. Dinotopian society is stable, assured, comfortable, and sheltered." The *Prenocephale*'s large green eyes glittered as he spoke. "I wanted more of a challenge than a life in the fields or administration offered. I taught myself to speak human, and I am also reasonably fluent in sauropod and hadrosaur."

"Not many big folk or duckbills out here," Chaz pointed out as the weight of their supplies settled comfortably into place.

The *Prenocephale* looked down at him. "I didn't know this was where I was going to end up. I just knew that I wanted to try something difficult, a different way of living."

"So you came this way," Sylvia observed.

"Yes." Turning slightly, Khorip gestured at the ravine that wandered off eastward. "Some time ago I made my way inland from the coast road. I found this place several months ago and have made my home here ever since. With a little water and a lot of attention, the Jova beans do well. That is fortunate," he added sternly, "since you have eaten so many of them."

"Sylvia said we were sorry," Will reminded their visitor. Chaz was nearly settled and ready to go. "There are yarns spun in the marketplace of hermits dwelling in the desert, but you're the first one I ever encountered who was anything more than just a tall tale."

"Don't you ever get lonely?" Sylvia shook sand from the hem of her tattered Orofani attire.

"Sometimes," Khorip admitted freely. "It's the predictability of Dinotopian life I'm trying to escape, not the people. I quite like the company of others."

"Yeah, we can tell," Chaz muttered under his breath.

"It's been very interesting to meet you." Approaching the *Prenocephale*, Sylvia extended a hand palm-up. Khorip placed his own, slightly larger palm against hers. "Breathe deep, seek peace." She smiled at their reluctant host as she spoke, and he returned the salutation.

A long moment passed without anyone moving before Chaz confronted his companions and inquired, "What are we waiting for?"

Side by side, Will and Sylvia were looking in different directions, he down the meandering ravine, she at a steep but negotiable hill slightly to their north.

"We're just trying to agree on the best way to go," Sylvia told him.

"Yeah." Yet again, Will wished for the assistance of Cirrus. "We want to make sure we pick the easiest, fastest route from here to the coast. Unless you'd like to do some additional, excess hiking in this heat."

His white-striped chest expanding, Khorip let out a heavy sigh. "Don't you know the way back to the coast road?"

"We did not come from the coast." Chaz drew himself up stiffly. "We have walked all the way from Canyon City, on the canyon of the Amu."

"Truly?" Will and Sylvia nodded concurrence. The *Prenocephale* was clearly impressed. "You chose a difficult and dangerous route. I wouldn't attempt it myself. So you really don't know the way to the coast road?"

Will shook his head. "We're trying to get to Hardshell, and from there we'll make our way north to Kuskonak."

"Well, you'll never get there if you keep following this ravine." Khorip gestured with his right hand. "It meanders in the right direction now, but after cutting through a few more hills it turns progressively toward the south and looses itself in a salt pan. I know. I've been there. In fact, I've been all over these hills." He deliberated as he considered his unwanted visitors. "I suppose there's nothing to do but that I'll have to guide you out."

"That's all right," Chaz snapped. "We can find our own way." He turned and started for the base of the hill Sylvia had been scrutinizing.

"Maybe you can—but that isn't it."

"Oh no?" The *Protoceratops* focused a jaundiced eye on their host. "And why not, pray tell?"

"Because," Khorip replied dryly, "while the slope on this side is climbable, on the far side it decays into a series of steep drop-offs." Once more he gestured, this time to the left of the grade. "The best way is to go is around here."

"But that gully curves to the west, back the way we came. If we follow it we'll be retracing our steps," Will argued.

"Only for a short distance," Khorip explained. "Then the wash widens and swings around back to the east. It's the easiest way." He shrugged leathery shoulders. "Of course, if you don't believe me, you're welcome to take any route you please."

"No, no," Sylvia responded quickly. The look she threw Will and Chaz was not quite murderous, but it was forceful enough to silence them temporarily. "Of course we'll take your advice. Furthermore, we'd be pleased and honored if you could see your way clear to guiding us the rest of the way, or at least until we are in sight of the coast road."

When the *Prenocephale* hesitated, she added, "If you want us out of your life as quickly as possible, showing us the way to the coast is the best way to accomplish it."

"Very well. As much as I desire to see you off, I certainly don't want you stumbling back here because you've lost your way." He glared at Chaz. "But I will brook no argument. Either you follow my lead, or you choose your own course."

When the *Protoceratops* kept his beak shut, Will prompted him warningly, "Chaz . . ."

"Oh, very well!" The ceratopsian sniffed pointedly. "I am just not entirely convinced that we should be entrusting our lives and continued well-being to an unknown, uncivil, anti-social hermit."

Khorip strode past him without looking down. "Were I as uncivil as you would like to believe, rest assured that I would not agree to guide you. As for being anti-social, it's attitudes like yours that drive individuals like myself to dwell in places like this."

"What's wrong with my attitude? Are you saying there is something wrong with my attitude? Is that what you're saying? Are you talking to *me*?" Scampering forward on four legs instead of two, Chaz had no trouble keeping pace with the surly *Prenocephale*.

"This is great," Will muttered as he and Sylvia fell in behind the two fussing dinosaurs. "Now we have to listen to not one but two whiners all the way to the coast."

She put a comforting hand on his arm. "Don't fret, Will. By the time we reach the sea they'll have become the best of friends. You'll see."

He covered her hand with his own. "Well, maybe," he ceded reluctantly. "But I wouldn't bet one finger of the Hand of Dinotopia on it. You don't know Chaz like I do. And neither of us knows much about this Khorip."

"That's so." She found herself watching the *Prenocephale*'s bobbing back as it strode along in front of them. "We don't know much about him at all."

At least they did not have to speculate much longer about Khorip's knowledge of the surrounding terrain. After removing from a cave a saurian-sized pack stuffed with recently picked Jova beans and swinging it up onto his broad back, the *Prenocephale* led them up the gully he had indicated previously. Within the hour it had turned north and then east exactly as he had said it would, and they found themselves once again progressing in the general direction of the ocean. The surface underfoot was hard-packed and level, and even Chaz had to admit that it made for easier walking than the twisting, narrow ravine or the steep-sided hill they had considered crossing before talking to the *Prenocephale*.

That did not keep the two dinosaurs from switching to a new argument every five minutes, however. Rather than admit he was mistaken about a subject, each of them would quickly change the subject to one they felt they knew more about. While it was unusual to witness such a childish display of intellectual one-upmanship among dinosaurs, Will had to admit that the arguments were elegantly contested.

With Sylvia close at hand, he chose to lag slightly behind. Since she paused often to examine a flower, or bug, or a particularly colorful outcropping of rock, they frequently had to break into a short sprint to catch up to their disputatious dinosaurian comrades.

"Look at them," he murmured in disgust. "What can they be hoping to accomplish by acting this way? They should save their strength for the rest of the trek."

Sylvia was more tolerant of saurian vocal peccadilloes. "Can't you see that they're having fun?"

"Having fun? The only time they're not arguing is when they stop long enough to think up new ways to insult each other."

She chuckled softly. "Doesn't Chaz just love to bicker, even when there isn't anything to bicker about?"

"Yes he does, and . . ."

"And Khorip clearly relishes a good dispute, and hasn't been able to participate in one in some time."

"That's probably true, but it still doesn't . . ."

"So," she concluded, putting a quieting finger to his lips, "leave them alone and let them have their fun. You're not going to get them to shut up no matter what you say, and you'll only make yourself upset over nothing." Looking up at the preceding saurian backsides, she concluded confidently, "By nightfall they will have worn each other out. You'll see."

"You'd better be right, Sylvia," he replied grimly, "or none of us is going to get much sleep."

She was right, of course. She usually was. By the time they halted for the day at a shallow waterhole shaded by a healthy thicket of surreal, many-limbed, spiny-leaved kokerboom trees, the two dinosaurs had pretty much exhausted their stock of mutual imprecations. Instead, they settled for throwing each other dirty looks while muttering darkly to themselves.

Relations grew a little less testy and a tad more cordial as everyone cooperated in making preparations for the evening meal and the building of the campfire. The addition of a little salt, Sylvia soon discovered, made uncooked Jova beans a lot more palatable. She envied Chaz and Khorip as they contentedly downed copious mouthfuls of the chewy legumes raw, without either the need or the desire for complimentary spices.

"Khorip, I don't mean to pry into your personal life, but there's something that's been bothering me since we started out this morning." With a charred stick she stirred the fire's embers.

"His presence?" Chaz could not resist volunteering.

"Chaz." Will chided his friend gently. "Be nice."

The ceratopsian looked up at him. "Why? It is not part of my job description."

Ignoring the jibing *Protoceratops*, Khorip replied courteously to Sylvia. "You evidently need to ask me a question. Go ahead. If I don't wish to answer, rest assured that I won't."

"All right." Her own unwavering stare met that of the *Prenocephale*. "You told us that you came out here because you found Dinotopian society boring. There are plenty of places in Dinotopia where one can go to find privacy. The Backbone and the Forbidden Mountains, the side canyons of the Amu, the wetlands of the north coast, the northwestern banks of the Polongo: there's no shortage of open, unpopulated expanses." She paused for emphasis. "The least hospitable of them is more accommodating than the Great Desert."

"I see." Khorip replied softly, sounding as if he was speaking from the bottom of a dark, shallow cave. "So naturally, you're curious to know why I chose to settle here."

"She's not the only one," Will put in.

The *Prenocephale* looked from one human to the other. "Very well. I'll tell you, but you'll laugh at me."

"Do not let that inhibit you," Chaz advised him. "Some of us have been laughing at you all along."

"At least I am not a permanent source of walking amusement," the bonehead replied. Before Chaz could riposte, Khorip continued.

"In my younger days I was an avid student. Even then I was by nature more of a loner than my contemporaries. Unable as a youth to satisfy myself by moving to a place like this, or one of the regions you mentioned," he told Sylvia, "I took to losing myself in books and scrolls.

"It was while reading for pleasure that I came across a series of ancient tales that piqued my curiosity in a way nothing has before or since. I'm not even sure what it means; only that I became obsessed with it. I discussed these old stories with fellow students, and with my instructors, but they all assured me that my findings were just that: nothing more than stories, mythology, legend. Refusing to believe that so much in the ancient records could be founded upon so little, I determined to try and resolve the conundrum myself. Instead of the Backbone Mountains or the Blackwood Flats, my studies led me here. This was fine with me, because it allowed me to pursue my obsession free of the pressure of taunts and unanswerable queries, as well as providing me with the isolation I've always sought."

A moment later Khorip confirmed the realization that had been building in Will's mind. The *Prenocephale* leaned forward, the light from the fire glinting off the slivers of semi-precious stones inlaid into the bony dome of his skull, and said, "Have you ever heard of the Hand of Dinotopia?"

At this Chaz threw back his head as far as his frill would permit and implored the evening sky. "Oh no—*not another one!*"

Khorip frowned as much as his leathery visage would permit. "What is he raving about?"

Sylvia looked at Will, who was shaking his head and grinning, and then back at their thoroughly mystified guide. "I guess we have a bit of a surprise for you, Khorip. You see, not only have we heard of it, we're out looking for the Hand of Dinotopia ourselves."

The *Prenocephale*'s mouth gaped wide. "You can't mean it! You're jesting with me."

"I wish they were," Chaz muttered tiredly.

"I found hints and leads in the old records too," Sylvia informed their guide briskly, "and came out here looking for evidence to support my discoveries." She chuckled ruefully. "No one would believe me, either."

Khorip nodded knowingly. "I can sympathize. Go on."

"The desert and I were getting along, but it wasn't what you'd call a really amicable relationship. Most of the Great Desert is only little known, and a lot of it isn't known at all. I didn't have a Jova bean orchard to sustain myself and had to carry all my food and water with me. Eventually, I fell in with a tribe of nomads called the Orofani, and that's where my fiancé and his friend Chaz finally found me." She smiled at Will. "They didn't believe me either, until we stumbled into the lost city of Ahmet-Padon."

Resting on his haunches, the *Prenocephale* stirred abstract designs in the ground with the tip of one claw.

"I know of Ahmet-Padon. It was mentioned in the old

tales." Straightening, he pointed back the way they had come. "It's over there, in the heart of the eroded mountains."

Sylvia nodded. "We did a lot of poking around streets and chambers."

"So have I, without finding much of anything. Beautiful carvings and wonderful dwellings, but nothing that anyone could call the Hand of Dinotopia."

"That's because the Hand of Dinotopia, whatever it is, doesn't lie in Ahmet-Padon," Will told him.

Khorip's gaze flicked in the skybax rider's direction. "What are you talking about? How do you know that? The ancient records tie numerous mentions of Ahmet-Padon to the Hand."

"That's because the abandoned city is a key to locating it," an enthusiastic Sylvia informed him. "But only a key. The Hand itself is elsewhere."

A noticeable tremor of excitement had crept into Khorip's voice. "You speak with a suggestion of certitude. If not in the lost city, then where?"

Sylvia sat back triumphantly. "On Outer Island."

"Outer Island?" An incredulous Khorip eyed them in disbelief. "No wonder I never found it in all my years of exploring the Great Desert!" Abruptly, he turned suspicious. "Wait a moment. How do you know this thing?"

Will had lain back on the sandy ground, locking his fingers behind his head to support it while he gazed up at the darkening sky. "We found a map."

"Excuse me?" Mustering cool dignity, Chaz looked up from where he had hunkered down for the night. "*I* found a map. *You* thought you had actualized nothing more complex than a swimming pool."

"Yes, that's right." Sylvia corrected Will. "Chaz figured out that what we had discovered actually was a map, Will—you might say that Will stumbled across it."

"But I don't understand." Khorip was clearly perplexed. "I'm sure that I visited every dwelling, every room in the abandoned city, and in all that time I never found anything that resembled a map, much less a map showing the location of the Hand of Dinotopia."

"It doesn't look like a map," Sylvia explained. "At least, not at first." She smiled gently. "It's kind of like making bread. Eventually you have to add water."

"And one very perceptive *Protoceratops*," Will added.

"Well, there would not have been anything for me to perceive if you had not activated the mechanism that released the water," Chaz avowed magnanimously.

"A hidden map." Khorip was murmuring aloud. "All those long, hot days I spent peering into dark chambers and squeezing down narrow passageways in search of the Hand, and all the time it was somewhere else."

"We don't know that for a fact." Will was quick to caution their guide. "We only know that we found what seems to be a map pointing to something that seems to have a lot to do with the Hand of Dinotopia. Until we actually get there and see for ourselves, everything is speculation."

"Speculation is the soul of discovery, my friend." Khorip continued to struggle with his disbelief. "The Outer Island. Who would have guessed?"

"No one," Sylvia assured him.

"Perhaps," Chaz ventured, "that is why it, if indeed there is an 'it,' was placed there."

It was something to ponder, which they did while finishing

their meal. When everyone was done and the small amount of debris had been cleared away, Sylvia put her other question to Khorip.

"The legend of the Hand claims that it shows a safe sea route away from Dinotopia."

The *Prenocephale* nodded vigorously. "That's exactly what my research asserted! The Hand is the key to a navigable route not only away from, but back to the Dinotopian lands. It's what I hope to confirm in person."

Will's response was somber. "Us too. If there's a way for vessels from the outside world to reach Dinotopia, that route should be monitored. I know from first-hand experience what can happen if travelers from the outside arrive here unexpectedly in a ship that's still intact."

He was thinking, of course, of the pirate Brognar Blackstrap and his cutthroat crew, who had made a successful if inadvertent landing on the north coast of Dinotopia the previous year. Most of that hapless riffraff and medley of transient blackguards were now living contented, reformed lives as adopted citizens of Dinotopia, but the next batch of unshipwrecked arrivals might not prove so tractable. What would happen, he had sometimes wondered, if a warship or two from a traditionally belligerent nation succeeded in anchoring off Dolphin Bay near Sauropolis? What would be the response of the degenerate monarchies and militaristic imperialists of the Old World to the unprotected riches of Dinotopia? Not for the first time, the images such a confrontation conjured up caused him to shudder.

But such an encounter was impossible. Only a freak series of coincidences had allowed the pirates' ship to make it safely over the perilous reef systems that girdled and protected

Dinotopia. A large modern warship, with its tall masts and heavy load of cannon, would never have survived the same wave that had carried Blackstrap and his crew to their unexpected haven in a shallow northern lagoon.

Unless—unless the legends that seemed to swirl around the Hand of Dinotopia were accurate, and that unknown, undefined hand did indeed point the way to a safe sea route into and out of Dinotopian waters. If such a route existed, the dolphins probably knew of it. But they were not about to inform any outsiders of its existence, and anyway, the dolphin schools that frequented Dinotopian waters tended not to stray very far from its familiar, comforting shores except to pursue the occasional migrating school of ocean-going tuna.

"You don't understand," Khorip was saying. "My interest in learning whether the old tales are true or false has nothing to do with setting up some kind of early warning system to watch for approaching craft. In fact, I would like nothing better than to encounter a visitor from the outside world."

"Now why would you want to do that?" A startled Will stared curiously at the eager *Prenocephale*. "As a recent immigrant to Dinotopia myself, I can tell you that you'd be regarded as a biological curiosity by everyone on board such a ship, and treated like an animal instead of a thinking, intelligent individual. I know," he concluded with feeling. "I saw it happen."

"I'm not afraid of such a confrontation." Their guide was supremely confident. "As you have seen, I speak excellent human. I'm sure I could communicate with visitors from outside, and once communication was established I know I could convince them of my intelligence. But even if that took some time it wouldn't matter to me. I wouldn't mind being treated like 'a biological curiosity.' Not if it would mean my being able to leave Dinotopia."

A shocked silence ensued. Will couldn't think of anything to say, and even the sweet-tempered Sylvia was unable to think of an appropriate comment. Which meant that it was left to Chaz to respond.

The *Protoceratops*'s response typified the tact they had come to expect from him. "See? I told you he was crazy."

"He's not crazy," Sylvia countered immediately. Then, less assuredly, she inquired of their guide, "Are you?"

"You really can't mean what you're saying." Will had finally recovered his voice. "Why on earth would you want to leave Dinotopia? Why would anyone? Mind you, I'm not saying that Dinotopia's perfect. We still have to deal with our Lee Crabbs and the carnosaurs of the Rainy Basin, and sometimes the weather is bad and the harvest is not what everyone expects. But I know better, Khorip. I was born outside Dinotopia, I studied books about the rest of the world, and I'm able to compare other places to here. Take it from me: Dinotopia is the best place there is."

He braced himself for a counter-argument. Instead, Khorip surprised him with a question. "And why is that, Will Denison?"

Will glanced at Sylvia, who nodded encouragingly. "There are plenty of reasons," he began doggedly. "Here everyone has enough to eat, everyone has some kind of work or study or craft to keep them busy, there's all kinds of entertainment and amusements to occupy time when you're not working or studying, and everybody helps everybody else.

Because of the discoveries that have been made here in biology and medicine, both people and dinosaurs live longer than they would in the outside world. There's great art, and music, and literature, and drama—what I heard my father once call a 'grand synthesis of the arts'—only with dinosaurs.

"Nobody worries about having to make enough money, because Dinotopia doesn't use money. Believe me, our help-and-barter system is a lot nicer." He thought a moment before concluding, "And best of all, Dinotopia doesn't know war."

"'War.'" The appallingly alien word did not even sound right emerging from a saurian mouth. "I've read about that in the ancient histories. The humans who were shipwrecked here from all over the world brought stories of war with them, but not war itself. Here in Dinotopia it just sort of died from lack of attention. From what I read of it, that's a good thing."

"Better than you know," Will told him with feeling.

"But war is only one thing they have in the outside world. The histories and old books speak of many other things. Wonderful buildings, and regal palaces. Spectacular mountains even higher than the Forbiddens, and great rivers longer than the Polongo, longer and wider even than Dinotopia itself. There are stories of grand works of art and vast cities, of strange animals and ancient monuments." Khorip's words were imbued with a long repressed craving. "I should like to see such things for myself, Will Denison."

Doing his best to try and understand, Will nodded empathetically. "There *are* fine things in the world outside, Khorip. But the problem is, you can't separate the good that's in the outside world from the bad, and the bad would mean the destruction of Dinotopia. It would mean your own ruination. You've got to believe me."

"I was born here," Sylvia added, "but many's the time I've listened to Will's tales of the outside world. I believe him. No one who was born and raised here, human or dinosaur, would be very happy or would survive for very long in the outside world."

"Speak for yourselves." Khorip was not to be dissuaded.

"It does not matter," Chaz interrupted. "You are all arguing about a state of affairs that will never come to pass. Because there is no safe sea route away from Dinotopia. If there was, it would have been rediscovered by now. And to prove it, we will track this so-called 'Hand of Dinotopia' to its end, and expose it for the ancient fraud that it is!"

"Then you'll let me come with you once we've made it out of the desert?" Khorip's eagerness to accompany them was painful to behold.

"Of course we will," Chaz replied before Will or Sylvia had a chance to say anything. The *Protoceratops* was clearly enjoying himself. "I am looking forward to the moment when you realize that the concept of a safe way out of Dinotopia is nonsense, that the notion is nothing more than ancient drivel and myth, and that you have been wasting a good many irreplaceable years in search of it." He drew himself up on all four legs. "I would not miss that opportunity for all the Jova beans in the Blackwood Flats!"

Their guide unhesitatingly countered with argument of his own, leaving Will to lean over and whisper resignedly to Sylvia.

"I thought Khorip was the only bonehead in our group—

but it seems pretty clear that there are two!"

"It doesn't matter what he thinks," Sylvia whispered back. "He knows the desert; where food can be found, where the waterholes are, which places to avoid and which allow for easier walking. Chaz's motives may be ignoble, but his instincts are right. We will be much better off letting Khorip guide us safely to the coast."

Will nodded agreement. "By that time we'll have talked him out of this crazy idea, or he'll have forgotten it all by himself. Once we get him into a nice, clean barn in Hardshell with fresh food and cool water, or better yet, in Kuskonak, any notions he might retain of abandoning his homeland will have faded away. He'll leave them behind in the Great Desert."

Sylvia was watching the *Prenocephale* closely. "I wish I could be as sure of that as you, Will."

Her fiancé's gaze narrowed. "You don't think he really means it?"

"I don't know." Her tone was cautious. "I'm a skybax rider, not a psychologist." Then her expression brightened. "But as Chaz says, it doesn't matter, because even if there is such a thing as a 'Hand of Dinotopia,' there can't be any safe way through the reefs and currents that protect us."

"Right!" agreed Will. "So there's no harm in letting him accompany us after we've made it safely back to civilization, because there's nothing dangerous for him to find."

"That's right," she admitted. "No harm at all." Even as she said it, she wished she sounded more convincing. Especially to herself.

# -XIII-

ccepted as a member of the little expedition, Khorip proved a knowledgeable and invaluable guide. Under his efficacious tutorship, Will and Sylvia learned more about the Great Desert in several days of hot, hard walking than they had known when they first had entered it. When he was not arguing with or engaged in exchanging mutual insults with the now garrulous *Prenocephale*, even Chaz had to admit that their new companion was a veritable walking encyclopedia of fascinating information on everything from the mechanics of dune formation to the edibility of decidedly unappetizing-looking plants.

Both Khorip and Chaz were also very fond of insects and other arthropods, from spiders to the scorpions that scuttled about at night and made everyone's sleep more exciting than might have been desired. Interestingly, Sylvia shared their enthusiasm for this fecund source of supplementary protein, but despite repeated attempts, Will had never been able to surmount the perception that eating anything with more legs than he had fingers on one hand constituted an unnatural state of culinary affairs.

"You really should try some of these, Will." Sylvia offered him a couple of the desert millipedes she and their saurian companions had roasted on hot rocks in the campfire the previous night.

He eyed the shriveled, toasted shapes and tried not to show how queasy the sight was making him feel. "No thanks. I'm not hungry."

"Of course you're hungry." They were hiking along a steep-sided arroyo that ran due west out of the hills. Within the day, Khorip had assured them, they would finally emerge from the rocky labyrinth they had been trekking through for days. If he was right, the coast road and the sea itself lay less than a morning's march beyond.

She extended the handful a second time. "Come on; try one. You eat crab and bugs and lobster and trilobites, don't you?"

His mouth began to water. "Don't tempt me with memories like that. Not here."

"They're all the same family. You tell me the difference between eating a crab and eating a tarantula."

He swallowed, eyeing the mottled strips uneasily. "I know it doesn't make any sense, Sylvia. But what people like to eat and what they won't rarely does."

"Now look here, Will Denison." Lowering her gaze, she fixed him with a challenging stare. "If we're going to make it all the way to Kuskonak we have to keep our strength up. That means eating whatever we can find that our bodies will tolerate. Spiders and millipedes in particular are very nutritious."

"I know," he admitted.

"They won't hurt you or upset your digestive system."

"I know."

"They're healthy food that won't make you fat."

"I know." More angry at himself than at her persistence, he snatched a couple of the cooked crawlies out of her open palm and shoved them in his mouth. "There! You satisfied now?"

A knowing smirk spread over her face. "I will be—when you swallow instead of tucking them up in your cheek like a grazing *Styracosaurus*."

Found out, he tried to do just that, but the crisp corpses in his mouth were too stiff to slide easily down his throat. Wincing, he bit down. The tiny toasted cadavers crunched tidily between his teeth and he swallowed the resultant scraps with great reluctance.

Much to his surprise, there was very little taste, and what there was reminded him of sun-dried peanuts and almonds. He blinked.

"Well? What do you think?" She was watching him closely, amusement in her voice.

"I think that when you're really hungry, you'll eat anything." He held out his open hand. "What else have you got?"

She searched the little satchel she had been carrying slung over her shoulder and produced another handful of assorted crispies. "I don't know what some of these are, but Khorip assured me they'll all edible, and Chaz confirmed it." She passed half the handful to him and began flipping the remainder piece by piece into her own mouth, chewing zestfully.

Half closing his eyes, Will imitated her action. If you

ignored the bent, shriveled little legs, he decided, you could think of the stuff as desert popcorn. As he ate, his mind continued to rebel. But his belly was grateful. Before he knew it, he found himself contemplating the most gruesome-looking desert dwellers with an eye toward their digestibility instead of their taxonomy.

It was while meditating on the nutritional value of a nest of large, black desert ants later that afternoon that he heard the noise. Frowning, he turned to Sylvia.

"You hear that?"

She listened for a moment, then shook her head. "No. Hear what?"

His mouth tensed slightly. "I'm not sure. It's like a rising wind."

The air around them was dead calm, and hot. "There is no wind, Will."

"I know, I know." Peering forward, he saw that Chaz had also halted. Khorip was looking back at the *Protoceratops*. The two humans hurried to catch up.

"What's the matter?" Sylvia inquired.

Khorip's delicate, beaked mouth clacked softly. "Your friend insists that he senses something. I don't sense anything." The *Prenocephale*'s gaze dropped as he gazed impatiently down at the small ceratopsian. "Are you going to stand there till nightfall, or do you want to get out of this desert?"

"Quiet," Chaz murmured. Unusually, the *Prenocephale*'s tone had failed to provoke the customary caustic response.

Will knew better than to challenge the translator. Chaz had his faults, but he did not invent things to get attention. If he insisted that he was sensing something, then there must be something to be sensed.

Whatever it was escaped Will's notice, however. "What is it, Chaz?"

By way of reply, the *Protoceratops* lifted first one front foot and then the other and stomped several times on the hard ground.

"A vibration. Underfoot."

Even as the distant whisper of a rising wind became more audible, Will failed to connect what he was hearing with what Chaz might be sensing. "What kind of vibration?"

"I do not know. But it is tangible." Turning his frilled head, he looked back the way they had come. "And it is approaching even as we speak."

Reflexively, everyone turned to look down the arroyo. It was empty, silent, barren of life save for its inconspicuous insects and silent scrub. In Will's ears, the wind had become a lowing rumble.

Sylvia heard it now, too, as did their saurian companions.

"What is it?" she wondered.

"I don't like it." Chaz's beak began to clack repeatedly, a sure sign of increasing nervousness among all ceratopsians.

Will turned to their guide for enlightenment. "Khorip?"

The *Prenocephale* continued to stare down the ravine. "I don't know. I don't recognize it."

The rumble abruptly became a roar, and the source of both sound and vibration revealed itself. It came thundering around the far bend of the arroyo, smashing into the sandstone walls and barreling toward them. It had no teeth and no claws. It did not even have feet. But it was quite capable of murder.

"Run!" Whirling, Sylvia sprinted desperately in the

opposite direction, the shredded vestiges of her colorful Orofani attire swirling like trapped whirlwinds about her legs and torso.

The exhortation was unnecessary. Instantly, they were all pounding down the ravine in frantic retreat, human thighs doing their best to match pachycephalosaurian stride while the stumpy-legged Chaz fought to keep up.

The diminutive ceratopsian quickly fell behind. Seeing that his friend was lagging badly, Will slowed and stopped.

Keeping pace with Khorip, Sylvia turned to shout back at her fiancé. "Will, hurry!"

"I have to help Chaz!" he yelled to her. "You and Khorip get to high ground!" That was a task easier said than done in the narrow, crumbly-walled ravine, he knew. Searching wildly for foot and handholds with which to climb to safety, he found none. But at least he could dig and scramble. The quadrupedal, fingerless Chaz could not even do that.

Staying close to his low-slung friend, he grabbed onto the nearest harness strap and pulled, trying to help the *Protoceratops* along. Chaz wheezed and puffed, doing the best he could. The thunder boomed in their ears now, clutching at their heels.

Then Will felt the surging torrent knock his feet out from under him, and both he and Chaz were swept up in the heart of the furious, raging flash flood.

The ferocious current pulled him under and he choked on swallowed water. Coughing and gasping, he held the harness strap in a death grip with his right hand, refusing to let go. Several times he and the struggling *Protoceratops* were slammed against one another. After what felt like ten minutes submerged, the roiling water kicked him to the surface. He had just enough time to gulp air and catch a glimpse of Chaz fighting to keep his own head above the waves before the flood sucked him down again.

Utterly helpless in the grip of that unyielding, aqueous hand, he allowed himself to be swept along, still clutching the harness strap. Though as helpless as his human companion, Chaz was a point of reference, a reminder of life in the dark, damp turbulence. Opening his eyes, Will found that he could only make out dim shapes as they rushed rapidly toward him and as quickly past. Rocks in the ravine, or perhaps the sandstone walls themselves, they sped by at astonishing speed. The squat, dumpy shape he clung to kicked stumpy legs in what seemed to be slow motion.

Bursting through the surface once again, he inhaled deeply. This time his kicking and flailing kept him afloat, though the flood continued to sweep him along helplessly. Chaz was up also, paralleling him and dog-paddling for all he was worth.

Turning, he saw that they had emerged from the far end of the ravine. As it spread out across the flat, sandy plain beneath the hills, the flood began to lose some of its strength. Swimming hard, Will and Chaz managed to kick themselves out of the main current. Gradually the waters subsided, spending themselves on the eager, thirsty sand.

Dragging themselves onto a low, earthen hillock, man and ceratopsian collapsed onto the saturated ground. Chaz's flanks heaved like a bellows while Will flopped onto his back and let the sun begin to dry him. Around them, the threnody of escaping water was still dominant. It was nearly half an hour before the flood began to fade from hearing as well as sight.

Only then did an exhausted Will lever himself up on his elbows upon hearing the sound of his name. Raising an arm become suddenly like lead, he waved weakly.

"Here! We're over here!" The effort depleted what little strength remained to him and he fell back onto his shoulders.

"There they are!" he heard a relieved voice shout. Moments later Sylvia was there, kneeling at his side. Her eyes roved from his feet to his hair, finally settling on his face. Bending over, she kissed him, then tenderly began to wipe strands of stringy, wet hair from his face and forehead.

"Will Denison, you look like a drowned rat!" As she made the joke he saw that she was fighting back tears. Reaching up, he did his best to reassure her.

"Hey, I'm okay. I've been looking forward to a swim for days." Grimacing, he forced himself to sit up. Muscles in his back protested vehemently. "I just thought we'd have to wait until we reached the ocean." Noticing the rest of her for the first time, he saw that she was barely damp. "You look like Nimbus suddenly appeared and plucked you right out of the flood's path."

"Hardly. Khorip and I found a way up the right side of the ravine just before the water reached us. We saw you go past." She swallowed tightly. "When you and Chaz went under and didn't come up I screamed at you to hang on. Mostly, I think I just screamed."

"I didn't hear you," he replied exhaustedly, "and unfortunately, the only thing Chaz and I had to hang onto was each other." Looking to his right, he saw that his ceratopsian companion was on his feet, shaking like an overgrown dog. Water flew in all directions.

The *Protoceratops* was able to perform the drying calisthenics only because there happened to be nothing on his back. There was nothing on his back because the waterbags, food satchels, and everything else he had shouldered so meticulously across the Great Desert had been swept away in the flood. All that remained of their supplies was a single harness strap: the one Will had clung to so tenaciously.

When he pointed out the loss to Sylvia, she waxed philosophical. "We'll find something to eat. Anyway, if Khorip is right, it's only a day from here to the coast. Surely we'll find food there."

Encouraged, he managed a nod. "I'm sure you're right, Sylvia. There are always mussels to be gathered, and snails." Despite his fatigue he summoned up a boyish grin. "When we're offered real food again, our stomachs won't know what to make of it." Rising, he turned and faced his fellow aquanaut. "Some ride, huh, Chaz?" As he spoke, the cuffs of his pants turned into downspouts as water drained out the inside of his pants.

*At least I'll be cool for a while,* he thought, trying to make light of what had been a near fatal situation.

"Only in your company, Will Denison." The *Protoceratops* shook himself again, the violent twisting starting at the snout and concluding with the short, stubby tail. "Only in your company could I reasonably expect to be offered the opportunity to drown in the desert. And not once, but twice!"

"Look at it this way." The *Prenocephale* loomed over the bedraggled translator. "That's half a kilometer less you have to walk."

"Oh it is, is it? As our resident authority on the Great Desert, perhaps you can explain how and why you failed to notice the drawing nigh of that minor deluge?"

Khorip replied thoughtfully. "The originating storm must have fallen far, far back in the high mountains. In all my time here I never experienced anything like it, so I had no precedent to warn me."

"Is that a fact? Or is it just that you are deaf, blind, and dumb as well as arrogant? Let me tell you, my bone-domed friend, that I *sensed* it coming while you were still standing there staring stupidly at nothing." The horny beak jabbed in Will's direction. "Even my friend here, who is not famed for his perspicacity, detected the coming flood before you."

"Now just a minute. . ." Will began.

Sylvia restrained him by putting a gentling hand on his arm. "Let him rant, Will. He's understandably upset, and agitated. He has reason to be, but it's not Khorip's fault. A flash flood is no one's fault. Even if he'd sensed it sooner *and* identified it, you two might still have been overwhelmed."

"Yeah. I suppose you're right." Will subsided. "Chaz's kind just aren't built for speed." Waterlogged hair fell across one eye and he idly pushed it aside.

She slipped her right arm around his waist. "Let's you and I just start walking. Khorip will follow, and then he'll take the lead again. Chaz will follow too, because he has no choice."

But she was wrong. The little *Protoceratops* did not follow. Instead, he paralleled their guide, occasionally even skipping on ahead so that Khorip would have to look at the *Protoceratops* as he continued to vent his displeasure. This went on for some time, with the *Prenocephale* enduring it patiently. Having made a private bet with himself as to whether the translator's voice or his vocabulary would give out first, Will was not surprised to see that it was the former.

Reduced by the restrictions imposed on him by mere flesh to mumbling dire threats and imprecations, the exceedingly irritated *Protoceratops* trotted alongside the bipedal *Prenocephale*, occasionally tossing his head from side to side to flick away the last lingering droplets of his involuntary swim. Holding hands, Will and Sylvia trailed behind, musing on the fact that the desert had provided them not merely with adequate water, but in quantities far greater than they had desired.

What unexpected surprises did the Outer Island hold, Will found himself wondering? He put the thought aside. If Khorip was right, they should soon encounter the first signs of Dinotopian civilization they had seen in some time. Better to concentrate on that. But despite that promise, they were not out of the Great Desert yet, and after all that had happened, he was not about to relax until they were resting safely in an inn or tavern in Hardshell itself.

# -XIV-

oth he and Chaz dried rapidly in the afternoon sun, and in the span of a few hours they had gone from being half drowned to wishing ardently for one of the waterbags that had been swept away. Sylvia had scavenged one, and Khorip another, but both had been severely shredded in the flood. Consequently, neither was capable of holding so much as a cupful of the precious liquid.

They drank their fill from lingering pools, but the parched sand had managed to absorb nearly all of the flood waters in the first hour. Now that they found themselves striding along over dry, rocky flats interspersed with ankle-high dunes, a sufficiency of water had once more become a concern.

"Don't worry." Trudging along stolidly beside her fiancee, Sylvia was in remarkably good spirits. Perspiration soaked her clothing and sweat streamed down her face. "There are water caches for traveling traders set out at regular intervals all along the coast road."

"I know." Will wiped moisture from his brow. "But as

I remember it, those intervals are substantial. Unless we're lucky enough to strike the road close by one that's been clearly marked, we'll have more walking to do even after we reach the coast."

"What road?" Nearby, Chaz resurrected his litany of complaint, gesturing with his snout at the way ahead while he did so. "I do not see any road."

"Soon," Khorip declared.

"Soon. Always 'soon'." Chaz snorted at the ground. "Any 'sooner' and we will all keel over, prostrate from the heat."

"I would almost welcome it," the *Prenocephale* responded caustically, "if it would mean that you'd shut up for a while. However, now is not a time to be quiet. Soon is now."

"What are you talking about?" Will inquired of their guide.

The bony head nodded at the desiccated landscape before them. "The sea. We've reached it. And not a moment too soon, judging from the rate at which your chunky friend's delivery of deprecatory adjectives is accelerating."

"Sea? What sea?" Chaz squinted at the eastern horizon. "I see no sea."

"Considering your stunted vantage point that's hardly surprising," Khorip could not resist observing. "But if it will make you feel any better, I don't see it yet either."

"Then how do you know we're almost there?" Sylvia wanted to know.

Reaching up with one clawed hand, Khorip lightly tapped his bulbous skull. "This is not all solid bone, you know. Like our close cousins the hadrosaurs, all pachycephalosaurs possess expanded nasal passages." To illustrate, he sniffed pointedly. "I know that we're close to the ocean because I can smell it. I've been smelling it for more than an hour now, but I wanted to be sure before I said anything. I didn't want to disappoint you."

"Oh, you couldn't possibly do that," Chaz noted sardonically.

He would have continued in that vein except that upon topping a low rise, a perfectly straight line of deep blue suddenly became visible. It was closer than Will had anticipated, and bluer, and unreasoningly welcome.

With a whoop, he took off down the beckoning slope, accelerating until he was running full out. Sylvia matched him stride for stride while Khorip kept up easily. Only Chaz lagged behind, lamenting the short legs that doomed him always to bring up the rear with his own.

It didn't matter. Rediscovered, the sea was not going anywhere. By the time the *Protoceratops* reached the coast road, his companions had fanned out in different directions, Khorip to the north and Will and Sylvia to the south. They were searching for the sign-marked, subterranean water caches that everyone knew were strategically positioned along the trade route to provide relief for improvident travelers.

It had never been intended that the coast road should remind one of the grand boulevard promenade in central Sauropolis. A dusty track no more than ten feet wide, it was unpaved for nearly all of its length. Swept clear of anything larger than a piece of gravel, it provided good footing for humans and dinosaurs alike, but little in the way of comfort.

As an out-of-breath Chaz was trying to decide whether to rejoin his friends, lambaste Khorip, or stay where he was, the *Prenocephale*'s engaging bleat drew him northward. By the time Will and Sylvia had rejoined their two saurian companions, both *Protoceratops* and *Prenocephale* were drinking their fill from the sunken cylindrical water tank.

Built of cut and mortared stone, the storage well was nearly full. The large bucket secured by a rope and pulley was repeatedly lowered and raised. The water it brought to the surface was of dubious purity, but cold and wet. Even though he knew better, Will drank until his side began to throb.

Sweeping down out of the interior, the dry hot wind of the Great Desert howled softly around them. Wiping lingering droplets of delicious moisture from his lips, Will contemplated their surroundings. Barren and deserted, the famous trade route disappeared southward and snaked northward devoid of visible trade or traders. In all that pristine vastness, nothing moved save the four travelers.

"If only we had an intact waterbag or two," Sylvia was saying.

"We could borrow the bucket and return it later," Chaz suggested.

Will quashed that notion. "It wouldn't hold enough to make it worthwhile, Chaz. Besides, it leaks, and uncovered, the water will quickly slosh out or evaporate."

"Maybe we can make something." Turning, Sylvia indicated the nearby shore. "A large fish bladder or stomach scraped clean would work."

"Of course it would," Chaz agreed without hesitation. "All we need now are several large, dead fish. Oh my," he finished sarcastically, "and I am just fresh out."

Will paid no attention to his tone. After so many days

of being compelled to endure it, he was now able to ignore the translator's jibes with comparative ease.

"We'll find something to make do with. There are big shells that would hold water, and like Sylvia says, maybe we can find something even better." Wishing there was traffic for him to avoid, he started across the sandy roadbed.

They found no suitable shells for carrying water, and certainly no fish, dead or otherwise, conveniently washed up on the desolate beach. What they did find, unexpectedly and in short order, were their spirits.

It started when Sylvia tripped on a concealed chunk of broken coral and went down face first in the tepid salt water. At the sight of his usually dignified fiancée sitting waist-deep in the shallows, Will burst out laughing. Seconds later he was coughing as she threw water at him with both hands.

Nor was the chortling Chaz spared. The *Protoceratops* retaliated for the dunking Will gave him with a wave generated by his tail, whereupon the inadvertently splashed Khorip quickly made his own presence known. Soon the four of them were flailing away at the water like mad, each doing his or her best to inundate their neighbor, and all of them squealing like children on vacation. Only when they ran out of energy did the aqueous Armageddon reach its conclusion.

"This is swell." Will could not keep the smile off his face at the sight of his companions. All of them were thoroughly drenched. "Nothing like working up an appetite when you're already almost out of food."

"We've made it to the coast road," Sylvia reminded him, "and the emergency well is more than half full." Turning, she inclined her gaze downward and began searching the water that swirled around her knees. "There should be plenty to eat here. We just have to look for it."

"I must say, it's a strange feeling to be standing in water after so many years spent in the interior of the Great Desert." Bending forward at the hips, Khorip joined her in hunting for something edible.

Never one to let an opportunity slip past, Chaz ventured his own observation. "Yes, I imagine wading must be a real novelty to you. Why not wander out a little farther and soak yourself right up to the nostrils? Or better yet, keep on going until this nice, refreshing water is completely over your head."

"Shut up, Chaz, and let's help Sylvia find something to eat." Bending over until his nose was almost touching the surface, Will began scanning the shallow bottom.

They had found the coast road, and water, quickly enough, but despite their expectations food proved harder to come by. The shallows featured a floor that was mostly sand, the flat surface broken only by the occasional clump of coral.

"This isn't working," Will finally decided, "and it's hot out here." Straightening, he nodded northward to where a clump of exposed rocks jutted seaward from the shore. "Let's try over there. Maybe there are mussels growing on the rocks." He kicked at the warm water. "There's nothing for them to attach themselves to here."

His companions followed him, but slowly, so they could continue to scan the sea floor as they walked. Leading the way, he suddenly espied movement beneath the surface and let out a whoop. Leaping forward, he got both hands around the slow-moving shape.

Twisting back on itself like coiled lightning, the shape also got a good grip on him, whereupon the food-gathering confrontation quickly became a battle for dominance between fish and fisherman. Except that Will was no fisherman.

Moreover, as he struggled to free himself, he saw to his wide-eyed shock that what had a hold of him was no fish.

One claw was locked painfully around his left ankle. No matter how hard he kicked, it would not shake loose. The other claw swung back and forth as its owner probed for a second grip. Compact, bristling mouthparts snapped angrily at the water.

Resembling a cross between a crab and a scorpion, the *Pterygotus* eurypterid was nearly seven feet long. Its shiny, segmented red and white body ended in a barbed tail. Though non-poisonous, it was big enough to deliver a wound more like a sword thrust than a bee sting. As the knifelike tail thrashed and jabbed, Will hopped about madly to avoid the tine and the barbs that lined both edges.

Kicking at the flat, blunt head was like kicking a rock. Flat, dull, primitive eyes goggled up at him through the roiling water. If it would just let him go, Will was more than willing to chalk the whole incident up to a case of mistaken identity and leave it in peace. But it was a meat eater, and while the eurypterids preferred to scavenge, the larger ones like *Pterygotus* could be active hunters.

Having long since swallowed his pride, Will continued to twist madly to avoid the second claw while yelling for help. Khorip arrived first on the scene, with Sylvia close behind.

"Kick it away!" she was shouting at him.

"What do you think I'm trying to do?" His movements slowed by the water, he was unable to dislodge the blunt but powerful claw from his ankle. Meanwhile he was tiring much faster than the eurpyterid.

Khorip tried to get behind the *Pterygotus*, but it was thrashing around so violently that churned up sand and silt obscured its movements and the *Prenocephale* could not get a clear view of it.

Working from the other side, Sylvia several times thrust both hands into the water in an attempt to get a grip on the eurpterid, only to draw them back dripping and empty. Aghast at her actions, Will waved her away.

"What are you trying to do, Sylvia? Are you crazy?"

She kept her attention divided between him and his attacker. "I thought if I could get a hand on the tail I might try pulling it off you while you kick at it!"

"Absolutely not! If your hand slides on the tail the barbs will rip you to shreds."

She dropped her hands to her sides. "Well then, do something!"

Wheezing hard with the effort it demanded to run through water, Chaz barely paused long enough to comment. "What this calls for is the sensitive touch of an experienced facilitator of communications between species."

Whereupon he stepped forward and, with commendable energy and precision, proceeded to stomp all over the dangerously aggressive eurpyterid with all four feet, using the same technique he had applied to the giant centipede days before.

Immediately, it let go of Will, who staggered and fell backward into the shallows. Sylvia was at his side in an instant. He hastened to reassure her.

"Don't worry, I'm all right!" Having spoken before bothering to ascertain the truth of the statement, he looked down at himself. His ankle ached, but there was no bleeding. Gingerly, he straightened, stood up, and found that he could put his weight on it with no difficulty.

Meanwhile Chaz was slowing down, the effort sapping his strength. But the eurypterid was in worse shape. Having contended wildly with Will, it was in poor condition to do battle with a more massive new opponent. Clawed arms and barbed tail flailed madly, but with progressively less energy. Eventually they ceased fluttering altogether.

Unpersuaded, Chaz continued to stomp the now inert *Pterygotus* until he too was out of energy. By that time the eurypterid lay flattened on the sea floor, its powerful claws stilled, several secondary legs snapped, the potentially lethal tail as motionless as a dead cod.

Arms around each other's waist, Will and Sylvia waded near for a better look. "Nasty looking thing," he muttered as silt settled around the segmented corpse. His ankle still throbbed.

"Yes, but delicious." Sylvia reached out to rest a comforting hand on Chaz's neck frill. The *Protoceratops* was still breathing hard from the unaccustomed exertion. "For a herbivore, you're not a bad hunter, Chaz."

"Thank you. I will be sufficiently pleased if this proves to be my first and last excursion into that particular realm of expertise." He shook water from his snout. "I may not be able to jump or climb, but there are certain advantages to being a stocky, heavy-set quadruped. He glared meaningfully at the watching Khorip.

The *Prenocephale* inclined forward slightly from the waist, simultaneously dipping his domed head. "I bow to superior design, my verbose friend. When it comes to the

235

business of stomping, there's no question that four legs are better than two." He eyed the battered eurypterid distastefully. "How can anyone contemplate eating something that looks like that?"

For once, Chaz was able to make common cause with his fellow saurian. "You know humans. Omnivores in the classic sense. They will eat just about anything."

"That's true." With Will's help, Sylvia had begun dragging the chitonous corpse toward the beach. "But eurypterids are not just edible, they're scrumptious. Mostly all white meat, and sweeter than trilobites."

"Ugh!" Khorip shook his bony skull. "If we can't find any grains, nuts, or berries, I'll settle for sea grass and kelp before I try to swallow something like that, thank you." He turned to Chaz. "Come. While these two mammals are preparing to eviscerate their catch, let's see if you and I can't find something decent to eat."

The *Protoceratops* nodded agreeably. "Certain kinds of kelp are quite tasty when properly dried and spiced."

"I prefer mine unsalted," Khorip replied, thereby sparking yet another argument. But this time their conversation was almost decorous, with none of the yelling and screaming that had characterized previous exchanges in the desert.

Sylvia watched them gathering and grazing while she helped Will build a cooking fire. "Do you think those two will ever stop bickering?"

Will looked up from the armful of driftwood he had already gathered. "I doubt it. Chaz is too opinionated to keep quiet about anything, and someone like Khorip who's stubborn enough to move out to the Great Desert for the avowed purpose of avoiding the rest of Dinotopian society is probably too headstrong to admit he's wrong even when he knows better."

Sylvia blew on the tiny flame she had succeeded in coaxing from slivers of dried bark, then sat back and fed it twigs handed to her by Will. "At least when they fight, they do so politely."

"What else?" Dumping his armload, Will wandered off in search of additional fuel. "They're Dinotopians."

Using a suitably shaped rock to crack the carapace, Sylvia set about extracting the firm, white meat from the legs and body of the eurypterid. Will found some green-lipped mussels which he added to the mix. By the time the meat and shellfish had been well cooked, Khorip and Chaz returned, burdened with greens.

"A humdrum repast, lacking in any of the civilized amenities," the fussy ceratopsian declared afterward. Having finished his meal, he lay sprawled on the sand cleaning his beak with his long, wet tongue.

Nearby, Khorip squatted and preened himself, using the claws on his forearms to assist in the hygiene. "But nicely filling. On this coast one has no choice but to seek food in the sea."

"And lucky we are to have it." Sitting up against a convenient rock, Sylvia patted the bulge of her belly. "Will, you need to make sure for the rest of this journey that every time you're attacked it's by something tasty."

He responded with a wan smile. "I'll try to arrange it." Lifting his gaze, he looked past her. The coast road was as empty as it had been when they had first espied it in the course of emerging from the interior. "Speaking of our journey, are we all agreed that we head north from here?"

"I would far rather go south to Chandara." Chaz squirmed deeper into the sand, seeking a more comfortable position. "Now there is a civilized city! But I suspect we are much closer to Hardshell, and that in turn is closer to Outer Island." He glanced over at Khorip, who was resting contentedly in the shade of a small eroded pinnacle. "That is unfortunately so, is it not?"

"I'm afraid it is." With the tip of one foreclaw the *Prenocephale* dug in the back of his lower jaw for a strand of reluctant sea grass.

"How far?" Will asked him.

Their guide looked to his right, squinting against the harsh sun, and postulated a figure. Will winced. Translated into the old English-American terms he remembered from his childhood days in Boston, the Dinotopian measurement worked out to between forty-five and fifty-five miles. A long, hot walk under the best of circumstances—which theirs were not. They had no waterbags, having lost them along with the rest of their supplies in the flash flood. That meant finding or fashioning carrying containers or hoping emergency water cisterns were frequent and not far apart between their present location and distant Hardshell.

Beachcombing turned up a couple of sizable Nautilus shells, but even the largest held less than a single drink for Khorip. Still, they were better than nothing.

After everyone drank their fill one last time from the replenishing well, the shells were topped off and they started on their way. Fate, Will was convinced, must be enjoying its treatment of them. In very short order they had gone from having plenty of water and no food to adequate food and practically no water.

"I'll be glad when I can sit down and ask someone to *bring* me something to eat and drink," Sylvia murmured after an hour of trudging along beneath the unrelenting afternoon sun.

"A shared sentiment if ever there was one." Chaz's broad footpads kicked up dust and sand as he shuffled along between the two humans.

Leaning over, Khorip put a hand on the ceratopsian's frill. "Anytime you want a strip of dried kelp, just ask me."

Chaz glanced up sardonically. "Oh, now there is an offer I can hardly resist. I have had my fill of kelp, thank you. A bouquet of fresh fruits now, garnished with mint—that I could really sink my beak into. Or one of those little gift baskets they hawk in the shops come New Year's, the kind that are full of cloves and nutmeg and fresh cut sugar cane." He was salivating helplessly. "Will, you have not lived until you have spent an hour or two leisurely nibbling mace off the outsides of nutmeg."

"That's all right, Chaz," the skybax rider responded, "but I prefer a different kind of salad." His voice grew misty with remembrance. "Lettuces and raddichio, endive and cucumber, jicama and hearts of palm. With a nice broiled Spanish mackerel laid right across the top of it all."

"Will both of you kindly keep your imaginings to yourselves?" Sylvia wiped at her lips and took the tiniest, most reluctant sip possible from the water-filled Nautilus shell she was carrying. "You can't eat memories, and talking about it only makes you hungrier."

"That is not a problem for me." By way of emphasizing the observation, Chaz's stomach growled. "I am wholly convinced I cannot get any hungrier than I am right now."

But he was wrong.

By the following morning their stomachs were knotted, complaining, or both. Will and Sylvia had finished the last of the edible eurypterid meat, and a few armfulls of dried kelp and sea grass did not go very far toward filling the bellies of hungry herbivores like Chaz and Khorip.

Pausing near a small rocky promontory that jutted seaward, Will eyed the water reluctantly. "I guess we don't have any choice. It's time to go fishing again."

"Just try not to pick up anything that fishes back." Sitting down on the sand, Sylvia began to roll up the hem of her Orofani attire preparatory to wading out into the water.

They were poking about in the shallows close to the beach with a conspicuous lack of success when Khorip abruptly straightened to his full height. Will noticed that the *Prenocephale* was staring silently southward. Flicking warm salt water from his fingers, he followed the bonehead's gaze. It took a moment for the movement he saw to register in his brain. When he rubbed at his eyes and looked again, it was still there.

"People?" he wondered aloud.

"Most certainly. I can't quite make out their configuration, or the style of their attire."

Sylvia waded over to join them. At the moment the sea was being parsimonious with its bounty, but at least standing in the gentle shallows kept them cool.

"Orofani?" She stared uneasily down the road.

"It's possible." Khorip shaded his eyes with one clawed hand. "No. No, I don't think so. It's starting to look more and more like a trade caravan." While he did a good job of keeping his emotions under control, he could not prevent rising excitement from creeping into his voice. "Yes, I'm sure of it now. There are sauropods in the lead." He glanced over at the human female standing next to him. "In my occasional contacts with the Orofani I don't recall any sauropods living with them."

"You're right, Khorip. There weren't any." She squinted hard as she tried to identify the newcomers advancing in their direction. "Of course, these could be representatives of some other migratory tribe. The Orofani might not be the only nomads wandering the Great Desert."

"Oh, that's nice," muttered Chaz from nearby. "Be an optimist."

"I really don't think they are desert dwellers," Khorip continued. "The nomads who inhabit the Great Desert tend to keep to the empty places. It's been my experience that they rarely, if ever, make use of the coast road."

"How can I greet traders from Chandara looking like this?" A disconsolate Sylvia peered down at herself, brushing fitfully at her tattered attire with both hands.

"Easy." Will was grinning. "You walk up to them, raise a hand, and say 'Breathe deep, seek peace,' and then you start talking."

"Very funny, Will Denison."

"What about me?" Chaz wondered. Being built closer to the water than his bipedal companions, the *Protoceratops* had to stay closer to shore. "There are formal greetings to be exchanged, and I am hardly in proper condition to follow through on matters of protocol."

"You two are worrying over nothing." Staring down the coast, Will watched as the advancing caravan began to resolve into individual shapes. "As soon as we tell them that we've crossed the Great Desert all the way from Canyon City, they'll forget all about our appearance."

"Maybe so." Sylvia was only partially mollified. "But *I* won't."

The caravan consisted of a dozen or so dinosaurs and their attendant humans. In contrast to the unlikely quartet they encountered waiting by the side of the road, the traders were suitably outfitted for the country they were traversing. Humans wore loose-fitting outer clothing and wide-brimmed hats while their saurian associates were equipped with shading headgear and the coolest pack materials available.

There were four big sauropods: one *Diplodocus*, a *Barosaurus*, and two apatosaurs. The bulk of the caravan's trade goods rode on their capacious backs. The remainder of the group's saurian contingent was comprised of ceratopsians, from hearty triceratops to a pair of loquacious Protoceratops. These two immediately clustered close to the relieved Chaz, all three of them trying to talk at once.

While the dinosaurs swapped stories and sorted out details, Will and Sylvia waited for a senior human to acknowledge them. This individual descended via rope ladder from a small howdah strapped to the back of the *Diplodocus*. The svelte sauropod on which she had been riding sported a double neckerchief of terrycloth-like material, the alternating maroon and blue colors giving his long neck a bright and cheerful appearance. The extensive strips of cloth served a purpose that was much more than merely decorative, however.

As they looked on, the sauropod reached back with its long neck to lift a sloshing bucket from an open cistern harnessed to its shoulders. When it had straightened completely, the human rider seated behind the small head took the bucket from her mount. Using a series of pulleys, she lowered herself halfway down the neck and began methodically applying water from the bucket to sections of the double neckerchief that had completely dried out. Soaking the winding towels served to cool the blood flowing up and down the elongated neck, which in turn helped to cool the entire massive body.

The sauropod rider greeted them with a jaunty smile and a rush of questions. Will felt she had entirely too much energy for someone traveling through desert country, and he and Sylvia were hard pressed to keep up.

They answered as best they could, explaining how they had come to be in the Great Desert, relating briefly their adventures there (but not mentioning what they had learned about the Hand of Dinotopia), and concluding with their recent arrival at the coast.

"And were you then planning to walk all the way to Hardshell?" Ndloma had laughing eyes to go along with her dazzling smile.

"Only as a last resort." Sylvia glanced meaningfully up at the *Diplodocus* as it luxuriated in its neck bath.

"Of course we'll be glad to accommodate you," Ndloma told them without waiting to be asked. "No one would think of leaving you to make that walk, especially after what you've already been through. We have plenty of room up top and it will be nice to have someone new to talk to. We're many days out from Chandara, on our regular run up to Proserpine. That's your intended destination, I presume?"

Will and Sylvia exchanged a glance. "Actually," he told

their new host, "we intend to stop in Kuskonak. Our sky-baxes are waiting at Pteros."

*There*, he thought. *That was truthful without being informative.*

"I see." The sauropod rider nodded vigorously. "I'm sure they'll be anxious to see you."

Indeed they will, Will mused, but Cirrus and Nimbus would have to wait a while longer yet to see their riders.

"But why are we standing here talking in the sun?" Turning, Ndloma pointed to the howdah high up on the *Diplodocus*'s back. "Come into the shade. You must be hungry and thirsty. How about some nice cold lemonade with some dates and dried fruit?"

Will tried hard not to drool openly as they followed their hostess to the bottom of the rope ladder.

As they mounted the gently heaving flank of the big sauropod, he saw that now Khorip as well as Chaz had fallen in with the two protoceratops who were part of the caravan. Chattering incessantly among themselves, the four smaller dinosaurs settled themselves between a pair of patient triceratops. The big-horned saurians ignored the babble of their smaller relations. Compared to a curious *Protoceratops*, Will knew, even a garrulous human like Ndloma would appear sedate.

The howdah was a haven in the sky, bigger than anything employed by the Orofani. The flat floor was covered with fine carpets fashioned by the skilled weavers of Proserpine, and the dark mesh walls and peaked roof let the slightest breath of air penetrate the single chamber. As soon as the caravan resumed its march, a gentle breeze sprang up, filtering the air within the howdah.

The slight side-to-side rocking motion was considerably more gentle than what they had experienced on the back of an Orofani stegosaur. Behind the howdah's living quarters, bales and sacks and boxes of goods from the southern and western regions of Dinotopia shifted hardly at all, firmly anchored to the *Diplodocus*'s broad back and hindquarters by an intricate tack of straps, ropes, and harness.

Selecting a date from the tray Ndloma placed before them, Will popped it in his mouth and chewed, the intense flavor exploding against his famished taste buds. The second date went down more easily, followed by a sweet chunk of dried papaya. Next to him, Sylvia was feeding as decorously as possible, considering her own hunger.

Reclining against a small pile of embroidered pillows, their hostess observed them with obvious amusement. "You four are lucky we came along. There won't be another caravan for a week, and it will be one heading south."

"We're more than grateful," Will avowed. "Chandaran hospitality is famous."

She chuckled. "Even when it's mobile? Well, we do the best we can."

"How often do you come through here?" Sylvia dabbed at her lips with a cloth napkin.

"Every few weeks. It depends on what cargo we can pick up. Usually we just go back and forth between Chandara and Proserpine, but I have conveyed obligations as far north as Osteo and south all the way to Bluebottle." She gestured toward the mesh. "We usually travel fully loaded. Not too many people, or dinosaurs, want to make the trip. It's hot, and after the first time or two, pretty boring. Myself, I like the solitude. I'm not a city person. Neither is Opaktia."

"Who's Opaktia?" Will sipped cooled fruit juice from an insulated tankard.

Ndloma slapped the carpet she was sprawled atop. "You're riding her. It's funny how much alike dinosaurs and people are. Some like the desert while others can't stand it. I think it must be much the same everywhere in Dinotopia. Everyone has their own personal likes and dislikes, and it doesn't matter how big or small you are."

"That's true," Sylvia agreed. "Will and I are partial to Waterfall City."

Their hostess made a face. "That soggy place? Too damp for me. The couple of times I visited there, *I felt* clammy every time I went to bed. Give me a dry climate any day. What about your companions?" She gestured forward.

"Chaz likes the cultural amenities of Sauropolis," Will told her. "As for Khorip, I think you'd find him a kindred desert spirit. He seems very comfortable here."

"Fond of it, even," Sylvia added mischievously.

Twisting to her left, Ndloma grabbed a handful of mixed cashews, macadamias, peanuts and almonds from a carved wooden bowl and munched on them as she continued to talk. "How long were you planning on staying in Hardshell?"

Sylvia shook her head diffidently. "Actually, we hadn't given it much thought. We were too concerned about just getting there." She glanced at Will, who was content to let her carry the conversation. "I guess we'll hang around until we can arrange transportation to Kuskonak."

Ndloma nodded approvingly. "And from there you'll make your way via the northern canyon road back to Pteros." Neither Will nor Sylvia bothered to explain that it was their intention to journey east and out onto the water from the well-known coastal port instead of west and inland. As was her conversational style, Ndloma did not give them much of a chance to reply anyway.

"If you don't mind waiting a day or two," she charged on, "while we conclude some business in Hardshell, I know that my colleagues would be delighted to take you all the way to Kuskonak."

"That would be wonderful," Will admitted readily. "It would save us the trouble of having to find transportation in Hardshell."

"We'd be ever so grateful," Sylvia added with feeling.

Ndloma put up a hand. "Tut! Happy to help out. You four would have a time of it trying to find alternate transportation in Hardshell, you would. Unless there was another caravan heading the way you want to go, you'd have to make private arrangements. Difficult, and not easy to come by. Hardshell's not Chandara. Of course, you could always walk to Kuskonak."

"No thanks." Will's response was immediate and heartfelt. "We've had enough desert hiking to last us a long time."

Ndloma's effervescent laughter filled the howdah. "I imagine you have!" Then she leaned forward and eyed them shrewdly. "Now then: as long as we're alone here, why don't you tell me what you were really doing out in the Great Desert? More than just exploring, I'll wager."

"We were looking for something." Sylvia lay back against the celestial softness of a large silken cushion. Will threw her a surprised, warning look, but she ignored him.

"Hah! I knew it!" Their hostess slapped one open palm against her right thigh. "And this thing you were looking for—did you find it?"

Sylvia nodded. "It was exactly the size I thought it would be."

Ndloma's brows drew together. "You have it with you?" Searching first Sylvia's recumbent form, then Will's, the trader did not find the enlightenment she was seeking. "But I see nothing. Where is it?"

"Here," Sylvia told her. Reaching up, she tapped the side of her head. "It's a legend. The legend of a lost city, and we found it. Ahmet-Padon."

The sauropod rider made a face. "Never heard of it."

Now it was Sylvia's turn to laugh. "I said it was a legend."

For a moment Ndloma was silent. Then her face split in a glorious grin. "You're having fun with old Ndloma, aren't you? All right, play your little games. But promise me one thing. Call it a partial payment for caravan services rendered."

"If we can," Will agreed guardedly.

"Promise that if and when you find something of more substance than a 'legend,' you'll find a way to let me know about it."

Sylvia lifted her tankard of juice to toast their hostess. "I promise that if in our travels we come across anything more interesting than the legend of Ahmet-Padon, we'll let you know about it."

"That's good enough for me." Ndloma's expression turned wise. "You two are the most interesting pair of sky-bax riders I've ever met. Usually your kind keep to themselves, and it's hard to carry on a conversation with someone when they're away up in the air. I wish you both long life, and good luck."

"Thanks," Will replied. "At least we won't have to concern ourselves with surviving in the desert anymore."

"No," concurred Sylvia readily enough, "but there'll be other things to worry about."

He looked at her sharply. "Other things? What 'other things'?"

But despite his most strenuous attempts to coax further information from her, she would only look at him and smile encouragingly.

# -XV-

aving never been to Hardshell or even seen pictures of the place, there was no reason for Will and Sylvia to be disappointed by it. Nevertheless, as soon as they set eyes on the town they were happier than ever that, thanks to the largess of Ndloma and her associates, they would not have to spend more than a day or two in its arid environs.

Situated in a shallow gorge between two opposing hills, Hardshell's appearance was that of a community that had seen better times. In ancient days the site had been an important trading center, but with the desiccating of the climate the Great Desert had encroached all the way to the sea, and numerous small coastal towns had gradually been abandoned as their populations sought out the more fertile lands to north and south. Of them all, along this vast stretch of dry Dinotopian coast only Hardshell survived as a way station for traders and travelers, and a reminder of a wetter, greener past.

"Can you imagine us spending weeks here?" Sylvia whispered to Will as they strolled through the humble marketplace. "Or trying to arrange for transportation to Kuskonak?"

Will eyed the simple stalls attended by humans and smaller dinosaurs alike. Large, colorful tarpaulins strung on poles provided shade from the sun. Many of the stalls backed onto the small homes of the vendors. These modest dwellings had been fashioned from local slate and sandstone. Sand and dust was everywhere. Though a small army of humans and saurians swept the town clean every morning, nocturnal winds deposited a fresh load of grit while they slept. To keep the Great Desert from reclaiming the townsite, the residents of Hardshell were forced to wage a never-ending battle against the elements.

And yet the citizens of the remote, isolated community delighted in their simple pleasures, in their privacy and seclusion. In such a place, Will decided, it was possible to combine the comforts of Dinotopian civilization with the solitude sought after by such as Khorip. Excusing himself, he left Sylvia happily inspecting the wares of a dealer in polished stone necklaces and bracelets so that he could go and talk to Chaz.

When she next saw him, he was breathless with excitement. Even the normally restrained translator radiated eagerness.

"Here," he told her. "Look at this!" As he spoke, he pressed something large and heavy into her hand.

It was a sculpture of a human forearm terminating in an open palm. On the inner section of the arm were scrawled a thin line of hieroglyphics.

"What is this?" She turned it over and over in her hands. "Where did you find it?"

"Not me." He patted the frill of the diminutive ceratopsian standing next to him. "Chaz spotted it in a stall full of antiques and relics."

"I recognized the inscription instantly," the translator told her. "It took a moment to decipher it all, and I wanted to make sure there was no mistake. It is quite straightforward." With his beak he nudged her hand. "It reads, in a well-known variant of ancient Neoknossosian, 'The Hand of Dinotopia.'"

"The Hand of Dinotopia?" Flustered, she studied the sculpture intently. "This?"

"Why not?" Will challenged her. "In appearance and shape it doesn't contradict anything we found in Ahmet-Padon. Nothing we saw there insisted that it had to be big." He looked down at the *Protoceratops*. "In fact, I don't remember you reading anything at all about its size or shape."

"Quite correct," Chaz agreed. "And now, right here in Hardshell, we find it."

"But I don't understand." Holding it up to the light, Sylvia searched for deeper meaning, for hidden directions or unrecognized symbology. "How does it point to a safe sea route away from Dinotopia?"

"Like this." Will took back the sculpture. Holding it out at arm's length, he pointed it in the direction of the unseen sea. After waving it around for about a minute, he passed it back to her. "There. It's all perfectly clear to me. Don't you see it, Sylvia?"

"See *what*?" By now she was thoroughly exasperated.

His lips quivered. "That I've been giving you a hand ever since the first time we met."

She started to reply, hesitated, and found herself looking hard from fiancé to friend. Realization dawned. "Why, you two . . . !"

Laughter spilled through the marketplace at the sight of the young woman in nomadic dress chasing her young male companion and the stumpy-legged *Protoceratops* between stalls and around piles of goods. The good-natured joviality redoubled when Khorip came over to see what was happening and a tight-lipped Sylvia formally presented him with the hand-hewn Hand of Dinotopia.

Only after the *Prenocephale* had been let in on the joke did Sylvia confront the two practical jokers without stone in hand. "Will, this is no surprise coming from you. But Chaz, you had me fooled completely."

The *Protoceratops* was still barking softly. "I may not exactly be everyone's first choice as a source of levity, but I assure you that I do have a sense of humor at least as well developed as these small horns that protrude from my lower frill. I simply choose to exercise it at only the most propitious moments. As a consequence I find that the impact," he concluded dryly, "is magnified by the exclusivity."

"And I was taken in as well." Khorip let the sculpture hang loose from one clawed hand. "Wherever did you find such a thing?"

"Like we told you, right here in the marketplace." Will was still breathing hard, and still grinning.

"And the 'hieroglyphics' on the underside?" Sylvia was trying hard not to smile back at him. She only partly succeeded.

253

"Who knows what they mean?" He looked over at Chaz. "Did you ever actually try to read them?"

"No. I did not want to waste any time in presenting it to Sylvia. Show it here." After Khorip proffered the length of shaped stone, the *Protoceratops* studied the inscription on its side carefully. "It is all quite readable. It says, 'carved by H.T. Suarez.'"

"And what is it for? Does it say that?" Sylvia wanted to know.

"It most assuredly does." Inclining his head upward, the translator whispered something to Will, who nodded and took the sculpture back from Khorip.

"Behold; the one true function of 'The Hand of Dinotopia'!" His grin widening, he placed the extended stone fingers of the graven hand against his spine and began to work it in an up and down motion against his back.

"Of course," Khorip murmured. "Once divorced from any possible relationship to distant legend, the object's purpose becomes immediately obvious. And to think I was so easily taken in."

"Hey, don't look like that. At least it's not useless," Will told the *Prenocephale*. "I'd hate to think we'd acquired something just for its gag value. Although," he added with a sly glance at Sylvia, "I think Chaz and I got our selection's worth in that department as well."

"I'm not going to let you forget this, Will Denison." She shook an admonishing finger at him.

"That's okay," he chuckled. "I don't think I'll forget it, either."

Khorip had straightened and was looking around. "It's getting late. We should rejoin the caravan at its bivouac on the north side of town. Ndloma and Chipbeak the *Torosaurus* both indicated to me that they would be leaving at sunup tomorrow. We don't want to be left behind."

"That's for sure," Will agreed. "They're being awfully nice to us and I wouldn't want to be responsible for delaying them."

The *Prenocephale* looked over at him out of saurian eyes. "We wouldn't. As accommodating as they've been, they're under no obligation to us and I'm sure they'd leave at first light whether we made our presence known among them or not."

"Then we'd best not be late," declared Sylvia briskly as she started off through the marketplace. Will followed, with Chaz and Khorip bringing up the rear. Occasionally he would reach out and try to scratch her back with the sculpted hand, and she would respond by pushing him away. It did not occur to him that the joke might be wearing thin.

The following morning Ndloma told them that if they wished, they could share her howdah again, but this time they chose to walk.

"For a while, anyway," Sylvia explained to their bemused hostess. "It's the proper thing to do. We don't want to abuse your hospitality."

"It's not just that," Will added. "Neither Khorip or Chaz can climb a ladder to share the space with us, and we're all supposed to be traveling together. Besides, why should your *Diplodocus* have to carry us? She has enough cargo on her back."

"That's very thoughtful of you," Ndloma replied, "and while I'm sure Opaktia wouldn't notice the added burden,

I know that when things are explained to her she'll appreciate the sentiment."

So they trudged alongside the caravan, advancing or letting themselves fall back the better to swap stories and share information with as many of the traders, human and dinosaur alike, as possible. Chaz and the two protoceratops who were members of the caravan generously shared their skills, thereby facilitating conversation among all concerned.

This wasn't so bad, Will decided as he marched along to port of a swaying, heavily-loaded *Apatosaurus*. All you had to do was keep clear of some supra-elephantine feet and walk in the lee of whomever you happened to be conversing with. An ambulating apatosaur cast plenty of shade.

As for the road ahead, it was flat and broad, a far cry from the gravel plains and low sand dunes they had been forced to traverse in their crossing of the Great Desert. Along the way, he and his companions took the time to carefully inspect every mound and hillock within easy walking distance of the road, but none turned out to be buried ziggurats or temples, none revealed anything more about their next destination than they had already learned in now distant Ahmet-Padon. Will began to think that they were searching for a dream on behalf of a legend. Not the sort of empirical evidence he would have preferred to base further journeying on, but it was all they had. His father would have been appalled. But then, he reminded himself, his father wasn't in love with Sylvia. *He* was, and love charts its own route on the map of life.

That was about enough rationalizing metaphors, he told himself firmly. He found himself hoping that they would find something, anything, on the Outer Island, if only to satisfy Sylvia that she had not led everyone else as well as herself on some wild gallimimus chase. Certainly the watery map they had discovered in Ahmet-Padon hinted at the presence of something significant offshore, even if it was not an imaginary sea route to and from Dinotopia. Whether Sylvia would be content with anything less remained to be seen. He hoped that she would, because both he and Chaz were convinced that no such fantastical path existed.

In terms of permanent residents, Kuskonak was not all that much larger than Hardshell, but its transient population of traders and barkers, fisherfolk and craftspeople, combined to give it the attitude and feel of a much bigger community.

Situated on a lovely, small bay with wide white sand beaches sweeping away to north and south, Kuskonak had been an important center of Dinotopian trade since ancient times. Here the only road that could be said to actually cross a portion of the Great Desert ran from the inland outskirts of town westward all the way to Pteros, and thence onward to Canyon City itself. To the north lay the important metropolitan center of Proserpine and beyond, the fertile lowlands of the Crackshell Peninsula. Boats exhibiting a diverse heritage of shipbuilding styles plied the rich fishing grounds of nearby Warmwater Bay while junks, dhows, galleys, outriggers, and Bugis pinsis transported cargo up and down the coast between Chandara and Proserpine.

In place of the rough rock habitations of Hardshell, the prosperous citizens of Kuskonak erected multi-story structures for themselves and their saurian compeers of fine stonework slathered with white-washed plaster, so that the entire town boasted a distinctly Mediterranean look. The presence of multiple chimneys on the modest skyline testified to the occasional invasion of a chilly winter's night, but for the most part the citizens of the port municipality enjoyed the balmy weather that was typical of eastern Dinotopia.

After offering a last round of thanks to their new-found friends, they bid Ndloma, Opaktia, and their colleagues farewell and allowed themselves the luxury of a night in a real inn. Chaz luxuriated in the soft hay bed most suitable for his kind while Khorip, used to rougher surroundings, had difficulty falling asleep. Eventually, he ended up sleeping on the hard pavement outside the barn. On the other hand, Will and Sylvia had no trouble adapting to the comfort of a real human bed, no trouble at all.

It was over breakfast the following morning that Chaz, having put it off for as long as possible, finally informed them of the decision he had reached the previous night.

"It is so nice to be back in civilized surroundings again."

"Sure is." Will was sipping a tall glass of cold chocolate flavored with cinnamon. Next to him, Sylvia was finishing the last of her wild grain pancakes. Khorip squatted alongside the translator, on the side of the table with no chairs.

"The road from here to Pteros is well-traveled, and we should have no difficulty making passage to there and then on to Canyon City," the *Protoceratops* continued blithely.

"No, we shouldn't," Sylvia conceded, "except that we happen to be traveling in the opposite direction."

"Speak for yourselves." Dipping his mouth in a cleansing bucket, Chaz swirled water across his teeth to clean them. "Myself, I have had enough of stumbling through inhospitable places in search of ancient legends. I long for the tidy barns and stimulating culture of Canyon City." He looked from one human to the other.

"I wish you well in your pursuit of anecdotes. When you have had enough of this running all over the most inaccessible parts of Dinotopia, you must drop me a line and let me know what you found. If anything," he added somberly.

"Chaz!" Leaning over in his chair, Will put his arm around the translator's thick neck. "How can you leave us now?"

"With ease and simplicity." The *Protoceratops* nodded in the direction of the arched entrance to the restaurant in which they were dining. "I will walk out that door and turn left."

"But we've found proof that the Hand is more than just legend," Sylvia reminded him. "There's the water map in Ahmet-Padon, and Khorip's research corroborates my own."

"The water map points to a location on Outer Island," Chaz argued, "not a sea route away from Dinotopia." Swiveling one eye, he peered up at the *Prenocephale* squatting next to him. "As for the 'studies' of our friend Khorip, they speak only to the legend of the Hand, not to its reality. A dozen independently researched legends still add up only to a myth. Call me contumacious, but I need to see something real before I can convince myself."

"That's why we're going to Outer Island." Will pleaded with his companion. "We may very well need the services of a translator there, Chaz. You have to come with us."

"No I do not." The *Protoceratops* was unshaken. "My mandate from the department in Canyon City was to convey you safely to a rendezvous with Sylvia. This I have done, and more. Nothing was said about assisting you in a crossing of the Great Desert, but I have done that as well."

Rising from his kneeling position, he backed away from the table and turned toward the doorway.

"I have more than fulfilled my instructions from the authorities, not to mention discharging any subsequently incurred obligations to you, Will Denison. I now look forward with considerable pleasure to joining the next convoy leaving Kuskonak for Pteros. I wish you all the best of luck in your continued journey. If there is an actual Hand of Dinotopia, and if you find it, I hope it proves of sufficient importance to justify all the time and trouble you are going through to search it out."

With that he turned his high hump of a rump to them and, with considerable dignity, waddled out into the busy street beyond.

Will exhaled sadly. "Well, I guess that's that. Whatever we encounter from here on out, we'll have to cope with it without the services of our own translator."

"We'll manage." Sylvia put a reassuring hand over his where it rested on the tabletop. "It's not always necessary to have a translator present."

"And I know several other tongues besides that of the pachy and the human," Khorip reminded them. "We will make out all right." He glanced toward the doorway where Chaz had taken his leave. "At least I won't have to put up with your erstwhile friend's incessant pessimism and criticism all the time." But it seemed to Will that even as the *Prenocephale* proclaimed his relief at Chaz's exodus, there was a note of regret in his voice.

"You know," he murmured, "Chaz does have a point or two. Maybe it would be better to return to Sauropolis and inform the Department of Archeology about our discoveries.

A formal expedition could be mounted, one with adequate supplies and preparation, and we could. . . ."

Sylvia's look stopped him cold. "Will Denison . . ." she began warningly.

He raised both hands defensively. "Okay, okay—it was just a thought." Leaning forward, he kissed her lightly on the cheek. "As soon as we're finished here, we'll head down to the harbor and arrange for a boat."

"It will be very strange to be on the open sea after so many years in the desert," Khorip declared thoughtfully. "I would hate to embarrass myself by becoming seasick."

"Don't worry about it," Sylvia told him. "Once, when I was making the crossing on the big ferry from Sauropolis to Baru, the weather turned rough really fast. There was a *Brachiosaurus* on board and believe me, when she turned queasy, you never saw a load of people move to the front of a boat so fast." Her expression twisted at the recollection. "Watching a fifty-ton sauropod violently empty the contents of its stomach over the side of a boat is not a memory that ranks among my fondest."

"Somehow that doesn't reassure me." Khorip straightened and stepped away from the table. "Hopefully the weather will be calm for the duration of our crossing."

Much would depend on the stability of their chosen craft, Will knew, but a thorough canvassing of the Kuskonak waterfront proved less than encouraging. The majority of boats that made the town their home port were either out fishing or making ready to join their industrious brethren in the task of reining in the bounty of the sea. It was the time of year when several species of edible armored fish were spawning, and bluefin migrated up the coast between the mainland and Outer Island. Busy with a bountiful harvest of everything from blue crab to trilobite, every boat seemed spoken for.

Those that were not looked less than seaworthy. Close inshore, the currents and winds that surrounded Dinotopia were easily navigable, but the further out one went, the more contentious they became. Traveling all the way to Outer Island demanded not only a sturdy craft, but a knowledgeable crew and experienced captain.

Driven by excitement, Sylvia and Khorip were prepared to retain any old tub, but Will insisted on holding out until they could make arrangements with a vessel suited to the crossing.

"It won't improve your chances of finding answers to your questions if we run into trouble halfway across the bay and have to turn back and start over," he argued.

"I know," Sylvia pouted, "but it's so frustrating to have come this far and now have to sit and wait." She was standing on the edge of the road that followed the curve of the harbor, eyeing the few boats that were berthed at the half dozen piers. Barnacles, limpets, and crinoids clung to the base of the stone jetties, while trilobites and crabs scurried about in the shallows.

"What about that boat?" Khorip pointed to a rectangular wooden shape drifting motionless alongside the nearest pier.

"That's not a boat," Will explained patiently. "It's a barge. See the hawsers around the sides? It's designed for moving a lot of cargo around the harbor, not for travel on the open sea."

"It floats," Khorip argued pragmatically.

"So does a cork from a wine bottle, but I'm not about to try and ride one all the way to Outer Island."

"If it's designed to carry heavy cargo, it would hold all of us easily," Sylvia pointed out eagerly.

"Now wait a minute . . ." Will began.

"The weather is dead calm and the sea is flat," Khorip pointed out. "Surely it could make the crossing."

"Probably, sure," a reluctant Will admitted, "if the weather holds. If not, you wouldn't have to worry about distinguishing yourself by getting seasick, because we'll *all* be throwing up. That's because all barges have flat bottoms. I'm no sailor, but I'd bet that in any kind of a swell something like that would rock and roll like crazy."

"Khorip's right." Sylvia had already chosen to side with the *Prenocephale*. "Right now, Warmwater Bay is like a lake."

"Yeah; right now," Will muttered.

"And barges aren't used for fishing, so it should be available for employment."

Will was not quite ready to concede. "What makes you think her crew is willing to sail that shingle all the way to Outer Island?"

"What makes you think they're not?" she shot back.

He rolled his eyes. "Great. Specious logic. How am I supposed to answer that?"

"You're not." Stepping forward, she put her arms tightly around him and peered deeply into his eyes. "You're supposed to tell me how beautiful I am, how you can't live without me, and how you're ready to support me in anything and everything I want to do because you love me fiercely, tenderly, everlastingly, with a love that's as deep and wide as the outer ocean itself."

"I am?" he replied disingenuously.

"Yes, you are." Unwinding herself from him, she stepped back and shook her head sadly. "But because you're a typical male, you won't. So I'll settle for us making arrangements to engage that barge to take us to Outer Island, and we'll worry about the motivation later."

"Well—I guess so." That was interesting, he thought. He'd clearly lost the argument and the funny thing was, he didn't even remember having had one. Together, the three of them headed for the pier where the homely craft was berthed. As they walked, Will could not escape the nagging feeling that he had somehow just been had.

# -XVI-

heir inquiries saw them directed to a water-front tavern, and it was there that they finally located the master of the barge. With his full beard and booming voice, he reminded Will of the ironmaster Tok Timbu, though Captain Manuhiri was of a gentler and less intense mien.

"Oh, she'll make the crossing, all right," he assured them as they left the tavern and found themselves strolling back along the waterfront. "She'll carry a pair of barosaurs side by side without tipping, and in a strong current at that." He scratched at his beard. "But if the weather turns on us, you landers are liable to have a rough time of it."

"We've already discussed the possible ramifications," Sylvia assured him. "We're prepared to deal with any difficulties we may encounter so long as we get to Outer Island."

"Oh, I'll get you there, all right," Manuhiri promised her. "Though what color you'll be when you step ashore I can't guarantee."

"That's our concern. But first we need to procure some supplies before we can leave."

Manuhiri eyed them speculatively. "Now why would you need to go and do that here when you'll be landing at Culebra? I know she's not much of a town, but you should be able to find anything you might need in her shops."

"We're planning on doing some exploring in the back country of Outer Island," Will explained, "and we can't come running back to Kuskonak if we forget something or can't find it in Culebra."

The beard bobbed as Manuhiri nodded understandingly. "I see. Exploring, is it? What sort of 'exploring'? No, never mind. You don't have to tell me, and I can see that if you wanted to, you'd have gone and done it by now. It's your business, and mine is just to get you there. So be it." Halting, he nodded out to sea.

"Make haste in your preparations, then, and be here by first light tomorrow. Outside the harbor the winds start to pick up an hour or so before noon, so the earlier we can leave, the better it will be for you."

Leaving the captain to see to his barge, the three travelers rushed through the shops and marketplace of Kuskonak in a hurried attempt to replenish the supplies that had been lost to the desert. At least water would not be a problem, reducing both their burden and their concerns. Outer Island was far enough to the east of the rain shadow of the Forbidden Mountains and its own peaks high enough to catch plenty of tropical moisture. According to Manuhiri, the island's heavily eroded central range was flush with streams and brooks, though none of the watercourses spawned enough flow to qualify as an actual river.

In the absence of visible masts, sails, or oars, Will had speculated about the barge's exact method of propulsion.

He found out the following morning as they were helped aboard by several members of the crew.

Manuhiri was busy near the bow with the rest of his people, helping them to secure a trio of temnodontosaurs in their towing harnesses. Active and alert as they were, it was difficult for the long-snouted, toothed aquatic reptiles to lie still long enough for their human partners to slip straps and buckles around their porpoise-like bodies. The temnodontosaurs bobbed and rolled in the water. Will quickly saw that a certain amount of good-natured splashing and slapping was prevalent among the members of both species. That explained, he decided, why the humans wore as little as possible. Because of the constant water play, they were nearly as wet as their ichythyosaurian co-workers.

An expansive Manuhiri walked back to greet them. "Welcome, my inquisitive friends! As you can see, the good weather has held—which means that your luck has held as well. It should be a smooth and uneventful crossing." He shook a finger in the air. "Furthermore, I have word that a cargo of fresh fruit and cane is sitting on the jetty at Culebra just waiting for some enterprising captain to pick it up. No one will be expecting a coastal barge to put into Tarabi Gulf, so we will both surprise and please the growers. Unlike your average fishing boat, we will be able to bring back the entire load."

"Then we came along at just the right time," Sylvia announced serenely.

"Indeed you did, young lady," replied the captain, giving her a hug that was entirely too friendly for Will. But then Manuhiri bestowed the same smothering embrace on him, proving that there was only good humor and nothing untoward in his actions.

Rearranging his bones, which had been temporarily realigned by the captain's bear hug, Will watched as the barge prepared to get under way. The temnodontosaurs stopped gabbing long enough to extend their harnesses. Attendant human sailors checked the buckles while others unwound the ropes that tied the barge to the pier from their restraining cleats. As soon as they were free and clear, sailors used poles to push off from the algae-stained stone quay. Khorip stood near the bow, as close to the Outer Island as he could get without swimming.

They were beginning to feel the ebb and pull of the slight current within the harbor when a loud bleating caused everyone to turn.

"Wait! Wait for me!"

Will did not have to search for the source of that frantic entreaty. He recognized the voice immediately.

"Chaz!"

Sure enough, the little translator was racing toward them at top speed, galloping down the pier as fast as his four short legs would carry him. Not having a hand to wave, he had to rely entirely on his voice to convey his zeal.

"I am coming, Will! Do not leave without me!"

Sylvia was entreating the captain. "We can't leave without our friend."

Pushing out his low lip, Manuhiri looked down at her. "Nothing was said about a fourth passenger. I don't know if I can accommodate you, Miss Sylvia. This vessel is extremely difficult to turn, and once Winken, Blinken, and Nod get water under their tails, it's almost impossible to get them to stop for anything short of dinner."

"But you have to!" she begged, trying to divide her attention between the reluctant captain and the sprinting *Protoceratops*.

Manuhiri stroked his beard. "Well now, m'dear, I suppose I could manage something—in return for a little kiss."

Sylvia's lower jaw dropped. "Captain Manuhiri! That's my fiancé right over there."

"And what if he wasn't 'right over there'?"

She drew herself up until she could almost, but not quite, look him in the eye. "Then I'd give you something else, and it wouldn't be a kiss!"

"All right, all right!" A jovial Manuhiri made placating gestures. "I was only teasing you, Miss Sylvia. Of course we'll turn back for your friend. I'm afraid it will take a couple of minutes to execute the maneuver, however. I wasn't twitting you when I said that it's a project to bring this craft about. She's not a racing scull, you know."

Unaware of the barge captain's intentions and believing himself abandoned, Chaz accelerated in the direction of the withdrawn boarding ramp. Will's eyes grew wide as he divined his ceratopsian friend's intentions.

"Chaz, no!"

Heedless of the warning, the translator planted all four feet on the boarding ramp, and jumped. Now, when it comes to jumping, ceratopsians belong in same class as rhinos and elephants, which is to say that a good high jump for any of them would fall somewhere in the range of several inches. But that did not dissuade Chaz. It should have, but it did not.

In the end, it was a miscalculation that saved him. In his haste to make the departing boat, he had neglected to allow for the fact that the barge's deck was about a foot lower than the top of the pier. It wasn't much of a discrepancy, but it made the difference between him landing hard on the departing deck and falling unceremoniously into the murky water between barge and quay.

Though slightly stunned by the impact, he scrambled to his feet and stood, panting hard, while he waited for his friends to join him. They had soon gathered around.

"That was a crazy stunt, Chaz!" Will didn't know whether to be relieved or angry at his friend.

"Yes," added Sylvia. "You could have come up just a little bit short and struck your head on the side of the barge."

The *Protoceratops* lowered the appendage in question. "What do you think this protective head-and-neck frill is for?"

"Not bumping into the sides of boats, I suspect." Will was surprised at how emotional he had become.

"Tut, tut, my friend. I am here and intact, which is all that matters."

"Not quite." It was Khorip's turn to contribute to the conversation. "What happened to your stated desire to return to Canyon City? What, in short, are you doing here?"

The translator's head dipped so low his beak all but scraped the deck. "The more I thought about it, the more I realized that I too wanted to get to the bottom of this Hand business. Much to my surprise, it developed into a need that could not wait. Even if there is no actual Hand of Dinotopia, I have discovered that I have to know for myself." Raising his head, he looked up at each of them in turn. "I have to find out, and I don't want to wait for the official report of your expedition. I want—I want to be a *part* of that official report, not a bystander to it."

Will rested an affectionate hand on the translator's frill. "You always were, Chaz."

"It is passing strange," the *Protoceratops* went on, "this desire to know the unknowable. Humans believe it to be a characteristic solely their own, but I can tell you that we dinosaurs thirst after knowledge just as intensely as do you."

"Khorip is proof of that," Sylvia reminded him.

"I know," Chaz admitted, "but I came back anyway."

"Don't stress yourself," the *Prenocephale* told him. "There's still time to turn around and put you ashore."

"That would suit you, wouldn't it, oh master of an impenetrable cranium."

"Truly it would, oh dispenser of superfluous commentary."

Watching them, Will was moved to remark to Sylvia. "Hard to keep good friends apart, isn't it?"

"Yes." She laughed softly. "They'll keep each other's minds off thoughts of seasickness."

The slight swell they encountered as they left the docks behind and headed out into the harbor proper had no effect on Will or Sylvia. As skybax riders, they were used to far more extreme jolts and bumps than mere waves could provide.

The three temnodontosaurs increased their pace, their broad tails waving in unison as they pulled the sledlike barge through the water. Seated on the pointed bow with his legs dangling over the side, one of their attendants sang out the solo to an old Dinotopian sea chantey while his comrades supplied the chorus. Fishing lines were cast from the stern and allowed to troll behind in hopes of providing a fresh lunch.

Will stood aft and watched as Kuskonak harbor receded behind them. From out on the water the entire town became visible, a crescent of white and pink-stuccoed houses snugged up against a low sandstone massif that provided protection from the blowing sand and wind of the inner desert. Higher hills beyond pointed the way to distant Pteros. The numerous springs at their base had assured that Kuskonak had been inhabited since very early in the history of Dinotopia.

Leaning on the railing that ran around the perimeter of the barge, he felt a hand on his arm. Sylvia joined him in bidding farewell not only to the town, but to the mainland.

"Strange to be out here," she avowed, "knowing that if one could just sail far enough eventually they would come to lands where dinosaurs are but bleached memories in rocks."

He nodded knowingly. "Where my father and I come from, the sight of a live dinosaur would be considered a miracle. Never mind a talking one."

"And they're so much older than us," she murmured. "They have hundreds of millions of years of history behind them, and we have so little."

"Maybe we can make a little history of our own." He put his arm around her waist and drew her close.

She seemed suddenly hesitant and he eyed her uncertainly. "Sylvia? What's the matter?"

"Nothing's the matter." She straightened, staring at the receding town.

"Come on, Sylvia. I know you better than that. Something's troubling you."

"It's just that—well, it's just that I'm starting to worry.

Kind of funny, isn't it? In the canyon of the Amu, in the Great Desert, I was always confident. But now that we're comparatively safe and so close to the end of the journey, I find myself wondering."

"Wondering what?" he coaxed her gently.

She turned to face him. "What if there is no Hand of Dinotopia? No mysterious, magical sea route away from here? What if Chaz has been right all along and it's just a fable, or a metaphor for something ordinary and every-day? I will have dragged you, and Chaz, all the way to Outer Island for nothing, and exposed you to all this danger along the way. I'm not concerned about Khorip's reaction because he would have come anyway."

"So would I, Sylvia," he whispered softly.

"No you wouldn't." Her tone was sharp. "Because there's nothing for you on Outer Island, no reason for you to go there."

"Yes there is."

"Oh? And what might that be?"

"You, Sylvia. You're going to be there. And that's reason enough for me."

They were silent then, the world filled with the sound of water slapping against the sides of the barge, of Khorip and Chaz debating some obscure point of archeology, and of the sailors singing. Then they embraced, arms wrapping affectionately around shoulders and waists, and for a few moments took the time to sing silently of themselves.

It was Sylvia who finally pulled away, pointing excitedly. "Look there, Will! Isn't it grand?"

He turned, and instantly understood her excitement. "I didn't know practice had begun."

Of all the celebrations and festivals that crowded the social and cultural calendar of Dinotopia, none was as eagerly awaited as the Dinosaur Olympics. Will had competed in them himself, as had Sylvia and everyone else they knew. Winning was not as important as doing your best, and the saurians they now saw practicing in a restricted section of the bay were certainly striving their utmost to achieve, if not athletic perfection, then at least physical feats worthy of the admiration of their peers.

As they cruised past, the human sailors on the barge let out several cheers, and the three temnodontosaurs who were supplying motive power to the craft joined in the acclamation with their own unique high-pitched whistles and shouts.

Off to one side, the local water ballet team was executing intricate practice maneuvers. Consisting of humans swimming in tandem with elasmosaurs and other pleisosaurs, the coordinated movements of human and dinosaur were an object of water-borne beauty. Due to the distance, those on board the barge were unable to hear more than a trace of the music the team was performing to, but the graceful swan-like sweeps of long elasmosaurian necks coupled with the intricate in-and-out darting of their partnered humans resulted in choreography that bordered on the mesmerizing. Will and Sylvia could have watched for hours, but the barge continued to move steadily out to sea.

Some distance away from the ballet team, squads of ichthyosaurs were racing through an oval obstacle course while humans in small attending boats timed them and offered suggestions and encouragement. Each team consisted of two ichthyosaurs swimming side-by-side. More than sheer speed was involved, since each pairing had one human partner balanced atop their slick, curving backs. The human rider kept each foot secure in a special boot harnessed just behind the ichthyosaurs' dorsal fins and held on to reins that both aided him or her in maintaining their balance while allowing them to guide their mounts.

Not that the ichthyosaurs couldn't see the course perfectly well on their own, but the human range of vision above water was greater than theirs, especially when several teams were racing around a course simultaneously, churning the water to froth. Above the roiling water, the human riders could see obstacles looming ahead and help to guide their team accordingly. Running the course well demanded a coordinated three-pronged effort between *Icthyosaurus* and human.

As those on the barge looked on, one team swung too far to the right. Changing course sharply to avoid a colorful, floating buoy that was one of the numerous course obstacles, one ichthyosaur drifted too far forward of its companion. With a wild waving of hands that failed to save her balance, their rider lost the reins and took an unavoidable spill. Immediately, both ichthyosaurs came about and returned to check on her, communicating in the high-pitched voices that made them sound perpetually querulous.

Once assured that their human partner was unhurt, they engaged in some serious chat while she treaded water. Then she remounted her team, carefully slipping first one foot and then the other into the waiting dorsal boots while both aquatic reptiles bobbed patiently side by side. Taking up the reins, she shouted something down to them and they accelerated, swimming slowly back to the starting gate to try the course again. Just as it did for the water ballet team, successful running of Olympic obstacle courses took a great deal of practice.

Out in the deeper water of the harbor they witnessed four mosasaurs divided into two teams apiece participating in an elaborate tug-of-war. Their powerful jaws agape, all four strained against the heavy harnesses that had been fashioned for the purpose by dexterous human hands. Just back of each massive skull, a human team member rode in a special saddle. While the mosasaurs pushed with powerful tails, their human counterparts offered advice on which way to turn, when to swim hard or simply try to maintain position, and when to put out a greater effort.

Between the practicing pairs, an old, nearly toothless *Kronosaurus* and several humans on a raft offered advice to the competitors, coaching both teams equally. In the water, a tug-of-war became a contest of strategy as much as pure strength. Waves foamed and crested around the contestants as they twisted and writhed like giant snakes.

They were the sea serpents of western lore, Will knew. In the waters around Dinotopia, mosasaurs were the equivalent of the great carnosaurs of the Rainy Basin, only much more amenable to civilized contact. Perhaps the bounty of the ocean rendered them naturally less aggressive. He knew that without their help, he and his father could never have reached and explored The World Beneath, the great caverns that underpinned much of eastern Dinotopia.

The harbor at Kuskonak was not extensive, so it wasn't long before they found themselves out on the open waters of Warmwater Bay. With the towing temnodontosaurs aided by a slight but steady following wind, Manuhiri was able to set a course almost due east for Tarabi Gulf and the port of Culebra.

At the speed they were making, the crossing would take most of the day. A simple but adequate shelter in the form of a rectangular wooden cabin dominated the stern of the barge. As passengers, Will, Sylvia, Khorip, and Chaz were able to take shelter there from the rising sun. Used to the unfiltered tropical rays, the crew busied themselves with sailors' tasks, clearing kelp and other growth from the sides of the boat, keeping the deck clean, and occasionally gathering up the delicious flying fish that, in their attempts to flee subsurface predators, stranded themselves on board when their attempts to fly over the wide wooden surface fell short.

Occasionally, one of the crew would haul in and unhook a more substantial catch from one of the fishing lines that trailed behind the barge. With little else to do until landfall, Will and Sylvia spent quite a bit of time watching the fishermen at their work. Those rainbow runners and bonito and mackerel the crew did not use to feed themselves or the hard-working trio of temnodontosaurs went into a communal tank for sale either in Culebra or back in Kuskonak. Some of the fine fish would be consumed locally while the rest would end up dried, salted, and shipped to distribution points further inland. The occasional big tuna would be retained for convoy use in the Rainy Basin, to be given as tribute to the carnosaurs who dwelled there in return for guarantee of safe passage. Tyrannosaurs, Will knew, were especially fond of tuna.

More than halfway to the Gulf, they had just finished lunch when a shout came from astern. While the rest of the crew were compelled by duty to remain at their stations, the passengers were under no such compunction. They gathered behind the wooden shelter to watch.

"What is it?" Rising up on hind legs, his front feet pawing at the air for balance, Chaz sought a better view of the action.

Will strained to see. There were now two crewmen fighting with the biggest of the fishing poles, with a third hurrying over to give them an additional hand. Astern of the barge, something big and powerful was churning the ocean to spume.

"I can't tell yet! There's too much foam."

Next to him, Sylvia brushed flying seawater from her face as she tried to see what the men had hooked. As she stared, something massive broke the surface for just an instant before disappearing back beneath the swells.

"I saw it! I think it's a *Dinichthys.*"

Will knew the ancient fish well. Powerful and heavily armored, it was also delicious eating. But it would not be easy to land. However, with the addition of a third set of muscles to the fishing pole, the tip of which was bent so far down it nearly scraped the water, the whooping, excited crewmen began to get the upper hand.

As they slowly and methodically began to bring the big fish in, Will saw that Sylvia's guess had been correct. It was a *Dinichthys* for sure, and a nice one at that. Not trophy size, but big enough to provide a decent meal for any carnosaur, not to mention a whole gathering of humans and smaller dinosaurs.

More than six feet long, the glistening armor plates that lined the sides of the great fish flashed in the sun whenever it broke the water. Powerful toothed jaws snapped futilely at unseen assailants. The crewmen struggled to land their prize before those heavy, massive jaws caught the line lest they bite it, or for that matter the heavy fishing pole itself, in two. They could also, Will knew, effortlessly do the same to a human arm or leg.

As the *Dinichthys* was hauled closer and closer to the stern, Will and Sylvia moved off to one side to give the straining crewmen as much room as possible in which to work. They would need a sizable portion of the rear deck to bring the fish aboard. Two other crew members had appeared, along with Manuhiri himself, to witness the catch.

Then the sea astern erupted as something truly gigantic thrust its head out of the water and bit the thrashing *Dinichthys* cleanly in half.

"*Megalodon!*" one of the crewmen screamed as he lost his grip on the pole.

Will stood stunned, Sylvia next to him, and gaped. Like everyone else in Dinotopia, he had heard stories of the rare, giant shark, but he had certainly never expected to see one. Many tons in weight, fifty or sixty feet long and armed with serrated six-inch teeth, a *Megalodon* could do battle on an equal footing with the largest kronosaur or with any of the migrating whales that sometimes visited Dinotopia's shores.

Like any shark, however, the *Megalodon* preferred scavenging to confrontation. Once hooked, the flailing, battling *Dinichthys* had involuntarily emitted the distress signals common to all fish in trouble, and the *Megalodon* had homed right in on them. Unfortunately, the rest of the *Dinichthys* was still attached to the stern of the boat.

At the unexpected appearance of the giant shark, the

crewmen had instantly abandoned their line and pole. The latter was secured by a metal brace to a footing in the deck. As the *Megalodon* gobbled down the last of the armored fish, it found itself hooked.

There ensued such a maelstrom of angry water, heaving deck, and flying epithets as Will had never known. As the *Megalodon* writhed and wrenched in its attempts to dislodge the hook now caught in its jaws, the stern of the barge heaved and plunged like a dancing *Dimetrodon*. Everyone was thrown off their feet, and only the seamen's experience kept them all from being cast overboard.

Looking around wildly, Will saw Sylvia sliding away from him, borne seaward on a carpet of foam. "Sylvia!" Starting toward her with hand outstretched, he felt himself tossed in the air as the deck was yanked out from beneath his feet. Landing hard on his shoulder, he rolled quickly enough to see her clawing at the deck, her feet hanging over the side as water swirled around her. She was yelling at him, but in the fury and confusion he could not hear what she was saying.

If she went over the side, with the furious *Megalodon* in the water. . . .

He threw himself in her direction even as he realized that he was too far away. Then other shapes appeared; both familiar, both non-human. As she slid halfway off the deck, sliding under the railing that ran around the outside of the barge, a powerful beak snapped shut on the collar of her dress. Four short, strong legs maintained their stance on the heaving, tossing planks while strong clawed hands clung to the *Protoceratops*'s short, thick tail.

Working in tandem, Chaz and Khorip managed to drag

Sylvia back on board. Keeping a grip on the wall of the cabin, Will fought his way across the water-swept deck to join them.

Together they worked their way around to the front of the structure. At least there they were safe from the snapping jaws of the *Megalodon*. Meanwhile the barge continued to thrust and buck beneath them, making it impossible for anyone but Chaz and Khorip to stand. The barge was as solid a craft as could be found in Dinotopia, but it was not unsinkable. If it went down, if her ribs or keel buckled, they would all find themselves so many tasty minnows helplessly adrift in the water.

Having slipped free of their harnesses, the three temnodontosaurs darted and swam around the *Megalodon*, harassing it with their cries and dashing in to nip at its tail and fins. The trouble was, they weren't doing anything the enormous shark did not already want to do itself. Having in two gigantic bites consumed the entire *Dinichthys*, it now wanted nothing more than to get away. It was the hook set firmly in its mouth that was preventing the escape everyone desired.

Through the roiling tempest of water and hysteria, Will thought he saw Manuhiri duck into the main cabin and re-emerge moments later. Another endless moment passed, and then, miraculously, the turbulent waters grew still. The air was filled once again with the cries of agitated seabirds and the sound of water slapping gently instead of frenziedly against the still intact hull. Waves no longer crashed over the gunwales, threatening to sweep everyone into the sea.

Holding onto each other for support, Will and Sylvia rose shakily. Fish cast onto the deck by the tumult flopped about madly in progressively weakening attempts to return to the water. Exhausted but relieved crewmen ran too and fro to check on the soundness of their craft and to recover lines and cargo that had broken loose.

Sylvia put both arms first around Khorip's neck, then Chaz's frill, hugging each of them in turn. "Thank you both. I love swimming, but not right now, and not here."

Chaz responded with a diffident twitch of his armored skull. "There are times when being built low to the ground has its advantages."

"As does having claws." Khorip displayed those on his hands and feet.

"Let's go see what happened," Will suggested. He kept his arm firmly around Sylvia's waist. "You okay?"

"No, I'm not okay," she sputtered, still spitting up sea water. "I feel like a waterlogged mastodon. But better to feel like one than be one." She summoned up a salty smile.

Together the four of them made their way around the cabin and to the stern. The scene there mirrored the chaos that had enveloped the rest of the craft.

Puffing hard, Manuhiri stood by the deck brace that now held only the stump of the heavy-duty, large diameter fishing pole. The ax that hung from the fingers of his right hand explained what had happened to the rest. Seeing that his passengers were all right, he was finally able to relax a little.

"I had no choice." He indicated the vanished fishing gear. "If the line had held, it would have pulled us under stern-first." His attention turned back to the now calm seas astern. "Better to lose a pole and hook than the whole boat."

"Ah, but Captain," remarked one of the battered crewmen standing nearby, "what a fish we would have had to show on the jetty at Culebra if we but could have landed it!"

"Hmph!" snorted Chaz. "It nearly landed us."

Khorip had walked to the edge of the deck and was gesturing for his companions to join him. "Look here, my friends."

A neat bite had been taken out of the upper part of the stern. The perfect crescent-shape cut-out was more than four feet across. Espying something sticking out of the wood, Will knelt and began pulling at it with his fingers. Working it back and forth, he managed to free it from the heavy timber in which it had become embedded.

It was a tooth, slightly more than five inches long, perfectly triangular and lined on both sides with razor-sharp serrations. Bits of whitish meat still clung to the light brown, blood-stained root. No human-forged utensil would have made a more efficient knife.

After showing it to Sylvia and Chaz, he ceremoniously presented it to Manuhiri.

"For you and your crew," he explained. "A little souvenir of the day's trawling. This is one fish story that won't be disbelieved for lack of proof."

Manuhiri accepted the gift gratefully. "I have caught fish that were smaller than this tooth." He indicated the damaged stern. "We're taking on water below, but slowly and only through cracked caulking, thank the sea gods. The main timbers and ribs are all intact." With one foot, he brushed affectionately at the deck.

"A prettier vessel would have gone down, capsized or swamped. Homely but sturdy, that's how I like my vessels. She'll have to be hauled out and fixed proper once we get back to Kuskonak."

Will looked at Sylvia, the unspoken corollary passing between them. "We don't want you to risk your boat, captain. If you want to turn back to Kuskonak now, we'll understand."

Smiling warmly, Manuhiri put a big, callused hand on each of their shoulders. "Nay, my friends, we're already more than halfway to our destination. I promise you that it is more sensible to continue on. The waters of Tarabi Gulf are more protected than those outside Kuskonak, and we can make temporary repairs at Culebra. Even if you were not aboard, I would still continue on this course. Rest assured of that." He turned somber.

"There is one change that we must implement immediately, however, and that everyone aboard must adhere to."

Will nodded solemnly. "Of course. What do you want us to do?"

A twinkle appeared in the captain's eye. "No more fishing! At least, not until we're within the more secluded waters of the Gulf. I love fish, but not enough to risk becoming one's dinner."

<h1 style="text-align: center;">-XVII-</h1>

he humans recovered more rapidly from the piscine encounter than did the agitated temnodontosaurs. Distraught at their inability to drive the *Megalodon* off, they repeatedly slipped their harnesses to circle the barge and inspect it for damage, all the while vouchsafing their apologies to those aboard. Particular attention was paid to the passengers, with the result that Will found himself growing embarrassed at the unrelenting solicitousness.

When Blinken swam over to request his forgiveness for the fourth, or maybe it was the fifth, time, Will leaned over the side and gazed down at the bright eyes and narrow, tooth-lined snout of the temnodontosaurus. Chaz stood nearby, ready to translate.

"You have nothing to be ashamed of," Will told the anxious icthyosaur via Chaz. "You and your friends did their best."

"We could have done better," was the squeaky reply as translated by the *Protoceratops*. "We *should* have done better."

"What could you have done?" Will wondered aloud. "The *Megalodon* was bigger than you, and unthinking. You can't have a rational conversation with unadulterated fury."

"Perhaps not," admitted Blinken reluctantly.

"No one was hurt, and the damage to your boat can be repaired. Captain Manuhiri said so."

"We know." The long snout absently flicked water into the air, the icthyosaurian equivalent of a human drumming fingers nervously on a tabletop. "But we cannot help but feel bad."

"I'd feel bad if I'd been eaten," Will replied. "Right now I feel pretty good."

"And you make me feel better," Chaz translated from the tribal temnodontosaurian. "It is good to have such understanding passengers with us. We haul mostly cargo and so we're not used to having strangers around. It's a refreshing change."

"And we're glad to be aboard your vessel." Will smiled. "Fishing particulars notwithstanding."

The huge porpoiselike reptile responded with a series of high-pitched gurgling sounds, the closest his kind could come to audible laughter. Throwing his head back, he sent water spraying away from the boat in a display of sheer good-natured exuberance. Then he swam effortlessly toward the bow to rejoin his companions in harness.

After that there were no more redundant abject apologies, either on the part of the temnodontosaurs or the human members of the barge crew. It seemed to Will that their speed increased by a half knot or two, and that the crew was finally able to throw themselves into their daily routine unburdened by the guilt that had been engendered by the perilous confrontation that had taken place earlier.

With the weather holding, the rest of the afternoon passed pleasantly, and it was not long before the high, sharp ridges and peaks of Outer Island hove into view dead ahead. True to the captain's prediction, the sea turned calm as a lake as soon as they entered the sheltered waters of Gulf Tarabi.

Tiny islets too small to be noted on the main maps of Dinotopia dotted the protected bay. Riotous coral bommies reached for the sunlight in explosions of subsurface color and form that delighted the passengers but caused Manuhiri and his crew no end of work. Beautiful they might be, but the flowerlike formations could easily rip a hole in the bottom of an unwary boat.

The approach to the Tracha Narrows was well-buoyed, however, and despite the inevitable occasional close call, they were soon closing on that remarkable geological formation. Culebra was situated on the shore of an ancient sunken caldera. Over eons, rain and tidal action had worn a gash through the flank of the volcanic wall. Once the ocean had gained admittance, it had filled the submerged caldera while simultaneously widening the opening to the sea.

But because of the tides, entry and exit was still a tricky proposition, not to be attempted by the amateur or unskilled sailor. At different times of the day, water from the caldera would rush outward in a veritable saltwater rapids, making entrance to the harbor and Culebra impossible. At other times, the sea would charge in. Arrivals and departures had to be carefully timed to take these powerful tidal surges into account.

At the moment the sea was calm and conciliatory, content

to rest upon its bed of sand and coral, neither boiling in or out. Towed steadily onward by the troika of temnodontosaurs, the barge entered the Narrows. Sheer walls of dark volcanic rock towered several hundred feet high on either side of the channel. Gas bubbles that had formed in the stone when the molten rock first cooled had filled over the centuries with rich, black soil. As a result, epiphytes and bromeliads covered the precipitous ramparts with a carpet of intense green and brilliant hanging flowers.

Will and Sylvia joined Khorip and Chaz in the bow. Close by, sailors were busy adjusting harness straps and lines to keep the towing temnodontosaurs as comfortable as possible. Those broad brown backs rose and fell in tandem as the big sea-going reptiles pulled the barge through the final stretch of the narrows.

Ahead, the rock walls gave way to the ten-mile wide Culebra crater, a veritable salt water lake that punched into the heart of Outer Island. Emerald-clad mountains soared on all sides, the dense tropical vegetation that covered them growing right down to the water's edge.

Sylvia was entranced. "What a beautiful place! I wonder why more people don't live here?"

"Because there is nothing here *except* beauty." Chaz bumped up against her right leg as he peered forward over the rising and falling arched backs of the towing temnodontosaurs. "I am oversimplifying, but that is the gist of it. Both humans and dinosaurs are gregarious creatures who enjoy the company of others and the culture that results." He gestured with his snout. "There is no culture on Outer Island. Only bugs, and rain, and unclimbable eroded volcanic ridges."

"Exactly," declared Khorip from behind him. "That's why I like it already."

Will smiled curiously at the *Prenocephale*. "Thinking of moving again already?"

"No. While the isolation tempts me, there are still too many people here. It is still part of Dinotopia, and as you know, my interest lies in leaving Dinotopia."

Will shook his head regretfully. "I can't believe you're still thinking about that, Khorip."

"Believe it, skybax rider. You were born in the outside world and remember what it was like. No dinosaur has experienced what you have experienced. I fully intend to be the first."

"Unmitigated foolishness," muttered Chaz under his breath. "I cannot wait to get back to civilization, and this bonehead cannot wait to leave it. Were ever two individuals with such diametrically opposed motives paired on the same expedition?"

Sylvia interrupted his griping as she pointed excitedly to starboard. "Look! There's Culebra."

"Yes," concurred a voice coming up from behind them, "and not a moment too soon, if I may say so." Captain Manuhiri joined them in the bow. "The seepage below deck has gotten worse. But don't worry: we'll make port in plenty of time." He gave Will a comradely slap on the back "You won't have to swim."

"Good!" snorted Chaz. "I had enough of that in the desert."

The captain's brows drew together and he looked uncertainly from the *Protoceratops* to Will. "In the desert? What does the no-horn mean?"

"We've had an interesting time of it," Will explained without really explaining anything. To change the subject he asked, "What should we do when we land?"

Manuhiri pursed his lips. "That depends on what your plans are."

Sylvia joined in. "We need to find transportation to a place in the high mountains near the center of the island."

Manuhiri gawked at her a moment, then threw back his head and roared with laughter. When he could speak again he put a friendly arm around her shoulders. Will's expression darkened but he said nothing.

"My sweet svelte skybax rider, no one travels to the center of Outer Island."

"Why not?" she inquired calmly. The weight of his encircling arm was not oppressive.

"Because there's nothing there, my dear. Nothing but impenetrable rainforest and cliffs so steep a commuting pterodactyl couldn't find a place to get a grip. There is only one road on Outer Island, if a road it can be called, and that runs around its circumference, except in the north where it turns inland, isolating the swampy Bamamba Peninsula."

"And there are no other roads?" Will pressed him.

Manuhiri turned thoughtful. "You really intend to follow through on this, don't you? Well, there *is* a branching that turns off the main circle track at its northernmost point, but it only goes about two-thirds of the way up to Cape Bamamba. In the southeast, an exploratory track runs inland and up into the mountains from where the main road borders the Great Eastern Bight. I believe that for part of the way it parallels one of the larger streams on the island.

"If I remember my history aright, it was started long ago by teams who hoped to find a route across the central massif, thus creating a land route between the Eastern Bight and Culebra."

"What happened?" Sylvia wanted to know.

This time he did not smile. "None of the construction crews ever made it across the mountains. Too steep, too wet, and too dangerous. But the remnants of the old road are still there, I believe, even though it is a road to nowhere."

"And no one uses it anymore?" Khorip inquired.

"Oh, it's used, my bulbous-pated friend. On Outer Island any access through the rainforest is prized. One of the principal activities of the island's inhabitants is the gathering of exotic tropical fruits for export to the mainland, where there is quite a market for such delicacies. I know; I have carried back many a delectable load."

Will was nodding knowingly. "I've seen Outer Island fruits in markets all over the mainland. They're not always easy to come by."

"If you really intend to try to make your way around the island and into the interior you'll see why," Manuhiri assured him. "Travel is difficult and harvesting is hard work." He finally removed his arm from Sylvia's shoulders. "Now if you will all excuse me, I must make preparations for docking."

Culebra was no Sauropolis or Baru, and there were only a half dozen or so craft docked or moored in the inner harbor. Fishing boats and small outriggers dominated, the latter used by their human operators to gather tridacna clams, lobster, and trepang from the coralline shallows. Manuhiri's boat was the only cargo vessel in sight, a discovery that pleased him because it all but assured him of a full load for the journey back to Kuskonak.

The tall pilings and elevated pier provided graphic evidence of the extent of Culebra's tides. Since it was currently near low tide, they had to ascend fifteen feet of wooden stairs to reach the dock. While sailors brought up their supplies, they bid farewell to Manuhiri and the rest of the crew. An amused Will saw that two of the sailors were already haranguing a port official with the story of their encounter with the raging *Megalodon*, while Winken and Nod were doing likewise to a pair of curious ichthyosaurs.

"By nightfall," he told Sylvia as they walked along the clattering planks toward shore, "the shark will have grown to eighty feet, with teeth a foot long."

"A hundred feet," Chaz corrected him from nearby, "with poison fangs and the bones of dead dinosaurs stuck in its jaws."

Chuckling, Will turned to Sylvia. "What now?"

She considered their prospects. "Find someplace to spend the night, I guess. In the morning we'll see about transportation. Obviously, if we're going into the interior, our best option is to head around the island and take that abandoned interior road as far into the mountains as we can. If there's no regularly scheduled transport to the east coast, we'll have to try and arrange something."

A thoughtful Khorip strode alongside, his tail waving lazily back and forth several feet above the ground. "I have no objection to walking, but I know that long marches can be difficult for humans. Besides, it would be nice to have the company of someone local who knows the area. Otherwise we might miss the interior road altogether."

"And wouldn't that be a shame," Chaz commented sarcastically.

They did not regret the time spent wandering in search of a suitable inn, even though it took most of the rest of the afternoon and on into early evening. Culebra was a fascinating town, quite unlike anyplace else Will had been in Dinotopia. From the quaint tropical architecture to the easy-going island attitude of the inhabitants, it was almost like traveling to another country entirely. Except for the inescapable presence of the saurian portion of the population, of course.

Culebra's main streets boasted multi-story edifices of wood, many with covered porches that overhung the streets below. After the white and pink stucco of Kuskonak, the bright tropical colors in which the buildings had been painted verged on the blinding. They strolled past apartment buildings and homes, inns and shops, all drenched in every color of the rainbow. There was no apparent organization to the riotous tints. Everyone painted their building whatever color they liked. Purple, vermilion, carmine, sun-yellow and sea-blue as well as numerous shades of green predominated, but they also saw wooden walls decorated with stripes and flowers.

One ramshackle three-story structure with an upper-floor balustrade of intricately lathed wood was painted entirely in bright blue. An artist with more enthusiasm than talent had filled the open spaces with energetic depictions of the sea life that swarmed around the island, from lowly starfish to cavorting kronosaurs.

Exotic flowers bloomed from planters and pots set out on the innumerable porches, and sweet-smelling vines dangled almost to street level. A full complement of Dinotopian citizenry filled the streets and shops, but compared to Sauropolis or Waterfall City, their movements seemed to take place in slow motion. Whether it was the isolated lifestyle or the heavy, humid air Will could not have said, but Culebra was definitely a place where everything happened at half the usual speed or less. Hopefully it would not affect their ability to get to the other side of the island in an expeditious manner.

Avoiding an ambling *Tentontosaurus* loaded down with a load of rosewood and purpleheart logs for the sawmill, they found themselves in the central market. Here the singular attractions of Outer Island were at their peak, for nowhere else in Dinotopia had Will and Sylvia seen such a concentration of exotic fruits and vegetables. Sauropolis and Waterfall City boasted greater quantity, and Treetown more diversity, but here the stalls were filled with fruits he could not even name.

"What're those?" He pointed to a heap of large green globes covered with stubby spikes that looked anything but appetizing.

"Durians, I believe," Chaz informed him. "They have a, shall we say, pungent aroma, but taste very much like custard. And those red cactus-like fruit are rambutan."

"Look at the pineapples," Sylvia gushed as they strolled among the busy stalls, "and the bananas! There must be a dozen different kinds of bananas."

"Coconuts," Khorip pointed out. "Mangoes, papayas, jicama, starfruit, sugar cane, breadfruit: the people here may not have much culture, but they aren't lacking in entertaining things to eat."

"That's for sure," Will agreed. "I haven't seen any skinny sauropods."

Chaz cocked a querulous eye at his friend. "Have you *ever* seen a skinny sauropod?"

"Well, no, not exactly." He held to his observation. "But if there wasn't enough to eat, there *could* be one."

Chaz uttered an annoyed grunt.

Along with the bounty of sea and land, they saw simple art and handicrafts for sale. Most impressive of the latter was the assortment of rattan furniture, including a tree swing big enough to hold a medium-sized ceratopsian or duckbill. Rattan stepping-stools were thoughtfully included to allow saurian access to the swing.

Wherever they paused, they sought information about the prospect of transport to the east side of the island, and without exception their inquiries were met with polite demurrals. Yes, it was possible to find locals who made periodic trips to the Eastern Bight and northern shores. No, to the best of the respondents' knowledge, no one was going that way today. Or tomorrow, or the next day, or later that week.

"We may be here longer than we planned." Will bit into the tangerine he had just peeled, carefully depositing the peelings into a public waste receptacle as they walked past.

"We could always hike." Sylvia gazed longingly eastward, toward the high central mountains swathed in their perpetual layer of cloud. "I don't see how we could miss as prominent a feature as the only road leading into the interior."

"Well, I do." Chaz objected strenuously. "People 'missed' Ahmet-Padon for centuries. If an abandoned city can be overlooked, so can an abandoned road. I absolutely refuse to go without local guidance."

"Chaz is right this time, Sylvia." Will gave his fiancée's hand a gentle squeeze. "Besides, if we have to carry all our supplies, we'll be exhausted before we even reach this road. Plus, we'll use up half or more of our provisions just getting there. I'm sure we can find fruit and fish along the way, but that takes time, too."

"I know." She sighed resignedly. "It's just that having come so far, it's hard to stop and wait."

Chaz did his best to appear understanding. "Many times, stopping and waiting will get you someplace faster than hurrying up and running. That may sound like a contradiction, but I assure you it is not."

"Easy for you to say," she muttered back at him. "You're not the one in a hurry."

"Come on." Will indicated the stall where their prenocephalean companion was beckoning for them to join him. "Let's see what Khorip wants."

What Khorip wanted was to allay their concerns, for he had found a vegetable vendor who knew of an ankylosaurian friend who often participated in wild fruit gathering expeditions. To the best of the vendor's recollection, just such an expedition was due to leave Culebra for a circumnavigation of the island within a few days. If they made the proper inquiries, they might very well be able to make arrangements to tag along.

Despite the lateness of the hour, Sylvia insisted they track down the *Ankylosaurus* in question and follow up on the vendor's recommendation. The armored dinosaur was just settling in for the night in a barn peaked at both ends, arranging himself on a bed not of hay but of palm and cecropia leaves. Other saurians were fluffing similar bedding nearby. The typically enormous structure was large enough to house several dozen dinosaurs of assorted species and size. The potent, familiar odor of saurian musk was pervasive.

The *Ankylosaurus*, whose name was Grinedge, welcomed them with the slight islander accent that sometimes caused imprudent mainlanders to refer to the inhabitants of Outer Island as hicks. But the affable anky, as his kind were colloquially known, saw no reason why they should not attach themselves to his group of traveling gatherers.

"We're always up to hear the latest news from the big cities," he informed them via Chaz's translation as he settled himself down on his bed of aromatic leaves. "It will be good to have some out-island company to talk to as we go. Now, tell me again where it was you wanted to be dropped off?"

"At the beginning of the old road that leads from the bight into the central mountains," Sylvia instructed Chaz to inform their new friend.

The anky's spiked skull bobbed slightly as the *Protoceratops* translated his guttural words. "That's the middle of nowhere, for sure. In fact, I've often thought on the occasions I happened to pass there that there should be a roadsign pointing inland. 'Road to Middle of Nowhere.'" He turned to Will.

"I missed the regular evening scrubdown." Clearly, it amused Chaz to translate this. "They do a good job at this inn. Would you mind?"

"Not at all." Will had performed similar services for

many dinosaurs. Selecting a long handled, thick-bristled brush from a nearby wall rack, he started at the clubbed tail and began working his way up the ankylosaur's broad back, making sure to work the bristles well down into the grooves between the armored scutes.

"Ahhhh, that's delightful." Grinedge's eyes closed in pleasure. "Keep that up, and I'll carry you around the island myself."

"You're sure we'll be welcome?" As desperately as she wanted them to be on their way, Sylvia did not want to impose. Accommodating guests meant someone else would have to carry extra supplies.

But as Chaz told it, Grinedge was entirely reassuring. "As long as you don't run out of news and stories, the only problem you'll have with my lot is making a break from them. They won't want to let you go until they've milked you for every last bit of news and gossip."

"That's fine with us." Grinning, Will used the scrub brush to indicate Chaz and Khorip. "We have a couple of friends who love to talk."

"When do we leave?" an anxious Sylvia had the *Protoceratops* inquire.

Grinedge blinked sleepily. "Barring any last minute complications, the day after tomorrow. You can use the time to acclimate yourselves to the island's humidity. Much of the interior is like the Rainy Basin, only higher. Or so I'm told, having never been to that part of Dinotopia myself. I'm island born and bred, and I like it that way." Tucking his legs beneath him, he settled into a sleeping position. "Of course, humidity's not such a problem for my kind. We don't sweat."

"We do." Will pulled his shirt away from his body. Like

the rest of his clothes, it was soaked with perspiration from the day's activities. But as he worked the brush back and forth against the ankylosaur's armored neck, he found that he no longer minded the discomfort now that they had secured guidance and transportation for the next leg of their journey.

Sylvia rose from where she had been sitting cross-legged near the ankylosaur's head. "We can't thank you enough, Grinedge," she had Chaz tell him.

"Don't mention it. Glad to have the company. I take it you were planning on walking a portion of the abandoned interior road?"

She nodded vigorously. "All the way to the end, and beyond."

Sage saurian eyes blinked open as Chaz growled Sylvia's response. "You—you're not serious?"

"Quite serious," put in Khorip from behind Sylvia once the *Protoceratops* had translated.

Grinedge's gaze flicked from *Prenocephale* to primate. "You are, aren't you?" He settled back down, his head coming to rest on a small pile of leaves fluffed up for that very purpose. "Well, I'm not in charge of the expedition, so I'll leave it to someone better qualified than me to disabuse you of that notion. No one goes beyond the end of the interior road. No one. It's too dangerous."

Sylvia was not discouraged. "We know all about the 'impenetrable' rainforest and the unclimbable mountain ridges. We're prepared."

"No you're not," Grinedge countered sleepily as Chaz translated, "because those aren't the dangers I'm talking about."

With that he fell into a deep and motionless sleep. Chaz was all for waking him and keeping him awake until they could get a satisfactory explanation of his last comment, but Will and Sylvia argued against it.

"He's been very kind and it would be most impolite to keep nudging him awake," she pointed out.

"I know," the *Protoceratops* started to argue, "but he was about to tell us of . . ."

"Probably flash flooding of mountain streams, or trying to find our way without a marked trail to guide us." Khorip was not concerned. "We'll find out what he was talking about tomorrow, or the next day, or along the way." The *Prenocephale* rested a clawed forehand on the little translator's spine. "Not to fret, my prolix *Protoceratops*. All will be well."

"Well, as long as *you* guarantee it," Chaz groused tartly, "then I'm *sure* we have *nothing* to worry about."

# -XVIII-

he members of the gathering expedition assembled early on the southern edge of town. Will and his friends found themselves in the midst of practiced but not hurried activity as humans and dinosaurs worked to prepare themselves for an island-girdling journey that would take several weeks. As Grinedge explained while two men clad only in bright red and blue loincloths loaded supplies and gear onto his curved armored back, there were many valuable fruits and medicinal plants that grew exclusively in the wilds of Outer Island and could only be obtained by expeditions such as theirs.

"I guess I don't understand." Will stood nearby, trying to keep out of the way. "Why don't any people live nearer to the source of supply?"

"Because they would be isolated," the *Ankylosaurus* explained in response to Chaz's translation. "No one wants to live away out in the forest with no one else to talk to. Living here in Culebra is much more pleasant." When he shrugged, his armored scutes made a dry rustling noise, like children playing in a pile of autumn leaves. "Better to live here and gather fruit elsewhere than to live elsewhere and visit here."

"Makes sense to me," Chaz agreed after rendering the ankylosaur's guttural explanation into words his human companions could understand.

"But not to me." Eager to get moving, Khorip kept turning to gaze southward. "I treasure isolation from the rest of Dinotopian society!" A tactful Chaz forbore from translating this bit of nihilistic psychology for their host. It would in no wise benefit them for the ankylosaur to realize that one of his guests was mentally unbalanced.

Will and Sylvia were surprised at the degree and extent of the preparations. After all, the expedition's avowed purpose was only to gather food and medicines. Something else about the arrangements kept bothering him, but he was unable to put a finger on it until mid-morning, when they were about to get under way.

It was Sylvia who prompted him to give voice to his concerns. "Will Denison, what are you pondering so hard? You look like your head is about to burst."

"Hmmm? Oh, I was just wondering at the makeup of our group. Notice anything unusual?"

She took a moment to study the assembling host. Dinosaurs were lining up two by two, each with a suitable number of humans in attendance. Each of the big quadrupeds was fitted out with empty baskets and bins, drums and boxes for holding the results of their gathering. Humans rode in intricate seats of bamboo and coconut fiber strapped to broad backs and strong legs.

In addition to the empty containers waiting to be filled,

several members of the party carried enough supplies for the entire expedition. These consisted of less than one might have expected so large a group to require, but on the lush Outer Island there was no need to haul water, and a certain amount of food could be foraged from the shore and jungle along the way.

"I don't see anything out of the ordinary, Will. What's your point?"

He nodded at the double row of saurians that was lining up in front of them. "Haven't you noticed the expedition's makeup? There are no duckbills, no iguanodonts, no sauropods; only ceratopsians and ankylosaurs."

"So? What of it?"

"Every one of them is an armored dinosaur capable of defending itself against attack."

She started to laugh, then caught herself. After all, what did they really know about the little visited, less explored Outer Island? Or perhaps she was remembering Grinedge's final comment before he had dozed off during their meeting the previous night.

"Maybe we'd better ask some questions," she decided warily.

"That's just what I was thinking."

Expressing their concerns to Chaz and Khorip, they started looking for someone in a position of authority who was not overwhelmed by last minute work. They found her in the person of Shree Banda, a senior leader of the expedition. She smiled in greeting as they confronted her, a small diamond sparkling in her left nostril.

"Yes, my friends. A fine day to go a-gathering! But then, every day on Outer Island is a fine day, unless it is raining, in which case it is no worse than a damp fine day." When no one laughed with her, she turned serious. "Such somber faces! Is something the matter?"

Chaz nudged Will with his snout, urging him forward. "We were just wondering," Will murmured, "why all the dinosaurs in the group were either horned ceratopsians or club-tailed ankylosaurs."

"Yes," added Khorip. "It's just a coincidence, isn't it?"

"By no means," Banda replied readily. "There are specific reasons for the restricted makeup of our party."

"Hah, there, you see?" barked Chaz knowingly. "I knew this little quest was becoming too easy."

Sylvia's reaction was considerably less volatile. "Why is that, Madam Banda?"

"If the rare wild fruits and medicinal plants were easy to obtain, people would have picked them all by now. In point of fact, that is exactly what has happened to those important plants that grow by the side of the Outer Island loop road. Casual travelers cull them to consume on the spot, or to trade back here in Culebra. In order to justify a full-scale harvesting expedition like this, much more than easily accessible roadside produce must be procured. We have to go deep into the rainforest to find untouched trees and bushes.

"Not only is the forest unbelievably dense in the flatlands and foothills, but it is protected by many kinds of thorn bushes and vines, like the same type of cane our rattan baskets and platforms are fashioned from. Unshielded humans would be cut to shreds trying to reach the best trees, and nobody wants to wear heavy protective leathers in the jungle. The same would be true for duckbills and iguanodonts and ornithomimids and even stegosaurs. Thick-skinned sauropods would fare better, but there are thorns and prickles in the rainforest here that would penetrate even their hides and feet."

"So that's it." Sylvia gave Chaz an arch look, but the *Protoceratops* refused to concede so easily.

"I can see an ankylosaur bashing its way through thorn brush without suffering any ill effects, but the skin of my fellow ceratopsians is no thicker than that of a young apatosaur."

"Ah, but you have armored heads," Banda pointed out. "Once the ankylosaurs break a crude path into the forest, our triceratops and styracosaurs and torosaurs use their long horns to widen the path and clear the debris out of the way. An ankylosaur can push through anything, but cannot clear it away. Using its horns for levers, a ceratopsian can do that easily. We humans clean up behind them, removing the small but still dangerous pieces that are too awkward for a *Triceratops* to shift.

"In that way we all share in the bounty as well as the hard work. And hard work it is, my friends. Hard, hot, and sweaty. But the rewards are ample: all the rare, exotic fruit we can eat, medicines for our families, and plenty of both to trade in the Culebra market.

"If this is such a worthwhile activity, why are there not more teams like yours out doing it?" Chaz wanted to know.

Brushing back long black hair streaked with white, she smiled down at the inquisitive *Protoceratops*. "I just told you, translator. Because it is hard, hot, sweaty work. And of course there is the danger."

The travelers perked up immediately. "Danger?" Chaz

responded. "What danger? We were told the journey could be dangerous, but nothing specific was mentioned."

"Why, there is danger from the carnosaurs, of course." Banda looked from one to the other, from *Prenocephale* to human and back again. "No one has mentioned anything to you about this, have they?"

"No," Will admitted. "Nothing was said about there being uncivilized carnosaurs on Outer Island."

Banda was clearly upset. "You ought to have been informed before this. Apparently those who should have told you assumed you already knew, or that someone else had already mentioned it. What did you think all the dried fish we are carrying was for?"

Suffering as he was from a steadily ballooning sense of ignorance, Will felt it incumbent on him to reply. "Traveling supplies. I did wonder once or twice at the quantity."

"The fish is for tribute, to assure us safe passage. I understand a similar procedure is followed by the caravans that cross the Rainy Basin on the mainland." This time it was Sylvia who nodded assent.

"I am very sorry," Banda told them. "You really should have been told. Under the circumstances, if you would like to change your minds about traveling with us, I am sure everyone in the group would understand."

"Oh no, not at all," Sylvia responded before Chaz could so much as part his jaws. "What kind of carnosaurs?"

"Not great lumbering tyrannosaurs and allosaurs like you have on the mainland," Banda explained, "but though smaller, they are threatening enough in their way."

Will was nodding to himself. "Another reason for traveling in the company of ceratopsians and ankylosaurs."

"They do give those of us not naturally endowed with armor and weapons a certain degree of protection," Banda agreed. "The rainforest is home to nothing larger than an occasional *Ceratosaurus* or *Baryonx*. Most of the local primitive predators are dromaeasaurs."

Will was taken aback and made no attempt to hide his surprise. "But on the mainland dromaeasaurs are as civilized as the plant-eaters!"

Banda shook her head slowly. "Not here. With the mantle of civilization confined to Culebra and its immediate environs, and that arrived only recently in historical terms, the local dromaeasaurs and other small carnivores were never swept up in the great march of Dinotopian culture. They have remained primitive meat-eaters.

"I have seen paintings and drawings of the great caravan groups that cross the Rainy Basin. Brachiosaurs and apatosaurs clad in elaborate suits of armor, with plated ceratopsians guarding their flanks. If I were walking through tyrannosaur country I would want that kind of protection, too. Here, a determined triceratops and an ankylosaur or two are enough to discourage most attacks."

"Most attacks." Chaz seized on the equivocal nature of their hostess's summation. "What exactly do you mean by 'most attacks'?"

She smiled seriously. "Hostilities of any kind are quite rare. Knowledgeable gathering expeditions always carry plenty of fish with which to barter for safe passage, and unknowledgeable expeditions never seem to travel very far. You have no need to worry."

"I don't need any need," Chaz replied darkly. "I can manufacture sufficient reasons for worrying all by myself."

"I don't care about the larger carnivores," Will told her, "but I almost hope we encounter some of these primitive dromaeasaurs. My father and his friends would find a first-hand account of them fascinating. Particularly a head librarian named Enit."

"We will see," she told him noncommittally. "I can hardly make any promises. Personally, I would just as soon that we do not. Not because they are any special cause for concern, but because such confrontations waste time and use up fish better suited to our own dinner tables." Turning, she gestured toward the double line of saurians. The formation, Will saw, was nearly complete.

"Since you have already made a friend among us, I've made arrangements for you to travel in his company. He was asked, and is agreeable. Go settle yourselves, and do not worry so much. I have personally made several dozen circumnavigations of Outer Island and have hardly ever had any real trouble."

"Hardly ever," Chaz piped up. "What precisely do you mean by 'hardly ever'?" But Shree Banda had turned on her heel and started off in the direction of a massive *Torosaurus* that was having trouble balancing its load on its back.

Deprived of the focus of his queries, Chaz shifted his complaining to his friends as they walked toward the indicated *Ankylosaurus*. "What do you think she meant by 'hardly ever'?"

"Put a cantaloupe in it, Chaz," an exasperated Will instructed his four-footed friend. As they approached the head of the line, he put up a hand in greeting. "Hello, Grinedge."

The ankylosaur did not understand human speech, but

the nature of Will's greeting and the expression he and Sylvia wore were easily interpreted. The armored dinosaur raised his left foot and extended it forward. Will's open palm flattened against it, his splayed fingers failing to reach the edges of the horny footpad.

"Oh well; breathe deep and seek peace, anyway," a gloomy Chaz instructed the *Ankylosaurus* in its own guttural tribal tongue.

Grinedge replied in kind. Squatting down, he invited the two humans to climb up onto his back. This they did, using one of the ankylosaur's knees as a step-up. The rattan and bamboo platform, seats, and protective railing mounted there were wholly in keeping with the tropical surroundings. With a back sixteen feet across at its widest point, Grinedge offered plenty of room in which passengers could move around. Once his new friends were safely aboard, the ankylosaur warned them to hang on as he straightened his short, powerful legs and rose once more to a standing position.

Will noted that they would be riding far closer to the ground than they would have been on the back of a sauropod, or even a large ceratopsian. This, coupled with Shree Banda's description of the "smaller" carnosaurs that inhabited the wilds of Outer Island, left him feeling less than completely secure.

No such apprehensions appeared to afflict the human or saurian members of the harvesting team. A few last-minute supplies were loaded, final adjustments made to harnesses and tack, and then the lead dinosaur, a weathered old *Styracosaurus* with several decorative pennants flying from the horns that lined his frill, let loose with a series of rumbling hoots.

Will grabbed for Sylvia as Grinedge started forward, causing the platform strapped to his back to lurch sharply. Neither of them had ever ridden an ankylosaur before, and because of their host's short legs, the motion was smoother than that of a stegosaur or sauropod. Once Grinedge was in full stride, modest as that was, there was very little in the way of a rocking sensation to disturb them. Will quickly discovered that he could stand up on the bamboo platform and walk around without having to hang onto anything to maintain his balance.

Chaz and Khorip ambled alongside, within easy hailing distance. Since they did not have to match sauropodian strides, they found it a simple matter to keep up with the rest of the troop. It was apparent that no one was in any hurry. The very word seemed the antithesis of everything Culebrian.

Shaded by several bamboo parasols affixed to the corners of the riding platform, Will and Sylvia allowed themselves to relax. A pair of triceratops led the way. Instead of empty bins and drums to be filled, they carried only a human apiece. These human-ceratopsian teams acted as scouts for the rest of the troop, scanning the rainforest for the fruits and plants they had come in search of. They also kept a sharp eye out for the potentially hostile, uncivilized country folk who dwelled in the emerald depths.

Culebra soon fell behind, the last of its colorful buildings swallowed up by an ocean of green. The road narrowed rapidly, becoming little more than a trail through the forest. Bleached a stark, sterile white by the sun, a paving of crushed coral prevented the surrounding verdure from reclaiming the road, as well as providing good footing for travelers.

The forest was frenetic with bird life, many species of which were new to the mainlanders. From their gently swaying perch atop Grinedge's back, Will and Sylvia had an excellent view into the trees. Khorip could see clearly as well, while Chaz was reduced to his usual grumbling about what little could be seen by someone afflicted with a perspective that was only a foot or so off the ground. His sympathetic companions did their best to share their discoveries with him.

Several kinds of birds-of-paradise in full mating plumage soared among the treetops, the males distinguishing themselves with astonishing calls and feather displays from perches on their favorite exhibition branches. Will and Sylvia had to ask Grinedge, via Chaz, for the Dinotopian names of each remarkable avis. They were especially taken by one bluish specimen that boasted a pair of long feathers that extended back from its head to three times the length of its body. Another showed even longer feathers emerging from its tail, while a third displayed a halo of yellow-gold froth as it pranced and tootled madly on an exposed branch in hopes of attracting a female.

Nor were the trees the only source of avian astonishment. As they turned a corner in the road, the troop startled a covey of massive *Aepyornis*. Ten feet tall, flightless, each weighing half a ton, they went pounding off into the forest depths nervously fluffing rust-colored plumage that was more like hair than feathers. Alert yellow eyes darted in all directions, trying to keep track of the plodding dinosaurs and their human companions.

They passed grazing dinornis, taller even than their aepyornis cousins but not as heavy, and a bevy of smaller flightless birds. Together these ruled the forest floor, far larger and more dominant than the small mammals that scurried out from beneath their feet. Actively hunting the small rodents and marsupials were a pair of massively built *Harpagornis* eagles, their distinctive black-on-white wing and body patterning a design that Will and Sylvia both recognized instantly. They were grateful that not all the life on Outer Island was exotic and alien.

At the southern tip of the island the hilly, forested landscape they had been passing through degenerated into a steamy Cambrian swamp, forcing the expedition to pick its way carefully along a roadbed that in many places had been overwhelmed by bog and stream. Huge amphibians like *Eryops* and *Greererpeton* lay just beneath the surface, waiting for unsuspecting smaller salamanders and frogs to swim or hop into their path. Peering over Grinedge's side, Will was grateful for his safe location atop the ankylosaur's broad armored back. Not even a hungry fifteen-foot long carnivorous amphibian like *Eogyrinus* would dare to challenge such formidable visitors.

Their position did not render them completely immune to assault from the swampy surroundings, however. Will was watching a school of yard-long diplocalus scuttle away from Chaz's feet, their bizarre boomerang-shaped heads twitching from side to side as they flailed frantically at the water, when he heard Sylvia scream.

Whirling, he sought the source of her distress, only to find her standing on top of one of the rattan chairs attached to the bamboo riding platform.

"Get it off, make it go away!"

Looking around, he saw nothing. But he remained wary. He had never known Sylvia to be afraid of anything. "Make what go away? I don't see anything."

"That!" She thrust a shaky finger at something unseen near the base of her chair.

Lowering his gaze, Will finally saw something scuttling about near the chair legs. He'd missed it at first because it was almost the exact same color as the honey-hued rattan and bamboo. Identifying it, he relaxed.

Grinedge growled a query and Chaz translated, barking up at Will. "Our friend wants to know what's going on up there."

"Nothing," Will assured the curious *Protoceratops*. "Tell him everything's under control."

"Like heck it is!" Maintaining a precarious balance while standing on the seat of the swaying chair, Sylvia gestured furiously at the intruder that was nosing around its rattan feet. Sylvia could whoop exuberantly while dangling upside down from the harness of a skybax doing loops at two thousand feet, but this had her frantic. "Will Denison, you get rid of that thing right now!"

"It's only a bug." Slowly, he advanced on the chitonous trespasser. Bending over with both hands outstretched, he attempted to shoo it over the side. It must have come aboard by tumbling onto the *Ankylosaurus*'s back as they'd passed beneath an overhanging branch.

"It's a cockroach!" She shuddered visibly. "I can't stand cockroaches, Will. You know that."

"I guess everybody can't stand something." As he chased the evasive insect back and forth across the bamboo platform, he decided she was making an awful fuss over one solitary bug. After all, she ate them fried or broiled on a regular basis. Just because it happened to be a roach.

Of course, it was a Cambrian cockroach, nearly two feet long, but he knew that mere size did not change its nature. It was perfectly harmless.

After a good deal of darting too and fro, he finally managed to chase the roach over Grinedge's left flank, watching as it fell to the moist ground and scurried away into the underbrush. Then he turned back to his fiancée.

"All right, Sylvia. It's 'safe' now. You can come down."

Cautiously, she stepped off the chair and back onto the platform. Refusing to rely on his word, she checked beneath the chair and in the surrounding rattan and bamboo. Only when she was completely satisfied did she resume her seat. When he offered her a drink from a waterbag, she sipped gratefully.

"I'm sorry." She passed the heavy bag back. "But I just can't stand those things. They make my skin crawl."

"Other insects don't. Why just cockroaches?"

"I don't know. I'm a skybax rider, not a mental health therapist. It's just something inside me." She shuddered slightly. "I think it must be the way they move."

Feeling a bit abashed at the lack of empathy he had shown, he sat down and put his arm around her. "Don't let it bother you, Sylvia. We all have something hidden inside us that we're afraid to let out." As he spoke, something large and iridescent flashed in front of his eyes. He twitched involuntarily as it landed on the front railing and remained perched there for them to admire.

There was much to ooh and aah at. The giant dragonfly had a wingspan of more than four feet. Its tapered, aerodynamic body glistened like a branch of polished black coral striped with crimson. The wings were sheets of purest gossamer shot through with iridescent purple and gold. It rested on the railing for several minutes, methodically exercising its incredible wings, before lifting off and disappearing across a shallow, torpid lake.

"What if a cockroach had wings like that, instead of dull brown ones?" Will asked Sylvia.

"It wouldn't matter. A cockroach is still a cockroach, no matter how you dress it up." She made a face. "Especially when they get as long as your arm."

As they journeyed eastward along the southern part of the island the land gradually changed back from swamp to lowland rainforest. The birds returned in all their feathered glory, and the first wild fruit trees began to appear among the cecropias and cycads. Will and Sylvia lent their limber primate fingers to the harvesting, assisting their hosts in picking only the best of the available bounty before moving on.

Bins and empty drums began to fill with fruit, nuts, and medicine plants as the expedition turned northward. The east coast of Outer Island was very different from the sheltered west. Since its shore was exposed to the open ocean, the travelers could see huge breakers smashing themselves on the fringing coral reef. Several kinds of dolphins surfed in the swells, and whale sharks cruised the outer drop-off in search of the zooplankton that fed on the coral bloom this time of year. The world's largest fish, the mature males and females were too big even for a mosasaur to tackle.

Only when they began to approach the center of the eastern bight did the visitors from the mainland find themselves anxiously examining the forest depths with renewed excitement. According to what they had been told in Culebra, Will knew that they must be getting close to the abandoned inland road. They would follow that road up into the high central mountains of the interior, where if the wonderful water map of Ahmet-Padon was to be believed, an ancient temple of unknown origins and purpose awaited them.

Or, he thought, they would wander around until they became fatigued, hungry, and bored, whereupon they would make their way back down to the coast road and wait for the next passing caravan to take them back to civilized Culebra. If the cynical Chaz was to be believed, that was the more likely scenario. Finding a map was one thing, the *Protoceratops* had been insisting continuously ever since they had made their way out of the Great Desert. Making a major archeological find where none was suspected to exist was something else entirely.

But skeptical as Will was, it was hard not to be caught up in Sylvia and Khorip's boundless enthusiasm. He found himself wishing that he had seen some of the old library texts they claimed to have accessed.

None of them knew quite what to look for: a narrow trail opening onto the road from the forest, a stone cairn marking the route, perhaps deep blaze marks on flanking trees. He certainly did not expect a wide, orderly offshoot of the main coastal thoroughfare itself.

But there it was: partly overgrown to be sure, but unmistakable in its artificiality and direction. Paved with crushed white coral just like its far more heavily traveled island-girdling cousin, the abandoned interior road boldly shouldered its way due west in the direction of the cloud-shrouded central mountains.

With a sizable grove of wild orange trees growing near the old road junction as well as isolated patches of a certain vine whose sap, when distilled and treated with heat, made an excellent poultice for treating burns, it was not necessary for Will and his friends to ask the expedition to make an extra stop. While ankylosaurs bulled their way into the dense vegetation and ceratopsians followed behind to make a path for their more vulnerable human colleagues, a worried Shree Banda and concerned Grinedge did their best to dissuade their new-found friends from attempting to penetrate the interior.

"There's nothing to be found in there anyway," Banda kept insisting. "Why risk that kind of danger and isolation for nothing?"

"We don't think it is for nothing," Khorip told her.

"And the rest of you believe similarly?"

Will returned her gaze stolidly while Sylvia nodded with enthusiasm. Behind them, Chaz contented himself with pawing at the ground and muttering under his breath.

"If you run into trouble, no one will find you. No one will come looking for you." The team leader eyed each of them in turn. "This isn't Pooktook, you know."

"We're prepared." Sylvia exuded confidence. "We've trodden far more difficult paths and come through without problems."

As a moody Chaz translated for Grinedge, the bulky ankylosaur sighed like a steam engine. "There's no place in Dinotopia like the high mountains of Outer Island. Sure, the Rainy Basin is dangerous. But at least it's flat. But you'll find out." He shook his heavily armored head. "At least you're not striking off blindly into the rainforest. You have the old road to guide you back out."

"Grinedge is right," Banda told them. "Just try not to

317

stray too far from it or you'll surely get lost." Indicating the hidden, cloud-swathed peaks, she added, "I hope you don't mind being wet all the time."

"Surely not all the time," Will murmured.

"Probably not—but after a day or two of morning, afternoon, and evening rain you'll feel like it's all the time." A bellow from a *Torosaurus* exiting the forest with several humans in tow caused her to turn. When she looked back at them her expression was set.

"You are good people. I'd hate to see anything happen to you."

"So would I," muttered Chaz under his breath.

"But I can see that your minds are made up. All we can do then is wish you safe traveling and good fortune." So saying she stepped forward and in the fashion of her family, bussed each of them fondly on both cheeks. Or in the case of Chaz, on his upper frill.

Grinedge added a doleful hoot and several times rapped the ground firmly with the club at the end of his tail, underlying Banda's parting words with melancholy saurian timpani. As word of the visitors' planned departure spread along the length of the caravan, several other humans and dinosaurs approached to offer their good wishes and encouragement.

When the last palm-press had been proffered, the final words of wisdom extended, the gathering expedition reformed their double line and resumed their northward trek, paralleling the sandy, tree-lined shore of the Eastern Bight. Will and his friends watched until the harvesters were out of sight; ceratopsian humps, ankylosaurian scutes, and human headgear alike swallowed up by the enveloping rainforest.

Then they were alone on the deserted coral-coated road.

To their left, the unfinished cross-island track beckoned. Small streams coursed on both sides, framing the crushed coral pavement. Chaz's backpack was stuffed with supplies and they were all healthy and intact. There was no reason to hesitate. Sylvia did not, heading inland without a word. Will hurried to catch up to her while Khorip and Chaz brought up the rear.

Ahead loomed unseen mountains, enshrouding mist and fog, unknown dangers, the source of an ancient, half-forgotten legend, and more adventure.

As the road became steep and slippery, Will found himself ready to trade all of it for a nice apple pie.

# -XIX-

mpressively, the abandoned concourse ran straight and wide up into the foothills and then into the mountains themselves, never varying in its width or intention. But as it climbed steadily higher, years of unrelenting erosion began to take their toll. Constant, pounding rain had sliced the once-smooth surface into rivulets and gullies, washing away the bright white coral paving to reveal the dark volcanic rock and soil beneath. Trees long unpruned overhung the open swath of the roadbed to catch the additional sunlight thus proffered, while bushes and forest grasses gnawed at its edges, turning the border ragged and uneven.

Like a battered boxer, the road continued to hold its ground even as the forest and the elements chipped away at its uniformity. Will knew that eventually, despite the best early efforts of Dinotopian engineers and builders, the vegetation would reclaim the forsaken project completely. In such matters civilization had intelligence and expertise on its side, but the forest had Time.

It took them days to reach the end of the road. When they finally came to the terminus, there was no mistaking it. A solid wall of green blocked their path. Close inspection of the soil at the edge showed no chunks of coral gravel among the roots. The rainforest here had not reclaimed a portion of the road. This was where its original builders had surrendered to nature and topography and all construction had ceased.

They were standing on a steep slope, the stream-etched road a wide white ribbon unfurled behind them, dense forest pressing close on all sides. For hours they had been enveloped by mist, warm and damp. Looking higher, it was impossible to judge the state of the terrain ahead. Fifty feet on they might run into a sheer rock wall, a steep gorge, or a volcanic pit. The only way to find out was to go there.

"What now?" Chaz had his head twisted back to study the underside of his rear right foot. The thick pad was caked with mud. As he waited for a reply he scraped it back and forth against the coral gravel, trying to remove as much of the accumulated muck as possible.

Sylvia and Khorip caucused. "If we remember the map correctly," she told him, "we need to keep moving inland until we hit a plateau near the top of this ridge. From there we can either go north or south to find the temple. The map wasn't exact, and of course this road wasn't on it. It's a much more recent construction."

Chaz shook water from his face. Rain had a disconcerting tendency to run down his neck frill and into his eyes. "That takes in a lot of territory. It would be hard enough to cover this kind of ground in *good* weather." He gestured with a forefoot. "We could pass within one *Diplodocus* length of a whole temple complex and walk right by it without seeing anything."

"Once we get to the top we'll spread out," she told him. "Always keeping each other in sight, but walking abreast. That way we'll cover a lot more ground." She nodded up into the mist. "We'll find the temple."

"If there *is* a temple to find," the tired *Protoceratops* reminded her.

"We've come this far." Though he did not feel as strongly as Sylvia about their prospects, Will felt compelled to support her. "It would be a shame to turn back now, without at least attempting the last leg."

"That is what worries me," the translator responded. "That I am on my last leg."

"What are you complaining about?" Sylvia shot back. "At least you have four of them." So saying, she chose a likely-looking gap in the trees off to the left and started upward. Will and Khorip went with her. Chaz lingered a moment longer, more to make a statement than out of any intention of remaining behind, before trotting off in their wake.

It was hard going in the forest, but not impossible. As soon as they got a little ways away from the road, the canopy created by rainforest trees reduced the amount of sunlight reaching the forest floor, thereby curtailing the number of smaller growths. The decrease in density supplied room for the travelers to pick a path upward.

Walking within the forest also proved drier than hiking up the open road, since the roof of thick leaves caught much of the falling rain. While the grade inclined steadily upwards, it never grew insurmountable. Sustaining the ascent became more a matter of endurance than skill.

Exhausted, they stopped for the night beneath a cluster of elephant-ear philodendrons that provided decent shelter from the nightly downpour. Without a dry stick of tinder to be found, they were unable to make a fire and had to content themselves with a cold supper. This was more of an inconvenience than a real predicament, since their supplies included only dried food or fresh fruit, and the temperature on the mountainside varied only slightly with the coming of night. Still, Will found himself wishing he could be as dry as the fish he and Sylvia were forced to masticate for their main course.

Sunset brought with it blackness of Stygian proportions, made worse by the lack of a fire and the lugubrious mist that congealed silently around them. Will and Sylvia huddled close together beneath a brace of overlapping leaves the color of deep ocean while Khorip settled down on his haunches nearby. Instead of the tick of a clock or the flutter of a fan, they were forced to rely on Chaz's ceaseless muttering to lull them to sleep.

"Just a couple of days, Will. That's all Khorip and I are asking for. If we haven't found the temple by then, or at least some definite clue that it exists, we'll start back down. I want to prove that this Hand of Dinotopia is real, but I'm not going to be obsessive about it to the point of foolhardiness."

"You're not?" Lying on the damp ground, he turned to face her. "I thought we'd passed that point a long time ago." To show her that he meant no harm, he grinned.

She fisted him in the shoulder, but gently. "You really

don't believe there's anything to it, do you? You still think it's an old maiasaur's tale."

"I don't know, Sylvia. I honestly don't know. But whether it is or isn't is not what's important to me. What matters is that we're together."

She snuggled as close as circumstances allowed. "You're quite a find, Will Denison. Even if you are a Newcomer who speaks in theatrical clichés at moments of high emotional confrontation."

"Hey, at least I try," he argued. "Believe me, I'd much rather say that I wish we were together on the beach at Cape Turtletail than here."

She hit him again, but it was much more of a caress than a blow.

The dissonant yet alluring screech of male arabis soliciting potential mates woke him from a deep sleep. The rain had stopped and the sun, intermittently visible through slits in the canopy, was out. Steam rose from leaves and branches, trunks and vines, as much of the nightly shower was sucked back up into the sky.

Glancing to his left, he saw that Sylvia was still asleep, her right cheek resting on her hands, her head curled child-like against his shoulder. Turning to his right, he found himself considering the heavy green-black leaves that had shielded them from the nocturnal deluge, some spiky palm bushes, clusters of pink and purple-lipped orchids, a single-file line of leaf-cutter ants toting their trimmings over their heads like miniature lime-colored bumbershoots, and the sharp-toothed countenance of a curious *Deinonychus* staring back at him with an intensity he had only rarely encountered before, and then only in the Rainy Basin.

He sat up fast.

Awkwardly jostled awake, Sylvia stirred next to him. "Will? What's going on?"

He spoke without taking his eyes from their soundless visitant. Near at hand he had not a club, not a rock, nothing but the vestiges of the previous night's meal. If the lithe, powerful *Deinonychus* chose to rush them, he doubted its attack could be beaten back with a handful of greasy cod bones.

"Wake up, Sylvia." He raised his voice deliberately. "Wake up, everyone! Chaz, Khorip—we have company."

In response, the *Protoceratops* rose from his belly onto all fours, and the *Prenocephale* straightened on his hind legs. Their reaction when they saw the visitor was the same as Will's: silence coupled with wary apprehension.

Still the *Deinonychus* did not speak. Resting on its haunches, it squatted close to Will and Sylvia. Both forearms hung down between its front legs, the fingers that terminated in curving razor-sharp talons untrimmed and openly visible, as were the claws on its feet and the great sickle-like killing spur at the back of the ankle. Much to Will's discomfort, this matchless weapon kept flicking repeatedly up and down as edgily as a switchblade.

A long spear trimmed with feathers rested in the crook of one bent elbow while a small pack fashioned from some woven fiber rode on the man-sized carnivorous dinosaur's sinewy back. A smaller pack drooped loosely from a waistband. Most remarkable was the paint, made from vegetable dyes, that streaked its face and upper body. The patterns were as unrecognizable to Will as they were to Sylvia and Chaz.

As he recalled books and magazines that he'd read avidly as a boy back in Boston, Will found the sight putting him in mind of something other than Dinotopian civilization. Something he had encountered often in those cheap novels and penny dreadfuls. Something that, as far as he knew, was unknown in and alien to the culture of Dinotopia.

War paint.

It was a very reluctant Chaz who stepped forward to initiate communication. "Breathe deep, seek peace," he ventured hesitantly in the tongue of the dromaeasauran tribe to which the *Deinonychus* belonged. There was no response on the part of their visitor. An ominous sign, as the translator hardly needed to point out.

Unable to stand the silence, he continued. "We come as friends, seeking enlightenment." With his beak, the *Protoceratops* gestured back the way they had come. "We are alone, and unequipped for hostilities." There was nothing to be lost by pointing that out, the uneasy *Protoceratops* believed, since the *Deinonychus* could see it clearly for himself.

This, at least, elicited a response. Rising to its full height, their visitor turned and hissed loudly into the forest. Instantly, a dozen similarly equipped and painted members of the same tribe appeared, their face and body paint whorls and slashes of color amid the green. Not all of them carried spears. A few hefted stone axes whose extremely functional appearance was no more reassuring.

In addition, most of them wore headbands that were not only decorated with geometric patterns, but boasted plumes and feathers taken from the most colorful of the rainforest birds. No one had to draw a picture for the travelers to explain the fate of the missing birds. The sickle-clawed *Deinonychus* was a superb natural predator. On the mainland, they had long since grown civilized enough to merge their primitive nature and instincts with the incomparable greater Dinotopian culture.

If appearances were to be believed, it seemed that here those edifying effects were absent. Unlike the larger carnosaurs such as *T. Rex* and *Allosaurus*, *Deinonychus* had always been a pack hunter. In the green depths of Outer Island, that archaic social structure had apparently given rise to a well-developed tribal culture.

The question of most immediate concern was, in what ways might that circumscribe or not circumscribe their diet? This was a matter of some pressing personal concern to Will and his companions.

The headdressless individual who had silently observed Will's return to wakefulness conversed briefly and in terse phrases with several of his comrades. The unsophisticated nature of their speech was difficult for Chaz to get a handle on and so for the present, at least, their intentions remained ambiguous. Disturbingly, none of them lowered a spear or ax.

Finally, the speaker stepped forward to confront Chaz. Will tensed, and Sylvia clutched hard at his arm, but the spearpoint remained aimed at the sky, the terrible claws retracted. The little ceratopsian held his ground. He might as well, Will mused, because they were effectively surrounded with nowhere to run.

Again the *Deinonychus* spoke, this time slowly and carefully. Chaz listened, hazarded a reply, and then remembered to translate for his friends.

"He says that he is Korut, son of Enots. The chief, or leader, of this tribe."

Will nodded knowingly. Enots was a sensible *Deinony-chian* family name. Enit, the head librarian at Waterfall City, was also a *Deinonychus*. Will wondered what that ultra-civilized, sophisticated dromaeasaur would make of this barbaric cousin, running about in the rainforest in feathers and paint.

"What else does he say?" Sylvia whispered.

"That we are trespassers on their hunting grounds, and therefore in violation of their laws." A noticeable quaver had crept into Chaz's voice.

If there was one thing Will had learned from his skybax training, it was never to hesitate when confronted with a difficult situation. "Tell Korut that we didn't know these were their hunting grounds, and that therefore we could not know of their laws. Tell him also that we are not hunters, but gatherers, and that we take nothing from their land that they themselves might use."

"I do not know how he will respond," Chaz replied plaintively. "This is not like debating in the public hall at Sauropolis."

"Try it," Will urged his friend. "What else can we do?"

Nodding, Chaz turned back to the chief. It was hard to keep his gaze fixed on the *Deinonychus's* face instead of those multiple talons, but the translator managed admirably.

Korut listened attentively, was silent for a moment, and then responded.

"He says," a relieved Chaz informed his companions, "that while ignorance of the laws is not an excuse, they can see that we are ill-prepared to be traveling in these mountains, and that we are therefore more to be pitied than confronted."

"Something to be thankful for." Like his companions, Khorip was more than willing to embrace the implied affront. "I'm happy to appear as helpless as they think we are."

"Think, nothing," Will responded. "We *are* helpless."

Korut was talking again, and once more Chaz took his time to make sure the translation was absolutely correct.

"They want to know what we are doing here. They are not the only ones. At the moment, I am asking myself the same question."

Sylvia stepped forward to stand alongside the apprehensive *Protoceratops*. As she spoke, she stroked his back with a soothing motion of her right hand. It helped to calm him, but only a little.

"Tell them the truth. That we are looking for ruins of an ancient monument or temple called the Hand of Dinotopia."

"I will try." Chaz did his best to convey the information to Korut and his fellow tribals.

The leader of the deinonychids listened attentively. When the *Protoceratops* was through, the chief turned to those nearest him and began to converse in low tones. Not a whisper so much as a carefully modulated growl, it made the hairs on the back of Will's neck crawl. In eons past that same guttural rumbling would not have contained intelligible words; only the raw passion of superbly designed saurian assassins preparing for the kill. Uncultured Korut and his people might be, but they were not complete throwbacks.

No indeed. These days they probably chose to debate the

possible ramifications before making a meal of their intended victims.

Korut evinced no such intentions when he finally turned back to Chaz and resumed talking. This time it was the *Protoceratops* who listened closely. Occasionally he would pause to ask for clarification of this or that barbarous phrase. Instead of growing impatient or losing his temper, the *Deinonychus* appeared to regard the translator's lack of ready comprehension as further evidence of the trespassers' inescapable feeble-mindedness.

But when the dialogue ended, Chaz turned to his companions with more than a hint of cautious optimism in his voice.

"Chief Korut says that they are not going to eat us."

"Well, that's encouraging," Will proclaimed dryly. "Just out of curiosity, why not?"

"He says it is because they do not eat stupid people."

Khorip stood a little straighter on his hind legs. "We are not stupid."

The *Protoceratops* favored the taller *Prenocephale* with a jaundiced eye. "Oh no? We are here, aren't we?" Turning back to Will and Sylvia, he continued. "I explained about our desire to find unvisited ruins and what do you know? He claims that he can help us!"

Sylvia eyed the noble *Deinonychus* expectantly. For his part, Korut gazed back phlegmatically. "They know where the Hand of Dinotopia is?"

"Not so fast," the translator cautioned her. "He says that they know where there are extensive ruins and structures. He and his people have known of them for as long as the oldest among them can remember. But they do not know who built them, or when, or why. They do not go there often. Not because they are afraid of the place, or because some ancient tribal taboo was laid upon it, but simply because the hunting there is bad."

"And they're willing to take us?" Smelling a catch, Will was reluctant to share his fiancée's excitement.

"Korut says that they are. Furthermore, he says that the surrounding country is difficult, and that there is only one way in that an inexperienced human or a four-leg like myself might manage. He insists that without the aid of his people we would never find it by ourselves."

"I can believe that," admitted Sylvia. "If the place was easily accessible, others would have found it by now."

Khorip concurred. "Itinerant fruit gatherers like our friends Grinedge and Shree Banda would have been all over such a place by this time. That only confirms how well hidden it is."

"Is, and has been." After a thoughtful pause, she pressed Chaz further. "Well, don't just stand there. Tell him we're ready to go."

"That is just the problem." The *Protoceratops* squinted up at her out of small round eyes. "Korut says that he and his people will guide us to the place—but for a price."

Will was taken aback. What did the *Deinonychus* have in mind? Money as he knew of it from his childhood in America was unknown in Dinotopia, having long ago been replaced by an elaborate and venerated system of barter. What could they possibly have that the ferocious-looking carnivores might want? Surely their stock of supplies was too small to interest the dozen or so carnosaurs, who could take it by force any time they wished. Baffled but curious, he put the question to Chaz.

"Fish," the *Protoceratops* explained.

The explanation was brief, but at least it made sense. Carnosaurs of every shape, size, and species had an insatiable craving for the fruits of the sea. Yet except for the occasional long-jawed *Baryonx*, they were ill-equipped to harvest the bounty that thrived in Dinotopian waters. Therapods in particular were designed to stalk and kill land-dwelling prey, a tactic that had with time and the acquisition of intelligence fallen out of favor among even the mainland carnivores. They all preferred the tribute and gifts of fish and shellfish that were handed out by passing caravans. To tide them over between visits, they scavenged the prodigious carcasses of the deceased.

Here on Outer Island there were far fewer noble dinosaurian corpses upon which to feast, and in the mountain hinterlands, none at all. To keep their unique tribal culture intact, these aboriginal dromaeasaurs had been forced to rely on the capture of birds and small mammals when unable extort a levy of fish from one of the infrequent passing fruit-gathering expeditions.

Once again Will was made mindful of their limited provisions. "I think we have only a couple of the dried fillets that Shree Banda supplied us with left, but they're welcome to them if that will convince them to lead us to the ruins."

Chaz shook his head. "It doesn't matter. That won't do. They want *fresh* fish."

"Fresh!" Will exclaimed. "What do they expect us to do? Drop everything and go fishing?"

The *Protoceratops* nodded slowly. "Precisely."

"It's absurd." Khorip protested vehemently. "It would

take us days, weeks even, to catch enough fish to satisfy the whole tribe. Even if we had the use of multiple hooks and lines, which we do not."

"Maybe we don't need hooks and lines."

Everyone turned to Sylvia. "What are you talking about?" Khorip looked as puzzled as he sounded.

She addressed her companions confidently. "When I was in school, one of our field expeditions was to the upper Polongo delta to go net fishing."

Will's expression softened. "I thought net fishing was done from boats."

"Not all of it," she explained. "There's an old procedure that can be used without boats, provided the water is shallow enough." She gestured back the way they had come. "It looked to me like there were plenty of suitable shallows in the inshore Eastern Bight. The technique is taught by Dinotopians whose shipwrecked ancestors came here from a place called Polynesia."

"That's swell," avowed Will, "but we don't happen to be carrying any nets with us."

"We'll make them." She spoke without hesitation. "There are plenty of suitable vines and creepers around. Look at those back and waist packs and headbands they're wearing. It's clear that Korut and his people are experienced weavers." She leaned over Chaz. "Go on; ask them if they're willing to try and make fishing nets, if I show them how."

Chaz conveyed the suggestion to the *Deinonychus*, who for the first time since Will had awakened showed something akin to real enthusiasm. A brisk babble sprang up among the tribesfolk as they considered the proposal.

As usual, it was left to their chief to reply for all. Will and

Sylvia waited anxiously for his response.

"Korut says that he and his people are willing. If you would demonstrate to them how to catch more than one fish at a time, they will not only show us the way to the ruins: they will be eternally in our debt."

"A few days worth of their indebtedness is all we need," Sylvia responded. "We'll need some larger vines for the heavy parts of the net. I wonder if those spears are sharp enough to cut through the bigger lianas?"

Chaz put the question to Korut, who by way of reply let out a disdainful snort, turned, and leaped six feet into the air. Taking aim at a nearby sapling, he slashed out with his right leg. By the time he hit the ground, the severed trunk was already toppling over on its side.

"I guess that answers that question." As were his companions, Will was suitably impressed by the impromptu demonstration of inherent deinonychian cleaving abilities.

Sylvia rubbed her hands together. She was full of energy and assurance, neither of which Will or Chaz shared. But she always seemed to know what she was doing, and he saw no reason to doubt her now. If she claimed she could teach a mob of unenlightened dromaeasaurs how to fish, then teach them she could.

He was more than a little curious to see how.

# -XX-

aving been joined by the immature juveniles and pregnant females who had been waiting in the forest, the tribe of skeptical but eager deinonychids now numbered more than twenty-five. As they descended back down the abandoned road toward the coast, Will found that he had to put up with the attentions of a pair of animated youngsters who had taken something of a fancy to him. They ran around and through his legs, occasionally getting tangled up in his pants or each other. This would not have been so bad had they not already possessed teeth, hand talons, and foot claws that were miniature versions of those brandished by their parents. He likened the experience to trying to outrace a runaway bucket of razor blades rolling downhill.

As they descended from the high ridges, individual members of the tribe cut and trimmed suitable vines under Sylvia's active direction. For a while, Will wondered if the whole exercise was nothing more than a subtle diversion intended to get them safely clear of the deinonychids' territory, but he soon saw that she was earnest about the endeavor and optimistic about its success.

"You are really going to try and teach these unenlightened carnosaurs how to fish, aren't you?" he whispered to her as they neared the coast. There was no reason for him to whisper, he knew, since neither Korut or any of his people knew more than a word or two of human speech. But whisper he did, anyway.

"I certainly am," she replied cheerfully.

He remained doubtful. "Darned if I don't think you're serious about this. Have you given any thought to what might happen if it doesn't work?" He nodded in the direction of the *Deinonychus* chief, who was striding along powerfully beneath a heavy load of cut and coiled vine. "Somehow I don't think Korut is the stoic, forgiving type."

"Will you relax, Will?" she counseled him. "I know what I'm doing. This *is* going to work. I'm sure of it!" With that she left him behind and moved to the edge of the jungle to supervise the cutting of one more large liana.

Will lengthened his stride to catch up to the little translator. "What do you think about this idea, Chaz?"

The pensive *Protoceratops* regarded him peevishly. "I think you two are meant for each other. Teaching aboriginal dromaeasaurs to fish! Next she will start a knitting class for tyrannosaurs." With that he broke into a jog and moved back in front, having had quite enough of human conversation for the moment.

It was fascinating to watch the assembled deinonychids fashion the big net under Sylvia's supervision. Talons capable of rendering flesh in a single swipe were employed at trimming and slimming vines. Powerful fingers quickly adapted to tying knots and passing finished rope through designated loops. Elongated rocks were fastened securely to the anterior cable. After some initial frustration, the proceedings began to take on a life of their own, with the members of the tribe entering wholeheartedly into the process of manufacture.

When the net was nearly complete, Korut broke away from his fellow tribesfolk to confront Chaz. Lacking hands, the *Protoceratops* was taking no part in the net-weaving operation, a state of affairs that suited him eminently.

He snapped to alertness when the *Deinonychus* approached, however. Despite thousands of years of civilizing influence, ancient fears still maintained their tenuous grip on the herbivorian psyche. Genial, gruff conversation notwithstanding, the diminutive *Protoceratops* still found it difficult to relax in the presence of all those teeth and claws. All Korut sought, however, was clarification.

"The final plaiting is nearly done, and so is the day. We will have to wait until the morning." Watching his busy people, he growled under his breath. "I do not understand how this is supposed to work. We have no boats, so how will we gather the fish?"

"I do not pretend to be familiar with the process myself," Chaz explained uneasily. "It is all in the human female's head."

"Strange creatures." Korut followed Sylvia's gestures as she moved among his fellow tribesfolk, using sign language and facial expressions to explain what she was after. "Slow and soft, with dull teeth and no claws. It is a wonderment to me that they have survived."

"Apparently they dominate life in the world outside

Dinotopia, if their stories are to be believed." While not exactly subsumed in a bonding experience, Chaz felt himself drawn a little closer to the carnivorous dromaeasaur. "They just have not, according to what I have heard and read, done a very good job of it."

"*Gerr-umph*!" Korut snorted. "I can believe that. But I will forgive anyone anything who helps us catch fish." With a mightily clawed hand he indicated the trees that covered the mountainside and marched skyward into the clouds. "Food is not so easy to catch anymore."

"You should come into Culebra," Chaz suggested, "and learn to partake of civilized ways."

"Pah!" the *Deinonychus* retorted with such violence that Chaz flinched involuntarily. "And live in shelters built of dead wood, and eat food grown in the ground?"

"Fish is available in plenty to those carnivores who are part of Dinotopian society," the translator told him.

"We will learn to catch our own." Piercing, raptorish eyes focused unblinkingly on the busy, unaware Sylvia. "If not, we can always find other things to eat."

"Um—yes," Chaz mumbled as he excused himself.

That evening the tribesfolk were able to demonstrate their skill in finding that most precious of commodities in the rainforest—dry wood. Fires sprang to life on the beach, and the rain cooperated by falling only on the higher slopes of the green-clad mountains.

Seated around the small but intense individual blazes, the travelers swapped stories of mainland Dinotopia for tales of hunting and exploring in the island's forests. Eventually the youngsters drifted off to sleep, and then the juveniles. By midnight only a few of the adults were still awake after the long, hard day's exertions. Among them were Kurot's mate, a senior matriarch, and Chaz, who despite his best attempts to relax, found that he simply could not do so surrounded by so much unsheathed fang and claw.

So it was that when morning arrived, the translator was groggy from lack of sleep while his human companions and Khorip awakened refreshed and ready to embark on the great piscine experiment.

With Will and Khorip backing her up, and Chaz doing his best to shake the sleep from his brain, Sylvia confronted the waiting *Deinonychus*.

"Everyone alert and ready? Then let's get to work. I know you're all hungry—I can see it in your eyes."

"Please," Chaz muttered from behind her, "don't speak of things like that. Not while we are sharing the company of this lot."

Ignoring him, Sylvia continued. "I'm ready for some fresh reef fish broiled over an open fire myself. Squirrel fish, parrot fish, and if we're lucky, maybe a patrolling mackerel or two. Now then: I need the youngsters and the smaller adults to take hold of the top of the net."

Under her supervision, the net was hauled out into the water and stretched to its full, impressive length. Stones attached to the lowest cable dragged across the bottom while holding the mesh taut and fully extended from sand to surface.

"You on the end there," Sylvia yelled from her position on shore, "move forward! That's it. No, just the two on each end. All right, stop where you are. Now turn and face the sea. Good!" Pivoting, she confronted the rest of the tribesfolk, who had gathered at the water's edge.

"The net is in position. Now it's up to the rest of us."

"Us?" Chaz blurted.

"Well, Will and I, anyway. Khorip, you can join us if you think you're able." She faced the expectant carnivores while speaking to Chaz.

"Tell Korut and his people that we have to swim out as far as we can and then form a line facing the net. Everyone should make their way out independently and as quietly as possible."

Chaz dutifully translated for the benefit of the *Deinony-chus*. When he was finished, Korut looked first to the male on his left, then the female on his right. A few words were exchanged before he addressed himself to the *Protoceratops* again.

"They want to know why they have to swim out past the net," Chaz informed her.

Sylvia smiled patiently. "Because that's where the fish are."

Again the diminutive ceratopsian translated. Korut nodded his understanding before replying.

"He says that they do not know how to swim."

Sylvia sighed. "Tell them to watch how Will and I do it. Those who can't copy our movements should wade out as far as they can. Tell them to keep their eyes on me. When the line has been formed and is in position, I'll wave my hands over my head and yell. When I do that, everyone is to start making as much noise as they can and start moving toward the net, slapping the water with their hands and tails as they advance. This will drive the fish forward."

"You hope," Chaz declared, adding hastily, "I will not translate that."

As soon as she was sure both the net holders and the fish drivers understood their duties, Sylvia led the way into the water. Will took up a position several yards away from her, the better to set an example for the tribesfolk in his vicinity.

The sun was bright, the morning hot, and the water warm as he waded out into the calm lagoon. White sand stirred beneath his feet and bottom feeders scurried away at his approach. Nearby, Korut and the rest of the designated drivers were advancing tentatively into the sea. The verdant slopes of the high mountains were their traditional home, not the water, and they were manifestly uncomfortable. But in addition to their hunger, they had their pride to drive them oceanward. No self-respecting *Deinonychus* would own up to a fear of going where a soft-muscled human readily trod.

When he felt he had alternately waded and swam far enough, Will turned to face the beach. Korut dog-paddled awkwardly in deeper water nearby. Then the air was split by Sylvia shouting at the top of her lungs. Will joined in, whooping and hollering as loud as he could. In an instant, the line of dromaeasaurs added their nominally terrifying shrieks and bellows to the general clamor.

Moving forward and closing ranks as they flailed and thrashed at the water, Will began to see more and more fish beneath the surface. Many darted past him, heading out to sea, but many more fled shoreward away from the noise and commotion. As they saw what was happening, the advancing deinonychids redoubled their efforts, some even plunging beneath the surface in wild attempts to keep any more fish from fleeing the snare.

Ahead, the tribesfolk handling the opposite ends of the

crescent-shaped trap began to advance into deeper water in accordance with Sylvia's instructions. Herded into the bowl thus formed by the net, frenzied fish slammed crazily into one another in furious attempts to escape.

"You two on each end!" Sylvia shouted, cupping her hands to her mouth, "turn toward shore! Now!" With Chaz unavailable to translate, she had to resort to exaggerated gestures and pointing to make her intentions clear. But the pantomime sufficed. Slowly, the net and its bulging burden of fish was turned toward shore. Deinonychid fish drovers clustered at either end and continued to raise hell, keeping the trapped fish cornered in the ever-decreasing space.

Lifting her knees high, Sylvia sprinted clear of the water, yelling at Chaz as she did so. "Tell the drivers to help with the net! Now, before we lose any more of the catch!"

Chaz not only translated as loudly as he could, he pitched in with the heavy work. Wading into the shallows as far as his squat posture would let him, he secured a grip on a vacant loop of the net with his powerful beak and began to pull, backing up onto the beach. Khorip also lent a hand.

With the net-handlers pushing and keeping the top of the net above water, and the drovers now pulling from the shallows, the distended, makeshift catchment was slowly hauled up onto the sand. Following a couple of concerted bellows from all present, the top of the net was pulled forward to turn it inside out.

The mass of sharply scented seafood that spilled out, flopping slickly onto the beach, rose higher than Chaz's head. While not as much as Sylvia had hoped for, it was more fish than the deinonychid tribesfolk had ever seen in one place in their whole lives. Delirious with joy, they broke into a barbaric, impromptu dance around the catch. Since an adult *Deinonychus* can leap twelve feet straight up into the air, it was a spectacular display.

Korut approached the exhausted but ebullient Sylvia and, with as much dignity as his dripping-wet form could muster, bowed profoundly. Chaz translated.

"Korut says to tell you that when you first proposed this, he had his doubts. Now he admits to you, snout to snout, that he was wrong, and seeks your forgiveness."

Sylvia was toweling her hair with a strip of bark cloth that had been provided by one of the tribesfolk. "Tell him that there's no need for me to forgive him, because I didn't know that he had any doubts."

When this reply was supplied to the chief of the forest deinonychids he did not exactly smile, but succeeded in conveying a sense of satisfaction nonetheless. It was just as well, because a smiling *Deinonychus* would have bared more lethal, pointed teeth than any onlooker would have found comfortable.

From their skillfully woven backpacks several of the dromaeasaurs produced musical instruments: flutes suitable for fingering with clawed hands, drumsticks to be energetically applied to the most convenient hollow log or tree, a small stringed mouth harp easily plucked by selective fangs, and a cleverly designed folding guitar-like device that could be played either with feet or hands.

Arranging themselves in a semi-circle before the small mountain of fish, the carnivorous quintet launched unbidden into a throbbing, droning chant that was as alien to Chaz and Khorip as it was to their human companions.

Certainly Will had never heard its like before. Music was extremely popular among all dinosaurs, but this half-civilized hymn to hunting harkened back to an era when the saurians of Dinotopia were just beginning to develop the higher intelligence that had become the hallmark of their unique culture. He saw that Sylvia was equally fascinated, and even the usually dour Chaz was captivated.

"Specialists from Waterfall City should come here and listen to this." Eyes half closed, Sylvia found herself swaying to the whine of the strings and the rhythmic pounding of the drumsticks. "I know at least one musical ethnologist who would give up his tenure at the Arts Library to be here right now." Opening her eyes, she indicated the intent deinonychid musicians. "These people constitute a missing piece of Dinotopian cultural history, a relic from ancient times. Their culture should be preserved, somehow."

Will concurred. "Someday someone will invent a way to record sounds just as the scribes record words. I know father has talked about trying to build such a device. One that can record pictures, too."

Sylvia made a face at him. "Your father is a dreamer, Will. Such a machine is impossible. Look at what happened to his heavier-than-air flying machine. He had to be rescued by skybax."

"But it flew for a little while," Will argued. "And there were the strutters and other devices we found in The World Beneath. Making machines like that function is just a matter of settling on a source of motive power."

"That's what da Vinci claimed. Have you ever read his *Codex Mechanica*?" Will shook his head. "It arrived here on board a Venetian trading ship that was wrecked on the west coast hundreds of years ago, not far from where you and your father swam ashore."

"Look," Will directed her, changing the subject. "They're really dancing now."

Given the innate athletic ability of all dromaeasaurs, Will and Sylvia were not surprised at some of the leaps and pirouettes the tribesfolk performed. But it was still impressive to watch them all but dance on air, propelled upward by leg muscles that would have been the envy of any human athlete. Their sleek, muscular bodies filled the air around the musicians and the brilliantly hued mound of fish, sunlight glinting off green-banded skin and vivid face paint. The wildly successful fish-netting operation had turned into a joyous celebration.

A startled Will found himself in the grasp of a female *Deinonychus*. Courteously keeping her curved, scythelike talons away from his fragile human skin, she whirled him around and around, the two of them spinning madly about a common center. Once, he felt himself flung skyward, only to be brought smoothly back to Earth by his chortling, inspired partner. Eyes evolved to separate fast-moving prey from enveloping camouflage stared back into his own, but now they were filled with amusement and delight instead of ancient murderous intent.

Nearby, he saw a laughing, breathless Sylvia being spun back and forth between two male deinonychids. Bladelike claws passed dramatically close to and all around her body as the man-sized carnivores made pass after pass at her without nicking so much as one of her fingers. In between one full-length body toss, she waved and yelled to him and he did his best to wave back. Khorip likewise had been inveigled into participating in the revelry. The teasing dromaeasaurs did their best to cajole Chaz into participating as well, but despite their most zealous efforts the impassive *Protoceratops* would have none of it.

"Look at these legs." He proceeded to lift first one forefoot and then the other. "They are designed for many things, but dancing is not one of them." Snickering gutturally, his amused tormentors finally abandoned their attempts to get him to join in.

The celebration continued well into late afternoon. New fires were lit, and much broiled as well as raw fish was energetically consumed. Sated to the point of gluttony, the tribesfolk laid down or collapsed all along the beach.

Belly distended, Korut was in no mood to talk, but Will and Sylvia insisted.

"We've done our part," she instructed Chaz to remind the chief. "Now let's see these ruins he's been talking about."

In response to the *Protoceratops*'s inquiry, the prone *Deinonychus* groaned. But Chaz, emboldened by the sluggard carnivore's self-inflicted discomfort, insisted, until the chief finally replied.

"We have to return to the place where we first encountered him and his tribe," Chaz explained. "Tomorrow he and six of his strongest hunters will take us to the site we seek. That is, if they can walk by then." The ceratopsian did not try to hide his disgust at the sight. All around the fish heap, the complaints of the glutted were beginning to make themselves heard, replacing and overriding the earlier songs of celebration and delight.

The noise as well as the sentiment was contagious. It was not long before Will, who had also eaten more than his share, decided that whirling and bounding like a dervish was not a particularly good idea on a full stomach. Holding his middle, he searched for an auspicious place in which to be ill. Sylvia looked on with a disapproving air, while everyone including Will was forced to endure Chaz's nonstop scolding.

Morning brought with it some relief from the discomforts of gluttony. Korut and his people appeared to have largely recovered from the eating binge of the day before. Will felt better as well, though his lower abdomen acted up just often enough to remind him of his earlier excesses, lest he forget them and try to eat some more. Leaving the majority of his tribe on the beach to gut and prepare the remainder of the piscine bounty, Korut and half a dozen stalwart colleagues led their new-found friends back up the abandoned roadway and into the mountains once more.

Upon reaching the end of the coral pavement they turned northward, following a hunting trail none of the four visitors would ever have suspected existed. Despite his best efforts to follow the track, Will lost sight of it every couple of yards. In his defense, he was used to tracking large features from the air, not imperceptible scratches in damp, dense undergrowth. Sylvia did no better, and Khorip and Chaz were even worse off.

By afternoon one thing had become transparently obvious: if their helpful guides chose to abandon them in this place, they might never find their way back out of the tortuous maze of gullies and ridges. Because of the enveloping mist it was impossible to sight on any significant landmarks, and one direction looked the same as any other.

In places where the dense understory completely blocked

the path, their guides politely widened the trail for the convenience of their guests. A *Deinonychus* had no need for bush knives or machetes, being equipped with sufficient inherited cutlery to do the job. Talons slashed efficiently at overhanging branches and vines, sending fragments of obstructing verdure flying in all directions.

The next morning, following a dank, humid night spent camped out in the soggy bush, they found themselves confronted by a sheer wall of black volcanic rock that marked the terminus of a foliage-filled cul-de-sac.

"Well, that stops us." His bone-domed head tilted back, Khorip studied the mist-shrouded upper reaches of the insurmountable obstacle before them.

"Not at all," Korut declared via Chaz. Unsure of what he had heard, the *Protoceratops* barely took the time to translate before re-querying the chief.

"Surely you do not mean to imply that we are going to try and go up this?"

The *Deinonychus* turned from addressing his companions. "Of course we are. What did you think?"

"That I was not a bird, or a skybax," the translator retorted. "I am of the tribe of ceratopsians. We walk. We do not climb."

"I understand, and I promise that you need not worry." Korut indicated his fellow tribesfolk, who were now busy cutting vines and flexible saplings with their claws. "It will be taken care of."

"Oh it will, will it?" Chaz stepped back from the chief. If the *Protoceratops* had possessed arms, he would at that moment have crossed them defiantly.

"What's going on?" Will walked over to stand next to his

friend. "What was that all about?"

With his beak, the translator indicated the sheer stone wall. "Korut says we are going up that. I informed him that I could not. He replied that it would 'be taken care of'. I do not know exactly what he means by that, but I am not sanguine."

"Look here." In front of them, Sylvia was running a hand over a portion of the rock face. "There are hand- and footholds chiseled right into the basalt!"

Chaz nodded purposefully. "That is clear enough, then. I have no hands."

As the sturdy basket began to take shape under the skillful hands of the dromaeasaurs, the meaning of Korut's assurances became clear. When the procedure they were preparing to implement was explained to him, Chaz was more than a little reluctant to acquiesce.

"If you will recall," he reminded Will, "the last time I came down to earth in something like this I swore it was an experience that I would never willingly repeat."

"But this basket isn't attached to a balloon," his friend helpfully pointed out. "You'll be securely fastened to a rock up above, on top of the cliff. There's no flying involved."

"Unless the ropes break." The *Protoceratops* remained obstinate.

"The ropes won't break," an exasperated Sylvia assured him. "You saw the net Korut's people wove. It would have held a good-sized pleisosaur. I'll help them refine the weave on this basket and rope arrangement as well."

"It's the only way up." Will pleaded with his friend. "Of course, we could always leave you here until we come back."

The *Protoceratops* was silent for a moment. Then he finally let out a resigned sigh. "Why is it that when I find myself in your company, Will Denison, I am always reduced to choosing the least unattractive option?"

Grinning, Will grabbed the top of the translator's frill and shook it gently. "It's because you're such a fine judge of character, Chaz. Don't worry—I won't let them drop you. I'll be above helping to pull you up myself."

"How very reassuring." The dubious ceratopsian remained unconvinced.

As impressive as the dancing deinonychids had been, it was downright startling to watch them make their way up the sheer cliff. Talons and claws not only made use of the existing hand- and footholds that had been incised into the black rock, they repeatedly made their own. Faced with a difficult place, a *Deinonychus* would simply jam powerful fingers or toes repeatedly into the stone, their sharp claws digging into the rock until a new grip had been secured.

After Korut and two of his companions had made it to the top, it was Will's turn. He picked his way carefully up the cliff, making use of every niche. Sylvia followed. A better rock-climber than he, she was soon crowding his heels.

At the top, they paused briefly to catch their breath before lending a hand with the improvised rope and basket arrangement. To prove to an irresolute Chaz that it was perfectly safe, Khorip allowed himself to be hauled up first. Then it was the translator's turn. He breathed a visible sigh of relief when the basket finally reached the top and he was able to amble clear of its claustrophobic confines.

"See?" Sylvia chided him. "Nothing to it."

"It was easier than the balloon," the *Protoceratops* admitted, "but you have to understand that my kind share an inherent fear of heights that is common to all who are built naturally close to the ground." He was looking past her. "Hopefully there will be no more such elevating experiences."

Much to the ceratopsian's delight, the path they now set out upon involved ascending a number of steep places, but nothing that required him to be ignominiously hauled aloft like a sack of potatoes. There were a couple of difficult spots where he required a helping hand, but nothing that proved insurmountable.

It was late afternoon when an exhausted Khorip called a halt.

"I'm sorry, but I guess I've spent too many years in the desert. This humidity is hard on me, and so is the altitude."

"We're all tired." Sylvia sat down on a nearby flat-topped rock. As she fanned herself with a plucked leaf, she instructed Chaz to convey their feelings to Korut.

The *Protoceratops* did so, then appeared to hesitate over his translation of the chief's response, as if unsure of what he had heard.

Will prompted him. "Something wrong? What does he say?"

Chaz turned to face his friends. "He says that he understands our weariness but that we can relax now. Because we are here."

"Here?" Looking around, Sylvia saw only mounds and hillocks of green-clad stone. "Here where? Where are the ruins he's been talking about?"

"Right here." The translator stomped the ground with

351

his right foot. "You're sitting on them."

Hopping off the rock on which she had been relaxing, Sylvia brushed at the concealing vegetation. Sure enough, as the clinging plant matter was scraped away, finely finished masonry was once again exposed to the mist-diffused sunlight.

"Well I'll be a doubting duckbill," Will whispered. "We would've walked right by without seeing it."

While they made their discovery, Chaz had continued his conversation with the chief. "Korut says that there are ruins all around us. The archaic structures have been reclaimed by the rainforest, but if we are interested he and his people can show us some especially inspiring sites."

When she looked up from the stone on which she had been innocently resting, Sylvia's eyes were shining. Behind her, Khorip stood straight and proud, suffused with an air of vindication.

"Oh, we're interested, all right." Her voice fairly vibrated with anticipation. "And, Chaz?"

"Yes, Sylvia?"

Stepping forward, she put a comradely hand on the chief *Deinonychus*'s shoulder. Her face was barely a foot from teeth that could kill in one bite, but she was not afraid. Instead, she smiled warmly at him.

"How does one say 'thank you' in dromaeasaur?"

# -XXI-

ot only the extent of the ruins but their layout gradually manifested itself. As they explored the forest-clad mounds and knolls it became clear that a great city had once covered the entire mountaintop.

Though heavily overgrown with rainforest, it was still possible to trace the outlines of parade fields and temples, storehouses and living areas. Architecturally the ruined city was much different from Ahmet-Padon, showing earlier and more middle-eastern influences.

"Early Classic Period human-saurian design, I would say," Chaz declaimed as they stood at the base of a step pyramid some two hundred feet high. Vines and creepers enveloped the crumbling structure, providing a foothold for less tenacious plants. Flowers bloomed where humans and dinosaurs had once trod. Insects hummed as they went about their work. From concealed perches, exotic birds sang enigmatically.

"Or meso-Greek." Sylvia pointed to a line of fallen pillars with badly decomposed cornices.

Kurot and his fellow deinonychids showed no fear of the ruins. They might admire the place, but they did not venerate it. To them the fantastical foliage and the stone playground was as familiar as any other part of the highland forests they called home.

Will saw the chief beckoning for them to follow. Having learned that it was sensible to comply with the *Deinony-chus*'s instructions, he began picking his way through the jumble of collapsed masonry.

Behind the pyramid they beheld the most impressive structures they had yet encountered on the crag-ringed plateau: a quartet of enormous statues hewn from dark stone. More than a hundred feet tall and executed in the style of the four colossal seated portraits of the pharaoh Ramses II at Abu Simbel, they had been placed back to back so that each one faced a different point of the compass. All four had human bodies but each boasted a different saurian head, very much in keeping with the ancient Egyptian fashion of placing the heads of animals atop the bodies of humans.

Only in this case, one male figure had the head of a *Triceratops*, another that of a *Corythosaurus*. There was a brachiosaur-headed mature female figure and one slightly younger and slimmer that wore the skull of a *Maiasaurus*. Towering over the central portion of the ancient metropolis, their stone eyes stared somberly off into the distance. Will was surprised that Kurot and his people did not regard such imposing figures with awe. With Chaz translating, he asked the chief why he was not more impressed.

The *Deinonychus* replied diffidently. "They are only creatures of stone. Big, to be sure, but not living flesh. You can only be hurt by stone if it falls on you."

Will nodded understandingly and then pointed at the nearest of the four figures, the one with the head of a *Maiasaurus*.

"And that," he asked evenly. "What about that?"

Receiving the translation, Kurot turned to gaze at the outstretched hand of the statue.

Each of the striking sculptures reposed on a throne with its right hand outstretched, fingers held together, thumb inclined out to the side. The Hand of Dinotopia, Will thought with satisfaction. They had found it at last. Broaching his conclusion to Sylvia, he was more than a little surprised at the sharpness of her reply. Not to mention its content.

"It's not," she told him. "It can't be."

"What do you mean, it can't be?" He indicated the unmistakably outstretched stone hands. A Princess Stephanie's arabis had built a nest between the middle and index fingers of the *Maiasaurus* statue.

"Because the ancient texts refer specifically to *a* Hand of Dinotopia. Not to a pair of hands, not to multiple hands, but to *a* hand." She gestured at the calmly contemplative quartet. "There are four hands proffered here."

An exasperated Will tried to reconcile what they had found with her certitude in the matter. "All right, so *one* of them is 'the' Hand of Dinotopia. One of them points the way to the imaginary sea route. Which one? Did the old scrolls tell you that?"

She would not be converted. "The legends speak only of a Hand of Dinotopia. Therefore these multiples can't be it. It must lie somewhere else within the city."

"Or maybe it points the way to still another forgotten

municipality," Chaz contributed from nearby. "And in that overlooked community we will find a hand, or a broken leg, or an inscription that points the way to still another ancient ruin. Myself, I have had enough of descrying antediluvian metropoli. It is time to go back, to return to the comforts of civilization, and to turn our discoveries, which I acknowledge are substantial, over to the proper departments so that they can make plans to carry out expert follow-up research."

"No!" Sylvia insisted. "*The* Hand is here somewhere. It has to be."

Khorip added his support to her resolve. "Sylvia is correct. We have come to the right place. We can't turn back now. I won't turn back now."

"Then stay, and see if you can convince Kurot and his tribespeople to put down their spears and pick up picks and shovels." Chaz ambled over to the foot of the nearest statue. "Because I, for one, am not about to participate in any protracted excavation of the premises. Why, it would take a crew of ceratopsians and sauropods working side by side more than a two-month just to clear away the overgrowth and reveal the best places to start digging."

"Not that long." A confident Sylvia was running her fingers over the fine stonework that formed the base of the monumental human-*Maiasaurus* sculpture. "These four statues with their extended hands are the key to everything. I'm sure of it."

"You're sure you're sure about being sure?" Chaz replied accusingly. Picking his way with his short legs over broken stone and exposed roots, he walked over to where the base of the *Maiasaurus* statue joined the base of the figure with the head of a *Triceratops*. "If this is the key, then where, pray tell, is the lock? Or are we just supposed to push one of these pretty carvings over and note which way its outstretched hand falls?"

So saying, he placed his snout against the junction of the two sculptures and shoved derisively. There was a click as a silent switch was thrown, and a stone slab slid upward and out of sight just to his right. The *Protoceratops* jumped involuntarily which, given the natural inability of his kind to elevate themselves very far off the ground, was almost as impressive as the sight that was revealed by his action.

"You have a real talent for finding things, Chaz." Will gave his stocky companion an affectionate pat on the back as together they considered the unexpected gateway.

Khorip was compelled to demur. "Wouldn't it be more accurate to refer to this problematic talent of the stumpy one as demonstrating 'fortuitous ineptitude'?"

As the tongue of a *Protoceratops* is quite large, it follows naturally that so was the raspberry it generated in response to the *Prenocephale*'s comment.

The passageway behind the stone led in and down. Approaching cautiously, they saw that the walls were filled with ancient hieroglyphic script, part original Egyptian and part hybrid Dinotopian. Despite the excellent state of preservation of the surviving inscriptions, this combination proved impossible for Chaz to decipher. Kurot and his followers, who until now had been utterly unaware of the passage's existence, were of even less help.

Surprisingly, there was light at the far end of the shaft. It entered from the left to illuminate the end of the tunnel.

Sylvia started forward, only to hesitate within the portal. "Will, Chaz—aren't you coming?"

The translator eyed the shaft dubiously. "I will think about it. I dislike venturing into an entrance when I have no idea where it will exit."

"Well, I do," she told him confidently. Bending slightly, she pointed down the tunnel to the far end. "See where the light is coming in from? Now look at the siting of the four statues. There all have to back onto the same opening. Their opposing backs form the walls of a small courtyard or something." She started down the tunnel. "Come on, Khorip."

The *Prenocephale* followed close on her heels, leaving Will and Chaz to ponder their hesitation. At least, Will mused, their desert guide did not have to worry about bumping his head on the tunnel ceiling. He came equipped with his own built-in construction helmet.

"Come on, Chaz." Will vied with Kurot to be next into the shaft.

"Where have I, much to my regret, heard that before?" With a sigh, the translator followed the two bipeds, one human and one saurian, down into the dimly illuminated narrows.

Letting them hurry on ahead, he lingered within the tunnel, drawn to the exquisitely finished hieroglyphs that covered both walls. Some still displayed their original coatings of paint, but jungle molds had eaten most of the color away. As to the underlying meaning of the intricate carvings, he could not tell. Despite his best efforts at understanding, they defied interpretation, resembling nothing he had encountered during his studies of ancient Dinotopian languages. That did not mean they had no mainland antecedents, however. Only that he was personally unfamiliar with them.

As soon as he exited the far end of the tunnel, he saw that Sylvia had been right. The backs of the four colossal saurohuman statues formed a small courtyard that had been taken over by invading rainforest. Under Sylvia's direction, Korut and his people were clearing away the thick foliage. Talons and claws flew freely, sending vegetation flying. Possessed of less knifelike nails, Will and Khorip helped by pulling the cuttings away. A mound of truncated greenery began to rise in one corner of the courtyard.

Chaz found the setting more than a little eerie. The high, smooth backs of the statues shut off all sight of the rainforest beyond, while the perpetual mist at these heights blocked out the sky. Not a breath of wind penetrated the confined, sheltered enclosure.

Several deinonychids were removing creepers and epiphytes from a mound of rock in the center of the courtyard when one of them let out a startled cry. Immediately, everyone else stopped work to see what the warrior had found.

The broad, circular stone was carved out of solid rock. Seven or eight feet across, it boasted an unmistakable and splendidly rendered relief map of Dinotopia. Will studied it admiringly.

"No need to flood this one with water to know what it is."

"No," agreed Sylvia. Leaning over the stone, she gestured with one hand. "See? There's the Polongo, and to the right, the Forbidden Mountains."

In order to see properly, Chaz had to raise himself up and rest both forefeet on the edge of the adamantine map.

"That smooth portion has to be the Blackwood Flats. But there are no cities."

"Maybe it's just supposed to show physical features," Khorip suggested. "Look at how deeply the Amu Canyon is carved into the stone."

"And there's Outer Island, where we are right now." Leaning forward, Will squinted at what appeared to be an unnamed mountain peak still covered in encroaching greenery. "That's funny. I don't remember there being a central mountain that high on any maps of Outer Island that I've ever seen." Stretching himself across the map, he pressed his chest and stomach onto the stone and began to pull at the greenery that clung to the central projection.

"Nor I." Sylvia looked on as he tore at the persistent plant growth.

"If anyone should know elevated topography, it is a pair of skybax riders." Chaz watched with interest, as did Khorip and the curious deinonychids.

A small vine had wrapped itself several times around the stone outcropping. Gritting his teeth, Will finally managed to pry it away from the rock far enough to slip his fingers underneath. It took several sharp tugs before the vine reluctantly relinquished its grip. As soon as the slightly greasy growth came away in his fingers the reason for everyone's confusion was made instantly clear. The carving that rose from the center of the map was not of an unknown mountain. It was another statue.

A perfect miniature, in fact, of the four great sculptures presently surrounding them.

The reproduction was unmistakable. There was the same human body, the identical seated posture with arm and hand

360

outstretched and pointing. From the neck up, the figurine had the head of a *Tyrannosaurus*.

It was pointing westward, toward the mainland of Dinotopia itself. Which, Will decided as he tried to make sense of what he was seeing, made no sense at all.

"The Hand of Dinotopia?" Khorip wondered aloud. "At last?"

"I can't imagine what else it could be." Will slid back off the stone map. "In which case the legend of there being a safe ocean route to and away from Dinotopia is nothing more than that: an old, groundless story handed down through the generations by imaginative tellers of tall tales."

"It can't be." A distraught Sylvia anxiously circled the map, looking for the clue she felt sure they had to be missing.

"What else can it be but that?" Keeping his forefeet on the edge of the rock, Chaz slowly worked his way around the map's circumference, following in Sylvia's wake. "It occupies a location of obvious importance here in the very center of this ancient metropolis. It is an outstretched hand within protective walls of outstretched hands. The fact that it points to the center of Dinotopia and not out to sea proves that it has nothing to do with any kind of oceanic itinerary."

Khorip was as discouraged as Sylvia. "Perhaps it indicates a course that takes as its departure point a site on the western coast of the mainland."

"No," Will reluctantly decided. "That makes even less sense. Why place a direction finder on the opposite side of Dinotopia from your leave-taking point? It would make a lot more sense to build it on the beach or in the mountains directly opposite the critical spot. Placing it here makes everything unnecessarily complicated."

Chaz let his forefeet slip off the stone. Resting again on all fours, he rubbed his flank against the curving stone to scratch an itch. "Whatever it is, we have indisputably found the thing. The Department of Archeology will be delighted. Perhaps their specialists can decipher the meaning of this place, and of your mysterious Hand." He took a couple of steps toward the tunnel opening. "Now it is time for us to return home. I would very much like to decipher the meaning of my own bed."

"No, wait!" As Will looked on in surprise, Sylvia climbed up onto the map and began crossing it on hands and knees. "There has to be more. There has to be!"

"Sylvia," he murmured gently, "there isn't anything else. There's just the map, and the little statue, and that's all there is."

She glanced back at him sharply. "You don't make a map like this and put it in a place like this with an obvious pointer in the middle of it unless it's designed to show you the way to someplace tangible."

"It does show the way to someplace tangible," he argued. "Somewhere inland. Maybe," he suggested in a minor burst of inspiration, "it's pointing to the site of Ahmet-Padon."

"Now that would make sense." Chaz complimented his skybax-riding friend. "The map in Ahmet-Padon points to here, and the map here points to Ahmet-Padon. They comprise a way of reinforcing the relationship between the two ancient cities. Perhaps they had trading arrangements, or carried out cultural exchanges."

"No." Sylvia had reached the relief carving of Outer Island with its miniature statue and was now kneeling next to it. She was still reluctant to give up her hard-won hypothesis. "It has to show the sea route. Otherwise the ancient texts make no sense."

"Exactly the point I have been trying to make all along," Chaz observed peckishly.

Will was growing impatient. "It doesn't have to show *anything*, Sylvia. What its carvers intended and what you want it to mean aren't necessarily the same thing."

"I don't understand." Kneeling on the stone, she stared forlornly at the finely-hewn figurine in its center. "I just don't understand."

"Let us take it back with us," the impatient *Protoceratops* suggested. "We cannot move these surrounding colossi, and a small chunk of one would mean little, but the miniature statue will delight the authorities at the Department of Archeology in Sauropolis. Perhaps they will have better luck deciphering its meaning."

"You're right, of course, Chaz. I guess it's better than nothing." Reaching down, she attempted to remove the figurine, only to find that it would not come away in her hands.

"Fastened to the map?" Will inquired.

Sylvia was staring hard at the little statue. "Yes, but it moved a little. Let me try again." She did so, and then sat back as if stung. Will was instantly alert. It had not occurred to any of them that the map, the tunnel, or any of their surroundings might have been booby-trapped by the ancients. Now that the thought had struck them, it seemed perfectly reasonable that the map garden was a special place, perhaps one that denied access to the unqualified. Such places often boasted protection in the form of unpleasant surprises.

"What is it, what's wrong?"

"Wrong?" She sounded dazed. "Why, nothing's wrong, Will."

"You said that it moved a little." Hurrying around the map, he had half climbed up to be next to her.

"That's right." She looked back at him. "But it didn't just move. It pivots."

"Pivots?" Khorip frowned. "What do you mean, Sylvia?"

"Have a look for yourself." Leaning forward again, she rested her fingers on one side of the figurine and gave it a shove. It responded by rotating freely before grinding to a halt.

"I guess the vine and the other plants that have been growing on it held it in place and kept it from moving." Will was kneeling alongside her now, gazing in wonderment at the statue. "It's a pointer, all right, but not a fixed one." Reaching down, he gave it a spin himself.

They took turns flipping it around with their fingers. With each new rotation it moved more freely, as grime and accumulated gunk fell away from the concealed pivot stone. Each time it stopped, it came to rest in the same position.

"It's balanced," Sylvia declared, "so that it points to the same place every time."

Will found himself nodding agreement. "Every time. And it's not pointing to the mainland anymore."

"Let me see!" Khorip was reluctant to climb up onto the map for fear that the sharp, heavy claws on his feet might damage the intricate carving. Will and Sylvia moved back so that the *Prenocephale* and everyone else could have a good look.

The miniature outstretched arm and hand were now gesturing, not westward, but to the northeast. Out to sea.

"Krachong," Chaz suggested. "It points to Krachong Island." A sizable landmass in its own right, Krachong was still a good deal smaller than Outer Island, or even Ko Veng Isle, a popular fishing locale that separated Warmwater and Sapphire bays.

Having flattened herself out on the map, Sylvia was squinting along the path indicated by the miniature stone hand. "No, it's not pointing at Krachong. The line lies farther to the east."

"Well then," Chaz continued, "if I remember my cartography correctly there are two small islets located north of Krachong."

Sylvia sat back up and shook hair away from her face. Her response was categorical. "I know the islets you're referring to, Chaz, and they don't lie in the line either. This points to a place a little farther east and much farther north." She tapped the map. "To another tiny island—here."

The *Protoceratops* was equally resolute. "There is no land above water further east of Krachong or the northern islets. Not until one reaches the outside world, anyway."

"I have to agree with the translator." Khorip looked as if he wanted to believe Sylvia's interpretation of the map, but couldn't.

"Well, you can agree with Chaz all you want," Sylvia responded, "but that doesn't agree with the map." She tapped a small carved outcropping where it protruded above the flat far western portion of the inscribed stone. "What's this blip way up here in the ocean if not another, previously unrecorded island?"

"A mistake by the carvers," Chaz suggested. "An imperfection in the rock."

Seeking support, she looked imploringly to her right. "Will?"

His jaw set, he spread himself out flat until he was staring down the line formed by the arm and hand of the rotatable figurine.

"Try it again," he instructed Sylvia.

Obediently, she twirled the statuette. No matter how many times it was spun, no matter at what speed or in what direction, it always came to a halt facing the distant spur of upthrust stone. After several minutes he sat up again.

"I hate to say it," he murmured to his audience of attentive saurians, "but I think Sylvia's right. The little statue points to a bit of land that's not on any map of Dinotopia."

"Except this one," she announced with growing confidence. "And we know that the Hand points to some place, because no one would go to all this trouble to build something this intricate to show the way to nowhere."

"Unless," Chaz pointed out, "it is broken. Or slightly askew."

By way of reply Sylvia spun the statuette again, several times. "If it was broken I'd think it would point to slightly different spots at least occasionally, Chaz. The same if it was slightly off-kilter. But it always stops with the hand pointing at that far-off island."

"If it is an island," the *Protoceratops* argued. "Please keep in mind that this map is as old as this city."

"You're right. So the only way to find out if the map is still accurate is to go to the place where it is pointing and see if, as the carving appears to indicate, there is an uncharted island out there."

"Oh no!" Chaz took a couple of steps back toward the tunnel entrance. "Crossing the Great Desert was one thing. Even here on Outer Island we are on known land." Turning, he gestured with his beak. "But once beyond Krachong Island the waters belong to the fish and the mosasaurs. I have talked to sailors and I know what it is like out there. The winds become unpredictable and the currents too strong to sail against. That is why no one goes fishing or shelling beyond traditional limits. Farther north than Crackshell Point a boat has no chance. It will inevitably be swept shoreward and smashed against the reef." He drew himself up to his full height.

"I," he declaimed with notable fervor, "do not wish to be smashed against the reef. Or drowned, or sucked down into a whirlpool. The next boat I step aboard will be one headed back to Kuskonak."

"I want to go on that boat too, Chaz." Sylvia's tone was calm, rational. "*After* we visit this unfamiliar island. Who knows what we might find there?"

"If it exists, I can guess," the *Protoceratops* muttered huffily. "Another map."

Sylvia turned to her fiancé. "Will?"

He took one last look at the intricate circular stone chart. "There don't seem to be any other prominent flaws in the stone, so why should the one you found be an imperfection instead of an island? And every time it's spun, the hand of the figurine points right to it. It's too much of a coincidence, Chaz. I think Sylvia's right. There's an island there."

"Good!" the little translator responded. "Let it stay there.

Let someone better equipped find and explore it."

This time Sylvia was grinning as she shook her head. "Can't do that, Chaz. Because no one will believe there's anything there, right?"

"Circuitous logic just makes people dizzy." Chaz folded his legs beneath him. "I am not going sailing to some mysterious anomalous point way out in the ocean, and that is final!"

"It's not anomalous," Sylvia pointed out. "Whoever built this city was meticulous about its design and construction." She indicated the map. "They would never carve a statue that points to some place they couldn't return from, because then they wouldn't have been able to come back and carve the statue to point to there in the first place."

The beaked, frilled head swiveled to face her. "You are an insidious female, Sylvia. Your reasoning squats on my mind like an old headache. Anyway, it does not matter, because we have no means of getting there. Or do you think that you will be able to hire a boat in Culebra? I told you; I have often spoken with sailors and fisherfolk. They fear traveling farther east or north than Krachong, and with good reason. They would not risk their craft, much less their lives, on such a chancy venture. Not for fish, not for lobster, and certainly not on the word of a couple of skybax riders and an ascetic bonehead with antisocial propensities."

"That's true." Sylvia looked downcast as she climbed back off the map. "I guess you're right."

Having crushed her hopes, the *Protoceratops* now tried to lift her spirits. "Do not look so forlorn, Sylvia. I am sure you can make arrangements to accompany the first official expedition to this unknown island—if there is indeed an island out there."

Leaning back against the map, she crossed her arms over her chest. "Come on, Chaz. You know what's going to happen when we turn in a report on what we've found. First the authorities are going to want to explore Ahmet-Padon. Then they'll come to Outer Island and set up a full-fledged study camp here in the old city. *Eventually* they *may* decide to check out the map. By that time I'll be an old woman!" She spread both arms wide, imploring him. "I want to go now."

Will commented as sensitively as he could. "*I'd* go with you right now, Sylvia. Today. But—it's a long swim."

Throughout the exchange Korut and his people had held their peace, letting the humans and their saurian companions argue back and forth. Now the *Deinonychus* chieftain confronted Chaz.

"If you will pardon me a moment," the *Protoceratops* explained to his companions, "Korut insists on knowing what we've been jabbering about. It should not take me long to fill him in."

Khorip explored the circumference of the map while Will did his best to comfort Sylvia. Meanwhile Chaz and Korut conversed. Occasionally one or two of the other deinonychids ventured a question or comment.

After some ten minutes of steady, even-toned conversation, the chatter took on a different tone. Leaving Sylvia to discuss specific aspects of the map with Khorip, a curious Will wandered over to observe.

As the level of discourse rose in intensity and volume, he suddenly found himself the subject of much gesturing and incomprehensible growling from Korut.

"What's he trying to tell me?" he asked the translator.

"*Nih chorg noh mecke* . . . I mean," Chaz corrected himself, switching from dromaeasaur to human, "it does not matter." He resumed talking to Korut. Arguing, it seemed to Will. Unmollified, he tapped the *Protoceratops* on his frill.

"What do you mean, 'it doesn't matter'? Chaz, you tell me what Korut is saying, and you tell me straight." When the *Protoceratops* appeared to vacillate he added, "It's your sworn duty as an officially designated translator to tell me. What would Bix think?"

"The distinguished Bix would probably think that I am mad for being here," Chaz replied. "Just as these aboriginal carnivores are mad."

"Mad in what way?" Will demanded to know. Again Chaz wavered, but this time he did not wait for his friend's prompting to respond.

"I have explained the situation to them in full and Korut says—this makes absolutely no sense, mind—that they know where we can get a boat."

# -XXII-

o qualify as fully-fledged skybax riders, both Will and Sylvia had been required to learn flight navigation. While differing from the methods a sailor or fisherman would use, there were enough similarities to persuade them that they could plot a course to the mysterious islet indicated on the stone map and, more importantly, follow it. Barring, as a disconcerted Chaz was quick to point out, destructive winds, hidden reefs, non-navigable currents, and obstacles they could not even imagine.

"It won't be so bad, Chaz." Sylvia tried to reassure the reluctant *Protoceratops* as she made careful notes with vegetable ink on a strip of bark. "It's not like we're trying to sail back to Will's birthplace. We're just going a little north and east of the last known point of land in Dinotopia."

"Of course," the translator muttered. "Nothing to it. A stroll in the park."

"We'll make it all right," Will chipped in. "I've been on plenty of boats."

"Sure you have." Chaz swiveled an eye up at his friend.

"On the Polongo, or in Dolphin Bay. It's not the same. None of us are deep-water sailors. In fact, there are no deep-water sailors in Dinotopia because deep water is too dangerous."

"As long as we don't stray too far east we can't get lost," Sylvia pointed out. "If we run into bad weather, or any other kind of unforeseen trouble, all we have to do is turn about and sail due west until we hit the mainland."

"Unless we're carried north of Crackshell Point." The agitated ceratopsian climbed to his feet. "Amu canyon was daunting, the Great Desert was lunatic, Outer Island is absurd, but this—this exceeds the boundaries of common sense!"

"All exploration into the unknown exceeds the boundaries of common sense, Chaz." Will put a succoring arm around his friend's neck. "That's why there are still places that are unknown."

"I would just as soon leave it that way."

Will straightened. "You can stay on the beach, by the side of the coast road, and wait for the next itinerant harvesting expedition to come by. We'll look for you on the way back."

"Oh no you don't." The *Protoceratops*'s gaze switched back and forth between humans. "You are not leaving me alone here with these atavistic assassins! I would rather perish at sea than be eaten."

"Really, Chaz!" Will was taken aback. "Haven't Korut and his people proved to you by now that they're our friends? They may be primitive, but they're not cannibals."

"An easy conclusion to reach when there are four of us standing together." The *Protoceratops* looked decidedly uncomfortable. "If confronted by danger, Khorip can wade far out into the water, and you two can climb trees. Whereas I am a slow-moving, ill-defended, walking supper."

"I wouldn't say ill-defended," Khorip told him. "Your words can draw blood at twenty paces."

"Where hunger is concerned I prefer not to count on an uncouth, head-feathered, face-painted *Deinonychus* being amenable to reasoned persuasion." He swallowed hard. "I will take my chances with the sea, foolhardy as I consider this proposal to be." He cheered slightly. "Anyway, when these quaint forest-dwellers say that they know where we can obtain a boat, that does not mean it will prove adequate to our needs. It may yet be that circumstance and common sense will carry the day and we will soon find ourselves on our way home."

It was a long, sodden hike out of the ruined city, down the broken cliffs, and back through the rainforest before they reached the upper terminus of the inland road and, not intolerably long thereafter, the coast. Drifting haze rose from several locations next to the deinonychid encampment. The pungent aroma of fish smoking over smoldering charcoal fires greeted the tired travelers long before they trudged into the camp itself.

There was much ritual tail flicking and head bobbing as those who had remained behind warmly greeted the quietly jubilant members of the tribe who had gone with the visitors. Feeling a sharp pain at his ankles, Will looked down to see that the two eager young deinonychids who had affectionately pestered him previously had once more attached themselves to his person. Literally.

Eyeing the makeshift smoking racks, Khorip was moved

to comment. "At least you won't have to worry about food while we're at sea. And I'm sure Chaz and I can find enough fruits and nuts to sustain us for the duration of the voyage."

"Anxious to diagram your demise, are you?" The fretting *Protoceratops* scanned the sandy white beach. "Where is this boat Korut seemed so keen on? I see nothing more seaworthy here than clumps of disorganized driftwood."

Shading her eyes with one hand, Sylvia strolled toward the water. "I don't see one either, but Korut insisted it was here."

Chaz felt vindicated. "And why should we not hold a primitive throwback to his word? I wonder if he even knows what a boat is?"

Seeking out the *Deinonychus* chief, they found him relaxing on his haunches with his mate and two offspring close by. All were feasting on chunks of delicious smoked reef fish. Sharp teeth made short work of even the toughest skin and bone, both of which were consumed with pleasure.

Seeing them approach, Korut's mate offered Will a cured, whole, skillfully filleted parrot fish. He declined the offering with a smile, whereupon she nodded, popped it between her own parted jaws, and bit off the rear portion. The remainder looked as if it had been professionally halved with a chef's cleaver.

Via Chaz, they inquired as to the whereabouts of the boat Korut had mentioned. His belly swollen from gorging himself on fish, the *Deinonychus* levered himself erect and beckoned for them to follow. One youngster clung briefly to the chief's stiffened, outstretched tail before Korut absently shook her off.

It was a short walk through the coconut palms, fruit

trees, and coastal brush to a small cove where the boat waited. Or boats, rather, for Will and his friends were astonished to see a veritable flotilla of small craft drawn up above the high tide line. There were several fishing boats, a couple of interharbor transports, and one small barge. None looked to be in fit shape to cross the lagoon, much less put out to sea.

In response to their queries, Korut explained that without having any specific use for such craft, his people were too fascinated by them to simply abandon them to the elements. So whenever one was found washed up on a beach, it was either dragged or pushed to this place, to be saved for possible future use. He and his people were particularly happy when they were able to salvage bits of metal, usually brass and iron, from the beached craft.

"I've heard that storms sometimes blow inadequately moored boats out to sea," Sylvia commented. "So this is where some of them end up—on the far side of Outer Island."

"I would not put out on the surface of a large bathtub in any one of those." Chaz eyed the salvaged wrecks mistrustfully.

Will put a sympathetic arm around Sylvia. "He has a point. None of them look very seaworthy."

Having come so far, Sylvia was not about to be thwarted by the shabby condition of the erstwhile deinonychian navy.

"All we need to find is one watertight hull. We can cannibalize the other boats and use the parts to make at least one of them seaworthy."

"So now, in addition to being explorers and archeologists, we are to become shipwrights?" Chaz made a rude noise that was unique to ceratopsians.

"It shouldn't require an extensive effort." Khorip was standing next to Sylvia, gesturing with one clawed hand. "I see plenty of solid decking on other boats, and there's rigging all over the place. That fishing boat there has an anchor we can use, and the one next to it has what appears to be an intact hull."

"And what do we use for tools to make these repairs with?" Chaz demanded to know. "Coconuts?"

Sylvia had already started toward the crowded cove. "There might be some on the boats. Come on, let's have a look!"

They did not find tools in abundance. No complete workshops had been swept out to sea with the missing boats. But there were a couple of battered, grungy hammers, and one hand-powered drill, and a particularly valuable box of nails that had been overlooked by the scavenging deinonychids. Half of these were given to Korut, who with suitably grand gestures promptly dispensed them to his delighted people.

Meanwhile Will, Sylvia, and Khorip concentrated on making the least damaged of the assembled craft ready for sea. Chaz grumbled all the while, but lent what assistance he could. Having committed himself to not remaining behind, he intended to ensure that the makeshift vessel was rendered as sound as possible.

The single mast was fitted with a cross-spar and sail salvaged from another boat. Long sweeps were placed in the rowing sockets bolted to the gunwales. Will was glad to see that the builders of the boat had made provision for oars. If they were caught in an adverse current, or becalmed, these would provide a means for breaking free. He had no idea how long or how hard he and the others could row, but it was nice to be able to set sail knowing that the option was available to them.

Dangling loose at the stern, the rudder was quickly fixed. The new anchor was loaded on board and attached to the fore capstan. A second successful fish drive allowed a stock of dried filets to be stored aboard, together with fruits and vegetables for Chaz and Khorip.

When all was in readiness and the tide was at its highest, they went to request Korut's help in launching the now heavily laden craft from the beach.

They found him standing among the trees that surrounded the little cove. He had come every day to observe their progress. Will noted that a light wind was blowing out to sea, which should help to speed their departure.

But when they asked for the tribe's assistance in getting under way, the chief had another surprise in store for them.

"No. I will not assist you in this manner of leave-taking."

As this was translated for them, Will and Sylvia exchanged a concerned look, as did Chaz and Khorip.

"What does he mean, they won't help us?" Sylvia prodded the *Protoceratops* to ask. Chaz promptly put the question to Korut.

"He says," the translator explained, "that he did not say they will not help us. What he said was that they will not assist us 'in this manner of leave-taking.'"

Will frowned. "And what's that supposed to mean?"

Again Chaz inquired. This time he hesitated over the translation.

"Well, what does he say?" As he spoke, Will watched the *Deinonychus* for some clue as to what the intelligent but uncultured carnivore might be feeling.

Surprise and astonishment colored the ceratopsian's reply. "Korut explains that because we helped them to gather food, we have become part of his peoples' extended pack. Therefore it would be churlish of them to allow us to risk our lives when they could help."

It was Sylvia's turn to express surprise. "I don't understand. They've already helped us by guiding us to the city in the mountains and by bringing us to these boats. Now we're ready to leave. What more assistance can they give us?"

"It strikes me as quite beyond belief, but Korut says that they feel obligated to help us to reach our destination, wherever that might be."

Will had to smile. "It's very good of them to offer, but you don't see even enlightened deinonychids working as mariners. It's been my experience that they prefer more learned pursuits, like library work or scroll writing."

"Surely they are not experienced sailors," Khorip could not resist adding.

"Not at all," Chaz clarified. "But Korut says they are willing to row."

The offer caught Will completely off guard. When they had restored and repositioned the sweeps that fit on the sides of the fishing boat, he had thought they might prove useful in an emergency, as a backup for the single sheet. It had never occurred to him or Sylvia that they might be used to supplement or even supplant the sail as the craft's primary means of propulsion.

He tried to see Korut in a new light. Deinonychids had strong arms and incredibly powerful legs. Given something to push against, he had no doubt one of the mature carnivores could drive one of the heavy oars against the weight of the sea. Given a willing contingent of rowers they might even be able to make headway against a prevailing wind, or a contrary current.

As he was considering how best to reply to the magnanimous offer, Sylvia beat him to it. "Of course we'll accept their help! With all our thanks."

A curved beak nudged her thigh. Glancing down, she saw Chaz peering up at her. "Uh, Sylvia, don't you think it might be better to consider the possible ramifications of this offer first?"

She blinked at him. "What ramifications?"

The *Protoceratops* swallowed. "I do not know about anyone else, but the notion of putting out to sea in the company of half a dozen or more rapacious, unrepentantly carnivorous primitives strikes me as highly questionable."

"Nonsense. Korut and his people have already proven themselves to be our friends."

The frilled head bobbed up and down. "Sure they have. In copaceptic, pleasant surroundings. But what happens if we find ourselves too long at sea with our supplies running low? Might we not be transformed in their eyes from friends into food?"

"If things get that bad," Will pointed out, "it won't matter."

"Besides," Sylvia concluded, "nothing like that is going to happen. We know exactly where we're going and how far away it lies."

"Oh yes," the *Protoceratops* conceded sardonically. "All minuscule unmapped, uncharted, unknown islands are a cinch to locate."

Sylvia refused to be baited. "This one will be. We copied

the course and location right off a map, remember?"

"You copied it off a block of rock, you mean." The little translator snorted and pawed nervously at the ground. "I said that I would come, and so I will. Anything is better than being abandoned to the company of unregenerate killers."

"Now Chaz," Will admonished his friend, "I'd say they're plenty regenerate."

"And do not try to make light of the situation with me, Will Denison." If he'd had a finger, the *Protoceratops* would have shaken it at his companion. "This is the most dangerous thing we have yet attempted in the course of this peculiar excursion you have set out upon. If it ends in failure, my passing will be on your hands."

"If it ends in failure," Will countered, "the only thing that will be on my hands is seawater. Would you rather rely on just the sail and our own muscles to get us to the island?"

"There are many things I would rather rely on," the translator snapped back, "but unfortunately, none of them are presently available to me. Therefore I am compelled to rely on you, Sylvia, one bonehead, and however many of our newfound 'friends' will be coming along." He shuddered openly. "Remember: your predecessors never served as food for the ancestors of our new acquaintances. Mine did."

"Those times are long passed." Will felt no qualms at reassuring his friend. "Korut and his people may not be ready to take their place in the Amphitheater of Knowledge in Sauropolis, but they're not newly arrived refugees from the Rainy Basin, either."

Chaz sighed heavily. "I suppose it does not matter. You have made this decision, and I must do my best to live with it. Because I fear I might not live without it."

Korut observed the verbal exchange silently and without comment, and no one thought it necessary to translate it for him. His offer of rowers formally acknowledged, he retired through the trees to garner suitable disciples. As they were to learn later, argument broke out among the tribesfolk when the chief made the announcement. It turned out that every mature member of the tribe wanted to go. Having spent a good deal of time near and in the sea, they all harbored a silent wish to see more of it.

In the end, Korut chose seven of the strongest members of the tribe to accompany him and their newfound friends. Seated four to a side, they comprised as impressive a rowing team as Dinotopia had ever seen. So strongly did they pull at the oars when the rest of the tribe finally succeeded in pushing the fully loaded craft out into deeper water, that the old fishing boat fairly shot across the surface. Khorip took it upon himself to prevail on them to slow down lest they snap the big sweeps right out of the oarlocks.

Even if their course had not taken them in that direction, the impassable barrier of the outer reef would have soon forced them to turn north or, alternatively, to the south. With the enthusiastic deinonychids bellowing the blood-thirsty hunting songs of the ancestral pack to help them sustain their stroke, the redeemed fishing boat burst out of the eastern bight and turned northward, keeping the verdant coast of Outer Island off its port side. Given the presence on board of such consolidated carnosaurian muscle power, deployment of the single sail seemed almost superfluous.

Chaz was fine (more or less) as long as the high peaks of the island were present to port and the sheltering reef to starboard. Behind the reef the water was comparatively calm, its motion tranquil. But once they left Cape Banamba behind, his discomfiture began to intensify. It worsened when, after a search of more than an hour; Will, Sylvia, and Korut selected a passage through the reef and the deinonychid rowers momentarily redoubled their efforts.

Since they were heading north, the fishing boat burst through the opening without difficulty, the really dangerous open-ocean breakers rolling in only from the east. But now they were exposed to those same swells, which came in heavily abeam. Instead of trying to fight the current, they continued on a northward tack while allowing it to push them slightly to the west. As soon as they gained the lee of Krachong island, the sea quieted once again.

Will knew it would be the last time they could rely on any kind of protection from the might of the open ocean. North of Krachong there were only scattered islets, none more than a mile in extent and most far smaller. If they could not successfully negotiate the winds and the currents, they would be driven ashore somewhere along the length of the Crackshell Peninsula. And if they succeeded in sailing past that point, they would be bereft even of any safe shore on which to run aground.

But if the tiny island they were attempting to reach was simple to get to, he reminded himself forcefully, it would have been rediscovered many times over by now.

The increased turbulence did not seem to trouble the deinonychids. They rowed and sang and gobbled their meals without so much as a complaint. To them it was all a great adventure, an exploration of new hunting grounds even though there was nothing in the immediate vicinity to hunt. Lines cast over the side brought in fresh fish to supplement the dried and smoked supplies they had stowed on board, while Chaz and Khorip sustained themselves on a monotonous but healthful diet of dried fruits and nuts.

No one would go hungry, but as one day merged imperceptibly into the next, drinking water started to become a concern. The active deinonychids needed plenty of fluids, and the tropical climate caused Will and Sylvia to perspire profusely.

By the time their store of fresh water had been drawn half way down, the deinonychids inaugural songs of challenge and defiance had subsided to a zestless drone. The only shade on the fishing boat lay beneath the single deck, and anyone who went below was out of position to row. To spell the now weary carnosaurs, everyone took their turn at the oars. Will and Sylvia did the best they could, but they lacked deinonychid musculature. Khorip performed a little better, but Chaz was of no use at all. No one blamed him for his quadrupedal posture, unsuited as it was to the business of rowing.

Like the rest of his people, Korut had long since set aside his elegant feathered headgear. Now he squatted by the mast while Will, Sylvia, and Chaz discussed how best to proceed. Taking his turn at the sweeps, Khorip was not present.

"Korut says that his people have done all they can for us, and that some of them are starting to wonder if this island of ours really exists," Chaz translated on behalf of the chief.

"Of course it exists," Sylvia instructed the *Protoceratops* to reply. "Several of them accompanied us into the mountains and saw it for themselves."

"They saw a stone with carving on it," Chaz interpreted. "They did not see an island. Korut says to tell you that he believes in you, but not all of his people are of the same mind. They are tired, and miss their families, and dry land. They have enjoyed their time upon the sea, but they are not dolphins or ichthyosaurs, to leap overboard and frolic in the waves." Turning his head, Chaz looked from one human to the other. "Then there is the water situation. Korut is their chief, but he says he is not an autocrat. If enough of his people say they want to go home, he will take them home."

"But we can't!" Even though she knew he could not understand her words, Sylvia implored the *Deinonychus*. "We've come so far, and we're so close!"

"Are we?" Chaz did not shout, did not badger. This time his words were calm, rational, reasonable. Under the circumstances, he felt that was all that was needed. "What if the map was wrong? What if we have drifted off the right course? The 'island,' if it exists, is so small it could easily be missed even by experienced mariners. It *has* been missed by experienced mariners. Yet you are confident we can sail right up to it." With a horizontal sweep of his beak the *Protoceratops* took in the surrounding open ocean.

"If our calculations are correct we have already sailed well to the north of Crackshell Point. If we were to now change our heading to due west we could sail right past the mainland of Dinotopia, or be caught in the northshore currents and wrecked off the Northern Plains like so many ships from the world outside." He spoke as considerately as he could under the circumstances.

"Face reality, Sylvia. If there is an island out here in the middle of nowhere, we have missed it. If there is not, to continue on this bearing would be worse than folly: it would be suicidal."

"It's out here." Rising, she turned to gaze over the bow.

On either side of the boat, determined deinonychids pulled methodically, rhythmically at their long oars. But, Will noted, several of them were watching the humans and the *Protoceratops* carefully. The aura of good feeling that had enveloped the boat when they had first set out was starting to dissipate. Though he tried hard to keep it out of his thoughts, he found he could not keep from thinking back to Chaz's nascent fears about traveling in the company of so many uncivilized carnivores. Sylvia would not want him worrying about such things, but he couldn't help it.

Chaz was right. They had done all they could, come as far as boldness and planning could take them. It was time to . . .

The rower occupying the first seat to port suddenly rose and pointed with a taloned hand. He was shouting something in the primitive deinonychid dialect. Quickly, his companions put aside their own sweeps and scrambled to join her, leaping lithely over oars, benches, and whatever else was in their way, Khorip included. Within moments every deinonychid on board, including Korut, was gathered in the bow, jabbering and gesturing excitedly.

At the risk of unbalancing the boat, Will and Sylvia joined them. Chaz crowded behind, straining to see, frustrated at his inability to peer past the mob of taller human and saurian bipeds.

Feeling the squat ceratopsian pushing against her, Sylvia looked back and down. "I don't see anything. What are they all so frantic about?"

"The one who stood up first says there is land." Chaz struggled to extract meaning from the guttural babble of aboriginal dialect. "I hope it is not a mirage, or a hallucination brought on by too many days at sea. I do not like to think how our 'friends' would react to the disappointment."

Pushing through the crowd of chattering, jostling deinonychids, Will finally gained a clear view over the bow. At first he saw nothing and feared that the *Protoceratops* might be right. Then Korut was at his side, holding him around the shoulders with one powerful clawed arm and pointing with the other. Sighting along the line made by the chief's hand, Will finally saw what all the shouting was about.

It was land, all right! An island, slightly to the west of where they had calculated, but unmistakable in its solidity and profile. Not very much land, to be sure, but land nonetheless.

He forced himself to stay calm and urged Sylvia to do the same. "After all, just because it's an island doesn't mean it's *the* island."

"Of course it is," she replied, refusing to acknowledge his attempt at circumspection. "It's right where we thought it would be!" Then, checking the position of the sun, she added in a more restrained voice, "Well, almost. But it's there!" Her eyes were shining. "It's real, Will. Khorip and I didn't imagine it, we didn't make it up. The Hand of Dinotopia is real."

He found himself staring speculatively at the distant rocky spire. Perhaps, just perhaps, he thought, this Hand story was indeed real. As real as Sylvia wanted it to be.

The question that remained to be answered now was— real what?

# -XXIII-

The sight of land gave the rejuvenated deinonychids new strength. Returning to their
seats, they pulled at the oars with the kind
of feral energy that had made their ancestors
among the most feared predators of the Late
Cretaceous. Will and Sylvia joined in the effort as well, dou-
bling up on the long sweeps in partnership with straining
deinonychids, sharing their benches as well as their oars.
The thunderous, bloodcurdling chant of a deinonychid pack
on the hunt once more rang out over the open sea.

Meanwhile Chaz leaned against the mast and muttered
to himself.

As they drew nearer, the island soon resolved itself into
a steep-sided pillar of rock crowned by three distinct
precipices. Looking back over the stern, Chaz found that
from their present position even the high snowy peaks of
the Forbidden Mountains were no longer visible. He felt
very isolated, and not a little afraid.

What was this place, so far from the Dinotopia he knew
and yet seemingly a part of it? What ancient, forgotten

secrets lay hidden beyond its inhospitable shores? Did he even want to know?

It did not matter. Sylvia wanted to know, and so did that persistent bonehead Khorip, and probably his friend Will as well. So it looked like Chaz the Translator was going to "know" whether he wanted to or not.

That is, he was going to if they could find a place to land. As they embarked on a slow, careful circumnavigation of the island, the prospect of not even being able to get ashore began to become a very real possibility.

The island was composed largely of limestone, and geologically recent limestone at that. The persistent, unceasing action of waves driving across open ocean had eaten into the base of the island, undercutting it, honeycombing it, and giving it the appearance of a gigantic, spike-topped, green-clad mushroom. Marching in from the east, foam-topped breakers smashed furiously against its flanks. The best sailors in the world could not have contrived a landing on such a shore.

"Maybe we'll have better luck in the lee," Sylvia said hopefully.

"If there is a lee." Will was more cautious. The strong currents swirling around the island were ragged, which meant that waves could attack the rock from any and every direction. If it was undercut this severely all the way around, they would have to concede defeat. After achieving so much and coming so close, that would be maddening. But attempting to land someone on the heavily eroded slopes in the midst of dangerously dancing waves would mean risking the integrity of the boat's hull, and that they could not do. Not under any circumstances. Not even for Sylvia.

As it turned out, he was spared the necessity of making that tortuous decision by the discovery of a single, tiny beach on the far western side of the island. The sandy inlet was only a couple of feet wide. Behind it, they could see where cascading rainwater had cut a fissure into the otherwise sheer, undercut rock face, providing not only a reasonably safe landing site but also a means of accessing the island's interior. Securing the boat with rope to holes that had been drilled through the solid rock by the action of the waves, they jumped into the shallows, waded ashore, and started inland, grateful after days at sea to be treading once again on a surface that did not dip and sway beneath their feet. For this, at least, humans and saurians were equally thankful.

The thin ribbon of rainforest that clung to the sheer sides of the deep ravine they were ascending was thick with well-known species. At least, Chaz reflected, the plant life on this isolated smudge of limestone was familiar. So were the birds that watched curiously while the long line of humans and dinosaurs made their way up the steep but negotiable slope. So were the small nervous mammals that scurried for cover at the plod of approaching footprints. Biologically if not physically, the island was a part of Dinotopia. An overlooked part, perhaps insignificant, but not an alien one.

As they left the pocket beach behind, the fissure broadened out until they found themselves standing on an uneven circular plateau that looked as if it might run all the way around the island. Bigger trees flourished here in profusion. Many were heavy with fruit that never had been, and in all likelihood never would be, gathered by the likes of Shree Banda, Grinedge, and their perambulating band of harvesters. Khorip and Chaz munched casually on what had fallen from the overhanging branches, selecting only the best and ripest of the unexpected bounty.

"What now?" Will wondered aloud.

Sylvia was studying the nearest section of cliff. "I guess we keep going up."

"Up that?" Will gaped at the nearly vertical pinnacle. At least a hundred feet had to be surmounted to reach either of the saddles where the mountain split into its three separate peaks. And if that could be attained, then what? An ascent of one of the three crags? For what purpose and to what end, he found himself asking?

"Sylvia, there's no reason to go up there. Which is good, because we can't. We don't have any mountaineering gear with us. Just the ropes on the boat, and we can't very well untie it to go rock climbing."

Tight-lipped as she was forced to contemplate the un-scalable pinnacles, she lowered her gaze and nodded reluc-tantly. "I know, you're right. But there *has* to be more here than just fruit and rocks and birds. Help me look."

For once, Chaz did not offer any criticism of what ap-peared to be a counter-rational, useless activity. Together with Khorip, he was too busy feasting on the fallen fresh fruit. Engaging the deinonychids in the enterprise, Will and Sylvia embarked on a thorough search of the plateau. Their diligent searching turned up nothing out of the ordinary. Just when even Sylvia began to fear that was what they were going to find, one of the saurian hunters called for everyone to come and have a look at something he had found.

Will's initial excitement turned to disappointment when

he saw what the *Deinonychus* had discovered. It was an opening into the mountain, and a sizable one, but there was nothing exceptional about it. Still, since it was all they had found, it was deemed worth exploring further.

Fashioning torches from the ample supply of available dry wood and setting them alight with a hand-sparked fire, they entered into a wonderland of speleotherms that instantly reminded Will of The World Beneath, that vast underground land underlying the mainland of Dinotopia that he and his father had explored previously.

Pure gypsum helectites covered the ceiling like frozen commas while soda straws dripped rainwater onto burgeoning stalagmites. Aragonite needles clustered in hollows and corners: forgotten fairy pincushions. Banded flowstone rippled along walls like huge slabs of raw bacon. His torch crackling and spitting above him, he bent to sip from the pure transparent water of a travertine pool.

"There's nothing here." Khorip did not try to hide his disappointment. "At least, nothing like what we were hoping to find."

Nearby, Sylvia and Korut held their torches close to the walls. The damp limestone threw back sparkles and color, but no enlightenment. Entering through unseen tubes and passages, the wind howled mournfully, carrying with it the scent of the nearby sea.

Lifting his head from the pristine pool, Chaz declaimed quietly but firmly to one and all. "This is all there is. A most engaging place. Charming, even, in its speleological fashion, but hardly peerless. If everyone has seen enough, I suggest we return to our boat before a hostile gust of wind or a belligerent wave tears it from its moorings and sweeps it away to maroon us here forever." Turning, he started back toward the entrance that was clearly delineated by the sunlight that came pouring through the uneven opening.

"Just a little farther," Sylvia pleaded. Holding her torch out in front of her, she carefully picked her way down the next slope.

"Careful." Will raised his own light high. "The formations are wet and the floor is as slippery as a sauropod barn before cleaning."

"I'll watch ou . . . oh my."

"Sylvia?" She had turned a corner and, just for an instant, stepped out of sight. "Sylvia, are you all right?"

"Yes—yes, Will. I'm all right. I—I've found something."

Behind him, the *Protoceratops* rolled his eyes. "Doesn't she always?" More steadfast of foot than his bipedal companions, he started down in Sylvia's wake.

When Will and the deinonychids finally arrived, they too momentarily lost the power of speech. Instead of finding themselves overwhelmed by size and spectacle, as had been the case at Ahmet-Padon and the forgotten city on Outer Island, here they were struck dumb by an exhibition of carving skill the likes of which none of them had encountered even in the great library at Waterfall City.

They stood at the bottom of a domed chamber, a common enough formation in caves. But here, all the marvelous natural formations so typical of limestone caverns had been cut away and replaced with bas-reliefs. Not an inch of the gently curving walls or ceiling had been left vacant. So small and intricate were some of the carvings that Will, who prided himself on his excellent eyesight, could not make out all the details. And as near as they could tell, that same degree of delicacy extended all the way up the walls to the very apex of the dome itself.

In the center of the chamber stood a single stalagmite, deliberately spared by whatever vanished people had fashioned this place. Some six feet in diameter, it was completely covered with still more of the incomparable incisions. Some of the tracery was so painstakingly refined that Will felt it could be destroyed by someone breathing on it.

And all of it was pure, unadulterated white limestone that reflected back the light of their torches like a million tiny mirrors.

Not all of the bas-reliefs were diminutive in stature. The largest individual carvings reached the size of a human fist, veritable monuments compared to the majority of etchings. Will let his overwhelmed attention wander unhindered among the stone tracings, his vision saturated with splendor. He would have gladly continued in that mode for hours had not Chaz demanded his attention.

"What is it?" he asked his stout friend. The *Protoceratops* seemed unnaturally subdued. "Something important?"

"Look at these panels here." Chaz gestured with his beak.

As soon as Will looked closely he discovered why the translator had not replied to his last query. No explanation was required. The carvings explained themselves all too well. It was hard to believe he was seeing what he was seeing, but the images in the rock, and the remarkable work of long-dead artisans, refused to be denied. He called Sylvia over, and Khorip, and lastly the deinonychids. Human and saurian stood side by side staring in silence at the carvings, and understood, and were hushed in the presence of a conjunction of ancient wisdom and tragedy.

The bas-reliefs showed humans and dinosaurs together. But not together as they knew it in present-day Dinotopia. In relief after relief, carving after carving, the representations of long-vanished individuals were engaged in frantic, desperate activity. An activity that had never come to pass on the mainland of Dinotopia, but which if the reliefs were to be believed had at several times in the past severely afflicted Outer Island. Swallowing, Will hardly dared conjure the long-unused, nearly forgotten word in his mind.

War.

Humans battled other humans and dinosaurs in image after image. Will recognized and pointed out for his companions precise depictions of Roman triremes and Chinese junks, perhaps blown off course from the South China and Arabian Seas. Arrows and spears flew from the decks of heavily armed ships, from the bows and fingers of frightened men. In response, huge sauropods writhed and died. Duckbills and smaller dinosaurs ran and were hunted down and killed. None were immune from the deluge of iron and bronze.

Following reliefs showed desperate, starving sailors and legionaries landing on the beaches. Instead of accepting the hand of friendship from the humans and saurians who were then living in peace and harmony on Outer Island, the invaders butchered and slaughtered the inhabitants, enslaving those they did not kill. Collateral carvings showed relief columns from the high interior of the island responding to the cry for help from the inhabitants of the coast.

"The forgotten city on the plateau." Will held his torch close to the wall, simultaneously fascinated and repelled by what he was seeing.

"Yes," whispered Sylvia. She pointed to another section of wall. "Look here."

Mounted on armored ceratopsians and preceded by ankylosaurs, the saviors from the highland city swept down on the invaders. With the overtures and appeals to reason proffered by their lowland relations having failed utterly to civilize the newcomers, the mountain folk reluctantly pushed them back into the sea. Some tried to escape in their boats but were pursued and sunk by enraged mosasaurs and pleisosaurs. Finally, as a follow-up to the catastrophe, all traces of the invaders' presence was carefully and methodically obliterated.

Then, appalled and ashamed by what they had done even though they had been given no alternative, the highland folk abandoned their beautiful city on the plateau and dispersed, mixing with the lowlanders. With the mass memory of unnatural death clinging inexorably to their land, the survivors eventually drifted back to the mainland, and Outer Island was forsaken by its original inhabitants forever.

Except, Will reminded himself, for a few lingering, isolated bands of recalcitrant individuals. Watching the enthralled deinonychids as they traced the story told by the bas-reliefs, it struck him like a hammer blow that standing beside him and around him were the sole survivors of the ancestors of that momentous, ancient tragedy. It wasn't that they had never been civilized. Abandoning their grand city and illustrious culture, Korut's forefathers had left behind a few scattered bands of iconoclasts who had slid back into older, half-forgotten ways. No wonder he and his fellow tribesfolk remembered how to hunt and kill. No wonder the highly sensitive Chaz had been so unremittingly nervous in their company.

Not so very long ago, in order to survive, their ancestors had been forced to hunt down invading humans.

"Away from here," he heard himself mumbling. "Let's get away from this place." Suddenly the extraordinary cavern was no longer so beautiful, its delicate tracery of carvings no longer endlessly attractive. Now it glittered and shimmered with all the disheartening dazzle of a dead butterfly. The pristine limestone stank of death.

Slowly, humans and deinonychids began to shuffle back the way they had come, heading for the entrance in the side of the mountain. Looking back, he saw that Sylvia was lingering by the central stalagmite.

"Come on, Sylvia. You found what you were looking for. I can't say that I care for it much myself. Let's get out of here."

"Just a minute, Will. Don't you see the import of these carvings? These—what did you call them?—Roman and Chinese ships, they landed here intact! They didn't break up on the reefs and their crews weren't shipwrecked. That means the legend is true! There *is* a safe sea route into Dinotopia. And if the part about there being a safe route in is correct, then the safe route out probably exists as well."

"And if it does, do you still want to find it?" With his torch he indicated the grim, brooding carvings. The silent walls seemed to press close around them.

"No." She lowered her head slightly. "No, I guess not. I suppose I'll have to be satisfied with confirmation of just part of the story." She took a step toward him, only to pause again.

He waved his torch to urge her onward. Sylvia was the love of his life, but there were times when he felt that she deliberately tried his patience. He did not doubt that there were times when she felt the same way about him. It was called, he had been told, a relationship.

"Now what?" Behind him, Korut and the rest of the deinonychids had already exited the cavern, with Khorip and Chaz close behind.

A passing glance at the top of the stalagmite revealed a series of beautifully carved hands. It struck Sylvia as not only significant, but downright blatant. Each hand had been posed differently by its sculptor, so that the fingers appeared to be waving. The dance styles of many cultures, from Southeast Asian to Incan, Monomotapan to Egyptian, featured waving hands. The Egyptian influence on the art and architecture of the mountaintop city on Outer Island had been especially pronounced.

Perhaps half of the upraised hands were human, the rest saurian. It was almost as if they were importuning her to say farewell. Feeling a little foolish as she did so but also the need to pander to the impulse, she began making her way around the stalagmite, pressing her palm in the accepted traditional Dinotopian fashion to each set of fingers that she passed.

Will watched, trying to make sense of her actions. "Sylvia, it's getting late. What are you doing?"

"Saying good-bye to a dream." Her voice echoed spectrally off the frosted walls of the decorated dome. "Telling this place, and whoever made it, to breathe deep and seek peace."

Chaz would have had an appropriate comment, Will

knew, but he could only wait, and watch, and smile at the empathetic antics of his beloved. She had labored long and hard to find this place. In all likelihood they would never return. He could hardly begrudge her a few moments of inner reflection.

In contrast to the torpid, tropical air that hung unmoving within the cavern, the graven limestone was cool and damp to her touch as she pressed her palm and fingers against each individual sculpture. Among the saurian hands, every Dinotopian species appeared to be represented. There were ceratopsian foot-pads and duckbill palms, flattened sauropod feet and delicate gallimimus digits, elongated pterosaur thumbs and even pleisosaur paddles.

Having nearly completely her circumlocution of the striking stalagmite, she prepared to palm one of the last hands—and hesitated. It was a therapod hand this time, not unlike those flourished by Korut and his tribe. There was no mistaking the slim, strong wrist or the sharp downward curving claws that protruded from the ends of three fingers.

Three fingers, three fingers. Her own hand continued to hover over the sculpture, so like those that flanked it on either side except in the number of digits. What, in particular, did three fingers suddenly put her in mind of?

Her lower jaw dropped slowly. Behind her and higher up she could hear Will calling to her. Initially impatient, he now sounded concerned. She ignored him, fighting to make a connection in her mind. Three fingers. . . .

She was standing beneath them. The three rocky pinnacles of the island! Connection—or coincidence? Without hesitation or further thought, she pressed her palm to the upraised saurian hand, exactly as she had done to the many others that lined the upper portion of the speleotherm.

As she exerted pressure, she felt the sculpture move beneath her fingers.

The mountain groaned. The noise reverberated through the dome and the surrounding cavern, repeating itself as it echoed off sculpted walls. A deep-throated rumbling came from beneath her feet, growing steadily louder, rising to the surface like a breaching whale. Bits of loose scree and some of the more delicate natural formations crumbled from the ceiling, bouncing off the ground, dusting her hair with powdery white sparkles.

"Sylvia!" Extending a hand, Will reached for her emotionally as well as physically. "Run!"

This time she did not hesitate. With the ground quaking beneath her feet, she stumbled and ran toward him. Around them, the shaking intensified.

Deep within the mountain great volumes of sand were being shifted as stone blocks slid from their moorings. Beginning with small keystones and tiny volumes of material, larger and larger blocks were displaced, freeing greater and greater reservoirs of sand. Limestone blocks slid down unseen, artificial chutes, knocking free a dozen keystones at a time. Each one released a compartment holding still more sand.

A complex system of counter-balanced rock and sand began to shift inside the mountain. A geological equilibrium that had appeared natural was being artificially disturbed. Great masses of rock were slowly displaced.

All the while, powdered limestone and aragonite needles continued to fall on and around Will and Sylvia, whitening their hair and shoulders. Somewhere high above the cavern, stone screamed as it was methodically displaced according to an ancient, preordained plan.

Despite the increasingly unsteady footing, she finally reached the frantic Will and took his hand. He gripped it tightly, intending not to let go this time until they were back on board the fishing boat and safely away from this place. Around them, the island was going mad.

Staggering outside, they found that leaves and branches were falling from those trees that were still standing. Every bird on the island had taken wing and was now aloft, screeching and screaming its displeasure. There was no sign of Chaz, Khorip, or the deinonychids. With his eyes shocked by the sudden re-emergence into full sunlight, Will had to squint while they refocused on their surroundings.

"There they are!" Extending his arm, he located the others. They were already making their hurried way down the rift. "They're heading for the boat. Come on!"

"But what's happening?" Allowing herself to be half guided, half dragged, Sylvia kept looking back over her shoulder toward the central part of the island. Behind them, the mountain growled like a tyrannosaur waking from a long sleep.

It also began to move.

Deranged images took possession of Will's thoughts. The mountain was rising up on concealed feet to wreak vengeance on those who had dared to disturb its rest. The ghosts of the departed sculptors were emerging from the depths to steal their souls. Zombified assassins from the time of the troubles on Outer Island were rising from their mass graves beneath the dome to resume their ancient reign of terror and destruction.

Actually, what was happening was at once more unbelievable and wonderful than any of his riotous inventions. It was a feat of ancient engineering sufficiently grand to astound the most jaded.

Before they had been compelled to abandon the civilization of Outer Island, its early inhabitants had tracked down the safe sea route used by the Roman and Chinese invaders. Tracked it, and marked it, in case anyone who came after them should need or want to know the way. Not for them simple maps or references in libraries. To mark it, they had used not paper or scroll but an entire mountain.

A mountain in the shape of a three-fingered therapod hand.

It made all the sense in the world if you just thought about it for a moment. Dinosaurs, not humans, had begun the civilization now known as Dinotopia. Dinosaurs, not humans, had nourished and maintained it down through the millennia until wandering humans had begun to be cast up on its shores. Why then at once conceal and reveal such a weighty secret with a human hand instead of a saurian one?

Three fingers Korut's ancestors had possessed on their hands. Three pinnacles dominated the top of the central mountain. As carefully positioned sand and rock deep with its core was displaced, it continued to shift slowly behind the frantically retreating Will and Sylvia. Loose rock spilled from its slowly inclining ledges and splashed into the sea.

Stumbling onto the beach at last, they found the anxious deinonychids seated and waiting at the rowing benches. Khorip had taken a place alongside Korut while Chaz could only dance impatiently as his friends made their way across the last stretch of sand.

"Hurry, hurry!" The shaken ceratopsian all but tied his

optic nerves in knots trying to watch the running humans and the slipping mountain simultaneously.

As soon as they were aboard, the deinonychids cast off. The uncooperative sail luffed against the mast, but long oars dug water and they pulled rapidly away from the beach. Almost as soon as they were clear, the danger vanished. Now inclined forward at an angle of nearly forty-five degrees, the uppermost portion of the mountain had finally stopped moving. It hung there, immobile as when they had first espied it, balanced on some unseen pivot. The Hand of Dinotopia.

Imitating the three fingers of a therapod hand, the three peaks now pointed in a northeastward direction. All that remained to provide final confirmation of the ancient fable was to follow it.

"We cannot do it," Chaz declared steadfastly when Sylvia proposed doing precisely that.

"It's the only way to confirm the legend," she insisted.

"I have no wish to confirm it with my life," the *Protoceratops* replied. "We have remaining water and supplies enough to get us back to the mainland. Not to Outer Island, but to Crackshell Point. That is good enough for me and if you have any common sense left, it should be good enough for you. If this route exists it means safe sea travel is possible both to and away from Dinotopia. If it does not, or if we stray into the wrong current, we will most likely find ourselves swept out to sea, there to perish far from home and family."

"Chaz is right, Sylvia. We can't risk it." Will gently rested both hands on her shoulders. "We can't ask Korut and his people to risk it. Not just to confirm a theory." Realizing the truth inherent in both their replies, she looked crestfallen.

"But," he added, "there might be a way that doesn't require us to put our lives at risk. At least, not any more than we already have."

Chaz gaped at him goggle-eyed. "Will Denison, I know how your mind works. I do not pretend to understand the process, but I am all-too familiar with the consequences. What tainted egg of an idea are you hatching now?"

Will was moving away from the bow back toward the middle of the boat. The deinonychids watched him curiously.

Reaching their limited stock of supplies, he began going through the accumulated pile of foodstuffs. Bananas, mangos, papayas, pineapples, oranges, potatoes, smoked fish—all were shoved aside in his search as he excavated their food. His friends beheld these goings-on with unalloyed curiosity, Sylvia no less than Chaz or Korut.

Eventually he found what he was looking for. Triumphantly, he held up the bunch of young coconuts.

Chaz gawked at him. "Let me guess. You are going to resolve Sylvia's conundrum by having a snack?"

"Not at all." Will grinned at him. "I'm just going to give these coconuts a chance to demonstrate how their ancestors settled Dinotopia—or how their progeny left it."

So saying, he moved to the side of the boat and tossed the armful of nuts over the side. They splashed as they entered the water and bobbed quickly back to the surface. Will, Sylvia, and everyone else who could see strained to follow their progress.

For nearly an hour the floating seeds of the coco palm bobbed aimlessly in the gentle swells, moving hardly at all. But as they drifted, the unseen tendrils of an unknown current were already plucking at them.

"Follow them," Will directed Chaz to instruct Korut and the deinonychid rowers. "Keep them in sight. But from a distance. And warn our friends to be prepared to pull hard if I give the word."

Chaz complied. Slowly, cautiously, the fishing boat trailed the progress of the floating coconuts. Within less than an hour they had picked up speed as they fell further under the spell of the subsurface river. Then they unexpectedly and visibly accelerated.

"Back!" Will shouted. "Tell them to pull back!"

As Chaz translated the order, the deinonychids rose and changed their rowing positions on the benches. Wooden sweeps pulled water. Even so, the boat continued to move forward, against the pull of the oars.

"Harder!" Will yelled. "If the full current catches us, we're lost!"

Throwing herself into a seat next to one of the female deinonychids, Sylvia gripped the oar tightly and pulled, jamming her feet into the foot brace to gain leverage.

With agonizing sluggishness, the fishing boat slowed, stopped, and began to reverse course. The deinonychids continued to row hard. It was a near thing, but before long they had pulled clear of the outstreaming current and were once more drifting in easily negotiable waters.

Too close, as Will acknowledged. Chaz berated him unmercifully.

The skybax rider was unrepentant. "It was the only way, Chaz." Reaching out, he gently caressed Sylvia's cheek. "I know my fiancée. She had to know, or she'd be on her way back here before you could say 'Nallab natters knowingly' three times."

Nodding, Sylvia turned to reflect on the section of sea that had nearly swept them away. The surface of the renegade water was as calm as that surrounding it, giving no clue to the power that raged just beneath. Borne relentlessly northward, the armful of coconuts was already out of sight.

"Cross-currents." Chaz was muttering aloud to himself. "One running out and away from Dinotopia, another rushing in. It is the latter that are prevalent around our shores. Only here can one make a safe landing, on this island, and from this place find calm water leading south to Krachong and then onward to Outer Island. It is the only place where the sea that surrounds the mainland is navigable in both directions." Lowering his head by bending on one knee, he bowed in Sylvia's direction and then, with considerable reluctance, to Khorip.

"You both were right in your suppositions. There is truly a Hand of Dinotopia, and it does indeed show the only safe sea route both to and away from our land. I offer my apologies for doubting you."

"You had good reason to doubt us," Sylvia told him. "It was a cockeyed hypothesis right from the beginning." She smiled at the little ceratopsian. "Just because it turned out to be true doesn't change that."

"The mosasaurs, the pleisosaurs and ichthyosaurs and dolphins must know of this place," Will pointed out. "Yet they have kept it a secret from the rest of us."

"The ocean-dwellers do not usually initiate conversation," Chaz reminded him. "Perhaps they have not so much been keeping it a secret as simply not volunteering information about it. Or possibly they have used this singular sea route in the past to visit parts of the World Outside, but have not done so since the invasion of Outer Island revealed to them what the outside world was really like."

"Sea serpents," Will murmured. Everyone looked at him and he explained. "There are many tales in the outside world of great sea-going monsters. People called them sea serpents. But no one has seen them in modern times." He nodded appreciatively at the *Protoceratops*. "That would fit with Chaz's theory that the mosasaurs and their cousins once freely visited the rest of the world's oceans but no longer choose to do so."

Taking Sylvia's hand in his, he walked her to the bow. Behind them, the deinonychids pulled steadily as the boat angled south, back toward Outer Island. Heading home again, they once more began to sing. Only now it was a hymn of pure exultation, celebrating their triumph over mystery and strange shores.

"What will you do now?" Sitting on the railing, he continued to hold her hand, as if afraid that by letting go he might somehow still lose her to the island of the Hand, or to her unrelenting curiosity.

"File a report with the proper department, I guess." She looked past him, gazing forward. Her incessant inquisitiveness satisfied at last, she was as anxious as anyone else on board for their first glimpse of familiar terrain.

Will nodded knowingly. "We'll work on it together. People need to know about this place; about its history, and its marvels, and its dangers. It needs to be watched, so that the disaster that befell Outer Island can never be repeated in Dinotopia." Feeling a new presence, he turned to find

Khorip standing behind them. Like Sylvia, he too was staring across the bow.

"Well, Khorip, you found what you were looking for. A way to leave Dinotopian civilization behind forever. A way to reach the World Outside." Will watched the silent *Prenocephale* closely. "What are you going to do about it?"

The domed skull inclined towards him. Limpid eyes, green and round, gazed back into his own. The eyes of a plant-eating dinosaur, intelligent and sensitive.

"I can't get those bas-reliefs out of my mind. What did you call the horrific activity they depicted?"

"War," Will reminded him.

Khorip quivered slightly. "Fighting and killing. So that is what the outside world is about."

"Not entirely," Will told him. "But even as a child I knew that was a large part of it. An important part."

Khorip nodded slowly, understandingly. "Such a small, short word for such a great, unimaginable horror."

"Then you're not going to try and leave?"

"No. Not now, not anymore. I think I have learned as much about the World Outside as I want to."

"What will you do?" Sylvia asked curiously. "Resume your life in the Great Desert?"

Contrite, the *Prenocephale* looked from one skybax rider to the other. "If you will have me, I think I would like to return with you. To Sauropolis, or Waterfall city, or wherever is your final destination. I know a lot about the little-known parts of the desert. I think I would like to share what I have learned." He drew himself up, his tail flicking from side to side behind him. "I think I would like to contribute once again to the civilization of Dinotopia."

Alan Dean Foster

He stumbled as something head-butted him from behind. Recovering his balance, he pivoted to see Chaz standing behind him.

"You will have to keep on your toes better than that to gain a hearing among the desert specialists in Sauropolis." Less contentiously he added, "But I will be pleased to support you, and help smooth your return to a cultured life. I might even, with a little effort, be persuaded to offer suggestions and advice."

"When haven't you?" Khorip quipped. Chaz retorted with a suitably acerbic asseveration and the two fell to fussing noisily.

Letting go of Sylvia's hand, Will raised his arm until it was draped snugly around her shoulders. She responded by leaning into him. They stayed like that for some time, both silent and lost in their own thoughts.

She was contemplating their life together, he decided as he gazed at her radiant face. The setting sun gilded her cheeks and brow. Doubtless she was thinking about what they were going to do tomorrow, about how they would at last have the opportunity to relax in each other's company as soon as they returned to safety and civilized surroundings. It was not surprising, because he was meditating on precisely the same things.

"We'll find some time together." He held her a little closer, squeezing with the arm around her shoulders. "If not in Kuskonak, then at Canyon City."

She blinked, looked up at him. "What?"

He frowned. "Wasn't that what you were thinking about?"

"Oh no," she replied in that ceaselessly chipper voice he had come to know so well. "Sorry. I was just wondering if a skybax and rider could make the flight from Crackshell Point to here. You know, if you swapped out the normal delivery perch for a racing saddle, I think it would be possible to . . ."

Using his free hand, he put a finger to her lips. "That's enough. I don't want to hear anything more about expeditions, explorations, hands of Dinotopia, shifting sea currents, forgotten cities, or even a misplaced hatband!" Then, seeing the look on her face, he added resignedly, "At least, not for a week or so."

Her pout metamorphosed into a smile, which he met intimately with his own.

# DATE DUE